# CARNAL SECRETS

# CARNAL SECRETS

## THE PHOENIX PACK SERIES

## SUZANNE WRIGHT

Text copyright © 2014 Suzanne Wright
All rights reserved.

Published by Montlake Romance, Seattle

www.apub.com

ISBN-13: 9781477849972
ISBN-10: 1477849971

Cover design by Anne Cain Graphic Art and Design

Library of Congress Control Number: 2013914168

Printed in the United States of America

*For Edward*

# CHAPTER ONE

He was going to get bad news today. Nick knew it in his bones. The "knowing" wasn't an unfamiliar feeling. He'd often *know* things. Sometimes it was just as it was right now—no more than a feeling, an itch at the back of his neck that warned him something was wrong but gave him no clue as to what. Other times it was more specific yet very mundane; he would *know* exactly where a missing object was, like the TV remote or the car keys. But then there were times when the *knowing* was a heavy weight in his gut, a warning that rang through his body . . . like that time when he was in the woods with his sister and he had *known* that if they didn't turn back, something awful would happen, something that would change everything.

Call it intuition, call it instincts, call it a gift—whatever. The point was that he knew that bad news was coming, and it was becoming harder and harder for the Alpha to keep his anxiety from leaking out into the pack link.

He was pretty sure that the two wolves in the vehicle with him had felt his edginess, but that was only to be expected considering that—as his brother and bodyguard—they were closely attuned to him. His wolf also sensed Nick's tension and was now pacing within him, as edgy and restless as he was. Well at least he and his wolf were on the same page, for a change—he'd missed that feeling. Nick Axton had always prided himself on the fact that he and his wolf were very much in sync with each other. There had only ever been one thing that they had been in total disagreement on—claiming Shaya Critchley, their mate.

His wolf's stance on the matter was simple: she was their true mate, therefore Nick should claim her and bond with her and make her their Alpha female of the Ryland Pack. But it wasn't as clear-cut as that. No, there was a host of issues surrounding this situation.

For one thing, making a submissive wolf an Alpha female was next to impossible. It wasn't that submissive wolves were weak or passive. Hell no. Despite their aura of calm, submissive wolves could be feisty, hotheaded, and mentally stronger than any dominant wolf, just as dominant wolves could be weak-minded or emotionally vulnerable despite their aura of intensity. But these differences in aura were partly why dominant wolves were always high in rank; a dominant's intense vibes could suppress and, thus, force the submission of *any* wolf they were more powerful than, thereby leaving submissive wolves vulnerable to them.

The other essential difference between dominants and submissives lay in physical strength—a submissive, no matter their inner strength, could never be physically stronger than a dominant wolf. As such, submissives were vulnerable to dominant wolves on two scores, but they were vital to every pack in that without the natural calming influence of submissive wolves running through the pack link, the dominants' natural intensity would leave the pack unstable.

As such, though Shaya was vital to a pack and had the inner strength to match any dominant wolf, she would be vulnerable in other ways. If she was Alpha female, she would therefore be challenged repeatedly by the dominant females in the pack for her position. Of course Nick could keep her safe by ordering that no one challenge her, but then she would never be respected or followed or acknowledged as Alpha female. That would leave her feeling on the outside looking in, which was absolutely unacceptable to Nick, as was the very idea of her in danger.

That left him only one option if he still wished to claim her: he would have to step down from his position as Alpha. Hell, Nick would happily give it up if it meant he could have his mate. The problem was that no one in his pack wanted the position, and no one wanted the responsibility of keeping the pack stable. The old Alpha had been like a cancer, and he'd corrupted the entire pack until he'd blackened the heart of it. Although Nick had challenged and killed him long ago, past events still haunted the pack, and old wounds still tormented it.

His wolf wasn't concerned with these details surrounding the matter. It was all very black-and-white for him—Shaya was his, so she must be claimed. As such, he was particularly angry with Nick. Not that it was unusual for his wolf to be in a somber mood. He had somewhat of a dark disposition, in fact. Well of course he did. Not only had he surfaced prematurely, but he had been born in rage and fear.

As a rule, shifters changed for the first time during puberty. Nick had been just five when, in one very bizarre moment, his wolf had surfaced to protect him. Having such a strong, powerful wolf was something Nick was extremely proud of, but it hurt to know that his wolf had been born that way, leaving scars on his soul—scars that had been deepened by the event that had later led to Nick spending time in a juvenile prison. Despite his wolf's anger, the animal wasn't wild or challenging. No, his wolf was still as controlled and composed as Nick, but he also viewed the world as a bleak, dark, harsh place. Shaya had been the only thing to ever stir strong emotions in his wolf.

Admittedly, she was the only thing that had stirred strong emotions in Nick. Much like his wolf, he could be hard, cold, and remote at times. It wasn't that he didn't have a conscience, and nor was it that he didn't know the difference between right and wrong. But Nick seemed to lack a little something—like there had been a glitch in his emotional development that made it difficult for him to bond with others, to connect like they did. He felt emotion the same as everyone else—or the same as most, anyway. But bonding was something he found difficult.

Maybe it was hardly surprising. His wolf had surfaced too early, surfaced at a time when his mind and body hadn't been ready. It would be much like a young child being plunged into the stages of puberty—it wasn't something they were psychologically or biologically ready for, and it would undoubtedly have a fundamental effect on their development as a person: mentally, physically, and emotionally. As such, Nick was tainted and broken in so many ways. His mate, however, was much the opposite.

Shaya reminded him of a butterfly: colorful, vibrant, graceful, and always on the move. She had a certain grace and ease with people, could mingle in any crowd and charm them with her sassy attitude. Not that she was Little Miss Innocent. Oh no. He'd heard all about her legendary temper. He'd heard that she could be just as crazy as her best friend and Alpha female, Taryn. But, still, Shaya was sweet and perfect, and so different from him it was laughable.

He could still vividly remember the day he'd found her. It had been the mating ceremony of her Alpha pair, and he had offered to perform the ceremony for them. He'd had an itchy feeling all day, a *knowing* that something important was going to happen. The second his gaze had landed on the beautiful redhead, he'd known what she was to him. The impact of the realization had been like a blow to the chest; possessiveness, joy, and need had hit him all at once. The pressing urge to claim her had climbed all over him, entered every pore of his body, and invaded every cell . . . and it hadn't left him. He craved her so badly that she was all he thought about, all he dreamed about. He itched with the need to have her, touch her, smell her, or even just be around her. The need could steal his breath, taunt his mind, and make his body restless. Basically, it was hell.

But the main reason he forced himself to endure that hell and resist claiming this one thing he wanted more than anything else was that she could find herself being burdened with a patient instead of a partner. His mother's words rung in his head: *The healing sessions are working, Nick. Don't forsake your mate out of fear. You're strong; you can fight this.*

There weren't many shifters whose animal surfaced prematurely, but each one of them shared something in common: their cognitive functions suffered for it in later life, slowly degenerating. There was no denying that the healing sessions were working for Nick. The headaches, memory lapses, muscle tremors, and episodes of mental disorientation had all eased off. In some cases of premature shifting amongst his kind, these degenerative aftereffects could be healed completely, but in some cases they couldn't. As his mother had said, he *was* strong. But his mother was right about something else: that fear remained . . . that fear that the improvement was only temporary, that the problem would eventually return.

His pack healer had warned Nick that this could happen. If it did happen and he was mated to Shaya at the time, she would find herself being his caregiver as opposed to his partner, watching him slowly deteriorate until he didn't even know who she was. He'd seen what it was like for his mother to live without a mate. She had survived the breaking of her true mate bond with his father after he died by centering her entire existence around her children, clinging to them like a lifeline. She was happy in her own way, but she was still lonely and only half alive. With Nick as her patient rather than her partner, Shaya would in effect be without a mate. He couldn't bear the thought of his spirited Shaya only half alive.

Although he didn't feel he could claim her, Nick was resolved that he would always watch over Shaya from a distance, always protect her. Her well-being would always be paramount to him. And that was exactly why he was, at that moment, in his SUV approaching the perimeter gates of Phoenix Pack territory. He needed to be sure that the "bad news" had no relation whatsoever to Shaya. He needed to know that it was not at all linked to her health or safety. And, yes, he could admit he needed to just see her, needed a small "fix."

He knew it wasn't fair to pry in her life if he wasn't going to claim her, even if it was in an effort to protect her. In fact, her Beta pair—the only members of her pack, to Nick's knowledge, who knew he and Shaya were mates—had quite rightly pointed this out. They had also warned him that if the Alpha pair found out, there was a good chance that a war between the packs would begin. But even that wasn't enough to keep Nick away.

As Trey and Nick were close allies, the shifter guarding the perimeter gate didn't flag them down; he simply gave them a respectful nod and let them pass through the gates of Phoenix Pack territory, which was disguised as a nature reserve. Nick's wolf relaxed a little—content in the knowledge that he would soon see his mate.

Eli, Nick's brother, drove the SUV to the mountain that was deep within the territory. Unlike most packs, including Nick's own, the Phoenix wolves didn't live in cabins. Instead, they lived inside the mountain—an ancient cave dwelling that had been modernized.

Once Eli had parked the SUV inside the concealed parking lot at the base of the mountain, Nick turned to him. "Stay here. Derren and I should only be fifteen minutes or so." Nick was always careful not to bring too many wolves inside the caves. The Alpha, Trey, wasn't the most stable of people, and his wolf easily felt threatened. As such, the arrival of three powerful, dominant wolves would instantly have him alert.

"Nick, maybe you—" Derren quickly cut himself off, sighing. "Never mind."

Grateful he wasn't going to have to listen to more of Derren's shit, Nick exited the SUV. Both Eli and Derren knew that Shaya was his mate. Being someone who stayed out of other people's business, Eli hadn't said much about it—plus, he knew that pressing Nick on anything was an exercise in futility. Derren, however, had raised the matter plenty of times, badgering Nick to stop letting fear interfere with his decision to claim Shaya. It was getting real old.

With Derren close behind him, Nick climbed up the steps that had been carved into the face of the mountain until he finally came to the entrance. One of the enforcers, Marcus, was there, holding the door open. He didn't look happy. That might not have given Nick cause to frown if it wasn't for the fact that the tall, dark-haired wolf was usually cheery and flashing everyone a clown-wide smile. When Marcus didn't even give him a nod of greeting, a feeling of disquiet came over Nick.

"Trey's in the kitchen," he said simply before gesturing with a tip of his head for Nick and Derren to follow him through the tunnels that would take them deeper into the mountain. After a series of turns, they eventually reached the very contemporary kitchen. Sitting at the long dining table were the other three enforcers, the Head Enforcer, the Beta pair, and the Alpha pair. Much like Marcus, they didn't look happy to see him, particularly Taryn. And that could only mean one thing: they all knew the truth about Shaya being his mate. So either the Beta pair had finally told them, or Shaya herself had.

Well, it had only been a matter of time. Not one to play games, Nick didn't bother with any pretense. Stopping in front of the table, he simply said, "So you know."

"Oh, we know," confirmed Taryn snappily. Her mate began kneading her nape, clearly trying to keep her from going for Nick's throat. The blonde might be small and dainty, but she was powerful. And scary, for that matter. In fact, most of the shifter community feared her as her once latent wolf had overcome that suppression and surfaced.

"I suppose this is the part where you order me to stay away from Shaya." If they thought they'd have any success with that, more fool them. Hell, he'd ordered himself to stay away from her, and not even that had worked.

"You owe her that," gritted out Jaime; the Beta female was a close friend of Shaya's. But that was his Shaya—she made friends easily, inspired loyalty and protectiveness in people, which was why the wolves in front of him were clearly fantasizing about killing him. He noticed that one of the enforcers looked particularly pissed with him. *Dominic.* Nick really did hate that wolf. Why? Because Dominic spent a lot of time with her—so much so that Nick had at one point suspected he was in a relationship with her.

Usually his wolf—who was prone to jealousy—would have most of his attention focused on the little prick, but not today. No, today his wolf was stressing over something and was annoyed with Nick for not realizing what his wolf had already sensed: Shaya's scent was faint. Extremely faint, in fact. Unease tingled down Nick's spine. "Where is she?"

"That's not important," stated Trey, his arctic-blue eyes drilling into Nick. "What's important is that you listen carefully. We're all very much aware that you and Shaya are mates and that you've both known it from the beginning. As it's obvious that you don't want to claim her, you are to butt out of her life and leave her alone. If you don't butt out, well, you must want a war between our packs."

The word "war" should have had him growling and on high alert, totally focused on Trey. But all Nick could think about was the fact that Shaya's scent was far too faint—faint enough to suggest that she hadn't been here for a while. "Where is she?"

Trey and his Beta male, Dante, exchanged looks that said they weren't surprised that Nick was unconcerned about the warning.

"Her whereabouts are none of your business," snarled Taryn. Tao, the Head Enforcer sitting beside her, nodded his agreement.

Nick's face hardened. His words were quiet but firm. "Shaya is, and will always be, my business."

That had Taryn jumping to her feet. If Trey hadn't twisted his hand in the back of her sweater, she'd have leaped over the table. "Yougoddamnmotherfuckingsonofabitch!"

"It's okay, baby," soothed Trey. One of the enforcers, Trick, went to her side and laid a supportive hand on her shoulder. It was only then that Nick noticed the tears swirling around her eyes. For Taryn to be so upset, Shaya hadn't simply gone on vacation or to stay with her family in her old pack for a little while. She'd left for good.

"No, it's not. My best friend has gone because of that rat bastard!"

Yep, that confirmed it. "Gone *where*?" demanded Nick, barely holding back a growl. His wolf began pacing inside him, clawing at him, wanting freedom, wanting to hunt down his mate—the only thing that really meant anything to him.

"Somewhere safe," Jaime told him. "Somewhere where you can't hurt her anymore."

Nick took one step forward, and each of the Phoenix wolves tensed, prepared to spring. Yeah? Well he didn't give a fuck. "You think I *want* to hurt her? You think it doesn't eat at me that I can't have her? You think I don't constantly wonder where she is, what she's doing, and if she's safe?"

All of the faces softened, but Nick didn't want their fucking sympathy. He wanted to know where his mate was. He zeroed in on Trey. "Tell me where she is." When he didn't answer, Nick placed his hands on the table and leaned forward, placing him eye to eye with the Alpha. All the Phoenix wolves growled low, but they didn't attempt to interfere—that would imply that their Alpha couldn't deal with his own shit. As it was, Trey was perfectly capable of fighting his own battles. But although Trey might be strong and powerful, so was Nick; he let the full extent of his dominance leak into his expression, communicating that he was just as powerful as Trey. In actuality, he was also as fucked up as Trey—he just hid it better.

The Alpha leaned forward, placing his face close to Nick's, meeting his gaze full-on. "I have no interest in dueling with you, Nick—you fought alongside me to help protect my mate, my son, and my pack. That's something I'll always be thankful to you for. I once had people try to keep Taryn from me, and I reacted just as badly, so I can understand how you're feeling to an extent. But if it's a duel you want, you'll get one."

"If this was Taryn, if I knew where she was and I wouldn't tell you, what would you do?"

Trey cocked his head. "That's the thing—I never would have left her. I'm not the noble type. If you want to be self-sacrificing, fine, whatever—but you do it away from Shaya."

Dante spoke then, crossing his arms over his muscular chest. "If we thought you wanted to know her whereabouts for the right reason, we'd tell you. But you don't want to find her so you can claim her. It simply suits you to be able to interfere in her life. That's not fair to her."

Jaime laid a hand on Dante's arm. "I know what it's like to feel you have to resist mating with someone because you fear putting them in danger, Nick." And she really did know. Her wolf had been so traumatized that Jaime had been at risk of losing her human half completely. If that had happened and she had turned rogue, she would have been killed. For that reason, she had resisted bonding with Dante, worried he wouldn't survive the link being broken if she died. Luckily, bonding with Dante had instead helped her wolf heal.

Of course her reference to "danger" meant the danger of Shaya being an Alpha female—she didn't know about Nick's health issues, or she would most likely understand. But Nick wasn't and never had been interested in other people's perception of him, so he had no intention of explaining himself.

"I know it hurts," continued Jaime, "but you should have claimed her and trusted that you'd be stronger together. Just because Shaya can't be physically stronger than a dominant female doesn't mean she can't still defeat them. There's more to combat than physical strength—take it from someone who was trained by the best." She gestured at Dante. "I've kicked Popeye's ass a number of times." Dante scowled at her for that comment.

Nick sighed impatiently. "The dominant females wouldn't even need to challenge her. All they'd have to do is hit her with their dominant vibes and she'd be automatically submitting whether she wanted to or not." And Nick hated the idea of it. When an odd expression surfaced on Taryn's face, he narrowed his eyes. "What?"

Taryn shook her head. Losing her scowl, she sighed. "Just leave her alone, Nick. She's safe. I give you my word that if anything ever happens to her, if she's ever hurt, I will contact you. But that's the most you're getting."

While he appreciated that, it wasn't enough. He'd been kidding himself if he thought simply being around Shaya from time to time would be enough. It was only now, as he was faced with the fact that she was gone from his life, that she would never be a part of it, that he might never see her again, that he realized he'd subconsciously nurtured a hope that he could find a way around their issues. He hadn't truly given up on the matter, not deep inside, but the present situation was forcing him to do so, to give up *all* hope. And he found that he couldn't.

Nick inhaled deeply, fighting to remain composed. But how could he? Dammit, it fucking hurt that she'd left like that. Not just because she was away from him, but because she'd so easily been able to run when he hadn't had the strength to stay away. And he was angry too. Angry that she could leave him behind and start a life without him, and angry with himself for pushing her in that direction. Also, he was panicking. Not knowing where she was, if she was safe, if she was happy was a torment all on its own. Whatever Shaya or any of these wolves thought, he did want her to be happy. More than anything, he wanted to be the one to make her happy.

And with all that came the determination to find her.

But Dante was right: finding her simply to know where she was, to have peace of mind, wasn't a good reason. The only chance Nick had of being in her life was to put right what he'd done, step down from Alpha, claim her, and take Derren's and his mother's advice and shove aside his fears rather than forsaking someone so important to him. That was exactly what he would do. If that meant the foundations of his pack began to crumble, so be it. Shaya was his; she was more important.

Of course it would be pointless to tell her pack that. They would never believe him—they would simply think he was feeding them shit so they would reveal her whereabouts. He'd have thought the same thing in their position.

Fine, he didn't need them to tell him. Nick was a powerful Alpha, and he had many contacts, knew a great many Alphas all across the globe. There wasn't one pack in the world in which she could hide where he wouldn't find her. Pivoting on the spot, he began marching out of the kitchen.

"Nick?"

Halting, he glanced over his shoulder, meeting Taryn's gaze. "Let her be."

"Not going to happen. If you want to end the alliance, start a war, you do that. But it won't stop me from searching for her. Nothing will." With that, he left.

Trey sighed at the sound of the main door slamming shut. They had hidden Shaya well, had taken her as far as South Carolina. Rather than settle her there, they had—cashing in a favor that another Alpha owed him—used a private jet to transfer her from there to Arizona. Their belief was that Nick would never think they would hide her in such a close location. Ryan, Trick, and Marcus had then created a false trail going from South Carolina to New York before allowing it to abruptly end.

They knew that Nick wouldn't give up when finding no sign of her in New York and might backtrack, but they also knew that Nick wouldn't be searching for a human with Shaya's description—which was what she was posing as in Arizona. He would be searching all the shifter packs. Trey had been pretty confident that Nick didn't have a hope in hell of locating her. But having seen the determination in Nick's eyes, Trey wondered for the first time if their efforts had been enough. Not that he could blame the guy for his persistence in locating his mate. No one could keep Trey from Taryn, and God help anyone who ever again tried.

He glanced down at her, giving her an "I told you so" look. Taryn had insisted that although Nick might be pissed to hear that Shaya had gone, he wouldn't bother taking the time to hunt her down.

She sighed at her mate's expression. "Okay. You're right. I'm wrong. You're smart. I'm dumb. You're tall. I'm . . . average height." She arched a brow, daring him to call her tiny.

"Do we contact Shaya and tell her that he's coming for her?" asked Tao.

Taryn shook her head. "No. The last time I spoke to her, she sounded happy enough. She likes her new job, and she's decorated her new place. She's starting to get settled. If I tell her that Nick's on the hunt, it'll have her panicking. Besides, there's a good chance he won't find her. He won't for one minute imagine that Shaya's hiding in the human world."

Dante winced, running a hand through his short walnut-brown hair. "I don't know. I've heard Nick's a talented tracker. He's also got a lot of contacts—not just through being an Alpha, but because of his time in juvie."

"Juvie?" Taryn's mouth dropped open. "How the hell did he end up in a juvenile prison?"

"When he was thirteen, he killed a human teenage boy and badly maimed two others in his wolf form while trying to defend himself and his sister."

"*Thirteen?*" she echoed. "How long was he in there?"

"He came very close to serving a life sentence, but Nick had acted in self-defense—that's a lot different than cold-blooded, premeditated murder, particularly when what could have happened to Nick and his sister had been cold and premeditated. But the human court ordered for him to remain contained until he was eighteen."

"Shit," said Taryn. Matters concerning shifters were dealt with by packs, but if the incidents involved humans in any way, the human authorities had a right to deal with it. "Time in juvie must have been hard as fuck."

Trey nodded. "Hell yes." Although humans had juvenile prisons specifically to contain shifters, they were run by humans who tried to make all their lives hell for committing crimes against their race. Trey had heard about the type of shit that went on in places like that, and he had to respect anyone who got out of them with their sanity still intact. Not only was Nick sane—or relatively sane—but he was an Alpha and a very good one.

"So when I say Nick has a lot of contacts, I mean it," said Dante. "In juvie, shifters tend to band together, forming little packs of their own. They all keep in touch when they're released—in fact, Derren's one of the shifters who served time in juvie at the same time as Nick. It might be best to warn Shaya so she knows to keep a low profile."

After a moment of thought, Taryn shook her head again. "What kind of life would it be to be constantly looking over her shoulder for the big bad wolf who broke her heart?"

Trick leaned back in his seat, frowning in a way that made the claw marks on his cheek seem to darken. "Nick's right, though. Claiming Shaya would put her in danger."

Ryan, a guy who somehow always looked grumpy and very rarely spoke, nodded. "A whole lot of danger—I've seen it happen before." And they were probably the only words the enforcer would speak for the day.

"I wouldn't be too sure about that," said Taryn.

Trey narrowed his eyes at the roguish smile that curved his mate's mouth. "What do you mean?"

She took a sip of her coffee. "Just trust me—Shaya's no fragile flower. Don't forget I sparred with her all the time growing up and taught her all my combat moves. And do you remember how talented I am with knives?"

How could Trey forget? When he'd pissed her off a few weeks ago, she'd hurled five knives at him—all of which buried themselves in the wall around him, framing his body. "Yeah."

"Shaya taught me that."

Dominic's brows flew up. "Shaya?"

"And you remember those stories Caleb told you about how my ex-boyfriends often found their cars had been vandalized?" Caleb was a childhood friend from Taryn and Shaya's old pack. Trey nodded. "That wasn't me. Shaya's good with a bat—thanks to Caleb teaching her how to play baseball. She's real good with a rifle too."

Marcus gaped. "You're kidding me."

"Her dad's actually human, so he knows what it's like to be targeted in a pack for being weaker. He didn't want that for Shaya, so he taught her a few things. Being a Navy SEAL, he had plenty of stuff to teach her. Plus, he's not totally stable."

Dante chuckled. "No wonder I sensed a serious amount of impishness in that girl—there's almost as much as there is in my girl."

Jaime gave him a mock scowl and flicked her long sable hair at his face, making him puff it away. "I guess it's an advantage that Shaya looks so sweet."

Taryn's smile widened. "Yeah, everyone's fooled by Shaya's innocent exterior. They never see the mad coming. If Nick does manage to find her, he's in for a few surprises."

# CHAPTER TWO

I *won't aim this hairspray at her eyes. I won't aim this hairspray at her eyes.*

Shaya Critchley chanted it to herself over and over as she made the finishing touches to her client's hair, pointedly ignoring the irritating woman at her side who was delivering snide remark after snide remark. It wasn't that Shaya gave a shit about the peroxide blonde's opinion. It was kind of hard to care what a person thought of her when said person's face was so caked in makeup that she looked like a warrior going into battle. But after a long, busy day spent mostly on her feet, Shaya simply didn't have the tolerance required to deal with Paisley right now.

Each of her fellow hairstylist's insults had been delivered with the most patronizing tone and the falsest smile, and the message was clear: Shaya's hair was too red, her body was too thin, and her skin was too pale. Yeah, well, at least Shaya wasn't smeared in fake, blotchy, unevenly applied tan. The girl looked like she'd rolled in Doritos.

Having Paisley hanging over her shoulder as she worked only served to increase Shaya's annoyance, and she had a feeling that Paisley was well aware of that. And why would she be so

17

set on driving Shaya insane? Simple: Although Paisley had been working at the salon for four years, Shaya had more clients than her. Sensing Paisley's distaste, Shaya's wolf bared her teeth—she could be sassy and snippy like that. Though her wolf wasn't a fan of confrontation or the type to begin brawls, she was quick to defend herself or those she cared about and had little tolerance for petty people like Paisley.

If Paisley knew that Shaya was a half-shifter, her attitude toward Shaya would be even worse. The girl and her family were all strong supporters of the human extremist groups that had been calling for certain laws to be put in place to monitor, control, and isolate shifters. There would be a court hearing in four months' time to address the matter. If the human extremists were successful, all shifters would be chipped, placed on a register like child molesters, forbidden from mating with humans, and confined to their own territory. It also meant that any lone shifters would be forced to live outside human society in what had been referred to as "gated communities"—it was simply a way to contain and isolate them.

As such, Shaya had ensured that no one other than Kent— her boss, friend, and a fellow half-shifter—knew what she was. Not even the local shifters were aware of her mixed blood, as she had ensured she was never close enough for them to sense it. Why? Easy. Members of the Sequoia Pack had a nasty habit of "disappearing." Given that their Alpha was a drug lord, it wasn't difficult to guess who was responsible.

"How's that for you, Mrs. H?" asked Shaya, angling a hand-held mirror at the back of the middle-aged woman's head so that the reflection would be seen in the large mirror opposite.

Mrs. Harley turned her head from side to side, touching her perfectly straight dark hair as she examined the reflection. Then she shot Shaya a beaming smile as she stood. "How you manage to make my hair look so smooth when it's usually like straw, I have no idea, but I love you for it."

Shaya laughed, removing the black waterproof cape from Mrs. Harley's shoulders. "It's not like straw."

"Oh it is, honey. Not like your beautiful hair. What I'd give to have curls like yours."

Paisley made a face at that comment, while Kent nodded his agreement and reached out to tug on one of the corkscrew curls. "They just make you want to play with them."

Shaya scowled playfully as she swatted his hand away. He did that a lot—mostly because he knew it irritated her. If he wasn't such a good friend, she might have chopped off his spiky blond hair. Years ago, she and Kent had studied hairstyling together at college, and they had clicked instantly—not sexually, though, seeing as he was gay and all.

They had never once lost contact over the following years, and he'd asked her to visit him plenty of times. When she had called six months ago and asked if he would allow her to stay with him for a while, he'd been delighted. More perceptive than Shaya was comfortable with, Kent had immediately sensed that it wasn't simply a social visit. She had admitted that she was hiding from someone but hadn't wanted to say more—she had promised herself that making a new start would include not dwelling on having been rejected by the Prick of the Century, otherwise known as her true mate, Nick Axton.

Being as fabulous as he was, Kent hadn't pushed her for more information. Instead, he had helped her find a place to live and had given her a job at his hair salon. In other words, she owed him big-time. But she still often found herself yearning to go back to California. She missed all her friends, especially Taryn, Jaime, Dominic, and Caleb. She often spoke with them over the phone or Skype, but it wasn't the same. And, though she would never admit it to Taryn because her friend would come to collect her, she wasn't happy.

It wasn't just because of Nick's rejection. Despite having a job, it didn't exactly pay well. Although the home she rented was cozy, it was also slowly falling apart. Shaya did *not* specialize in DIY. Of course it was her landlord's responsibility to fix the problems, but he was extremely good at dodging that responsibility. Then there was her hypochondriac of a mother and her constant calls to deal with. Each call was the same—she would moan about all her "ailments," complain that no one cared, send Shaya on a guilt trip for leaving, and then become insulting when Shaya refused to return. It wasn't that the woman was pissed about not knowing Shaya's location or even that she missed her. She didn't even care that Nick hadn't claimed her. The woman just didn't like not having someone to fuss over her and cater to her every whim. How nice was that. Shaya had taken to ignoring the calls altogether.

And then, of course, there was the fact that she missed the social touch her packmates had always provided. Her wolf, too, missed that closeness. Nonetheless, Shaya had no intention of returning to California. No intention of ever again coming face-to-face with Nick, even if he was the other half of her soul.

Shaya had already lost part of her soul before she was born. That was exactly what Mika, her twin who had died in the womb, had been—an integral part of her. All her life, Shaya had felt an emptiness inside like a part of her was missing . . . because it was. She had always felt the sense of being "alone" much more acutely—something that had been worsened by the incident that happened when she was four.

The guilt had lingered deep inside—guilt that she had survived and hadn't been able to save her twin, despite how little sense it made. "Vanishing twin syndrome" people called it. During her teens, that guilt had led her down a path of self-sabotage as Shaya had felt that she hadn't deserved to be happy. With support, she had eventually given herself permission to live a full and healthy life, honoring her twin and using her as her motivation. But the pain, the emptiness, was still there.

Losing Nick before she'd even had the chance to know him was exactly like it had been with her twin. She hadn't had the chance to know Mika, to have a life with her . . . and now she would never have a life with her mate either.

Her wolf was going through a similar pain. She didn't understand why Nick hadn't staked his claim, and she viewed his actions as a rejection. But although her wolf was angry with Nick for rejecting her, she was also angry with Shaya. Her wolf still wanted to be in close proximity to her mate, not understanding that Nick had no intention of ever claiming her and that he would make life difficult. Awkward animal.

Snapping out of her ponderings, Shaya walked to the reception desk to say good-bye to Mrs. Harley, who was at that moment taking her receipt from Paisley. When Mrs. Harley tried to give Shaya a most generous tip, she shook her head. "That's too much."

"Honey, I've been going to have my hair done regularly for a long time. Usually, my stylist patiently listens as I moan and groan about all the trouble going on in my life—things that were always difficult to talk about with family members."

"You don't moan," objected Shaya. If anything, the woman was a delight.

"Not around you," agreed Mrs. Harley. "Because for the two hours that I'm with you, I totally forget all about my problems and find myself laughing and joking with you. What's more, you always have me walking out of here feeling good about myself. So, honey, you *will* take this tip." She forced the large tip into Shaya's hand, winked, and walked right on out the door.

"You have a way with people," Kent told her. "They like being around you, even seem to gravitate toward you. Considering you haven't been here very long, you've built yourself a nice clientele. You should be proud of yourself. I've never known anyone to form connections with people so easily."

Yeah, she was quite good at forming connections with people—lasting ones, in fact. She just had a really hard time forming *deep* connections. Although she craved one, she was too distrustful and guarded to allow it to happen. Was that really any wonder when her first real relationship had been an absolute mind-fuck?

She'd been just sixteen when she met Mason. She had been infatuated with him, practically worshipped him. He had told her he felt the same, that they were true mates. Still plagued by a feeling of emptiness after losing her twin, she had been so desperate to feel some sort of connection that she'd bought it hook, line, and sinker. Later she had realized that she had given her virginity to an asshole who liked to target young females and convince them they were true mates.

After that, she had flitted from guy to guy, never letting anything deeper develop. Not that she'd been a slut or anything, but she hadn't been in a serious relationship—determined to wait for her true mate . . . a guy she had spent the past half year trying desperately to hate. She was failing miserably with that. How could she possibly hate her mate, even if he was a prick?

Well, at least she didn't cry herself to sleep anymore. That was an improvement. She'd even started dating again. Not that the dates had amounted to anything, as apparently she was flypaper for losers lately. The world seemed to be against her meeting a decent guy. As much as it would make sense for Shaya to want to keep things simple and stick with meaningless encounters or short affairs after Nick hurt her the way he had, she wanted more than that.

Yes, part of it was that she wanted someone who could cancel out the mating cravings, someone who could fill the space that her true mate would never fill. But another part of it was that seeing her friends so happily mated made her hunger for the same. She wanted a guy who would care for her, a guy she could trust and depend on. Was that really so bad?

Apparently so. Either that or he simply didn't exist. Ah, maybe that was it.

Shaya almost banged into the reception desk as a ticked-off Paisley accidentally-on-purpose bumped into her as she passed.

Oh, for the love of God. Shaking her head, Shaya went over to her station to clean and tidy it. It was as she was sweeping up the hairs that were scattered on the floor that Paisley returned to her side. "I was just wondering, have you always suffered from ginger-vitis?"

Shaya rolled her eyes. The red hair comments were a regular thing, and she was used to them at this point, though she was tempted to point out *again* that her hair wasn't ginger in any case.

"I guess it must be nice being Ron Weasley's sister, though."

Sigh. "Seriously, Paisley, you don't need to keep this up. I honestly couldn't like you any less than I already do." Shaya walked to the trash can and emptied the clump of hair into it before returning the brush and dustpan to the cupboard.

Paisley trailed behind her. "As if being a carrottop isn't bad enough, you're—"

Shaya sighed again. "Can't you see I'm trying to pretend you're not here? When you speak, you kill the illusion."

Paisley curled her upper lip and made a move toward Shaya, but Kent was suddenly there. "That's enough," he told the blonde.

"She's only been here, like, *two* minutes and everyone's fussing over her!"

Shaya shrugged. "If what you want is the same treatment, maybe you could try *working*. Just sayin'."

Snarling, Paisley sharply twirled and returned to the reception desk, but the comments didn't stop. By the end of her shift, Shaya had come close to stabbing the blonde with her own scissors. Instead, she grabbed her things, gave Kent a hug and a kiss on the cheek, and left. As her car had died recently and she couldn't afford to fix or replace it, she made the fifteen-minute walk to her home. For a change, her closest neighbor—who was a hundred yards away yet still managed to be a pain in her ass—wasn't holding a house party that could wake the dead.

She let herself inside her home, secured the door shut behind her, hung her jacket on the coatrack, and kicked off her shoes with a groan of relief. The fluffy, magnolia-colored carpet felt amazing under her throbbing feet. Although coming back to an empty house never gave her any pleasure, it was certainly nice to let her feet breathe.

She had only walked two steps into the living area when she realized she wasn't alone. At the same time as it registered just who the familiar scent belonged to, a deep, rumbly voice spoke.

"Do you always leave your windows open when you go out?"

Abruptly, she turned to the corner of the room and gaped at what she saw. A contradictory mixture of shock, pain, anger, and—though she hated it—a slither of happiness hit her, almost stealing her breath. Sprawled on one of her cream leather armchairs, with his arms crossed behind his head as if he owned the space around him, was the last person in the world Shaya wanted to see. *Holy fucking shit.*

So beautiful. She was so damn beautiful that it almost hurt Nick to look at her. Despite not being small, she was petite and almost pixie-like with her heart-shaped face, small nose, clear skin, and clusters of adorable freckles that he wanted to trace with his tongue. His wolf was pacing—content yet also restless, and more alive around Shaya than in any other situation. Nick was feeling much the same.

He'd found her. He'd finally found her.

A fierce longing—both emotional and physical—pounded through him, making his body roar to life. He raked his gaze over her, reacquainting himself with every line and curve. "Hello, Shay."

Shaya almost jumped as that goddamn masterful voice snapped her out of her stupor. He had the most authoritative voice she had ever heard. It didn't demand compliance, it expected it. And it called to the submissive side of her nature. "What are you doing here?" He looked as he always did—dangerous, alluring, and deceptively relaxed. Nick Axton was *never* totally at ease.

Nick shrugged. "You're my mate. You're here. Where else would I be?"

He'd said it like it was a mathematical equation. Shaya's irritation was overshadowed, however, by the lust creeping over her. His appraisal of her was so thorough and intense that she felt as if he'd touched her. It reminded her of the night they had first met—he had barely taken his eyes from her, had watched her like a hawk. The difference was that there was now a determination in his gaze, a promise that she didn't understand.

Shaya inwardly groaned. Why didn't the universe like her? She didn't think she was bad, as people went. She recycled, and she donated to charity, and she didn't use products that had been tested on animals. Why, why, why couldn't fate have kept her hidden from him?

As Nick stared into those shock-filled bluish-gray eyes that were usually twinkling with an impish benevolence, he raised his brows. "You look surprised. Did you honestly think I wouldn't find you? Did you really think I wouldn't come for you?"

At those words, a surge of anger shot through Shaya. He had no right to be here, no right to seek her out when he didn't want her. She didn't need to have him watching over her and meddling in her life. That wouldn't *be* a life. He would never allow her to find someone else and be happy, regardless of the fact that he didn't want her for himself. He'd proven that by trying to scare off Dominic when he'd mistakenly thought they were a couple.

She knew that even if he mated with another female—a shaft of agony speared through her at just the thought of it—he'd never let Shaya have her own life. He'd left her no choice but to leave, and now the bastard wanted to mess up the life that she'd managed to make for herself here. Unfortunately, her wolf wasn't moved by those details. Now that the shock had worn off, her wolf's primary instinct at that second was to go to her mate, to touch him and take him inside her; to allow him to claim her, and to claim him in return. Great.

What *Shaya* wanted to do was snatch the nearest heavy object and hurl it at Nick's head. But she wouldn't give him the satisfaction of seeing her lose it. No. He'd made it clear through his past indifference that he didn't want her. She'd give him that same indifference now. She spoke in a crisp, cool voice. "Well you've found me. You've seen me. You know that I'm fine. Now you can leave." Before he could respond, she headed for the oak kitchen and quickly switched on the coffee machine. She sensed that he had followed her into the room, felt his power almost burning her back, but she paid him no attention as she fixed her drink.

"I didn't come here to check on you," he said. "I came here to take you back."

She chuckled humorlessly. "I'm not going back to the Phoenix Pack just so you can always know where I am and be in my business, scaring guys away. If you think I'm going to live life as a spinster, you're about as bright as Alaska in December."

The very idea of her with someone else always made Nick see red. His wolf, who was still pacing predatorily and eager to get to his mate, growled at the idea. Nick's voice was quiet but dangerous. "*Is* there a guy, Shaya? You better hope there isn't, or he's dead. And don't think I don't mean that."

She knew he meant it, the interfering bastard. Cup in hand, she pivoted to face him. Although he hadn't taken more than two steps into the room, his large, powerful build practically dominated her kitchen, making Shaya feel cornered. Like a prey by a predator. Involuntarily, her eyes briefly darted to the door. Nick, still staring at her with an intensity that would unnerve any female, stepped in front of it as though to block her avenue of retreat. Wow, did he actually suspect she'd run like a frightened little fawn? He should. She was seriously considering it. "Who I'm with and what I do is none of your business."

He took one slow step toward her. "You'll always be my business, Shay. You're my mate, you're mine."

Although his voice had been gentle, there was steel in his words. That steel only served to fuel her anger. But the anger wasn't enough to drown out the lust heating her body. Hell, *lust* wasn't a strong enough word. The closest word she could think of was *desperation*. Yes, she was absolutely desperate to jump on him and run her fingers through his short ash-blond hair; desperate to feed the need, feed the urges, and to answer that yearning for total completeness that she knew he could give her. She was actually shaking with it.

Shaya wished she could say that the only reason she wanted him was because he was her mate, but that would be a lie. No, this male who radiated authority was walking temptation with his powerful muscular build, sensual mouth, and penetrating dusky-green eyes that demanded total attention. Power hummed around him, and he exuded dark, primal, animal energy. Moreover, he was charged with a raw, magnetic sexuality. His natural dominance was like a magnet to her submissive side, and it promised to answer every craving she had. In other words, he was her personal wet dream . . . which meant it was vital that she got him out of her home.

Giving herself a mental slap, she returned her focus to the conversation. "Yours?" She snorted. "I don't think so."

Nick arched a brow. "I might not have claimed you, but you're still mine." His voice was soft and controlled, but even he heard the menace in it.

The possessiveness practically emanating from him pleased and seduced her wolf, just as his natural dominance that promised total safety did. But it wasn't enough for Shaya—her submission wasn't something he'd earned on any level. "I never had you down as the delusional type. Huh. I guess you never can tell. You can let yourself out."

Her dismissal pissed Nick off, but he'd known this would happen. He'd anticipated her resistance and anticipated that she would be eager to get a few things off her chest before even considering leaving with him. He could sense that, despite how calm she looked, she was absolutely livid. "This is a nice place," he said as he took a turn around the dining area that was attached to the kitchen. The house was warm, stylish, and bright. "How've you been?"

The genuine interest in his voice surprised Shaya, considering the impression he'd given her was that he saw her as nothing but an object to whom he had rights. Sipping her coffee, she watched through narrowed eyes as he strolled around like he owned the place. His casual body language displayed a quiet, relaxed confidence; there was no fidgeting, no wasted movements, no twitchy motions with Nick. Every single movement was sure, fluid, and deliberate. God help her, she found all that confidence and control sexy as shit.

It galled her that she was drawn to this person whom she would happily shoot right in the head. She forced a chirpy tone. "Great, thanks. I'll feel even better once you're gone." Her wolf, on the other hand, didn't like that idea. A little voice in Shaya's head insisted that she didn't either, but she ignored it.

"Aren't you going to offer me a coffee?"

"No. You're not a guest, you're an intruder. Plus, there's no point, since you're leaving right this second. Have a safe journey."

Nick grinned. He liked her sassy attitude. "Sure. I'll leave. Get your stuff together."

He'd clearly been held back a few grades if he thought that would ever happen. "Whoa there, did you not hear me before, Beavis?"

"Beavis? Are you saying I'm dumb?"

"It's not your fault."

Seeing the pain in her eyes that her aloof tone was trying to hide, he sighed. "Baby, I know I hurt you, so I don't blame you for being severely pissed at me—"

"I'm not pissed at you—although I've visualized you sliding down a barbed-wire banister a couple of times."

He winced. "That bad, huh?"

She nodded slowly, her voice hard. "That bad. But hey, don't beat yourself up about it. I'll do that."

Nick believed her. There was that temper he'd heard all about. "I'll make it up to you, I swear. Once I get you back to California, we'll—"

"I already told you, I'm not going back to the Phoenix Pack."

"I didn't come here to take you to the Phoenix Pack."

Okay, he'd *totally* lost her. Something in his expression made her wary. "I don't understand. What do you want from me?"

"I want you. All of you."

The flash of determination in his eyes made her suck in a breath. No, he couldn't possibly mean what she thought he might. "What does that mean?"

"I'm here to claim you." The last thing he'd expected was for her to hurl a teaspoon at his forehead. Shit, that actually hurt.

"Claim me? Now there's a fucking joke. I'd rather French kiss a goddamn barracuda than mate with you!"

Nick cursed in surprise as Shaya lifted one of the wooden breakfast stools and launched it at him. He barely ducked in time to dodge it. When he stood tall again, it was to see another stool coming at him. He caught that one, using it as a shield against the next stool. Then she was racing out of the room.

Before she could escape from the house, Nick dashed after her. But she didn't open the front door. She reached behind the rack of coats in the hallway, pulled out a baseball bat, turned sharply, and swung it at his head. *Motherfucker.* He jumped backward, barely avoiding it. "Dammit, Shay!"

Where had his sweet mate gone? Having a bad temper was one thing, but the female in front of him was a merciless psycho. Proving that, she swung the bat again—this time at his abdomen. Although he jerked away, he only managed to dull the impact of her swing. It still connected hard with his abdomen, making him instinctively bend over as the breath whooshed out of him. That was when the bat came flying at his head again.

Pissed-fucking-off, Nick caught the bat and yanked it toward him. He'd expected Shaya to try to keep hold of it, expected that his move would have tugged her to him. It didn't. She let go of the bat and made a dash for the living room—God knew what weapon she was hiding in there. Not wanting to find out, he flung the bat aside and dove at her.

When a hard body folded around Shaya and tackled her to the carpet, she growled a string of profanities. Unsheathing her claws, she twisted her body slightly and took a swipe at Nick's face. The prick was fast—he dodged the move and then clamped his hand around her wrist, pinning it above her head. Most likely suspecting she would try the same move with her free hand—he would be right—he shackled her other wrist. Then he locked his teeth around her shoulder in a very dominant move. Not biting, not breaking skin or marking . . . just cautioning her, snatching her full attention. It worked; both she and her wolf froze.

Putting his mouth to her ear, Nick spoke quietly. "I know you're pissed at me, and I don't blame you, but we need to talk. I'm going to sit you on the sofa, and we'll discuss this like adults. We can do this the easy way or the hard way. Choose." When she sank her teeth into his arm, he got his answer. Of course he could throw his dominant vibes at her and suppress her, but he would *never* do that to his mate. Not seeing any other option to calm her down, he used his free hand to put pressure on her baroreceptor in the carotid artery at the base of her neck where it met her shoulder. Pretty soon, she was limp beneath him.

As Shaya woke to find herself slumped across the sofa, she frowned in confusion. That frown deepened when she saw that Nick had moved her armchair so that he was now directly opposite her and watching her with shrewd eyes. It took only a split second to recall what had happened—he'd sent her into the land of the fairies when she wouldn't talk with him. She was actually kind of surprised he hadn't simply used his dominant vibes to suppress her. Huh.

Abruptly she sat upright. And that was when she realized something else. Her wrists were secured together in front of her with black fur-lined cuffs. She gaped at him. "Oh, you sick bastard."

He winced. "I was hoping I wouldn't need to use them . . . but I can't say I don't like the look of them on you. Notice that I didn't pin them behind your back. I don't want you uncomfortable. I just want us to be able to talk without you grabbing a bat and swinging it at my head."

"Thanks for the small mercy," she spat with heavy sarcasm.

Wearing a forlorn, hopeless expression that plucked at Nick's heart, she dropped her head and her shoulders sagged. Then she was sniffling. *Shit.* Guilt prickled his skin. He did the only thing he could do. He rose from his seat and went to her. Shocking the shit out of him, she suddenly sprang to life; she stomped hard on his foot, used her wrists tied in front of her to deliver a mean blow to his jaw, and then kicked his kneecap hard, making him stagger backward. Before Nick could reach for her, she was up and heading for the kitchen.

Nick should have been pissed—not only had she played him by acting the sad, stoic victim accepting of her fate, she had run from him. Instead, he found himself smiling at her deviousness. He could respect deviousness.

He was going to catch her. Shaya knew it. That didn't mean she was just going to lie back and take this shit. That wasn't who she was. Still, it was no more than five seconds later when a hard body folded itself around her from behind and she was tackled to the hardwood floor, pinned onto her stomach with her arms squashed beneath her. This was familiar. "Get off me, you son of a bitch!"

"You're fast, I'll give you that." Nick grunted as she jammed her elbow into his rib cage. He placed more of his body weight down on her, but if anything, that only intensified her struggles. "There's no point in doing this, baby. Stop."

She snickered, forcing herself to ignore the authority in his voice. "Fuck you!" She reared her head back, smirking as it connected hard with his forehead, and he cursed again. When wooziness momentarily came over her, she realized that that might not have been wise.

"Christ, woman, will you stop!" That move had hurt like a *bitch*. Ignoring the trickle of blood he could feel spilling from the top of his forehead, Nick trapped her cuffed wrists above her head. "I swear if you don't stop struggling, Shay, I'll spank your ass." She didn't stop. Of course she didn't stop. So he slid his free hand down to rest on her ass. Well, "rest on" wasn't quite accurate. More like he'd cupped her ass. He could say with all honestly that it was the hottest ass he'd had the pleasure of touching.

"What the fuck?" Shaya wished she felt as outraged as she sounded.

"Stop trying to fight me or I *will* spank you. Don't test me." He was hoping she did. "I never make a threat that I don't intend to follow through." Did she stop? No. She tried to head-butt him again. Nick *tsk*ed and sharply brought his hand down on her ass, smiling when she gasped and froze. "I told you not to test me. Or maybe you wanted me to do it." He placed his mouth to her ear and spoke in a teasing tone. "Maybe you like that. It'll be no hardship for me to spank you again, so if you don't like it, quit fighting me."

As much as she hated to acknowledge it, there was no way that Shaya could get out from under him. She was just so tired, and he was so strong, the asshole. Her wolf lowered her head and tail, acknowledging his dominance. Shaya couldn't bring herself to openly admit defeat to him, so rather than speaking she simply went lax beneath him.

"Very good." Nick's voice was thick with the lust he felt at watching her submit. "Now, we're going to slowly stand up." He should have known that she'd try to run again. He should have expected it merely because the female could clearly be counted on to do the exact opposite of what he told her. Being much faster than she was, he caught her easily enough, looping an arm around her and pulling her back against him. "Now that wasn't very good behavior, was it?" The crazy bitch bit into his arm, kicking him wildly. Grunting, he slung her over his shoulder and landed a harsh slap on her ass as he stalked back to the living room.

Shaya's outraged gasp turned into a lengthy growl. "Put me down, you asshole!" She clawed at the skin of his lower back.

"Just so you know, I like it rough. But I should point out something. You've used your claws and teeth a few times on me. If you do it again even once—whether it's out of anger or not—my wolf is finally going to rise to that and push me to mark you right back. With the mating urges beating at me and your scent wrapped around me and your skin under my hands, I know for a fact that I won't be able to resist biting you any longer. If you don't want that, stop."

The warning had been delivered in such a soft, sensual, velvety voice that a tremor rippled through Shaya. She hated knowing he'd feel her need for him.

Returning her to the sofa, Nick looked down into Shaya's snarling face and sighed inwardly. She was beyond pissed, which was the last thing he wanted. Conscious of the blood trickling down his forehead, he snatched a tissue from the box on the coffee table and used it to stanch the flow.

Realizing she was scowling at him, Shaya lowered her eyes—a submissive wolf wouldn't be able to hold an angry dominant's powerful gaze for very long. However, she wasn't an average submissive. There were things about her that many people didn't know. But as she had no wish to tell him, she forced herself to look away. "You'll regret this, Beavis."

"I'll remember to watch my back," he said with a smile.

"Oh no. When I come at you, I'll come at you from the front."

Her sassy response made his smile widen. "That's my girl." Sitting on the armchair again, he watched as she struggled against the cuffs. Sighing, he dug out the key from his pocket and unlocked them. At her suspicious look, he shrugged. "I think at this point you're as tired of all the running around as I am . . . although it was fun to chase and spank you."

"Had you honestly expected me to be quiet and compliant like a good little girl? I might be submissive, but I'm not a pushover."

"Oh, you're definitely not a pushover," he agreed. "I never, for even one minute, thought that you were." She had the strength of will to match any dominant female, to match his.

"You can't ignore me for months and then expect me to welcome you with open arms."

"I didn't ignore you—"

"You didn't even *look* at me, let alone speak to me or—"

"Because I didn't trust myself not to pick you up and carry you off." He sighed. "You're not dumb, Shay. You know that your being submissive is a problem. If the situation was reversed and claiming me would put me in danger, what would you have done?"

"Talked to you. I'd have talked to you and explained how I felt. If I hadn't thought that there was a way I could be with you, I'd have given you the space to live your life, but you couldn't even give me that."

He arched a brow. "Are you going to tell me that you're not feeling the same pull as I am? That your wolf isn't hounding you? That the urge to mate isn't close to controlling you? I can see you shaking with it, Shay. So don't make out like staying away from you should be simple for me. It never was." He inhaled deeply, wanting that scent he'd missed to be nestled deep in his lungs. God, she smelled like the ocean, fresh crisp air, and home. He had to fist his hands to keep from touching her. It was painful to resist.

He took a calming breath, inhaling deeply again. And that was when he smelled it—her arousal. It was the sweetest smell that seemed designed to torture both him and his wolf. He wanted to find out if her taste was just as alluring. His wolf was clawing at him, growling at his lack of action, at not claiming what was *theirs.*

"My name is Shay*a.* And yes, I do feel that same pull. Yes, the urges are a pain in the ass. And that's exactly why you're here—for the wrong reasons. Not because you truly want me, but because your wolf's pushing you too hard and the urges are bugging you too much. Well that's not good enough for me."

"I stepped down from Alpha."

She was so startled she couldn't speak for a few seconds. "What?"

"My old Beta is now Alpha."

She'd met his old Beta a few times, sensed his very dominant wolf, and she'd sensed something else too—extremely dominant or not, Jon was nowhere near as powerful as Nick. She wasn't sure whether or not he was lying about having stepped down from Alpha, but she knew one thing: "Your wolf wouldn't be able to take orders from someone less powerful than he is—he wouldn't obey him. Plus, everyone in your pack would still see you as the person to go to and answer to because you're more powerful than Jon."

"I know. That's why I left."

She gawked. "What?"

He spread his arms wide before crossing them behind his head and leaning back in his seat. "I'm now a lone wolf."

Her mouth bobbed open and closed a few times. What he'd done wasn't by any means a small thing. Not that she believed Nick had ever or would ever actually *need* anyone, but to be without a pack or territory or the social contact provided by a pack would be hard as all shit for any shifter. If Shaya hadn't been half human, she was pretty sure the lone-wolf lifestyle would have been too much for her to handle. As it was, she found it pretty difficult, but that wasn't so much to do with her shifter side as it was to do with her issue with being alone. "But . . . why?"

"Because if being Alpha means I can't have you, then I don't want the position. *You're* what I want."

Struggling to think clearly, she got to her feet and began to pace. She honestly didn't know what to say, what to do. Here he was, claiming to have made some *major* changes to his life just for her. Hell, he'd left his pack, his family, his territory, and his position behind! She would have been impressed, but it made no sense. If she had really been so important to him, he would have done this in the very beginning . . . which made her wonder if this was nothing more than a grand gesture. Even if he truly intended to never return to his pack, she very much doubted that it would work for him or his wolf. It would only be a matter of time before the urge to go back became too much.

He rose from the chair and went to her. "Come back to California with me. I don't have to tell you how dangerous it is to be a lone shifter right now—the human extremists are making themselves a huge problem. So if you want to return to the Phoenix Pack, fine, I'll go with you. I won't lie—obeying Trey would be hard because I'm as powerful as he is, but as he's not weaker than me, it could still work. Come with me."

Shaya looked at the hand he held out to her and swallowed hard. She could admit to herself that the temptation to go with him was like nothing she'd ever felt. Six months ago, she'd have given anything to hear those words. But not now. It was too late; betrayal still sat like lead in the pit of her stomach. She shook her head. "You walked away from me."

"And you ran from me." He slowly reached out and gently straightened one of her red corkscrew curls, watching with an inner smile as it bounced back into place. It took him by surprise how soft and silky her hair was. "But it was the best thing you could have done." At her questioning look, he elaborated. "It made me realize a few things. Namely that living without you isn't an option."

"Because the urges won't ease."

"Because you're more important than anything else," he corrected, taking a step toward her so that there was only a hairbreadth between them. As her scent wrapped around him, he barely resisted the temptation to bury his face into the crook of her neck. "I've missed your scent. It drives me crazy." Drinking in every detail of her face, he smoothed the pad of his thumb across her cheekbone. "I've missed looking at you. Watching you."

She told herself to step back, but it simply didn't happen. As if the mating urges weren't enough to deal with, she now had his scent—the guy smelled like cedar, cinnamon, danger, and a dark masculinity—swirling around her. The scent caressed her senses and made her tingle all over. Finally her legs began to work, and she backed away, shaking her head. "I want you to leave."

His wolf growled at not only her words but the distance she'd created between them. Nick quickly closed it. "I can't do that. Six months I've searched for you. Six fucking long months. I didn't do it just to walk away from you."

She snorted. "Why? You did it easily enough the first time."

"Nothing about it was easy." He ran his hand through her curls, glad when she didn't step away. "You're so full of life, and I'm broken and jaded, so you deserve better. But I've discovered that I'm not selfless enough to leave you alone." Resting his forehead against hers, he cupped her neck and began breezing his thumb up and down the column of her throat. "I'm a bastard for what I put you through, and I'm sorry. I won't let you down again, I promise. Just come with me."

Her chest ached at the plea in his eyes—eyes that always looked so haunted and shadowed that it made her wonder what he'd been through that had stained them that way. His thumb traveled up to her mouth and traced the outline of her lips as if he was claiming them. Shaya had every intention of pushing him away. Any second now she would do it.

"Since the first day I saw you, I've wondered if your lips are as soft as they look." A low growl rumbled up his chest when she nervously licked her bottom lip, making him want to do the same. She had the most enticing mouth—soft, sensual, and plush. He realized he wasn't going to be able to move without tasting it. "And I've wondered if you taste as good as you smell."

Oh shit. Shaya tried shoving him away, but it had zero effect. In fact, he didn't seem to notice. By the way his body tensed as if to spring, she had expected him to jump into action, for his hands to skate all over her and his mouth to come down forcefully on hers. Instead, he simply began to sip from her lips and nip at the curve of her inactive mouth. When he sucked her bottom lip and bit it gently—a total weak spot for her—she couldn't hold back the low, contented sigh.

Then he was sipping from her lips again . . . seducing her mouth, she suddenly realized. And it had worked. Although she had told herself that she would push him away, she was actually chasing his mouth with hers, wanting more, but he pulled back each time. She understood the message: she'd get what he gave her, nothing more. Instead of using his physical strength to assert his dominance, he'd literally seduced her into submission. Sneaky. Fucking. Wolf. She would have pulled back, but then his mouth landed on hers and took total control of it.

Nick groaned as her taste burst on his tongue, practically imprinting itself into him. He slid his hands into her hair and tugged, feeling her shiver against him. For so fucking long he'd wanted this, wanted *her*. Touching her wasn't easing the urges as he'd expected. Instead, sensations were crawling all over and through him. Worse, he was being taunted by a crushing, primal need all tangled up with a heavy sense of possessiveness and a fierce drive to *own*. He was thinking of pushing her against the wall and ripping the clothes from her body when he felt her suddenly tense in his arms.

Surprised by her own strength, Shaya abruptly tore her mouth from his and used the hands that had been plastered to his chest to push him back—the effect was more of her bouncing backward. "Enough." Hating that she had responded so enthusiastically to his touch, she skirted around him to put some space between them again, holding her hand up to warn him off. It didn't work. He advanced on her. Not quickly, but slowly and stealthily, like a predator prowling toward skittish prey. "It's too late."

Hating the pain in her eyes, he wanted to punch himself. "You're not the only one who's been hurting, Shay. Yes, it's my fault—I have no one to blame but myself. But I won't ever hurt you like that again."

A part of Shaya wanted to believe his promise, was hooked on how earnest he looked and sounded, and was totally hung up on just how much more alive she had felt in these moments with him than she had in the last six months. But she was simply too hurt and wary to take the gamble. "Just go."

"Not without you."

"You have no choice in the matter. I can't go with you."

"Why?"

"Because I don't trust you!"

Nick felt as though she'd punched him. The breath left his lungs in a whoosh. It didn't matter that it was his own fault, and it wasn't even a surprise, but it still hurt like a motherfucker.

"I don't trust you not to hurt me. I don't trust you not to leave me again."

Something about the way she'd said the latter words had Nick narrowing his eyes. This wasn't just about him. Being left was a big thing for her, and there was clearly a story behind that. He cupped her chin. "That's not going to happen."

She snickered, slapping his hand aside. "How do I know that? Huh? How do I know you won't suddenly decide that not being Alpha isn't working for you? That you need to leave me behind because it's 'not safe' for me to be your Alpha female? I'm not going through that shit again. You had your chance to claim me, and you fucked it up. Now go."

Not a thing could have made Nick move from where he was except for the tears now filling her eyes. He wanted to hold her and comfort her, but if she didn't trust him, the last thing she would feel was comforted. So far, he hadn't respected any of her wishes. If he had any chance of earning her trust, he needed to start now.

Forcing himself to ignore his wolf's and his body's demands, Nick stepped back and held his hands up in a placatory gesture. "Okay. If that's really what you want, I'll go. But I'm not leaving for good, Shay. I'm not abandoning you again." He could see that his words had surprised her. "Repeat that to me."

Scared that he would sense that a small part of her wanted him to stay, Shaya turned her back to him. "Just go."

"Not until you repeat it. Not until I'm positive that you understand I'm not leaving you again."

Prepared to do whatever it took to get him away from her, she mumbled, "You're not leaving."

Nick gave a satisfied nod. "I'll see you soon." When he reached the doorway, he called out, "Oh, and don't think about running. I'll only find you again. Feel free to call Taryn and ask her to come get you, but I won't let her or anyone else take you. I'll kill anyone who tries. I've hurt you, I get that. We can take this as slow as you want. But I *will* claim you, Shay. You're mine. I'm not staying away from you anymore."

When the front door closed behind him, Shaya let loose a string of curses. But this time, she wasn't cursing Nick. She was cursing herself. It was pathetic how easily and strongly she had responded to his touch. Maybe it would be fair to say that it was only natural, given that he was her mate, but it still galled her. His touch had left a tingle of fire in its wake, and now her cheeks were flushed and her entire body was crying out for him.

Her gaze moved to the cordless phone on the coffee table, and she briefly considered making a call to Taryn. The thought left her mind even quicker than it came. She could easily anticipate what would happen: Taryn, Trey, and some of the enforcers would appear, and every one of them would go ballistic at Nick. He would defend himself, and being as powerful as he was, he'd do extremely well at it. In other words, people she cared about could be hurt. Although she was mad at Nick, she didn't want him to be seriously hurt either. All she wanted was for him to stay away from her, to let her live her life.

*But is that* really *what you want?* asked a skeptical voice inside her head—one that totally supported her wolf's urge to claim him.

Yes, it was.

*Are you sure about that?*

Oh, for God's sake. As if it wasn't bad enough that she was having a war with Nick, she was also having one with herself and her wolf. This was not good. Not. Good. At. All.

# CHAPTER THREE

R eaching the end of Shaya's driveway, Nick exhaled a heavy breath. Well, things could have gone a lot worse. The bat could have knocked off his head, for instance. That merciless streak had been a shock. Maybe he should have paid more heed to her yard warning sign: TRESPASSERS WILL BE SHOT, SURVIVORS WILL BE SHOT AGAIN. And then there was the COME BACK WITH A WARRANT doormat. Yep, it was fair to say there had been some hints.

The fact that he'd had to place his mate unconscious for his own safety was something he'd never forget. Both Nick and his wolf loved that spark of fire in her. Despite being a submissive wolf, she hadn't hesitated in challenging him verbally or physically. That was a good thing—it was important to him that his mate never feared him or his level of dominance. It would cut him open if that were to ever happen.

As he walked a short distance and rounded the street to find his motor home, which had been his place of residence for the past six months, he noticed that someone was leaning against it—a very familiar someone.

Derren's muscular form stepped out of the shadows. "How

did it go?" When the ex-bodyguard's dark gaze fell on the small wound on Nick's head, he grinned. "Not so well, huh?"

Nick smiled; he was actually proud of her for bloodying him. "Didn't I fire you?"

"Multiple times."

In reality, Nick hadn't hired Derren in the first place. Back when they were in juvie together, Nick had saved Derren's life. The wolf had then taken it upon himself to appoint himself as Nick's bodyguard and escort him everywhere—which it seemed he intended to do until he finally returned the favor. It hadn't mattered what Nick had said or done, he hadn't been able to shake Derren off. "I asked you to stay with Jon. He's Alpha now, and he'll need you."

Derren snorted. "Jon can take care of himself. So can you, but you're stuck with me—you know this already."

Sighing, Nick shook his head. "I told you, you don't owe me anything." As usual, Derren ignored Nick's grumbling. "How did you find me anyway? I would have noticed if you had been following me."

"I stayed with Jon long enough to be sure the pack didn't give him any problems. As I'm sure you already know, he's doing fine, and he's been accepted. Though everyone misses you, they understand why you had to leave. As soon as I heard you'd located your mate, I tracked you down using the info you gave Jon this morning. I only got here about ten minutes ago. It must piss you off to know that you've been driving from state to state and she was only five hours away from your home."

It did. But something else pissed him off more. "It's not going to be easy to get her to leave with me."

Derren's expression was sympathetic. "You already knew that. Maybe if you told her everything—and I mean *everything*—it might help her understand."

"You're right. But there's a problem with that."

"Which is?"

"Shaya has a big heart, and she'd immediately feel sorry for me. I don't want her to give me a chance because she feels bad for me."

"You want to earn her trust."

Nick nodded. "And that may take a while." As a particularly sharp, agonizing pain sliced through his head, he winced.

"Headaches getting more frequent?"

The truth was that the headaches had started again two months ago and had very gradually increased in frequency and intensity until he often had one or two each day. Yes, chronic headaches had been a major problem when his cognitive functions first began to degenerate, but that didn't mean that the same thing was happening again. Headaches could be caused by plenty of things—stress, exhaustion, and emotional tension. There was no denying there had been plenty of that in his life lately. Plus, his father had suffered from chronic headaches most of his adult life; it could be hereditary. "It doesn't have to mean anything."

"Of course it doesn't. As long as it's only headaches we're talking about. If the memory lapses, muscle tremors, or periods of mental disorientation come back, you can't ignore it."

"I won't." But he refused to let fear keep him away from Shaya ever again. So unless the other symptoms returned, he wouldn't allow himself to even speculate if the headaches were anything to be worried about. Unlocking the door to his motor home, Nick said, "I need painkillers and sleep. *You* need to go home. Once again, I'm firing you."

Derren gave him a curt nod. "If that's what you want."

What Nick wanted was Shaya. But he fully understood that the process of winning her trust would be gradual. She was upset, confused, and angry—and justifiably so. He knew he was going to need to be patient, understanding, and sensitive. Patient he could do—he was more patient than most. Understanding and sensitive . . . He wasn't much good at that stuff, never had been, so this would be new territory.

He'd have to resist kissing her again. He wouldn't stop touching her altogether—he needed her comfortable with and used to his touch. But if he laid another heavy kiss on her, she might think he was trying to use their attraction against her to persuade her. Being that they were mates and the urges were so strong, it probably wouldn't be hard to seduce her. But he didn't want that to be why she came to him. He wanted it to be about more than the physical side of things. Unfortunately, resisting her was going to be hard as all shit since he was literally hardwired— body, mind, heart, and soul—to want her.

Groveling wouldn't do him any good—not that he knew how to grovel anyway—because the last thing Shaya would ever be attracted to or respect was someone worthy of pity. His and his wolf's pride would balk at it anyway. There was apologizing, and there was acting like a desperate, creepy asshole. He'd done the whole apologizing thing, and now he needed to show her that it hadn't been an empty apology.

To achieve that, what he needed right now was a solid plan of action. Nick had always been good with plans. He'd have to insert himself in her life, show her he was there to stay. Words would never be enough, particularly since she didn't trust him. He would need to be persistent, but not push her, not seem as though he was putting pressure on her as that would only worsen the situation.

God, he was going to have to do the gift thing too, wasn't he? He was bad at that. He knew that Shaya wouldn't want clichés. No, she was the type to appreciate personal gestures. But what were personal gestures? Shit, this was going to be hard as hell. Nick didn't *do* romance, never had.

Another thing he would be sure not to do was expect anything in return. He would take things at her pace . . . but he wouldn't let her make him give up. He couldn't. He truly hadn't known it was possible for him to feel pain on this scale, hadn't realized it was possible to feel so torn up inside. He'd known different types of pain in his life, but none of it equaled this—not what had happened to make his wolf surface, not what had happened that got him sent to juvie, and not even finding out that his cognitive functions were degenerating. None of it equaled the pain of being without his mate. He knew without a doubt that nothing could.

She was going to be late for work again. Groan. On the upside, it was the earliest that she'd ever been late. In pretty much a daze after a crappy night's sleep, Shaya left the house and began walking briskly down her driveway. And came to an abrupt halt at the sight of something parked at the end of it. It looked like a humungous bus. Coming close, she tried to peer through the blackened windows, but they were too high up.

Seeing movement in her peripheral vision, she swerved to see a Mercedes convertible pulling up behind the bus. Then the bane of her existence was waltzing toward her, carrying Starbucks takeout. Again he looked dangerous and indomitable. Again he emanated an unflappable confidence. Again he had her traitorous body heating and tingling, readying itself for him—so not good.

Why couldn't he look like Sloth from *The Goonies* or something? She scowled. "You're still here?" At his presence and scent, her wolf stirred and stretched out inside her, her dark mood lifting.

Nick arched a brow at her tone. "Good morning to you too, baby. And yes, my head healed nicely, thanks." His wolf liked her sassiness, was even amused by it—and it took a hell of a lot to amuse his wolf. "Coffee?"

She barely refrained from shivering at the sound of that masterful voice that she was sure had been designed to taunt, intimidate, and arouse. Determined to ignore the effect he had on her, Shaya moved her attention to the cup he was holding out to her and wondered if he'd known she was a sucker for Starbucks coffee. "What flavor is it?"

"Caramel macchiato, of course."

Yep, he'd known. And he thought buying her a cup of coffee would help even things out? *Pfft*. Still, it would be a shame to let the coffee go to waste. It would certainly be unreasonable to refuse to drink it based on the buyer. So she snatched it.

"You're welcome."

Feeling something lick her free hand, she jolted. Glancing down, she found a panting, playful-looking, tail-wagging Labrador. She'd been so transfixed by Nick that she hadn't even sensed the dog . . . a dog that was now being happily stroked by Nick. She shot him a questioning look.

"Shaya, this is Bruce. Bruce, Shaya."

"Bruce? He's yours?"

He scratched the dog between his ears. "He was *supposed* to be my brother's dog, but for some odd reason, he's always followed me around. I'm better with animals than I am with people." And he preferred animals to people, actually.

Frowning, she watched as Bruce scratched at the door of the large bus. Taking out a set of keys from his pocket, Nick unlocked it and the dog trotted inside.

"He's a lazy shit. Likes to lie in front of the TV all day."

"Wait, this bus is yours?"

"It's a Winnebago," he corrected, resisting the urge to reach out and touch her. He wasn't a touchy-feely person, but Shaya's skin called to him. Seemingly of its own accord, his gaze flicked to her sensual lips. God, what a mouth. He wanted to taste it again. Thoroughly and commandingly. Then he would bite that bottom lip, mark it.

"A Winne-what?"

"A Winnebago."

"Like the one in *Meet the Fockers*? Hang on, how can you drive this *and* the Mercedes?"

"It has a garage for the car. Whenever I want to stop off somewhere for a while, I park the motor home and then use my car to get around. Want a ride to work?"

Every hormone she had yelled, "Yes!" Lord, he was so gorgeous and masculine and alluring she could cry. But she couldn't allow that to shake her resolve. "What I *want* is for you to leave. I made that pretty clear last night."

"Did you really think I would?"

"No. I wouldn't dare expect you to take my feelings into account." She ran a hand through her hair. "I guess I shouldn't be surprised that you're playing this little game."

He pinned her gaze with his. "This isn't a game to me, Shay. You said that you don't trust me not to leave you again. As much as I hate that, I can understand. So it strikes me that I need to make sure you know I'm serious. I need to prove to you that I'm not leaving you. So that's exactly what I'm going to do."

The words were so final, left no room for negotiation. Although she'd half expected him to pester her for a little while since dominant males didn't drop matters easily, she hadn't expected him to be so committed. Her wolf, who was becoming a real pain in the ass, liked that he had come to her and had every intention of claiming her. As such, she wasn't particularly happy with Shaya for resisting him. Yeah, well, Shaya wasn't particularly happy with Nick. "I don't want you here."

"A part of you does, Shay." He'd sensed it, and he was so damn grateful for it. "It might be small, but it's there. Beneath all your anger, there's still a desire to make this work."

He was right, the asshole. If he was just any guy, she might have been easily able to forget about him—after all, there were plenty more out there. But she only had one mate, and this was him; a part of her wanted him near and wanted to believe him. But hell would freeze over before she admitted it. "I have to get to work." Before he could again offer to take her, she raised a hand. "I like to walk."

"Suit yourself. Although I should point out that it looks like it's going to start raining any second now." He leaned back against the motor home and took a long sip of his coffee, ignoring the tap-tap-tapping of her foot.

When he made no move to drive off in his Winne-whatever-it-was-called, she counted to ten in her head, praying for patience. "Well . . . are you going to move this . . . thing?"

"Nope."

Patience all gone. "Nick, seriously, you need to—"

"You're going to be late for work if you don't hurry."

She glanced at her watch and cursed. "This and *you* had better be gone by the time I get home." Nick simply shot her a lopsided smile. The guy was a menace. How the hell did you get through to someone who had selective hearing? No, actually, it wasn't selective hearing. He heard and understood every single word; he just didn't give a crap.

Sharply she turned and began striding down the street. No more than a minute later, the rain started. Great. The sound of an engine made her turn her head. Nick had parked his Mercedes at the side of the road with the convertible top now up and was opening the passenger door in invitation. She wrestled with herself for all of five seconds before jogging over to the car and jumping inside. "Letting you give me a ride to work doesn't mean anything."

Nick gave her a reassuring "of course not" look, but inside he was smiling. He wasn't dumb enough to let it surface—he knew he was on shaky ground.

When he started the engine, she turned to him. "The salon where I work is—"

"It's okay, I know where it is," he told her as he began driving. His wolf let loose a growl of satisfaction—he liked having her in his space, liked having her scent surrounding him.

"How?"

"You're my mate. I'm naturally going to want to know everything about you." He shrugged; it was simple. "That includes your

49

address, where you work, and your cell number—just thought you should know so you won't be surprised if a text message from me arrives."

She gaped, both offended and shocked. "You can't just pry into people's lives like that and find out all their personal details. And *how* did you find them out anyway?"

He shrugged again. "I have contacts in the right places."

"So, what, you're a stalker now?"

"I prefer the term 'intense investigator.'" Before she could give him any more grief, he gestured to the vehicle. "Like it?"

"It's all right, I guess."

His mouth curved at the sound of her reluctant appreciation. "I'm more into all-terrain vehicles, but I couldn't have fit one in the motor home."

She frowned. "Then why not just use an SUV or something instead of that big hulking thing?"

"Because an SUV wouldn't have been much good as somewhere to live over the past six months."

"You've been living in the Winne-thing?" she asked, shocked.

He nodded. "So when you said you'd spent six months looking for me, you meant it literally?"

He gave her an odd look. "Of course I meant it." Realization quickly dawned on him. "You thought I meant I'd had other people tracking you for me."

She shrugged one shoulder. "You're an Alpha; you have shit to do."

"Not anymore, remember. I gave it up the day I found out you'd left. I've been searching for you ever since." Casting a glance at her, he saw her skeptical look. "You don't believe I gave up the position?"

"I believe you'll go back." She wasn't sure about the rest, but she was pretty certain about that. "Living without your pack and your land is hard."

"Living without you is harder."

Instead of sounding soppy or pathetic, it had instead come out sounding cutely possessive and protective.

"Besides, if you want the truth, I don't much like company."

That had her double-blinking in surprise. "You don't like company?" she echoed disbelievingly. "You're a shifter."

"People annoy me. I like being alone." Yeah, he knew that was odd for a shifter—they craved contact and thrived on it. But he'd never felt the same satisfaction from social contact that the rest of his kind did. Then, after spending five years of his life in juvie where there were no such things as space, privacy, or quiet, he'd eventually come to crave those things as opposed to social contact. And he wasn't good at bonding anyway.

Shaya was about to question how the hell someone who liked solitude could have acted as an Alpha when she caught sight of something in the side mirror. "Is that Derren in the SUV behind us?"

Nick sighed tiredly. "Yes." He'd noticed his "bodyguard" minutes earlier.

Turning in her seat, she regarded him through accusatory eyes. "Aha. You said you'd left the pack."

"I have."

"If that was true, you wouldn't still have a bodyguard," she pointed out impatiently. "Which means you've only been telling me all this to fool me into mating with you."

"Sorry, Nancy Drew, but you're wrong on that one. I've been trying to get rid of Derren for years."

"Why would he stick around to protect you if you're not Alpha?"

"It was never anything to do with me being Alpha. It's a personal thing."

"Really?" she drawled, skeptical. "And what is this personal thing?"

He'd rather not say, would rather not tell her about that period of his life in case it scared her off. "You know, you didn't answer me last night when I asked you if there was a guy in your life."

Thrown off-balance by the complete change of subject, she was silent for a moment. Instead of answering, she hit his question with one of her own. "Is there a female in your life?"

Nick would have insisted on hearing her answer first, but it killed him to see the distrust in her eyes. "There hasn't been anyone since I first saw you."

She snorted and turned her head away. "Yeah, right."

He tugged on her hair, demanding her full attention. "I wouldn't betray you like that."

She spluttered. "But we aren't mated."

"Doesn't matter."

"You *chose* to forsake me."

"No, I chose to put your safety above everything else. It didn't change the fact that the only person I wanted was you."

If that was true, he was going to be seriously pissed off by her answer, and then she'd be stuck in a car with a raging, too-damn-dominant alpha male wolf. That was never a good situation, and her wolf wasn't looking forward to it. When he raised a questioning brow at her, she averted her gaze as she admitted, "I dated a couple of times." She braced herself for an explosion. There wasn't one. Risking a glance at him, she saw him looking calm and cool. Only his white-knuckled grip on the steering wheel betrayed his inner turmoil. "Why aren't you yelling?"

"How can I?" His words were like crushed rock. "All you were doing was trying to get on with your life."

And now she felt bad. She shouldn't. She knew that. If he'd yelled at her, she could have rightly pointed out that if he hadn't wanted her to date anyone else, he should have claimed her. But although he was undoubtedly angry, he'd turned that anger inward, had directed it at himself, and was taking responsibility for what he'd done. Dammit. She wanted to stay pissed at him, and he was making it hard.

As he smoothly pulled up outside the salon, Shaya glanced at him to find that he still wasn't looking at her. "I never slept with any of them." No, she hadn't owed him that detail, but he could so easily get to her. It wasn't just because he was her mate, either. It was his eyes . . . those pools of dusky green had dark shadows there—scarred by a pain that no person would ever want to feel. Any female with a heart would want to reach out and take that away, not intensify it. She was hurt, but she wasn't bitter and twisted and didn't relish the idea of making anyone's pain worse.

Fighting to keep his touch gentle when anger was overwhelming him and putting a sour taste in his mouth, Nick briefly breezed his thumb across her cheekbone. "Thank you for telling me that."

"I can't forgive you for abandoning me."

"I wouldn't expect you to."

"Then why come here? Why do this?"

He swallowed hard, squeezing her thigh gently. "Because I'm determined to earn a second chance."

"And if you don't get it?" She tensed as a lopsided, mischievous smile surfaced on his face. It promised bad-boy stuff.

He leaned toward her slightly. "What you don't understand about me, Shay, is that when I really want something, I'll do whatever it takes to make it mine. Like it or not, you already belong to me; I intend to make sure that's not something you want to fight anymore."

Her wolf liked that. Liked his determination. Liked the idea of being the sole focus of his attention. Liked the idea of the chase. To her utter dismay, a part of Shaya kind of liked it too, but anger and betrayal overshadowed that. Besides, she couldn't trust anything he said or did.

Resisting the urge to kiss her, he moved back. "Go on, or you'll be late. I'll pick you up after work."

"I'm perfectly capable of getting myself home," she snapped indignantly.

"Of course you are. I'll be here waiting when you get out." He smiled when she growled before getting out of the car. Once she was inside the salon, Nick drove farther down the street and parked outside the diner. He hadn't been sitting inside a booth for more than thirty seconds when Derren came strolling in. As he approached, grinning, Nick shook his head. "I distinctly recall firing you. Again."

"I'm trying not to be offended." He slid onto the seat opposite Nick. "She let you give her a ride to work. Progress."

"Yeah. This is going to happen in baby steps."

"How does your wolf feel about that?"

"The wait's killing him, but he understands that she's hurting. Like me, he wants her to come to him in her own time."

Derren gave a satisfied nod. "Your mom has called me three times in the past twelve hours to ask how you're doing and if your mate has accepted you yet. It would really help if you could answer your cell phone so she's not using me as a go-between."

"Why would I do that? If you're going to linger like a bad smell, you can make yourself useful."

Derren laughed. At that moment the waitress appeared, and they both ordered coffees and breakfast. "Your mom found Roni, by the way."

"Good." When Nick's sister was in her wolf form, she would often disappear for weeks at a time. Sadly, Roni spent most of her time as a wolf—she had done so since the incident that led to him serving time in juvie. Although his sister was strong enough to cope with anything life threw at her, it seemed that that one thing would always torment her. It was understandable.

"Your mom's trying to coax her to change back, but she's not having much luck."

"Has Amber tried?" Amber was the pack healer and, as such, the person who had healed Nick. The young female was also a good friend to Roni.

"She's tried, but she hasn't been successful. I spoke to Amber briefly. Her theory is that Roni's reacting badly to you leaving and has shifted to escape facing the true brunt of the pain."

And didn't that make him feel like shit. "I can't go back, Derren."

"I know. I told Amber that when she suggested you could at least go back for a little while."

"Good." Nick folded his arms across his chest. "Totally off the subject . . . We're being very closely watched." A group of four male wolf shifters in the corner booth had been casting him curious glances since he arrived. Furthermore, a trio of male wolf shifters at the rear of the diner was doing the same.

"The locals are going to want to know what you're doing in their territory. With or without the status of Pack Alpha, you're still a born alpha, and it's obvious in the way you conduct yourself. Hell, you're like a beacon to shifters with all the power practically humming around you." Derren paused as the waitress appeared with their orders. Once she was gone, he leaned forward. "Have you noticed there's a specific divide in the wolf shifters in here?"

Nick nodded. "Either there are divides *within* the pack, or we're dealing with two local wolf packs."

"Two wolf packs in one town . . . I don't see how that could work."

"It's not. Hence the tension."

Derren considered that for a second and then shrugged, switching his attention to his pile of pancakes. "Well, I know the main pack here is the Sequoia Pack, so I know who at least one of the Alphas in this town is: Petrus Hadley."

It took Nick a moment to connect the name with a face. "Ah, the Nazi."

"Why was he nicknamed the Nazi?"

"Because he's a Nazi."

"It's the 'drug lord' rumor surrounding him that bugs me."

Yeah, admittedly, it wasn't comforting.

"I'm surprised he hasn't approached your mate and insisted she join his pack or leave." Derren took a sip of his coffee. "You know, her wolf's not easy to sense. If I hadn't already known she was a half-shifter, I doubt I would have picked up on it." That was Derren—he missed nothing. "Maybe that's why she's been left alone."

"Her father's human," Nick told him after swallowing a piece of toast. "I found that out when I was searching for info on her to try to guess where she might be hiding."

"You know what that means, don't you?"

"That the urge to mate won't be as painful for her." Half-shifters had heightened senses and accelerated strength and speed just as full shifters did, but they differed in that their animal and primal instincts were diluted. "That's a good thing. I don't want her in pain."

"But it also means she won't be able to appreciate the kind of pain you're in by being around her and not claiming her. She'll be uncomfortable and restless and horny, but she won't have any idea of what you're going through. Won't have any idea how hard life's been for you since you laid eyes on her."

That was true. Shaya had it in her head that things had been an easy ride for Nick, that he'd found it simple to step aside. It was half the reason why she was so pissed at him. After demolishing the remainder of his breakfast, he said, "Like I told you last night, I don't want her to come to me because she feels sorry for me."

"But if she understands that you haven't, by any means, had an easy time, she might be a little less harsh on you." Derren took a long swig of his coffee, having finished his pancakes in record time. "*And* I still think you should tell her everything. The bigger picture would help."

Smiling, Nick snorted. "What, you're trying to be my advisor now, too?"

Derren cocked his head. "Do you think I'm smart enough?"

"Fuck you." There was no heat in his words. "I need to use the bathroom." Seeing that Derren was about to accompany him—most likely due to the gathering of snarling shifters—Nick threw him an impatient look. "I don't need you to hold my hand while I take a damn piss."

Derren chuckled. "Have fun, then."

Oh it *would* be fun if one of the shifters confronted him. Blowing off steam would be pretty helpful.

He got his wish. Nick had just finished buttoning his fly when four dominant male wolves entered the restroom. Not intimidated by their scowls or aggressive postures, he ignored them, went to the sink, and washed his hands. As he dried them, they formed a semicircle around him, blocking him in. Turning, he looked at them all curiously . . . like they were bugs. They didn't like that.

The one in the middle stepped forward slightly, tilting his bald head. "Who are you?"

"*You* guys are confronting *me*. I'll ask the questions. What do you want?" That seemed to have knocked his confidence a little. Good. Stupid shit was dominant, but he wasn't an alpha, and yet here he was practically challenging one, endangering himself and his packmates. He should know better. He should have been *taught* better.

"Our Alpha would like to speak to you."

"Really?" drawled Nick. "And why is that?"

"You're on our turf." He clenched his fists, snarling fiercely. "He wants to know why."

"Is that right?" Nick ensured he sounded bored. In truth, he was. When he was Alpha, there had been lone wolves who had drifted in and out of town occasionally. Unless they had bothered him in some way, he had left them alone. And if he had needed to speak with them, he hadn't done this whole song and dance in an effort to intimidate them. There was nothing big and bad about it. In fact, it was plain disrespectful and showed a lack of good leadership.

"So you need to come with us."

Nick stepped toward him. "If your Alpha wants to speak to me, he's welcome to come and find me."

"You really don't want to play this game. We're members of the Sequoia Pack. Our Alpha is the Nazi."

Nick just looked at him blankly. "As I said, if he wants to speak to me, he's welcome to come find me."

"You have no idea who you're fucking with."

"Neither do you."

He narrowed his eyes. "You're either very brave or very stupid."

"I'm bored."

"You're crazy," he decided.

Nick smiled. "How can you tell?"

"Listen, I follow orders. That means I'll take you to him conscious or unconscious. Do the smart thing and make the right choice."

No one was taking him anywhere. In a sharp yet fluid movement, Nick delivered a hard punch to the wolf's temple, knocking him out cold. Before any of the others could react, he yanked the hand dryer from the wall behind him and bashed it over the head of the wolf on his left, sending him dizzily crashing to the tiled floor with a hard thud. Just as Nick turned, one of the others charged at him. But Nick was faster. He used the hand dryer to shove him backward and simultaneously knock the wolf behind him off-balance. Nick then dealt his opponent a solid kick to the ribs, pretty sure at least one of them cracked. As the wolf keeled over slightly, Nick grabbed him by his hair and bashed his head on one of the urinals. The male went instantly limp and slumped to the floor.

Nick cursed in surprise when water suddenly sprayed at his face; the remaining wolf had turned on the faucet and curled his hand in the flow of water to make it spray at Nick. Taking advantage of Nick's distorted vision, the wolf aimed a mean kick at his face. Nick managed to dodge the move, but the kick still caught him on his shoulder. Totally pissed, Nick grabbed the next leg that came at him and twisted sharply, breaking the bone. The wolf screeched through his teeth and fell flat on his ass, satisfying Nick's enraged wolf.

Nick glanced around, taking in the scene in front of him. The wolf with the broken leg was getting paler by the second. Both the bald wolf and the one who had a close encounter with the urinal were still unconscious. And the male who had suffered a blow from the hand dryer was on the floor, moaning and cradling his head. He looked at Nick, who then arched a brow at him, daring him to get up. He didn't.

Nick sighed. "And that, children, is why you shouldn't pick a fight with an alpha—whether he's outnumbered or not. Your own Alpha should have taught you that. Consider this a lesson learned that your own Alpha should have taught you."

Strolling out of the restroom, Nick cast a quick glance at the three wolf shifters at the rear of the diner. They looked back at him, but there was no challenge in their gazes. Satisfied, he continued to his table.

Spotting him, Derren rose from his seat. "Did you let them live?"

Nick placed the money for his food on the table. "If I hadn't, then they couldn't explain to their Alpha that I'm not an easy target, could they? I don't need this shit right now."

"Not that I disapprove of you teaching the wolves a lesson," said Derren as they exited the diner, "but if you want to win your mate over, it makes sense to stay alive rather than go around pissing off drug lords."

"I don't know—I think she might prefer me dead."

# CHAPTER FOUR

Y ou seemed a little distracted today," Kent told Shaya as they
were slipping on their coats at the end of a long shift. "And
you look real tired."

She gave him a sardonic smile. "Such a polite way of telling
me I look like shit."

"Come on, tell me what's wrong. You're supposed to confide
in me and make me feel important and special." When she didn't,
he hit her in the chest with her own purse. "Spill."

Hanging the purse over her shoulder, she frowned at him.
"Hey, I don't harass you about your private business. If I was
going to do that, I'd say shame on you for flirting outrageously
with another one of your clients."

"I wasn't flirting. I was being particularly nice to a particularly hot guy."

"Uh-huh. Just try not to sleep with this one, okay?"

His mouth fell open. He followed behind her, spluttering, as
she headed for the door. "I did not have sex with Mark."

"No, of course not. . . . He had sex with you."

"As a matter of fact, Mark's not actually my client, he's
Paisley's client. I was just filling in that day."

"So it was you who did the filling and he who took—?" Stepping outside, her smile froze, as did her whole body, as she noticed the familiar figure leaning against a vehicle, waiting. Nick. Her stomach did about three flips, and her wolf instantly sat up, satisfied.

A part of Shaya had wondered if he'd keep to his word and come to give her a ride home, but that idea had been ruthlessly squashed by the distrustful part of her that had been born when Mason betrayed her; that part of her couldn't bring herself to invest any hope in Nick. She wasn't sure whether she was pleased or disappointed that he'd come, just like she hadn't been sure earlier whether she was happy or annoyed when she had received a text message from him:

I had the urge to text somebody who's smart, hot, and sweet . . . but sending messages to myself is just pathetic, so hi.

She had promised herself she would not laugh, but she hadn't been able to hold back a smile. She really didn't know what to do with this guy, but she knew one thing: she sure as hell wasn't giving him any encouragement by getting in that car with him . . . even though her feet were throbbing and it was cold and she was exhausted and she knew from earlier that his car was so warm and comfortable.

Kent, being nosy, strained to see over her shoulder. "Could he be the source of your distractedness, I wonder." She could hear the smile in his voice.

Moving aside, she allowed Kent to pass so he could shut the door and lock it behind them. Meanwhile, Nick was strolling slowly toward her with a predatory glint in his eyes. Although Kent was standing right there, Nick looked only at her. Having his intense focus on her was both daunting and thrilling. Her wolf loved it—the dangerous vibes he emitted didn't faze her wolf at all, because she was confident her mate would never harm her.

Shaya wished that the possessiveness in that gaze could have annoyed her, but it instead comforted her . . . eased something inside her. Insecurities that she wished she didn't have. His deep, rumbly, authoritative voice almost made her jump.

"Ready to go?"

"I'm praying someone spiked my coffee with some sort of hallucinogenic—the alternative that you're truly here is much too depressing."

If Nick's wolf could have laughed, Nick was pretty sure he would have. Only Shaya ever had this effect on the animal's mood. "I told you I'd be here when you finished work."

"And I told you that I'm perfectly capable of getting myself home." She noticed that Kent was staring at Nick in total admiration, fanning his face. When Kent looked at her, he mouthed, "Oh my God." Typical.

"It's just a ride." Nick smiled innocently, shrugging. "Like you said earlier, a ride doesn't mean anything."

She narrowed her eyes. He was twisting her words and using them against her. Oh, that was sneaky. And smart, she could concede.

Kent offered Nick his hand. "As Shaya's being rude, I'll introduce myself. I'm Kent."

Finally moving his gaze from Shaya, Nick shook what he knew was her boss's hand—as he'd told Shaya, he'd ensured he knew what there was to know about her life. "Nick." When the guy's brow furrowed in confusion, Nick realized that Shaya had never spoken of him. And didn't that hurt like a bitch. His wolf growled at that, wanting his role in her life to be noted. Nick was none too pleased about it either and thought about making it known right then. But he wanted Shaya to be the one to say who he was to her, wanted to hear her say it with pride rather than reluctantly through gritted teeth. "You're a half-shifter," observed Nick.

Kent nodded. "Very good. Not a lot of shifters are able to pick it up."

Shaya was kind of surprised that Nick hadn't firmly stated he was her mate. The guy was an extremely dominant alpha— the last thing he would want was any misconceptions about such a thing. Strangely, she found herself a little offended that Nick hadn't cared enough to clear it up. He wasn't even explaining that he was in town to see her. No, as he chatted to Kent, he was extremely vague, leaving his acquaintance with Shaya open to interpretation. Kent would undoubtedly think she and Nick had met in the last day or so. Again, she was offended.

God, what was wrong with her? One minute she wanted him gone, and the next minute she wanted him to declare she was his mate. But . . . maybe it wasn't all that odd, considering that her pride had taken a huge blow when he rejected her, she mused. His failure to acknowledge what she was to him had stung like hell, and it seemed that a part of her still wanted that acknowledgment, wanted to know he was proud that she was his mate.

As if he sensed her inner struggle and was taken over by a reflexive need to comfort her, he came closer and began casually toying with one of her curls as he and Kent chatted about the local pack and the local group of human extremists. She slapped at his hand as if it was an annoying fly, but Nick either didn't notice or didn't care because he didn't stop. So she slapped his hand harder. Without even glancing at her, he closed his hand around her offending one and nipped her ear punishingly. He then held her hand to his side, ignoring her struggle to reclaim it. Oddly enough, he seemed amused rather than frustrated.

"I wouldn't be surprised if the Sequoia Pack wants to talk to you, wanting to know what you're doing in town," said Kent. "You're not exactly inconspicuous."

Nick smiled. "I've already had that 'talk.'"

"What?" demanded Shaya. "You talked with the Sequoia Pack?" And why had "talk" sounded more like "fight"? "Nick, those guys aren't good. Please tell me you're not thinking of joining their pack."

Liking the concern in her voice, Nick ran the tip of his finger over her bottom lip. "I have no interest in joining their pack or any other." He chuckled when she slapped his hand again.

"If you ask me," began Kent, "the humans have a good chance of getting those laws put in place. It's shifters like the ones around here that give us a bad name."

"Is there more than one pack here?" asked Nick.

"No. The rebels are a small number of wolves who left the Sequoia Pack, but they refuse to leave town, so fights break out often between them and members of the Sequoia Pack. The human extremists use it as evidence to support their argument that we're wild and dangerous. The humans also know how the Nazi makes his money, but they have no way of proving it, so they follow him everywhere, desperate to pin something on him. The rebels are closely watched by humans too, but they don't have a permanent tail."

"So the extremists in this town are particularly active?"

"Yes." Kent gestured over Nick's shoulder. "And I think they wish to speak to you. They're at the end of the street, and they're slowly coming this way."

Nick had sensed them approaching before Kent's response. A white van had been following him and Derren around all day, and he'd figured it was the extremists—shifters wouldn't have delayed a confrontation for that long. He'd known it would only be a matter of time before they came to speak to him. Turning, he replied, "So I see."

The dark edge to his tone made Shaya shiver. In a millisecond, he had gone straight from gentle and cool to commanding and assertive. But that was the thing about Nick. Despite his casual posture, despite how supremely composed he seemed and his way of always seeming at total ease with his surroundings, he was never truly relaxed. He was constantly alert, ready to act. That dark energy he was loaded with was now radiating from him. It was a reminder of just how dangerous he was—like she needed that reminder. Although with her he could be gentle, she got the feeling that she might be the exception.

"Shay, I need you to get in the SUV with Derren." His wolf growled at the sight of the hateful humans slowly and cautiously approaching; he didn't want them anywhere near his mate.

"Derren?" she echoed, confused. It was only then that she noticed his SUV was parked behind Nick's Mercedes.

"Take Kent with you."

Before Shaya could say a word, Kent slipped his arm into hers and began dragging her to the SUV. Derren was out of the vehicle and holding the rear door open for them.

"In," urged Kent, shoving her inside.

A part of her wanted to stay with Nick, particularly as her natural soothing aura might just stop the confrontation from escalating. But she had to consider that her presence out there might instead cause the confrontation to get out of control—for her to be around the extremists would make Nick's wolf frantic enough to snap easily. Besides, presenting a united front was what mated pairs did, and they weren't mated. Her wolf growled and snapped her teeth at Shaya, unhappy with her refusal to stand at their mate's side in any case.

When Derren returned to the driver's seat, Shaya frowned. "Shouldn't you be out there with him?"

"He'll be fine."

"You don't think they'll attack him?"

He shot her an odd look in the rearview mirror. "Would you care if they did?"

"Of course I'd care." She might not want to mate with him, but she didn't want him hurt.

Derren returned his eyes to the spectacle outside. "If they have any sense, they won't dare threaten him, let alone attack him."

Distracting her, Kent elbowed her and gestured at Derren. "Sorry, Kent this is Derren, Nick's bodyguard. Derren, this is Kent, my friend and boss."

Kent cocked his head, confused. "Nick has a bodyguard?"

"Actually, he said he fired him."

Derren smiled. "He did. Repeatedly."

"So why do you stay with him?" She remembered Nick had said it was "personal."

Without removing his gaze from what was happening outside, he replied, "A few reasons. The main one is I owe him my life."

That had been unexpected. "And you're going to stay with him until you've returned the favor," she guessed.

"No. I want to ensure that there's never a reason for me to have to return the favor."

"In other words, you'll always be at his side trying to protect him." Which was weird. "Are you, like, gay?"

"Depends if I'm in prison or not." Hearing her gasp, he threw her an amused sideways glance. "Kidding. Be assured I have no designs whatsoever on your mate."

Kent gawked. "Nick's your mate?"

Derren gave her an indecipherable look in the rearview mirror. "You didn't tell him?" There was a big dose of disappointment in his voice. "Whatever you think about Nick, he didn't choose the position of Alpha over you. He never wanted the position in the first place."

That surprised her. "Then why did he take it?"

"You'll have to ask him."

Seeing that the crowd of humans was now directly in front of Nick, she asked, "Are you sure you shouldn't be with him?" Derren merely shrugged carelessly.

"You don't know your mate very well if you think he needs me."

That comment hurt . . . because it was true.

"Nick's a very powerful shifter," Derren continued. "Much like his wolf, he can be cold, remote, and calculated when he needs to be. Put all that together, and you have a lethal individual. That's why when he's angry, people pay attention. And he's not happy right now."

"If you truly believe he doesn't need you, why look out for him?"

"The problem with Nick is that he'll do anything he has to do to protect the people he believes he's responsible for. Anything. It means he can be a little reckless with his own life."

Seeing the almost rabid look on Nick's face, she asked, "Reckless, or just plain crazy?"

Derren's lips twitched. "A bit of both."

"Wow, he's practically bleeding power," said Kent with a gasp.

"Yup," said Derren. "Let's sit back and watch the show. Wait, is that . . . ? Son of a bitch!"


It wasn't the first time Nick had found himself surrounded by a group of prejudiced humans. But it was the first time that he was close to losing his self-control—and all because the leader of this particular extremist group was very familiar, and very much despised by Nick and his wolf. He knew he was vibrating with anger; it was taking everything he had not to gut the bastard.

Wearing a ruthless scowl, the human stepped forward, practically spilling hatred and senseless narrow-mindedness. But there was also fear there. "I know you're a shifter. Don't bother denying it. I can easily identify one. What I don't know is your name."

"You get three guesses," replied Nick. "But if you get it wrong, your firstborn's mine."

"Well, we've established that you're a smartass."

"Only around stupid people. I'm guessing you're the leader of the prejudiced humans."

"Not prejudiced," the human told Nick. "Enlightened. I want to know what you and your friend are doing in my town."

"As I told the Sequoia Pack, my business is my business."

The human's expression hardened. "This is my town. Trust

me when I say that out of the Nazi and me, I'm the one you need to worry about."

Nick arched a brow. "Really? Then why are you so afraid I can smell it?" His wolf loved the scent of his fear, wanted more of it.

The human froze. "You think if you make my men here believe I'm scared of you, they'll leave my side?" he scoffed, taking a few aggressive steps forward. "It's very much for your own good that you leave."

"Oh, is that so?" As Nick came toward him and invaded the human's personal space, the guy's confidence faltered at the power and dominance and alpha energy that spilled from Nick.

The human's voice was shaky as he continued. "Understand right now that if you choose to stay, I will be watching you. The first mistake you make, I'll be on you so quick, you won't know what hit you."

"Forgive me if I'm not quivering with fear, Logan." Seeing the surprise on the human's face, Nick smiled. But it wasn't a nice smile. "You don't remember me? Because I sure remember you," he rumbled.

The human cocked his head, studying Nick intensely. Then his eyes widened. Wariness crept into his expression, and the fear in his scent intensified.

"That's right," said Nick, his voice thick with anger. "I also remember how you get your kicks, just like I remember defending myself from you a number of times. Funny isn't it that you say you hate our kind, but you sure enjoyed sexually abusing the shifters in that place?"

"What's he talking about?" one of the humans asked Logan.

"I'm talking about the time that your leader worked as a guard in a shifter juvenile prison. Logan has a thing for young boys. I fought him off a number of times. Yeah . . . those aren't good memories for me." Nick gave Logan a pointed look. "So that presents you with a problem."

"Are you threatening me?" Logan swallowed hard.

"I'm merely pointing out the facts." Nick shrugged. "Trying to take me on always ended badly for you in the past. You simply might want to take that into consideration. It's a smart man who learns from his mistakes. Speaking of mistakes . . . how's your shoulder? Many people say that once you have an injury to the shoulder, it's never the same again. That true?" On one of the occasions that the sick prick had tried to touch him, Nick had dislocated his shoulder.

Logan's bitter expression confirmed that Nick was right. "How can what happened be abuse when you're not people, you're animals?"

Nick raised a brow. "So it's bestiality that gives you your kicks? Wow."

After a tense silence, Logan backed up a little. "I'll be watching you, Axton. You'll slip up, and I'll be waiting."

"Sure you will." Nick's expression warned him to move away. Logan wisely retreated, along with the others. Only when the humans had driven away did Nick move his eyes from the white van. Striding over to the SUV, he saw a scowling Derren lowering his window. "I take it you recognized Logan." Nick's words were barely understandable while anger was still bubbling inside him.

Gritting his teeth, Derren nodded. "All I wanted right then was to jump out of the SUV and rip his throat out."

Nick sighed heavily. "I have more self-control than most people, but I nearly killed the bastard myself."

"You were right not to," said Derren. "There are too many witnesses. His time will come."

"You know him?" Shaya asked Nick and Derren.

Forcing down his anger as best he could, Nick opened the rear passenger door. He didn't move to let her pass, though. "Unfortunately, yes. You okay?" He knew his voice was still strained with anger, but he couldn't soften it yet. He inhaled deeply, taking Shaya's scent inside his lungs and using it to calm him. But the only thing that could totally calm him right then was the feel of her, and that wasn't something he could indulge in.

Shaya nodded, wanting to know how he knew the human but conscious that his wolf was extremely tense right now. Revisiting what just happened would make things worse. "Fine."

"Derren's going to give you a ride home." Nick didn't trust himself alone with her while he was this wound up. The impulse to kiss her and hold her was too strong to ignore, especially when she would provide the calm he so needed.

The overprotectiveness got her back up. Making her even more pissed, Shaya found that she actually wanted to be with Nick and wanted to comfort him. It was instinctive—he was her mate, and something was clearly paining him. But that instinct made her want to slap herself. "He doesn't need to—"

Nick ignored her. "Kent, do you need a ride home?"

"No, thanks," he replied as he hopped out of the other side of the vehicle. "I have my MINI Cooper."

Nick gave him a brief nod and then returned his attention to Shaya. "I'll see you in the—"

Frustrated, Shaya went to get out of the SUV, but then she froze at the low warning growl that rumbled out of him.

"I can't be around you right now, Shay. And I think you know why. But if you really insist on Derren not taking you home, I'll do it myself regardless. The problem is I can't guarantee I won't touch you." There was no way he'd let her walk home on such a cold evening. No mate would. When she opened her mouth to object again, he gave her a look that said he'd argue with her all night if he had to. Eventually she sighed and slumped in her seat. "Good girl. I'll see you in the morning."

"Go squat and piss up a tree, asshole."

He almost smiled at that. "Right."

A few hours later, Nick was in his motor home tossing several pills into his mouth. These days, he took so many pills so often that he was surprised he didn't rattle as he walked.

Derren shook his head from his seat at the U-shaped black leather dinette. "You didn't tell me the headaches were happening so close together."

Nick forced a careless shrug. "Why would I? It's not important."

"You can't afford to be flippant about this, Nick."

"The healing sessions worked, remember? As I recall, you were one of the people telling me not to let fear rule my actions and to go after Shaya."

"I was also one of the people who heard Amber tell you the symptoms might return."

Nick slumped onto the black leather sofa bed opposite the dinette, his eyes shut, pinching the bridge of his nose. Bruce joined him on the sofa and butted his shoulder, hinting for some attention. With his free hand, Nick began scratching him between the ears. "They're just headaches, Derren. Bad, yes. Frequent, yes. But they're still just headaches."

Exasperation filled Derren's voice. "Look, I get why you're refusing to consider this might be something to worry about. And I get that you don't want to let Shaya down again. But this is one time you can't afford to risk yourself for other people. This is serious."

Nick's eyes flipped open. "You think I don't know that? If at any time I'm convinced the symptoms are coming back and the healing sessions failed, I'll leave. I don't want Shaya being my caregiver. Unless that happens, I'm staying where I am."

There was a short pause before Derren sighed. "Fine. Off topic, do you think Logan will be smart enough to leave you alone?"

"Nope. He has a score to settle—not just because I dislocated his shoulder once, but because I always managed to fight him off and intervened many times when he tried abusing other shifters. Plus, I'm guessing he knows just how badly I'd like to hurt him. It would suit him if I retaliated, and he probably thinks that it won't take much to make that happen."

"You think he'll spend his time trying to rile you, trying to get a violent response from you to support the extremists' argument?"

"Think about it: If he can rile me enough to attack him, he can present an argument to the court that an alpha male who spent time in juvie isn't reformed after all, that he'd attacked humans again. That will go a long way to proving that the current way of dealing with offending shifters isn't working and that some changes are necessary."

Derren shook his head, blowing out a breath. "Shit, Nick, you really need to leave this place. Any shifter with any sense is keeping a low profile while the court hearing is due."

"I said Logan wants a reaction—I didn't say he'd get it." No matter what Logan or the other humans did, nothing would provoke him enough to retaliate. Not simply because being cooped up in a prison again would most likely send his wolf totally over the edge, but because behind bars would count as leaving Shaya again. He couldn't do that. Nor could he add fuel to the current fire created by the human extremists—he would be letting down his entire race if he did that.

Derren rested his arms on the cherry wood table that the dinette framed. The wood ran throughout the entire motor home. "What if Shaya doesn't come around? She's angry, Nick."

"She has a right to be."

"No, she doesn't, but she *thinks* she does because you haven't told her everything. Right now, when she looks at you she sees a person who rejected and abandoned her. She sees someone she can't rely on and who has every reason to suffer. When she finds out she put you through shit you didn't deserve, she's going to be pissed with you, and she's going to feel guilty when it's not her fault. That's not fair to either of you."

"You don't like her, do you?"

"I don't like that she's not willing to give you a second chance."

"Wait until you find your mate," said Nick with a half smile. "Any emotion you feel is magnified tenfold, particularly pain. She's right to be so reluctant."

Derren gave him a "whatever" look. "I still say you should tell her everything."

"I heard you. Now, are we playing poker or what? I've missed kicking your ass at it."

"There'd be no sport in winning against a guy whose head is pounding so badly that he can't even see properly. But as I don't have a particularly fussy conscience, let's play."

# CHAPTER FİVE

Finding Nick again waiting by his car with a Starbucks coffee for her the next morning, Shaya thought he looked a lot calmer. She, by contrast, wasn't so calm. "You know, you and Derren are unbelievably alike. Neither of you can take a hint, and neither of you pay any attention to what other people want." She still snatched one of the coffee cups, though.

As always, Nick and his wolf were amused by the snippy side of her nature. "Such charming manners." When he tucked a stray curl behind her ear, she predictably slapped his hand away.

Shaya went to take a sip of the coffee but then stopped. "Wait, this isn't the one you've been drinking out of, is it?"

"You ask that like I have an infectious disease or something."

She shrugged. "I just don't like sharing straws or glasses or cups with other people."

"Really?"

"It's one of my quirks."

He raised a brow. "You have others?"

"Yes. I paint my nails when I'm extremely pissed off. I sleep diagonally. I have a serious issue with birds. I always lose my pens. And I *hate* using public bathrooms—I would rather hold it in until I get home. Even using the one at work is hard."

Laughing, Nick opened the passenger door and gestured for her to hop in. Bruce was inside, lounging on the backseat. "I'll give you a ride to work again."

"I'm perfectly capable of getting there by myself, thanks." In honesty, though, the offer was tempting since she was exhausted after another restless night—stress was a bitch. Not even going for a run in her wolf form in the wooded area behind her house had helped.

"I'll even let you drive."

That had her attention, and his smug smirk said he knew it. "Yeah, right."

"Why wouldn't I?"

"Because boys are weird like that—they don't like anyone else even *touching* their car."

"You're my mate. What's mine is yours." He dangled the keys in front of her, watching her try to wrestle back her eagerness. But then movement in his peripheral vision caught his attention.

As his expression switched from playful to alert, she followed his gaze. Three males were gathered at the end of the street, casting subtle looks their way. "Aren't they the rebels?"

Sensing her wolf's nervousness, Nick closed the small distance between them. "It's fine." They didn't appear to be looking for trouble, but he wouldn't risk Shaya's safety. "Well, are you driving or am I driving?"

Shaya regarded him curiously. "You're not going to turn into an overprotective caveman and shove me in your car because strange males are lurking nearby?" It would be a typical reaction for a dominant male wolf.

"No, but I am hoping you'll do the sensible thing and accept a ride."

She wanted to, but that might insinuate to him that he was making progress with her. "I like to walk." Rather than explode, he shrugged one shoulder.

"Then we walk."

"I didn't mean—" She growled. "Do you have to be such a pain in the ass?"

Cupping her chin, he ran his thumb over her bottom lip and seized her gaze with his. "Shay, I don't know what those guys want, but I do know that I have no intention of letting them harm you. If that means pissing you off this morning by sticking by you as you make your way to work, that's what I'll do. I need to know you're safe."

She could point out that he had no right to appear after six months and appoint himself as her guardian, but that would be futile because he'd stick to her side no matter what she said if he believed her safety was at risk. Arguing with him would be fruitless and would only make her even later for work than she already was. "If I'm going to suffer your company this morning, I'll do it in the comfort of your car. You drive. I want to drink my coffee."

Satisfied, Nick nodded. She grumbled something about paranoid dominant males as she slid into the passenger seat. Now that she was in the safety of the car, he shot the rebels a challenging stare, but they didn't respond. So what the hell did they want? Shoving aside the issue for now, he hopped inside the car.

Noticing Derren in the side mirror making his way from the motor home to his SUV, Shaya asked, "Did he sleep there last night?"

Pulling out onto the road, Nick nodded. "I told him he could use the comfort of my home to get a good night's rest if he promised to go back to California this morning."

"You know he won't go, don't you?"

Nick sighed. "Derren does what Derren wants to do. He's always been like that."

"He doesn't like me." She cringed at how petulant she sounded.

"He can't make that assessment—he doesn't know you."

"Neither do you."

"That's where you're wrong, baby. I know that you love dancing, drink mainly cocktails, have more stilettos than is reasonable, you don't like mushrooms or anchovies, and you enjoy listening to music and sketching clothes."

Startled, words failed her. He'd always ignored her, sometimes even looked right through her, so how could he know anything? "But . . . but how? You asked Taryn?"

"I told you the first night I came here that I'd missed watching you. I might not have spoken to you whenever I went to Phoenix Pack territory, but I was always paying attention to every single thing you did."

And that got to her, soothed her wolf's damaged ego. He was *supposed* to be an ass so she could continue rejecting him.

"I know you thought I didn't give a shit." He briefly massaged her nape. "That's my fault. Derren used to poke fun at me for how much and how hard I watched you."

Shaya tried to hold back from asking, but the matter had been playing on her mind since Derren had mentioned it. "He said he owes you his life. Is that true?"

"He owes me nothing. Maybe when he finds his mate, he'll finally stop following me around." Derren deserved that kind of happiness, but Nick wasn't sure if his friend would even recognize his mate while his loyalty was so completely and unnecessarily devoted to Nick.

Part of the reason that Derren was so grateful to him for being alive was that he had been completely determined to track down and kill the person responsible for him being locked up— it had been the only thing keeping Derren going while he was in juvie. Having heard his story, Nick had been able to understand why. That was why he had helped Derren track the bastard down—a bastard who was now very much dead. The problem was that it had made Derren feel even further indebted to Nick. Dumb asshole.

She should leave it alone, Shaya knew. She should act disinterested. But as she was way too curious for that, she lasted only a few minutes before blurting out, "How did you save his life? In a pack war or something?"

Nick inhaled deeply, hesitating to speak. He really didn't want to tell her about his past, but he was already keeping so much from her. Telling her at least *some* things would be fair. Plus, being tight-lipped would lessen his chances of her letting him in. "When we were in juvie—"

"You were in juvie?" Shaya practically squeaked.

"—a group of human guards cornered him and were torturing him with electrical rods and Taser guns while at the same time beating the shit out of him. It looked like they intended to rape him too before finishing him off. That kind of thing happened a lot. Many shifters die in juvie. I intervened and stopped Derren from being one of those very unlucky shifters."

It took at least two minutes for her to recover from the surprise of his admission. It hadn't just been what he'd said, it had also been the way he'd said it—emotionless, flat. But she knew better than to think that Nick was aloof about it all. She'd quickly come to understand that the more enraged Nick was, the more toneless his voice became. After giving him a few minutes to calm down, she finally asked, "How did you end up in juvie? What happened?" When he didn't answer, she pressed him. "Nick?"

"We're here." He pulled up outside the salon, relieved to be able to escape the conversation.

Feeling like she'd been dismissed, both Shaya and her wolf bristled. If he wanted to be cagey, fine. Whatever. But, really, it wasn't fine. Not simply because she was extremely intrigued, but because she wanted to know more about him. Wasn't that her right?

Realizing she was again being weird, she cursed herself. She shouldn't be sulking because he hadn't confided in her. This should be what she wanted. Sharing stories would counteract her effort to keep a distance between them. Trying for nonchalant, she shrugged. "I shouldn't have asked. Your past is your business." Before she could open the door, a hand was curling around her throat and turning her head slightly. At the dominant move, her wolf backed down a little.

"I'm not disregarding you," Nick told her in a low voice. "I just don't want to scare you off. I don't have pretty stories wrapped in red bows, Shay. I don't have fun memories to exchange with you. I wish I did, but I don't." He drew circles on her throat with his thumb. "I meant it when I said you deserve better, but I also meant it when I said I wasn't selfless enough to leave you alone. I can't risk you running even faster than you already are." As she nervously licked her bottom lip, a growl rumbled out of him. "Do you have any idea how much I want you? Any idea how much I want to know what it's like to be buried deep inside you?"

At that moment, Shaya had that deer-in-the-headlights feeling. His strong hand was around her throat, tension was riding his body, and his hungry gaze was trained on her mouth—feeding the need that was twisting her insides. It occurred to her just how vulnerable she was—how easily he could hurt her, and just how *badly* he could hurt her. But he never would, she was certain of that.

Before he lost control and kissed her, Nick released her throat and leaned back. "You need to go."

Swallowing hard, she nodded. "Thanks for the ride. Bye, Bruce." The dog merely looked at her blankly.

Once Shaya was inside the salon, Nick moved his gaze to the rearview mirror. Yep, the red Rolls-Royce was still a little distance behind Derren. The car had been following them for the past two minutes. Irritatingly, a white van was also following—the same white van that the human extremists used. Deeply suspecting that the Rolls-Royce was the Nazi's car and that he had something to say, Nick drove away from the salon, not wanting him anywhere near Shaya. As he suspected, the Rolls-Royce followed him to the local park where Nick had yesterday taken Bruce. Similarly, so did the white van.

As Nick parked in the small, half-empty parking lot at the edge of the park, Derren's SUV took the space on his left, and the Rolls-Royce took the space opposite Nick's car. The van pulled up a few cars away from the Rolls-Royce. As Nick got a glimpse of the driver of the van, he noticed the familiar profile. Logan. *Fucker.*

Ignoring the two vehicles, Nick and Derren began walking along the narrow dirt path through the wooded area with Bruce at Nick's side. A few minutes later, five wolf shifters came close enough to warrant a reaction—one of whom was the bald male shifter who had confronted Nick the day before. In response to the tension, Bruce growled at the strangers.

"I don't think he likes me very much," said an olive-skinned male with deep-brown eyes. If Nick hadn't vaguely recognized him, he would have known it was the Nazi by the dominant alpha vibes emitting from him. "But that's fine. Not many do." He looked hard at Nick, attempting to stare him down, to intimidate him into lowering his gaze. Like that would ever happen. "You attacked four of my wolves yesterday."

"They were irritating me," said Nick dryly.

"That made me very unhappy."

"As it's your fault, you might want to take up that matter with yourself."

He laughed. "*My* fault?"

"You ordered them to *summon* a wolf who is not only much more dominant than them, but an alpha. What did you expect would happen?"

The amusement fled from his expression and tone. "I expected you to be smart enough to speak to me."

"I have no interest in you or your pack. But if it's a brief conversation you want, we can have that now."

"I suppose we should start by introducing ourselves. I'm Petrus Hadley."

Nick could see that Hadley expected some sort of reaction, so he didn't give him one. "Nick Axton."

Hadley went into deep thought for a moment. "Nick Axton, Alpha of the Ryland Pack?"

"Previous Alpha of the Ryland Pack. I'm no longer Alpha or part of the pack."

"You've joined another?"

"No."

"A Pack Alpha's turned lone wolf? I have to ask myself why an alpha as powerful as you would live without a pack. You're too powerful for anyone to have forced you out, so you must have left of your own accord." Hadley shook his head. "I don't get it."

"You don't need to. It's not your concern."

Hadley stepped forward. "This is *my* turf. Therefore, any of your business—"

"Is mine and mine alone," Nick firmly stated. His wolf growled his agreement.

A minute of complete silence passed. "There are only two things that make men do stupid things—women and greed. After spotting you with a redhead, I'm guessing that in your case, it's a woman. I'm also guessing that while you're here, you won't involve yourself in pack business." That was more of a pressing suggestion than a query.

"As I said, I've no interest in you and your pack."

"Good. If things remain that way, you and I won't have a problem. But if they don't . . . What's your redhead's name, by the way?"

*Son of a bitch.* Nick stepped forward. "You know, if I didn't know any better, I'd think you were threatening my mate. But I have to be mistaken, because if that was the case, I'd have to kill you—and I'm pretty sure you'd prefer to live."

A smile spread across Hadley's face. "She's your mate? Well that explains everything. And now I feel so much better." His expression turned grave as he continued. "That's not all that I wanted to speak to you about. I'm sure you've heard the 'drug lord' rumor and how many of my wolves abruptly vanish."

"Rumor? You're saying it's untrue?"

"Although you haven't been in town long, you may have noticed that the human extremists here are somewhat eccentric. They started the drug lord rumor in an effort to blacken my reputation. It makes me the perfect suspect each time one of my wolves goes missing."

Hearing the pain and anger in Hadley's voice, Nick's skepticism began to fizzle away. "You have nothing to do with their disappearances?"

"It took me some time to figure out what was happening. The humans running this thing are very smart and very careful."

"Running what?"

"A game preserve."

His wolf went still. "Game preserve?"

"From what I've learned, they kidnap shifters, dump them in the middle of nowhere, and then track them and chase them, running them down like they're dogs."

Derren studied Hadley through narrowed eyes. "What about the trio of packless wolves who hang around town, the rebels? If the rumors about you are untrue, why would they leave your pack?"

"Each of them lost close ones to these humans," replied Hadley. "The longer I went without finding the people responsible, the more the rebels began to wonder if I truly had something to do with it, so they left. I have some of my wolves keeping watch over them. Out there all alone, they're easy prey."

"Why haven't you shut the preserve down?" asked Nick.

"I haven't yet found it. As I said, these humans are smart and careful. Imagine how much money they can make from charging prejudiced and hateful humans to hunt us like that? They'll also be very much aware of how bad the repercussions would be if their little secret was discovered—not only would they have shifters on their ass, but their own kind. Currently extremists are making out like *we're* the monsters. If that place is exposed, it would pretty much cancel out their argument."

And exposing it would therefore be the answer to the prayer of every single shifter in the world. "I'll contact some people I know, ask them to find out what they can about this preserve and see if they can locate it."

"People you can trust to keep it quiet? I don't want the humans being tipped off that we know. It would give them the time to pack up and run."

"Yes, people I can trust. Keep me updated on what you know, and I'll do the same."

Hadley considered that for a minute, studying Nick and Derren intently. Then he nodded. "You should be careful. You may be powerful, but you're easy prey without a pack, just like your friend here. If your mate is a shifter, she'll be in similar danger. I'd feel uncomfortable leaving you unprotected, given that you're on my territory."

"Protection won't be necessary."

"I've heard a lot about you, heard just who and how many shifters you're allied with—including shifters other than wolves, which is a rare thing. The last thing I need is something happening to you and then a horde of pissed-off shifters turns up here, holding me responsible to some degree for not protecting your ass. So if it's all the same to you, I'll be putting some people on you in any case." Before Nick could respond, Hadley was walking away.

When the Nazi and his wolves were out of hearing distance, Derren said, "At first I thought he might be talking shit about the preserve, but he was definitely telling the truth."

Nick could agree with that. "I wouldn't be surprised if Logan has something to do with it. I remember full well just how he and the other guards liked to chase and hunt the shifters back in juvie."

"Me too," growled Derren. "It would make sense that extremists are behind its creation, even if Logan isn't personally involved."

"Whatever the case, it needs to be stopped."

"It will be. Many of the Nazi's wolves have been lost to this preserve—no Alpha would let that alone. I'm not surprised he's put guards on you."

"Great," snorted Nick. "*More* people following me."

Derren grinned. "You've always had a natural talent for getting people's attention."

"Now it's time to get my mate's attention. Let's just hope my little plan works."

As Shaya once again looked at the gift Nick had sent her, she resisted the urge to groan. He hadn't bought her flowers or chocolates—things she could have rolled her eyes at, considering how little thought and creativity would have gone into the gifts on his part. Nor had he written her a soppy poem or a lovey-dovey card—corny things she could have scoffed at. Nor had he bought her jewelry or perfume—expensive stuff that would have given her an excuse to claim he was trying to buy her. No . . . he'd bought her something funny, something that would make her laugh. Something that Kent was again playing with, making her want to snatch it back. So she did. "Hands off."

"Ooh, possessive." Kent chuckled and went back to tidying the salon, ready to close up. "I think this is hilarious."

"What's funny about a Public Toilet Survival Kit?" In truth, the only reason she wasn't chuckling with him was that she was annoyed—Nick was being nice, something he most likely wasn't experienced at. But he was trying. For her. And it was getting to her.

"I'm guessing you told him about your phobia of public toilets." She had only told him this morning, and already he was on top of it. There was no denying he was sharp. The gift hadn't been the only thing to make her smile. No. Not long after the gift had arrived, she'd received a text message from him:

Ever played Simon Says naked?

She wanted to feel furious with him for sending her messages when not only had she not given him her number, but she'd made it clear that she wanted to leave. Instead—like yesterday—she found herself trying and failing to stifle an amused smile whenever she thought of the text.

"Why are you so irritated?" Kent asked quietly, conscious of Paisley's presence. "Your mate bought you something that would make you smile—what's bad about it?"

"I don't want him to make me smile," she said, sounding petulant. "I want to keep detesting him."

"He's who you ran from," Kent said in sudden realization. "Tell me everything."

So she did. But Kent's reaction wasn't what she'd anticipated. Rather than being outraged on her behalf, he was sighing dreamily. "It's so romantic, isn't it?"

She gaped. "How do you figure that?"

"Well obviously the rejection part wasn't nice. But look what he's done for you. He didn't just give up his position of Alpha, he gave up his pack, his home—everything. Then he spent six months tracking you down and didn't give up. He hasn't asked you to go back to his pack, and he's even offered to join yours. Do you have any idea how hard it would be for someone like him to be in a pack and *not* be Alpha? Yet he's willing to do it. He's practically camping outside your house, and he's trying to make himself part of your life while still going at your pace—going completely against every alpha instinct he has. You're not looking at things this way because you don't want to; you don't want to be tempted to give him a chance."

She spluttered. "Would you?"

"Hell yes, he's devastatingly hot! He's got such a commanding presence, hasn't he? I'll bet he's just as commanding in bed. I've never been with an alpha before. Can I borrow him?"

Hearing herself growl, she wanted to slap herself for the knee-jerk possessive reaction. She was *so* mixed up right now. She had almost asked Taryn for advice when they had chatted over Skype last night, but she was too worried that Taryn would react extremely badly to finding out that Nick had tracked her down.

"What are you two whispering about?" asked an approaching Paisley, wearing her usual bitchy scowl.

"The weather," replied Kent.

Paisley rolled her eyes. "Don't think I don't know that you're talking about me behind my back. I'm not stupid."

Shaya and Kent exchanged an amused look. "Of course you're not," he assured the blonde, patting her hand. "No one would ever insinuate otherwise."

Appearing slightly mollified, she gave him a nod. As Kent went off to grab his coat, Paisley threw Shaya a look filled with utter contempt. "I don't blame *him*. It's *you*. Don't think I'll let you turn him against me. I can't believe he's even friends with you. His mom should have told him not to play with matchsticks."

*Oh, enough with the red hair jokes!* "Don't things like you hibernate?"

Paisley smirked. "Easy there, ginger ninja."

"You do realize that my hair isn't actually ginger, don't you? It's red. As a hairstylist, you should know the difference. No, as a person with eyes, you should know the difference."

"Whatever you say, Agent Orange."

*Bitch.* "Oops, I've dropped my clip by your feet." Crouching, Shaya gently placed her hands over Paisley's black pumps. "Spread 'em, blondie. Bet you've heard that a lot before."

She gasped. "How crude!" Paisley looked about to snap when something over Shaya's shoulder caught her attention and she smiled in admiration. "My, my, my."

Clearly an attractive guy had just walked in. Shaya stood, turned . . . and gaped as Nick breezed into the salon. His eyes immediately found her, and a small smile curved his mouth. He took slow, confident steps toward her. Off-balance by his totally undivided attention, Shaya might have backed away if she hadn't felt rooted to the spot by that unblinking stare. Her wolf, too, had frozen.

"Can I help you?" Paisley's voice was seductive and filled with promise. She had also put on her best invitational smile, but Nick didn't spare the bitch a glance; he continued to stare at Shaya as if no one else was of any importance. Shaya kind of liked that.

Coming to stand in front of Shaya, Nick fought back the urge to reach out, drag her to him, and take what was his. The need emanating from her wasn't helping. Spotting his gift at her station, he grinned. "So it came." Humor danced in her eyes, making his grin widen.

"Oh, hi," drawled Kent as he returned to Shaya's side, smiling widely at Nick. "I take it you've come to give her a ride home again. Fabulous. It's chilly out there." He shoved at Shaya's back. "See you tomorrow, bright and late."

Shaya scowled at her supposed friend. "I don't need a ride. I'm—"

"Perfectly capable of getting yourself home," Nick finished. "But why would you want to walk when you can be chauffeured around?" Curling an arm around her shoulders, Nick led her toward the door.

Shaya might have fought him—then again, she might not have—but the expression on Paisley's face stopped her. There was a little too much admiration and lust there for Shaya's liking. Although Shaya didn't want to want Nick, she didn't want Paisley thinking he was available either. Maybe that was petty. . . . Okay, it was definitely petty. But she did *not* like the thought of Nick with someone else, and she especially did not relish the idea of another female pursuing him.

Inside the car, Nick asked, "Well, did you like your gift?"

Shaya snorted. "It has to be the least romantic thing I've ever been given."

He grinned. "It made you smile. Admit it. You like it."

Admit it? *Pfft.* "You can take it back, in any case. I don't like receiving gifts." It always made her feel awkward.

"You better get used to it, Shay, because I plan to do it again."

She was about to give a cocky comment when she noticed he was staring right at her mouth. Her breath seemed to get trapped in her throat, and instantly the memory of their kiss assailed her. The heated look on his face said that he was recalling it too.

Shaking off his fantasies of just how Nick could use that sensual mouth of hers, he began driving en route to Shaya's home. "Hungry?"

*Depends what kind of hunger you're referring to.* But Shaya knew what he meant—she had smelled the spicy curry the second she got in the car. He had clearly gotten takeout and was hoping they could share it together. "I told you yesterday—letting you give me a ride somewhere doesn't mean anything."

Nick frowned. "I don't understand."

"Giving me a ride and then buying me Indian food isn't going to make me suddenly let you into my home."

Realizing where her thoughts had taken her, he drawled, "Oh. I'm afraid you're a little mistaken. I didn't buy you takeout. I cooked you a meal—a meal *for you*, not for both of us to enjoy together." He had no intention of pushing things, pushing *her*.

"You cooked me a meal?"

"You've been on your feet all day. I figured the last thing you'd want to do was cook at the end of it. This means you have one less thing to worry about when you get inside."

Shaya really didn't know what to do with that. There was no denying he had an ulterior motive—he was trying to win her over; he'd already informed her of this. But he wasn't doing the alpha thing and being pushy, nor was he doing the mate thing and invading her personal space. He had done something sweet for her and wasn't expecting anything in return. He was merely hoping to demonstrate that he'd meant everything he said to her, backing it up with actions.

She knew he could have no real idea just how little words meant to her. Mason had given her plenty of words, told her just how special and beautiful she was, and just how proud he was to have her as his true mate. He had given her all the words she could have wanted to hear, using her need for a connection to get what he wanted.

Only actions would make her even consider believing Nick. But she didn't want him to give her actions; she wanted to stay mad at him and give herself every reason to keep him at a distance. So she wasn't a happy bunny right now, knowing this big, bad, powerful, and often remote alpha was focused on having her and had done something considerate for her.

*But he didn't tell Kent you were his mate*, a voice in her head reminded her. *He's not proud to have you.*

"You're angry that I cooked you something?" asked Nick, sensing her mood shift. He tried examining her expression, but she was busy staring out the window. His wolf tensed, honing every sense on her.

"No. It was sweet." And very convenient because she was an awful cook and she tended to exist on cereal, noodles, and takeouts.

"Then why are you mad at me?"

She folded her arms across her chest. "I'm not mad."

"Yes, you are."

"I'm not. I told you, what you did was sweet."

Then why did she sound like she wanted to rip out his heart and use it as a mallet? "You're mad that I did something sweet?"

"No."

"So what's the problem?" She didn't answer, just continued to stare out the window. His wolf growled with impatience. "Shay, you gotta help me out here. How can I apologize if I don't know what I've done?"

"I don't want your apologies anyway."

"Shay, tell me."

The dominance and power in his tone made her shudder, and before she knew it, the words came flying out. "You didn't tell Kent I was your ma—" She quickly cut off her words, annoyed with herself.

"And that pissed you off?" He didn't understand women and probably never would. "Shay, I'm not good at this. When I was with females in the past . . . They weren't relationships. I kept everything casual. Giving any kind of commitment to another female would've felt like cheating on my mate. I know some are open to imprinting, but I wasn't. I wanted to find you."

"Then I guess I'm a big disappointment to you, huh?"

Taken aback, he said, "Excuse me?"

"It's always been obvious that you don't think I'm good enough for you and that you look down on me." She lurched forward as he suddenly pulled the car to a complete stop at the side of the road. "What the—"

"Would you mind repeating that?" The words rumbled out of him.

"Come on, Nick, you acted like I didn't exist, like I was nothing to you. What I don't understand is why, if I wasn't good enough for you back then, I'm suddenly good enough for you now."

"Is that really what you think?" he asked in a low voice, shocked. "That I think you aren't good enough?" He leaned back in his seat, literally feeling like he'd been felled. "Jesus, Shay."

"Why else would you have totally snubbed me?" she asked rhetorically. There was no anger in her voice as she continued, just exhaustion and sadness. "I can understand how me being submissive is a problem, but that wouldn't be a reason to ignore me the way you did. It wouldn't be a reason to drive me to leave. And now that I've built a life for myself here and I'm happy, you turn up and say sorry, you've changed your mind and you've given up your Alpha throne. It makes no sense."

Sighing, Nick scrubbed a hand down his face. He'd had no idea that she'd interpreted his actions that way. *Shit.* The only way she would understand the truth behind those actions was if he explained everything to her, explained *all* the reasons that had kept him away—even those that he would rather she didn't know. But that would risk her giving him a chance out of pity. In fact, she might even think he was trying to guilt her into giving him a chance. He wanted to earn that chance, wanted to earn her trust. They'd have no shot without trust anyway. "We need to get one thing straight."

Although his tone was gentle, the authority there had Shaya instantly giving him her full attention. She couldn't have ignored him even if she had wanted to. His gaze held hers; there was a hint of anger there. She wasn't sure if he was angry with her or himself.

"You are everything I ever could have wanted—everything I didn't even know I wanted. Beautiful, smart, independent, loyal, and you have this sassy, effervescent charm that I wouldn't have thought would appeal to me. If I thought you weren't good enough, if you were something I could resist, something I could be without, I wouldn't be here." As a familiar ache suddenly began to build behind his eyes, he almost cursed aloud. Great.

Another headache was creeping up on him. "Don't ever again think differently."

Shaya wasn't sure what to say to that, so she said nothing.

"My great-uncle from another pack recently died." Seeing that Shaya was ready to offer her condolences, Nick put a finger to her lips, needing to make his point. "He'd never mated. He told me once how he almost imprinted a long time ago, when he was twenty-one. The reason he hadn't was that he'd wanted to hold out for his true mate. He never found her. My point is that many take it for granted that they'll find their mate, but not everybody does. We're lucky to have found each other. I know I fucked up. I've said I'm sorry for hurting you; I meant it. I promised you that I wouldn't let you down again; I meant it. You might not believe that right now, but you will in time—I won't have it any other way. You're mine, and I refuse to live my life without you in it."

Neither of them spoke during the rest of the drive home. Even when he finally pulled up behind his motor home, he opened Shaya's door without a word and handed her the large tub that contained the meal he'd cooked. He didn't look angry with her, but there was hurt there. And another pain too . . . a pain she didn't understand. It made her wolf whine, wanting to comfort him. He then merely gave Shaya a nod and gestured for her to go inside. She wanted him to talk to her, wanted to know what that pain was that he seemed to be trying to hide. But showing concern for him could give him the wrong idea, couldn't it? So she ignored her wolf and her own concern and simply said, "Thanks."

As the pain in his expression seemed to intensify, she was about to ask what was wrong, but then Derren appeared at his side. His body language was supportive and protective, and again there was disappointment in his gaze as he looked at her.

Derren turned to Nick and gestured at the motor home. "Fancy a game of poker?"

Nick quickly realized that Derren—who never missed a trick—had detected that he had one of his headaches and was urging him to go inside to take some painkillers. The urging wasn't necessary. Not when his vision was starting to darken around the edges. "Sure." He again gestured for Shaya to go inside her home, having no intention of moving until he saw that she was safely inside. Then, hearing a car pull up close by, he glanced briefly toward the noise . . . and tensed. "Oh, you've got to be kidding me."

Confused, Shaya spared the Chevy a brief look before asking Nick, "What?"

Derren winced, earning both of their attention. "Wow, I didn't think she'd really come."

Nick rounded on him. "You knew she was coming? You knew and you didn't think to tell me?"

"Who?" demanded Shaya.

Turning back to Shaya, Nick sighed. "My mother."

"She called me earlier," said Derren. "She wanted to know how you were doing and what was happening with you and Shaya. As I know you're private about personal stuff, I was pretty vague. Apparently that wasn't the wisest move."

Clearly not, because she'd come to find out the answers for herself. Nick cursed.

"What's so bad about it?" asked Shaya. "Don't you guys get along?"

"It's not that. I came to Arizona to find you, make things up to you, and claim you. I kind of wanted some privacy, and no one seems to want to give it to us." And his mother would undoubtedly pressure him to tell Shaya everything when she realized he hadn't yet done it. She might even blurt out a thing or two, believing he'd already told Shaya. He couldn't have that. "Why don't you go inside, baby. I'll take care of this."

"You don't want me to meet your mom?" Shaya didn't particularly want to do the whole "meeting the parents" thing, especially considering the way things stood with her and Nick, but she couldn't help feeling wounded by his behavior.

Seeing the insecurity in her eyes and knowing she most likely still feared he thought she wasn't good enough for him, that he was embarrassed by her, Nick growled. "Now you're making me want to bite you." His wolf felt much the same. "I just don't want people interfering. She thinks being my mother gives her the right to do so."

The click-clacking of heels along the pavement was quickly followed by Kathy Axton launching herself at him, kissing both cheeks. "Derren assured me you were fine, but I had to see for myself." Turning to Shaya, she smiled widely. "You must be Shaya." Then she was hugging the breath out of Shaya too. "I'm Kathy, Nick's mother. I knew you'd be beautiful, and you are. And I knew you'd understand his reasons for holding back."

The latter sentence was more like a question, so Shaya nodded at the small brunette with Nick's green eyes. The bubbly, affectionate woman was so unlike her own mother. "It's nice to meet you." Though mighty awkward, given the circumstances.

"Behind me are Nick's sister, Roni, and our pack healer, Amber."

Seeing only one female, Shaya frowned. Then Nick crouched down and stroked a graceful dark-gray female wolf, cooing gently and whispering. Before Shaya could ask who was who, the tall, purple-haired dominant female fit for a catwalk came from behind Kathy and threw her arms around Shaya.

"You must be Shaya, hi!" Pulling back, she said, "I'm Amber—a good friend of Nick's. His mom has told me a little about you. You sound perfect for him."

The way she looked at Shaya was almost adoringly . . . but there was something else in those eyes. Something that surprised her: jealousy. Well, well, well, the pack healer had a thing for Nick. Shaya's wolf wasn't at all pleased about that.

As Amber's eyes drifted to Shaya's neck, her face pulled into a frown, and she looked down at Nick. "You haven't claimed her?"

"When Shaya's ready, I will." Having no intention of explaining further, Nick tugged on Shaya's hand until she got down on her haunches beside him. "Shay, this is Roni, my sister. Roni, this is Shaya. My mate."

The dark-gray wolf studied Shaya for a moment before butting her hand. Understanding, Shaya gave her a brief stroke.

"Don't think she's being rude by not greeting you properly; Roni spends more time in her wolf form," explained Nick, swallowing hard. He suspected that it wasn't just the trauma of the attempted rape that she repeatedly tried to escape from by remaining in her wolf form for long periods, but the trauma of watching her brother violently tear people apart in front of her very eyes. She had already been terrified after being nearly assaulted, and then he'd made that terror even worse, despite that all he'd been doing was trying to protect her. He hated himself for what he'd done to his own sister.

As Roni's nostrils flared, she glanced around him. Nick had no sooner heard Derren's "Hey, Roni" than the she-wolf was beside him; the two of them were good friends.

"It's so great to see you!" Amber said when Nick stood. She hugged him before he could stop her. Unlike him, she was a touchy-feely person. Detaching her from him, he set her back by her shoulders and simply gave her a nod—letting another female touch him was suicidal when his mate was right there, and irritation was rolling off her in waves.

He passed his keys to Derren. "Um . . . you guys go wait in the motor home while I say goodnight to Shaya." His mother and Amber looked at him curiously, obviously confused that she wouldn't be coming inside also. Had it not been for the fact that he needed to warn his mother to back off and not to let certain details slip to Shaya, he would have invited her inside. He doubted she'd have accepted the invitation, but he'd have asked all the same.

Both his mother and Amber looked about to comment, but a raised brow from him had both of them nodding instead and following Derren into the motor home with Roni trotting behind them. "Oh, and Roni, Bruce is inside—don't chase him around again," he called, though he wasn't optimistic that his sister would listen.

Turning back to Shaya, he slowly closed the distance between them and cupped her face with one hand, sliding his thumb over her mouth. "I'll make sure they're gone by tomorrow. But for tonight . . . For tonight, I need to let them stay in the motor home." And that was really, really bad, because one of those females wasn't related to him and was also unmated. "I can't turn them away. My mother won't budge until I've spoken to her anyway."

"It's fine," lied Shaya. How could it be fine when she knew that the dominant female in his motor home wanted him? And now Shaya had a primal urge to touch him in some way, to leave her scent on him—something that would warn away the other female. Ordinarily, such shifter primal instincts weren't so strong for Shaya, but this one was fierce. Her wolf was *demanding* it.

*But I don't want him*, Shaya insisted to herself. However, like with Paisley, that detail wasn't relevant when it came to the idea of other females wanting him. God, she was so freaking mixed up, and she hated it.

Still, she forced the distasteful words out. "You don't owe me any explanations. What you do and who you do it with is your bus—" She gasped as his mouth descended on hers and his tongue shot inside. The kiss was hard, deep, intense—not punishing, but a kiss designed to get her total and utter attention. It worked. She told herself to move away, but she couldn't. Not with mating urges riding her and with her insecurities and confusion badgering her; the contact with her mate soothed and reassured her. When he pulled back and bit her lip hard, she gasped again.

"What did I tell you only minutes ago, huh? You're everything I want. *All* I want. Just so you have it totally straight, I *am* your business, just like you're mine ... which is why I'm explaining to you that I'll be letting them sleep in the motor home with Derren while I sleep in his SUV."

"I just meant that—Wait, what?"

"You really thought I'd sleep in the vicinity of an unmated female when I knew you'd hate it?" If she'd wanted to allow an unmated male to sleep in her house without Nick there too, he'd have been totally pissed.

"You don't have to do that. You don't *need* to do that. It's stupid and—"

"Has given you peace of mind—admit it."

Okay, yes, it had relaxed her slightly. Her wolf was also mollified, though she still wanted to take a bite out of Amber. But Shaya didn't like the idea of him cramped in the SUV all night long. "Really, you don't need to."

"Yes, I do."

"But . . . you'll be uncomfortable."

His laugh was short and soft. "Shay, I was in juvie—I've slept in way worse places." He licked over her bottom lip. "And with your taste on my tongue and your scent all over me, I'll sleep just fine."

Her scent all over him . . . Her wolf was smug at that. It also served to further relax Shaya. Surprising her, Nick suddenly spun her around and slapped her ass, urging her toward the house. "Hey!"

"Go. And make sure you eat every bit of that meal." Amused by her mock scowl, he didn't move his eyes from her until she was inside the house.

It was at that moment that his mother's head peered out of the front door of the motor home. "Nick, what's this Derren's saying about you keeping things from Shaya?"

*And so it begins.*

# CHAPTER SIX

Two hours later, Nick was still arguing with his mother about his decision to hold back certain details from Shaya. Yes, Kathy had a valid point in saying that it was wrong for there to be secrets or lies between mates. And, yes, a lie of omission still counted. And, yes, it would be far easier to make Shaya forgive him if he told her the truth. But Shaya was worth the hard work. Plus, he'd never know if she'd given him a chance because she felt sorry for him or because she *wanted* him—he needed it to be the latter. "You won't make me change my mind," he told his mother. "Let it go."

Her eyes held his, staring at him to the point where he began to feel uncomfortable. Kathy Axton had a way of making people feel guilty even when they hadn't done anything wrong. When his dad had been alive, she'd been an expert at getting him to apologize for something when the fault really lay with her. She was also extremely good at getting her own way—usually by talking people in circles—but then so was Nick.

Finally, Kathy threw up her arms in a gesture of exasperation and sank onto the sofa, arms folded. "There never was any point in arguing with you over anything. You're stubborn as hell, just like your brother."

"He tried to talk you out of coming here, didn't he?" Nick sat at the dinette, where he was feeding Bruce scraps of meat. Eli was the type to stay out of other people's business, no matter who those people were—which made him the exact opposite of their mother.

Kathy's growl confirmed his suspicion. "I wanted to know how you were doing, and I wasn't going to be talked out of checking on my own son."

"*Now* who's stubborn?" She was more than stubborn. She was a force of nature. But he supposed she'd have to be as the mother of three dominant shifters.

She merely sniffed at him. "It's little wonder Shaya found meeting me awkward. Maybe if you let me—"

"No, you are not interfering here."

"I wasn't proposing that I tell her anything." Her face was the picture of innocence, earning her a laugh from Derren, who was lounging in the black leather recliner. Derren knew Kathy well enough to know that she'd already have a plan cooked up in her head. "Merely that I spend some time with her and get to know her a little."

"And then 'accidentally' let a few things slip?" scoffed Nick. "No way. You can get to know her after I've claimed her. Tonight you can sleep here. Tomorrow you go home."

"I'm not going home until I've had the chance to meet her properly." Which of course gave the woman an excuse to stick around. "There's a shifter motel nearby. I've heard it's a nice place with lots of land. Roni, Amber, and I will stay there. Then if you need us or get a little lonely, you have us nearby."

She'd made it sound so reasonable, but Nick knew the real reason that his mother was determined to stay for a while. Being away from him for long periods of time reminded her of what it had been like when he'd gone to juvie. It had been six months since she'd last seen him . . . which was why she had held on to him for at least ten minutes when he first entered the motor home.

He sighed, feeling mentally drained. "If you want to stay at the motel, fine. But you keep your nose out of this, Mom. I mean it. No turning up at Shaya's house. No trying to talk to her privately. No going to the salon where she works to get your hair done as an excuse to talk to her." The sheepish look on Kathy's face confirmed that he'd been right to suspect she'd do that. "No interfering, not for any reason. It's the last thing I need."

Finally her face softened. "Okay. I'll stay out of it. But I can't promise the same for Roni. You know how protective of you she is." Her devious smile made Derren chuckle.

"Yes, Roni's protective of me—which is exactly why she won't spy for you."

"Do you feel like you're making progress with Shaya?" asked Amber, who was sitting opposite him.

He gave the healer a pointed look. "What goes on between her and me isn't something I intend to discuss with anyone else."

"So that's a no, then," she mumbled beneath her breath.

"Excuse me?"

She exhaled heavily. "Like your mom, I just want you to be happy."

"I'll be extremely happy when you guys are gone tomorrow, because more than one night in that SUV is going to kill me."

Kathy looked surprised. "You're not going to sleep here because of Amber? Well, Shaya certainly runs a tight ship. I approve."

Nick cast his mother an annoyed look. "She hasn't ordered me to sleep outside. I'm doing it because it's the fair thing to do."

"I think it's shitty of her not to offer for you to sleep on her sofa or something," said Amber. "But rejection's not something a girl forgets."

Wasn't that the truth. But then, he could easily understand. Over and over Shaya had rejected him, and though he'd expected each and every one, they'd all hurt like a son of a bitch. As such, he wasn't surprised she hadn't offered him her sofa. Though, knowing Shaya, she'd probably feel a teensy bit guilty for not doing so. She had a heart of fucking gold, and he wanted a part of it.

It turned out he'd been right to think that being able to taste her and smell her would help him sleep, despite being without the comfort of his bed. Still, he'd woken up aching in several places and with a pounding headache. Needing to wash and change so that he could drive Shaya to work, he returned to the motor home and found everyone sitting at the dinette eating a huge breakfast that Amber had cooked. Declining his portion as he didn't have time to eat, he retreated to his bathroom to wash, dress, and take some pills. Then he was striding through the motor home toward the front door, brushing off his mother's attempts to speak to him and promising her he'd talk to her later. When he reached the front door, Amber appeared in front of him, blocking his path.

"Is everything okay?" she asked quietly, her expression one of concern.

"Fine." When she reached out to touch him, he dodged her hand; he wasn't touchy-feely, and Amber knew that. Besides, he knew better than to go to his mate with the scent of another female on his skin.

"You really don't look good, Nick."

"I said I'm fine."

"Don't insult my intelligence. I'm a healer. I can sense your pain."

Seeing that the others were deep in conversation, he admitted, "It's just a headache. It's a pain I can deal with, so therefore I'm fine."

"With pills?" she scoffed. "Let me take the pain away."

He backed up. "No." Because that would involve her touching him, and then Shaya would freak. He'd take the pain over that. Plus, the pills would kick in any second now.

Amber rolled her eyes. "Come on, Nick, *you're in pain*. I'll bet it's not just the headache either. The mating urges must be painful too, since she won't let you claim her—which I think is plain cruel. I know she was upset because you didn't claim her in the beginning, but you've given up everything and—"

"Amber, that's between me and Shaya," he stated firmly.

She gave him a slight smile. "I'm your friend, Nick. I don't want you to be hurting. I want you to be happy."

"Shaya makes me happy."

"It doesn't look that way from where I'm standing."


When Shaya had come outside to find no Nick in sight, she hadn't been surprised since she was fifteen minutes early. She'd love to say it was because she was working on her punctuality, but the truth was that she'd known Nick would have to go inside the motor home at some point this morning to change clothes and clean up, and she didn't like the idea of Amber around him. Yes, that should be inconsequential considering that Shaya didn't want to mate with him, but it *was* consequential whether she liked it or not.

How could the idea of her mate with another female be anything but agonizing?

Her anxiety and restlessness had given her the jumpstart she'd needed and quickened her movements. Her wolf was eager to see him, to get him away from the other female, and was urging Shaya to go to him. But when Shaya came up close to the motor home, she froze at the sound of two voices talking.

"Shaya makes me happy."

"It doesn't look that way from where I'm standing." *Amber.* Bitch.

Rather than barging in there and making her presence known, Shaya didn't move a single muscle, intending to listen closely and hear how the conversation played out. It was the best way to find out more about Amber and her "friendship" with Nick. Her wolf didn't agree—she wanted to barge in there and bare her teeth at the female, dominant wolf or not.

She heard Nick then; his voice was soft and gentle—*too* soft and gentle for Shaya's liking. "What're you doing awake so early? You were always a late sleeper."

A quiet, tinkle-like laugh that had a hint of flirtatiousness to it. "That's true. There's just so much going on, and with the court hearing looming . . . it's enough to disturb anyone's sleep. Roni's missed you so much. So have I."

"Oh, you've missed me, huh? Good. I missed you too."

Red-hot anger surged through Shaya and her wolf. It wasn't just Nick's words that hurt, it was the depth of emotion there. He clearly cared a great deal for Amber.

"I wish you'd come back home, Nick,"—oh, fucking did she now?—"Jon's great as Alpha, but it's not the same there without you. Everyone misses you. You know how much Roni would love it if you came home."

A short pause. Then he spoke in that same soft, gentle voice again. "So you still like being stroked there."

A blast of rage exploded in Shaya's mind and zoomed through her body. Oh, she'd slaughter them both! Amber for being a slut, and Nick for betraying every promise he'd made since he arrived. In seconds, she was up the steps and opening the front door. Stunned, she stopped dead and frowned. Nick looked up at her from his spot on the gray vinyl floor where he was crouched, petting Roni, who was still in her wolf form. And that was when it fell into place. He hadn't been talking to Amber, he'd been talking to Roni while Amber looked on, chatting away. Relief washed over Shaya, making the rage subside. Her wolf wasn't totally relaxed—her focus was on Amber, the interfering bitch.

Sensing Shaya's anger, Nick frowned. "Everything okay, baby?"

Shaya forced a smile, still recovering from her brief attack of panic. "You weren't outside waiting. I just came to see if something was wrong." She could tell he didn't believe her, and maybe Roni didn't either, because she came to Shaya and rubbed against her leg in a move that felt supportive. She then sat in front of Shaya almost protectively, staring at Amber, as if making it clear exactly where her loyalty lay. Appreciating that, Shaya reached down and stroked the she-wolf's neck. Sensing eyes on her, Shaya raised her gaze to Kathy and Derren, shooting them both an awkward smile. Had she not been feeling so off-kilter right then, she may have commented on how the motor home was a lot more luxurious than she would have ever expected.

Nick's eyes danced from Shaya to Roni to Amber and back to Shaya. If Shaya felt slightly threatened by Amber as an unmated female, he wouldn't be surprised; it was only natural for her possessive streak to trigger a jealous reaction. But he didn't want Shaya to ever be under the impression that he wanted anyone but her. So, getting to his feet, he immediately went to her. "Come on, baby, I'll give you a ride to work." Shaya nodded once but didn't move, as if to ensure that he didn't intend to linger.

After nuzzling his hand slightly, Roni then trotted over to the TV, bumping Bruce out of the way. Without a backward glance at Amber, Nick ushered Shaya outside the motor home. It wasn't until they were in the privacy of the car that he spoke. "You don't ever have to feel insecure about us. I don't want anyone but you."

She almost snapped, "There is no *us*," but instead she found herself confessing, "I heard you both talking. I thought you were saying those things to Amber, not Roni."

Confirming his suspicion and pleased that she'd been honest with him, Nick reached out and kneaded her nape. "There never has been, and never will be, anything at all between me and Amber."

"She wants you." Her expression dared him to deny it. To her surprise, he looked genuinely confused.

"I know she's a little . . . overaffectionate, but that's all it is. She's like that with everyone."

Shaya snorted. "Trust me, she wants you."

That made no sense to Nick since dominant females weren't at all subtle when they wanted a male. "I don't think so, baby. Amber's never given me even the slightest indication that she's interested; dominant females are pretty forward."

Okay, Shaya could concede that. "If you can think of any other reason why she's jealous, let me know."

Nick still wasn't convinced, but he had no interest in arguing with Shaya. "In any case, they're leaving today. Unfortunately, they won't be far. My mother wants to stay in the local shifter motel for a while, but don't worry, she'll leave you alone."

Shaya was actually kind of surprised that he wasn't encouraging his mother to give him some kind of character reference in the hope of softening Shaya's response to him. When he suddenly stopped the car after only a minute of driving, she frowned in confusion. Then she realized they were outside Starbucks.

"Wait here while I go get us some coffee. You didn't get your caramel macchiato from me this morning, and that's unacceptable."

She rolled her eyes, though she was touched. "I think I can cope without coffee for one morning."

"But you don't want to and you don't need to, so why should you have to?"

With that, he got out of the car and went inside, leaving Shaya feeling a contradictory mix of happy, confused, and angry. Happy because he made her that way with these little things he did. Confused because although she told herself she didn't want to be with him, she wasn't so sure of that anymore. And angry because she didn't want him to make her happy . . . or did she?

Hell, she *really* needed to get her shit together. Needed to remind herself just why she was refusing him. In fact, she spent most of her morning at work trying to do just that, but he blew that out of the water when another gift arrived from him. Not anything romantic or expensive or corny. No. It was a Dead Fred pen holder. If you stabbed the red chunk of silicone rubber that was shaped like a dead body, it would hold the pen right there just like that.

Clearly he'd remembered her little quirk of always losing pens, and she knew this would sit nicely near her hallway phone at home. Nick's note had suggested that she could pretend the rubber body was him and get out all her anger by stabbing the pen holder over and over. She did. It was pretty therapeutic. Kent also had a go at it, pretending it was his boyfriend's mother. Again, Nick had made her laugh. Idiot. She had then received a text message from him while on her break:

Missing me?

Though she had promised herself she would never, ever, *ever* reply to his texts and encourage what she should consider annoying behavior, she had found herself responding:

Sadly, yes, my aim seems to be off lately—either that or I need a new rifle.

Then she had waited in anticipation for a response—irritated about the whole "anticipation" part but unable to help it. She'd soon received one:

I'd ask how you're doing and if you've been busy today, but these new binoculars work great—a "must-have" for all intense investigators.

And, once again, she was fighting a smile. Once again, she failed. What further irritated her was that when he turned up at the salon at lunchtime, she was pleased to see him.

Apparently, so was Paisley, because she was immediately at his side, trailing along as he made his way to Shaya. "Are you here to book an appointment, sir, or were you hoping to—"

Nick looked at Paisley. "I'm not here to get my hair done. I'm Shaya's—"

"Boyfriend," blurted Shaya before Nick could use the term "mate" and, in turn, reveal that she wasn't totally human. After her grumbling last night about him not stating that she was his mate, he would undoubtedly have been clear this time.

Paisley's surprised gaze shot to Shaya. "Boyfriend?"

If she had said friend, it would have pissed Nick off. "Boyfriend" would placate him and prevent him from saying more. Forcing a casual smile, she nodded. "Nick, what are you doing here?"

Picking up that Shaya was hiding her shifter blood from her colleague, Nick dropped the issue. He came close and began toying with her hair. "Have lunch with me."

It hadn't been a request or an invitation—it had been a soft command. "I can't, I have a client coming in now."

"I'll wait. I can be very patient when it comes to getting what I want."

She knew he was talking about more than just lunch. Agitated that both she and her wolf found his persistence and determination attractive, Shaya almost growled. It was one thing for him to give her a ride to work, or to cook her a meal, or to buy her gifts. It was completely different to go somewhere with him—this might not be a date, but it was close enough to count. "Nick, I don't think—"

Nick placed a finger against her mouth. He'd anticipated that she would resist, and he understood why. But he couldn't win her trust if he didn't get opportunities to prove that he was trustworthy. That meant them spending time together. "Shay, you need to eat. I need to eat. Eating together makes perfect sense."

The tricky asshole made it sound so simple and innocent.

This was the thing about Nick: he wasn't overbearing, oppressive, and tyrannical like a lot of alphas. He mostly expressed and exercised his dominance in a subtle, smooth way. He led with words and influences, projecting a calm assurance that he would get his own way and didn't need to raise his voice or browbeat anyone in order to get it. The power radiating from him also warned that he was indeed capable of taking care of anyone who refused to do as he'd asked.

She wished she could say that his power and his subtle dominance wasn't a turn-on, but it damn well was. It promised safety, security, and sexual satisfaction she'd never before experienced. His tone might have been reassuring, but his mischievous expression was anything but. "Kent might not like it if I—"

Her friend and boss waved a hand dismissively. "I'm totally fine with it. No need to worry." Traitor.

Satisfied, Nick nodded at Kent and then turned back to Shaya. "I'll be waiting on the chair over by the reception desk. When you're done, we can leave."

He was gone before Shaya could say anything else. The entire time she worked, he watched her. Watched her with eyes that missed absolutely nothing—eyes that hid nothing of his need for her. For once, Paisley wasn't hovering over her while she worked. That would have been a good thing if Paisley wasn't instead spending her time flirting with Nick. But Shaya wasn't surprised by the blonde's behavior. Nick's quiet confidence, total self-assuredness, raw magnetism, and calm assertiveness tangled together to create a package that would appeal to any female.

In the past, Shaya had been with dominant male wolves, but their dominance didn't even come near to equaling Nick's level. Also, they had been nothing like him. Whenever there had been a problem, it had never been their fault—oh no, it had always been someone else's fault. Dominant wolves could be like that, too proud and egotistical to ever admit to any weakness. But apologizing wasn't really weak, was it? It took strength to admit to having been wrong, to admit to having made a mistake. And Nick was strong enough, man enough, and adult enough to be responsible for his own actions, to accept blame and to apologize. And he had.

Similarly, her past partners had tried to bully her into giving them their own way. Shaya might be a submissive wolf, but she wasn't weak-minded, and she had a backbone as steely as—or even steelier than—any dominant wolf. Rather than respecting that and treating her as their equal, those partners had felt that her being submissive meant that she shouldn't have her own mind, and they had tried to domineer her.

Nick, on the other hand, was totally different. Sure he *expected* things to go his own way and he *expected* to be obeyed, but he didn't become angry with her when she resisted. Instead, he coaxed her and subtly exercised his will—accepting her wishes while still working to get his own way, not being put off whatsoever by her resistance. He gave her the space to be her own person. She hadn't expected that.

The second she was done with her client, Nick was on his feet. Then, of course, her sixty-two-year-old client noticed him. "Is this your man?" Vivien chuckled and gave Shaya a knowing smile. "I didn't think they made them like that anymore. Someone that masculine will make any woman feel feminine. Look at those broad shoulders and that devilishly handsome face. You're lucky. But then, so is he. I hope you intend to treat her right," Vivien said to him as she went to the reception desk to pay. "She's a special girl." Nick's smile had the woman blushing.

"I couldn't agree more. That's why I have to have her. I won't stop hounding her until she's all mine."

Vivien turned to Shaya, smiling, and forced a tip into her hand. "Oh, I like him. If I was forty years younger . . ." She sighed dreamily as she walked out, making Nick grin.

"I mean it, you know," Nick said to Shaya quietly when she came close. "I won't stop all this until I have you."

Her voice was low and strained. "You can't make up for what you did. You can't fix it." She was surprised when his grin didn't falter.

"Prove it."

"Huh?"

"Don't fight me on trying to fix it. Show me it makes no difference." He held out his hand, but whereas with anyone else it might have been an invitation, with Nick it was a challenge. Shaya had never been one to back down from a challenge. Besides, what harm could it do to have lunch with the guy she wanted with every fiber of her being and who could get her horny with just his very presence? She was so fucked.

*You wish you were being fucked,* teased that daring part of her.

*Now's not the time for your shit,* she responded sharply.

Hesitantly she placed her hand in his, and she received a smile filled with approval and pride as he interlaced their fingers. She would bet he could get people to do anything just to receive that rewarding smile. After Kent handed her purse to her, Nick led her to his Mercedes and opened the passenger door. Just then she hesitated, wondering if allowing him to make them spend time together was really worth her pride at not turning down a challenge. She was effectively helping him with his cause to wriggle his way into her life.

The sensation of a thumb brushing over her chin snapped her out of her thoughts. Nick's expression was gentle, but there was no room for compromise when he spoke.

"In the car, baby."

A shiver wracked her body at the natural dominance in his tone. Making it worse, he skimmed his nose along the curve of her neck, inhaling deeply, and followed it up with a lick that almost had her knees buckling. But she had to make him believe his efforts were making no difference, she reminded herself. It didn't matter that it wasn't true—she *had* to make him think that so he would leave sooner rather than later, because he *would* leave. Knowing her legs weren't going to hold her up much longer, she slid onto the passenger seat. He gave her another of those rewarding smiles.

They drove in a companionable silence, although occasionally he would look over at her and wait for her to meet his gaze as though he wanted to make sure her mind wasn't elsewhere. It surprised her that although Nick had a strong, imposing personality and could be quite intense, she didn't find his presence suffocating. If it wasn't for the fact that she was trying so hard to keep him at a distance, Shaya might have felt relaxed around him.

Arriving at the diner, Nick possessively shackled her wrist with his hand and kept her to his side as they strolled toward the entrance. The physical contact served to further uplift his wolf's typically dark mood. She gave him an odd look and tested the strength of his hold. When his grip didn't slacken, she sighed in surrender—as if indulging him was the easier thing to do in this instance. It was.

Once they had placed their orders with the waitress, Shaya spoke. "What did you do with your morning?"

Nick sat back in his seat opposite her and folded his arms across his chest. "First Derren and I went for a run in our wolf forms through the woods on the edge of town. After that we took Bruce for a walk in the local park. Then we had some fun losing the two wolves that the Nazi has following us."

Inwardly, Shaya shook her head in wonder at how even when he sat, he maintained a powerful stance—head up, chest out, gut sucked in, feet wide apart. Then what he'd said penetrated, and her eyes widened. "He has people following you?"

Nick shrugged one shoulder. "I'm a stranger on his territory. He wanted to know what I was doing here." He saw no need to worry her with talk about the game preserve. As long as the humans believed she was one of them, she was safe.

"Maybe he's worried you'll help the rebels, organize them and make them into a proper pack. Will you?"

"No. I told you: you're more important to me than being in a pack."

"You expect me to believe that you don't miss being Alpha? That you don't miss your old territory and your family and friends? Your mom and sister have come to visit, but your brother's still back there."

Nick raised a hand. "Three things. One, I never wanted to be Alpha. Two, my family is important to me, but so are you. Three, I don't have friends."

She double-blinked in surprise. "What do you mean, you don't have friends?"

"Exactly what I said."

"Then what's Derren?"

"A pain in my ass. I told you, I don't like company—except for yours, obviously." He truly did enjoy being around her. His wolf, too, enjoyed it, even to the extent that he relaxed slightly when she was around.

A shifter who didn't like company . . . Yeah, that was definitely a new one. "You do know that's weird, don't you?"

He shrugged. "I was never what you'd call social. But when I came out of juvie . . . I just didn't feel like I could relate to other people. Derren, sure. But the others . . . they spent their teenage years going on dates, attending proms, and sneaking out to parties. I spent those years trying to stay alive in prison."

Her wolf growled at that idea, not liking it any more than Shaya did. He had spoken so matter-of-factly—there was no sense of him feeling sorry for himself, and that just made the whole thing even more heart-wrenching for her. "I've heard stories about what those places are like. Is it as bad as the stories say?"

"Shifter juvie centers are inverted communities where the mayors are sick-minded prison guards who have taken your rights away and have total control of your life. But it's not just them you have to worry about. There's what you might call a 'prisoner code'—break that, and you can be killed by your own kind.

Fighting becomes a survival tool. The center that I went to . . . it wasn't interested in rehabilitating us, wasn't aiming to help us become well-adjusted adults. All it did was breed anger and hate and a hunger for vengeance. On the other hand, it's a place that will teach you how to be street-smart, how to survive in the worst circumstances." He gave her a grim smile. "Like I said, I don't have pretty stories to tell you."

"Maybe I still want to hear them."

"So you can have more reasons to try to keep me away?" He shook his head. "You're too important. I have to have you."

"You're sure this isn't simply pride, stubbornness, and possessiveness talking? After all, it comes with being an alpha and the mating urges. I mean, you almost attacked Dom—" She stopped as he leaned forward and put a finger to her lips.

"Don't say his name, Shay. You don't know how hard it was not to kill the flirt."

She might have snapped at him for that comment if she hadn't noticed a hint of pain in his eyes. The idea of her with Dominic had hurt him, she realized. Not just pricked at his possessive instincts. It had hurt him. Maybe she shouldn't have cared, but then she remembered that Nick hadn't dated anyone since first seeing her. He hadn't even sought comfort from another female when he thought she was with Dominic, despite that pain and what must have felt like betrayal. "He's just a friend. That's all he ever was."

"I know. Your old packmate, Ryan, assured me of that."

"Ryan?"

"I saw him with the flirt at a club one night. I think Ryan was worried that I was going to attack his packmate—which I was—so he told me the facts in an effort to instill some rationality into me. Ryan then said he'd hate to hurt Shaya's mate, so if I could leave the flirt alone, that would be great. Still, hearing you say his name makes me want to bite you." To mark her, remind her that she didn't belong to Dominic, she belonged to him. "I think you'd like that."

Blushing and stifling her smile, she snapped, "Fuck you."

"What, you mean right now? In front of all these people? I guess I could."

She slapped his arm, and he laughed. Eager to change the subject, she said, "You need to make some friends. Whether you like company or not, it's important to have friends."

"Why would I want friends when I have you?"

"You don't have me."

"I will. Do you want to know what makes me so sure of that? Because no other situation is acceptable to me." His life had been a dull time without her. He didn't want to go back to that. Even arguing with her made him feel alive. It was the strangest feeling to have his wolf in a bright mood, but that was what she did to him. "Nothing you say or do will make me give up. Like I said, you're too important to me. The sooner you accept that, the happier we'll both be."

The resolve in his tone and expression practically petted her wolf. Their food came then, and it seemed that Nick's interest in chatting was over. With any normal person, it might have been because he was ready to tuck into his meal. But Nick wasn't normal, and apparently what he really wanted was to up the level of sexual tension between them. If he wasn't feeding her and then watching her chew as if riveted by the movement of her mouth, he was holding her hand and fiddling with it or nipping at her palm. In between all that, he would reach over and play with stray strands of her hair or snatch some of her fries, knowing she didn't like to share her food. Then he tried playing footsie under the table, but after she lost her patience and stomped hard on his foot, they just ended up playfully kicking each other instead.

Shaya had been shocked to find that she was actually enjoying herself. She spent more time laughing and smiling than blushing, which was no small thing, given the filthy thoughts traveling through her mind. Of course that smile faded somewhat when they walked to the car and found a human guy with cold eyes and a cocky countenance waiting there with two other males, his hateful gaze trained on Nick. She recognized them as some of the human extremists from the other night.

She wasn't surprised when Nick easily held the leader's frosty gaze, not in the least bit intimidated. Nor was she surprised when he stood in front of her slightly in a very protective move. Derren seemed to appear out of absolutely nowhere on Nick's other side, as expected. What *did* surprise her was that rage was radiating from both Nick and Derren. Sure, the humans were cruel and prejudiced, but this . . . this rage had a different source.

The human smiled at Shaya, creeping her out. "It's clear to me that you're Nick's girl. What's not clear to me is whether or not you know he's an animal."

"Being a shifter doesn't make someone an animal," she replied. Her wolf bared her teeth at him.

"Oh, so you're a shifter groupie." The humans all laughed. "There sure are plenty of them roaming around."

She was about to correct him and declare that she was a half-shifter and proud to be, but then Nick took her hand and squeezed lightly. She understood the signal: He didn't want them to know in case they targeted her. Neither did she but, dammit, this jabbed at her pride.

"How can it not bother you that he's inhuman? You're a traitor to our race."

"And you're a pedophile, a rapist, and a sadist . . . aren't you, Logan?" said Derren, ending the sentence with a snap of his teeth. "You have a fondness for young boys, as I recall."

Shock crashed into Shaya as the implications of that comment settled in. Now she understood where Nick and Derren knew him from, just as she now understood the source of Nick's and Derren's rage. She also understood that if Logan had succeeded in abusing either Nick or Derren, they wouldn't have allowed him to speak—he'd have been dead before he could blink. And she'd have looked on, clapping. Sick bastard.

Logan's attention shot to Derren. He narrowed his eyes, his expression nostalgic. "I should have known that his guard is you. You always did follow him around."

"So did you." Derren cocked his head. "But you weren't like the other guards at first, were you? No, in the beginning, you wouldn't play a part in the torture that went on in that place. But then eventually you gave in, and you found that you liked it. But you hated that you liked it, hated that you enjoyed sick shit like that. A little voice in your head reminded you it was wrong. So it had to be someone else's fault, didn't it? It had to be the shifters' fault that you got a hard-on for them, that you couldn't stop. And *that's* why you truly hate us—what you did to the shifters in that place made you see who you really are and how sick your desires are. The truth is, though, that you have the same desire to hurt humans, don't you? The people who should be isolated from society are sick motherfuckers like you."

At this point, Logan had turned an odd shade of purple and looked close to hyperventilating. The other humans seemed uncomfortable and confused. "The laws will be put into place— make no mistake about that."

"Maybe they will," said Nick. The only thing that stopped him from throwing accusations about the game preserve at Logan was that he didn't want to make the people behind it nervous. If Logan *was* involved, he would tell them. "But you'll still always be an evil bastard who lost his right to live a long time ago."

Both Shaya and her wolf shivered at the silky menace in Nick's voice.

"Now back the fuck off," growled Nick. Very wisely, the humans returned to their van. They didn't drive off, clearly intent on remaining on his tail.

"No one who abuses another person, particularly a child, deserves to live," stated Shaya firmly. "No one. But you can't let him trick you into attacking him."

Nick stroked a hand over her hair. "I know. Don't worry, I can be patient. Come on, let's go—your lunch hour's over, and you need to get back to work."

Once in the car and clicking on her seatbelt, Shaya tilted her head as she considered the situation. "So . . . you have two of the Nazi's wolves watching you, human extremists are tracking you, and you also have the rebels hovering around you."

Nick smiled, though his mood was grim. Only Shaya could have made him smile right then. "I thought you wanted me to make friends."

"This isn't in the least bit amusing. You have dangerous people on your ass."

His expression fierce, he assured her, "I won't let them harm you, if that's what you're worried about."

She rolled her eyes. "It's *you* I'm worried about, Beavis."

Nick smiled again. "I knew you cared."

It was no surprise to Shaya when he later appeared at closing time to give her a ride home from work. She resisted, of course . . . though, if she was honest, she resisted more because she *thought* she should than because she *wanted* to. He played her well, using her own words against her that giving her a ride was totally innocent. He also did the whole "show me I'm making no difference" thing, too. The bastard was good at this.

Minutes later, she was sliding into the passenger seat with a huff. Instantly, the delicious smell of Bolognese wrapped around her. He'd cooked for her. Again. Asshole. "You know, I'm perfectly capable of fending for myself," she said when he joined her inside the car.

"It doesn't mean I can't cook for you and make your evening simpler, does it?"

"You already commandeered my lunch hour. Wasn't that enough for you?"

"Nope."

She shook her head. "You are so selfish."

"Not selfish, baby." His expression was all innocence. "I just like things my way. As long as they are, I'm very reasonable and accommodating."

All she could do was growl. When they arrived at her house, it was to be greeted by the deafening noises coming from her neighbor's place. Great. He was throwing another house party.

"What the fuck is that?" asked Nick.

"It's Eric's Friday-night ritual, though sometimes he has a party on a weeknight too."

"That's not a house party. I've heard quieter concerts than that." Outside the car, he asked, "Haven't you said anything to him?" Not liking the odd look on her face, he pressed, "Shay?"

Huffing, she replied, "Of course I've talked to him." The first time it had happened, she'd nicely asked him if he could turn down the music. He'd said of course he could . . . but that he wouldn't and she could fuck off—and all because she'd politely declined his offer of a date. So she'd argued with him a little, and usually Shaya was pretty good at negotiating with people. But this guy was determined to make her pay for being "stuck up" and rejecting him. He'd even spat at her.

Shaya hadn't done too well with that, and her response had been to dig out her baseball bat and attack his car; the amount of noise coming from the house meant he hadn't even heard her. Naturally he'd turned up at her home the next day, automatically suspecting it was her. Naturally she'd denied it, as time in prison wasn't appealing. Since he hadn't been able to prove it was her, the police hadn't acted.

"And?" prodded Nick.

"And nothing. He's an ass to me."

"He's *an ass* to you?"

It turned out that telling him that had been an extremely bad move on her part, because then Nick was marching toward her neighbor's house. She hurried after him. "Nick, just leave it."

"Leave it?" he scoffed without breaking stride. "Not a chance."

"It doesn't matter."

"Of course it matters." That kind of disturbance would be bad enough for human hearing. For shifter hearing, it was painful.

"He's doing this to get a reaction because I pissed him off by rejecting him and vandalizing his car. Don't give him that reaction."

"You vandalized his car?" He'd bet that her beloved bat was involved.

"It's just a party."

"That's not a party. That's an attempt to aggravate you."

He was right about that. "Did you forget that two of Logan's men are watching you?" The last thing she wanted was Nick being violent right now.

In truth, for a few seconds, he actually had. "Not a problem. They'll just assume we're going to the party. And if they look to be suspicious, Derren will know to distract them." Then Nick was marching up the driveway of her neighbor's house.

"Nick, for God's sake, listen to me!" But he didn't. Instead, he began pounding his fist on the front door. A few seconds later, the door swung open and a tall blonde dressed in . . . pretty much nothing was eying Nick like he was a snack. Shaya didn't like that. So she growled. As if to reassure her, Nick closed his hand over hers.

Keeping Shaya close, Nick pushed his way inside and closed the door behind him, not wanting the extremists to see anything. "Where's Eric?" he asked the blonde.

Looking suddenly nervous—though it didn't seem to stop her from ogling Nick, which pissed Shaya the hell off—the blonde pointed down the hallway. "He's in the kitchen."

With a tight hold on Shaya's hand, Nick strode toward the kitchen. His expression must have been bad, because people parted to let him through as he advanced down the hallway. He'd gotten a glimpse of her neighbor a few times, so he knew exactly who he was looking for. No sooner had he spotted the guy than

Nick was in front of him with his free hand curled around his throat.

Shock took over Eric's face, and his eyes bulged. "What the—"

"Don't speak. Just listen."

The chattering in the room suddenly stopped, and Shaya was pretty sure that if Nick had been anybody else, people would have intervened. But it was like Derren had once said: When Nick was angry, people paid attention. At that moment, he was absolutely livid, and only a fruit loop would have wanted Nick's wrath shifted to them. Her wolf was feeling pretty smug about the whole thing, liked that her mate was protecting her; it was important to her to know that he could.

"You can see Shaya beside me," growled Nick. Eric's eyes briefly flickered to her. "So I don't think I need to explain why I'm here or why I'd like to snap your neck, do I?"

Eric did what was typical of any bully—he stood down the second someone stronger than him confronted him. Rather than fighting Nick's grip, he stayed very still. "No."

"I don't think I need to explain what will happen if you don't stop making yourself a problem for her, do I?" When Eric's eyes again moved to Shaya, Nick tightened his hold on the bastard's throat. "Don't look at her. Look at me. Now answer my question. I don't need to explain what will happen, do I?"

Eric shook his head as much as Nick's grip would allow.

"Tell me," rumbled Nick. "Tell me what I'll do to you if you ever even try to upset her again."

His voice came out strained and hoarse. "You'll beat me up."

Nick *tsk*ed. "Wrong. I'll slash you open, rip out your intestines, and string you up by them. Because Shaya's very, very important to me. And you know that voice in your head that tells you not to do wrong? I have one of those, but it doesn't give a shit about right and wrong when someone upsets her."

Seeing that not only was Eric likely to piss himself but that Nick was having difficulty staying in control, Shaya squeezed

Nick's free hand lightly and supportively, whispering low enough for only him to hear, "It's okay. Let him go." His hold on Eric loosened, but he didn't release him. "Let him go, Nick. Come on." She squeezed his hand again, pressing herself against his side. Inhaling deeply, Nick released Eric and locked his arm around Shaya. She should have moved away, but instead she melted against him, knowing he needed it. "Let's go." Turning, she realized that—no surprise—Derren was in the doorway of the kitchen.

He raised a questioning brow at her and Nick, asking, "Everything okay?"

Nick began leading her out of the house with Derren at their side. "Just making friends. Shay thinks I should get some."

She snorted. "Shaya also thinks you should be keeping a low profile right now, *not* confronting idiotic humans." He simply shrugged, like that was irrelevant when the subject matter was her. He truly was a law unto himself. And that was when something occurred to her. She'd originally thought he'd give up on winning her over after a series of rejections, but now she wasn't so sure. Outside, she turned to him. "You could never be 'handled' by anyone, could you?"

Derren barked a laugh. "People have tried."

Having thrown Derren a scowl, Nick met her gaze. "You're beginning to realize that getting me to leave won't be as simple as you thought," he surmised. "Good. By all means keep trying to push me away if you feel you must, baby. But it won't make a damn bit of difference." It was a warning as much as it was a vow. He trailed the tip of his finger from her temple, down her cheek, over her jaw, and along her neck until he reached the collar of her T-shirt. "I won't give you up. Not for anything. Not even for you."

# CHAPTER SEVEN

Nick had never had so much trouble putting one foot in front of the other. But while an ass like that was right there in front of him, he had no interest in moving anyway. As Shaya was bent over riffling through a shelf of canned foods, Nick simply gazed at her ass in awe. What he wouldn't give to know what kind of underwear she wore under that skintight denim. Normally he didn't like jeans on a woman; they didn't allow him easy access and they hid way too much, but with Shaya it was a sweet torment having it all left to the imagination. He looked for a panty line but couldn't make one out. Maybe she was wearing a thong. Maybe she was going commando. *Fuck.*

As usual when he was around Shaya, he was assaulted by a number of erotic images. He could imagine her being bent just like that, but naked and over a table while he was slamming into her. Or sprawled across his lap while he spanked her ass over and over until she begged him to take her.

And now his cock was hurting like a son of a bitch.

In the middle of a damn grocery store.

Knowing she didn't work on Sundays and she was always so exhausted after working long shifts, he'd figured she would sleep most of the morning. Apparently his Shaya liked to be up at the crack of dawn on Sundays to go shopping. He had been on his way to the gas station when he'd spotted her heading inside the store.

Either she'd picked up his scent or had sensed someone's gaze on her, because she suddenly glanced over her shoulder. He almost laughed when her eyes widened and she straightened abruptly. No doubt she had a good idea of the kind of thoughts and pictures that had been forming in his mind.

"What are you doing here?" asked Shaya, flustered—and annoyed with herself for being flustered. She knew she sounded particularly cranky, because she *was* cranky. Menstrual cramps could do that to a girl. "Are you following me?"

"It's harder than I thought."

"If I were you, I'd do the intelligent thing and fuck off," she growled.

"No."

She growled again. "Has anyone ever told you you're unbelievably stubborn?"

"Frequently. But, really, it's not stubbornness. It's just that I can say no without feeling guilty."

His lopsided smile miraculously made her want to smile back, but she would *not*. "What do you want?" His eyes went slumberous.

"You. In my bed. Naked. And wet and ready for me." When she gaped at him, he shrugged innocently. "You asked."

She closed her eyes for a moment, seeking patience. But she simply wasn't a patient person. "I don't have time for this. Move out of my way."

"I'm here to help."

Her words came out through clenched teeth. "Nick, not today, okay." The asshole actually put a jar of Bolognese sauce in her cart. She returned it to the shelf with a huff. "You can harass me again tomorrow."

"I don't harass you, I just show up wherever you are."

She growled when he put the sauce back into her cart and also a bottle of garlic oil. "Stop putting things in my cart!"

Picking up on her wolf's unusual prickliness, he frowned. Sure Shaya and her wolf were snippy, but this was different. "What's wrong with your wolf? She's a little . . . off today. Come to think of it, so is your scent." He leaned in and brushed his nose against her neck. "*Oh.*"

"Yeah," she said with a sardonic smile. At least one good thing would come from her menstrual cycle starting: he'd leave her alone for a few days, knowing seducing her wouldn't be possible. And he wouldn't send her a message similar to the one he'd sent last night that went a little something like:

If I was lying in bed with you now, if I had my hands on your body, where would you want me to touch you first?

Her traitorous body had responded to that, just like it was responding to his very presence now. But getting him to go away would be simple enough. Not simply because seduction wouldn't be possible, but because no wolf liked to be around menstruating female shifters. Shifter PMS was a bitch—a time filled with excessive fatigue, mood swings, irritability, cramps, bloating, aching breasts, tension, increased appetite, sleeplessness, and hot flashes.

"So that's why you're snippier than usual," said Nick. "It explains what your pretty ass is doing out of bed so early, too—you usually have major trouble getting up in the morning." It also explained why her breasts were bigger than usual. But he wouldn't comment on that. He wasn't stupid.

She gasped, indignant. "I get out of bed just fine each morning, thanks. And I'm *not* snippy."

If he was sensible, he'd walk away. Female wolves with PMS were likely to eat someone's face off at the slightest provocation.

But this was *his* female wolf. And right now, she needed someone to take care of her, whether she'd admit it or not. He curled an arm around her shoulders and used his free hand to push the cart. "Come on, baby. Tell me what stuff you need, and I'll help you get this over with. Then you can go home and lounge on the sofa all day. Doesn't that sound good?"

It did, actually. Nonetheless, she snapped, "I'm perfectly capable of putting items in a freaking shopping cart."

"Of course you are. But if I help, you'll get out of here sooner." Despite her grumbles and the string of unprovoked insults she flung at him as they strolled down aisle after aisle, Nick aided her in loading the cart and then helped her bag the items. When he offered to pay, he thought she'd break his jaw.

"I'm not a charity case," she hissed. Slightly mollified by his apologetic look, Shaya fished the money from her purse and held it out to the cashier . . . who was staring lustfully at Nick and wearing a seductive smile. Shaya cleared her throat particularly loud. "Do you see something that you like, because he doesn't," she spat. Apparently the guy waiting to be served behind her thought that was pretty funny. Shaya wasn't at all amused.

Holding the grocery bags with one arm, Nick gently but firmly took Shaya's hand and pulled her to him. "Ready to go home, baby?" Her response was a low growl that made him smile. As she ranted in the parking lot about how much she liked to walk thank-you-very-much, he placed the bags into the trunk of his car and then guided her into the passenger seat.

She continued ranting all the way home, and he did what any wise male shifter did when his mate had a PMS-induced tantrum—he kept his mouth shut and nodded along. She was still ranting when they pulled up outside her house. When he retrieved her bags from the trunk of his car, Shaya went to take them from him, but he shook his head and advanced up her driveway.

Shaya growled. "I'm—"

"Perfectly capable of carrying your own bags," he finished soothingly. "But that doesn't mean I can't do it for you, does it?"

"Stop with the therapist tone!" Realizing that something about the yard was different, Shaya took a moment to study her surroundings. "Did you mow the lawn?"

Nick shrugged. "It kind of needed it. You only just noticed? I did it yesterday while you were at work."

Huffing, she marched to the front door and unlocked it. "Do you have to be so fucking nice and helpful?" she growled.

"Now, Shay—"

"It's hard to hate you when you're nice and helpful!"

"Good. I don't want you to hate me."

Ignoring the murderous look Shaya shot him, he walked right on into the house like he had every right. She followed him, watching with growing agitation—like she wasn't agitated enough!—as he began puttering around her kitchen. "Okay, look, you've earned a gold sticker for ass-kissing. Now get the hell out and—" She gave a startled yelp as he lifted her, sat her on the kitchen counter, and then stood between her legs.

Nick handed her some Tylenol and a glass of water. "Here. Take these." It was most likely sheer stubbornness that made her hesitate. "You're in pain, baby. Take them."

There was enough authority in the latter words to make her bite back a snappy comment. Her wolf reluctantly backed down too. Conceding to herself that she did in fact need the pills and that refusing would be stupid, she sighed inwardly and snatched them from his hand. Once she'd washed them down with the water, he took her glass and placed it on the counter.

"Good girl." He moved his hand to her stomach and gently massaged it, hating that she was in pain and feeling totally help-less. "Now . . . would you rather curl up on the sofa or go lie down in bed?"

"I'm not an invalid."

"Every male shifter knows that when his mate has PMS, it's best for her to curl up on the sofa or in bed and enjoy doing absolutely nothing."

"I'm not your mate." Her wolf sassily swished her tail at her for that offensive comment.

Wearing a reprimanding expression, Nick *tsk*ed. "Yes, you are, baby," he insisted softly, tapping the tip of her nose. "You always will be, no matter what. You were made for me, belong to me in a way you could never belong to anyone else." He soothingly combed his hand through her red corkscrew curls. "I love how soft your hair is. Like silk." The compliment seemed to disarm her, and he got the feeling that she hadn't gotten a lot of them in her life. "What will it be: the sofa or the bed?"

She sighed, slumping in defeat. "Sofa." Her eyes widened as he curled her legs around him and carried her to the living area. He placed her gently on the sofa, where she immediately curled up like a fetus, and handed her the TV remote. Instead of leaving the house, he disappeared back into the kitchen. Hearing the banging of the cupboard doors, she realized he was unpacking her groceries. A part of her wanted to yell at him to get out, but then she'd have to do the unpacking herself, and she'd much rather stay where she was. So, instead, she turned on the TV and began flicking through the channels until she found something she wanted to watch.

When Nick returned to the living room a little while later, it was to find that she was crying. Putting the chocolate bar and cup of coffee he'd brought in onto the table in front of her, he crouched down and cradled her face with his hands. "Hey, what's wrong?"

"This damn movie," she said, sniffling. "The dog just died."

It took everything he had not to smile. He kissed her hair. "Maybe you should watch something else."

"I can't believe they called the movie *My Dog Skip*—it sounds like such a happy movie, doesn't it? You don't think the dog's going to die."

He swiped her tears away with his thumbs. "That's a good point."

"I know you're trying not to laugh, Beavis."

"How about we talk about something else? Distract you from the movie?" She looked about to snort at that, but then her expression shifted from annoyed to speculative. "You want to ask me something." She shrugged, as if it wasn't important. "Ask."

Shaya bit her lip, unsure. When she noticed that Nick's eyes had tracked the movement and he was staring at her mouth, she quickly released her lip from her teeth. His eyes moved to hers, daring her to ask her question. "Why were you sent to juvie?"

He sucked in a breath. "Ask me anything but that."

"I want to know." His hands slipped away from her face as his expression closed down. She could almost feel him pulling away emotionally. When he went to stand, she fisted her hand in his T-shirt to stop him. "You can't expect to earn someone's trust if you keep things from them."

Knowing she was right, he sighed tiredly. "Why do you want to know? Do you really need more reasons to think badly of me?"

"You can't call me your mate and then deny me the right to know these things," she said softly. "Tell me." A minute or so later, he finally nodded, but she didn't release him.

Nick inhaled deeply, preparing himself to go back to a time that he hated—preparing himself to reveal something that might make his job to earn a place in her life even harder. "I wasn't born in the Ryland Pack. My family is originally from a pack in Manhattan. They don't have a plot of land; they purchased an apartment block that's near a wooded area. The entire pack lives inside the block, and they use the wooded area to run in. One day, I was walking with my sister through the woods when we came across four human males. Their ages ranged from seventeen to twenty-one."

"How old were you?"

"Thirteen. My sister was twelve. They knew what we were, and like many humans, they weren't too happy about our existence. But they were happy enough to rape my sister—or, at least, to try. Two of them held me back, wanting me to watch, while another pinned my sister down. They threatened her that if she shifted to her wolf form, the others would kill me. In turn, they threatened me that if *I* shifted, they'd kill *her*. The fourth one was ready to record the whole thing."

When his eyes took on a faraway quality, she prodded, "Nick?"

His focus returned to her. "I shifted. My wolf was too enraged to hold back, and I didn't want him to. They were going to hurt her anyway, so obeying them seemed pointless. I killed the kid who'd tried to rape her, and I badly maimed two of the others. The fourth human ran off and got help." He waited for disgust to contort her expression, or for fear to enter her eyes. But she said nothing, and her expression remained blank.

Hopeful, he continued. "I might have been executed rather than sent to juvie, but the video clearly showed what the humans' intentions had been, and that it was self-defense. Still, I was thirteen and I'd killed a human and maimed two others on my own. The human authorities were nervous about it. I think they thought the likelihood was that I wouldn't get out of juvie alive, so problem solved."

"But you did get out." And she was proud of him for that. How could he have thought she'd judge him for doing what most shifters would have done in his situation? Hell, Trey's wolf went feral pretty often.

"I quickly realized that the guards were being paid to target certain shifters—most likely by relatives of the humans who'd been hurt at the shifter's hands. So I encouraged all the shifters in the place to band together into one pack rather than existing in small groups. It gave us more protection. While each one of us always had someone looking out for them, it made it extremely hard for the guards to target anybody."

"And you were their leader, their Alpha," she easily guessed. He was a natural leader. He truly was born to be an Alpha . . . and yet he'd left that position behind for her. The question was for how long?

"At first, no. Another wolf acted as Alpha, but the other shifters didn't really follow Merrick. They just didn't want to challenge him, didn't want a psycho on their case. And he made everybody's life miserable in that way that bullies do."

"So *you* challenged him."

"I killed him." And he'd always hate himself for it. "I didn't mean to. I really, really didn't. But he wouldn't submit, wouldn't back down. He was *enjoying* the fight, the blood, even the pain—it was weird. Merrick was totally messed up in the head. It went too far."

Shaya's voice was soft, nonjudgmental. "If he wouldn't submit, what choice did you have?"

"It's still more blood on my hands, Shay. Like I said, Merrick was messed up . . . but did he really deserve to die for that? He was only fifteen years old."

"And you were only thirteen, and you were in a life-or-death situation. You chose your own life over his. Anyone else would have done the same thing." To her dismay, he didn't look convinced of that; too much guilt stained his expression. "It can't have been easy to tell me all of that. Thank you." He simply shrugged. "How did you end up becoming Alpha of the Ryland Pack?"

"My family moved there while I was in juvie—they didn't want to be near the bad memories. Unfortunately, it was taken over by another Alpha three years after they settled there. He was the type to rule by fear and intimidation. He punished the slightest transgressions, caused divides within the pack, isolated the weaker members, and forced many of them to fight in the underground fighting club he owned—including Eli.

"After spending nine years cooped up in that fucked-up place, my wolf wasn't in the best frame of mind. Leaving juvie to find my family suffering like that . . . it knocked him over the edge. I challenged and killed the Alpha"—more blood on his hands—"but I didn't want the position. The trouble was that no one else wanted it. The pack was a mess, and no one wanted the responsibility of fixing it. I'd killed their Alpha. I had no choice but to do what was right by them and take that position. So I did."

Shaya could only begin to imagine how hard it must have been for him to have come straight out of juvie only to find himself suddenly Alpha of a pack. It was more or less exchanging one prison for another. Being Alpha was a huge responsibility; everyone else came first, and he always had to be strong for the pack, no matter his own problems. Nick had never had time of his own, never had a breather. Maybe this little vacation from the position would be good for him. She couldn't allow herself to trust that this was anything more than a vacation.

"Told you it wasn't a pretty story."

Shaya swallowed hard. "You protected your sister. No one can blame you for that. No one can blame your wolf for turning feral at a time like that."

His short laugh was bitter. "I hadn't turned feral, Shay. I knew exactly what I was doing. I didn't have to kill one of them. I didn't even have to hurt any of them. They were spooked enough by me shifting that they were ready to make a run for it—they'd clearly been confident that I wouldn't shift. But I wasn't satisfied with scaring them off. I killed that human because I wanted to, just like I attacked the two who had tried restraining me because I wanted to. If people hadn't turned up and intervened, I might have done more than maim them."

A chill suddenly came over Shaya. But, oddly enough, it wasn't because of his confession. It was because of how lonely he looked right then. She understood loneliness all too well. Could she really blame him for wanting to hurt people who had intended to rape his little sister? A *twelve*-year-old girl? Maybe other people would have, but Shaya found that she couldn't. "Of course you wanted to hurt them. They—"

"I'm not sorry I did it, Shay." It was better to find out now if she could or couldn't accept him as he truly was. He knew, however, that if she tried using this to push him even further away, it wouldn't work. "I never have been. Not even when I was put in that hellhole, not even when I thought I'd die there . . . I wasn't sorry. I don't think I ever will be."

There was that loneliness in his expression and voice again, that feeling of not having anyone who could understand and accept him. He was wrong. "I think of Taryn as a sister, and I know that if anyone tried to hurt her, I'd be prepared to stab them through the fucking heart."

Seeing the vigor in her expression, he could believe that. "You're *half* human, Shay. Those people I hurt are half yours."

"But I'm *half* shifter, too. And they tried to hurt your sister and you. That's not something I would ever find excusable." He was *hers*, whether she wanted him to claim her or not. He was still hers, and the idea of anyone hurting him simply wasn't something she could ever tolerate or forgive.

The total lack of recrimination was a balm to his wolf's scarred soul. Nick wanted nothing more than to take her mouth, but he forced himself to resist. Needing some sort of contact, he leaned his forehead against hers and traced her cheekbone with the tip of his finger. "See, you deserve better. But I'm going nowhere. I know that makes me selfish. I know another male shifter might have walked away. But I can't do that, Shay. I tried it once—it didn't work. Don't you get it yet? My life's worth shit without you in it."

She did her best to ignore his words, to not let them worm their way inside her—she really, really did—but they crept into that lonely spot she had, warming it. The possessiveness in his eyes melted her wolf. As he rubbed his thumb over her bottom lip, Shaya almost shuddered. Having him invade her personal space like this, touching her, should have annoyed her, but it was instead arousing her. Her nipples were hard, and her clit was tingling. God, she had been one big G-spot since he arrived. The wise thing would have been to pull back, but she sensed that the physical contact was calming him, chasing back the memories. How could she refuse to do that for him? Besides, if she was honest, she didn't want to pull back anyway.

The lust glimmering in her eyes made Nick groan. He scrunched a hand in her hair, digging deep for restraint and using the feel of her to do it. "You can't look at me like that, Shay. I'm hard as a rock here, and you're making it really difficult not to bite this mouth. But you like that you do that to me, don't you?"

Her blush gave her away. "Asshole."

"At least I have the comfort of knowing I'm not the only one who's horny." When she snorted, he arched a brow at her and said quietly, "Shall I tell you what I'm thinking about right now?"

Flushed, she squeezed her eyes shut. "I really wish you wouldn't." The mating urges were becoming harder and harder to deal with, and she didn't need him making it worse—particularly when she was feeling so restlessly needy. Her wolf, on the other hand, was extremely curious.

"I'm thinking about how gorgeous you would look tied to my bed. Want to know what I'd do to the nipples that are poking through your T-shirt? I'd suckle on them and bite them until you were arching off the bed and begging me to fuck you. But I wouldn't fuck you. Not yet. First, I'd taste you. You can't have any idea how badly I want to know how you taste. Only after I'd licked you to orgasm would I bury myself inside you and take what's mine. There'd be nothing gentle about it, Shay. It would be fast and hard and raw."

When she opened her eyes again, Nick saw that they had darkened and her pupils were dilated. To add to that, her lips were parted, and her breath was coming in short, soft pants. He had to wonder why he was doing this when he was tormenting himself just as much as he was her. Clearly he had a masochistic streak he hadn't known about until now.

Shaya took a steadying breath before speaking. Her voice was embarrassingly raspy. "You're a teasing, cocky asshole."

He laughed, forcing himself to get to his feet and end the torture. "Story time is now over. Eat your chocolate and rest. I have a juicer to fix." With that, he left the room and she turned her attention back to the TV. The plan hadn't been to fall asleep. But that was what happened. When she woke, it was to find that it was dark and that Nick was sitting on the sofa with her feet resting on his lap, watching the TV on a low volume. He must have sensed she had woken, because his eyes moved to hers.

"Hey, baby. Feel any better?"

She did, actually. The cramps had gone, and the edginess had eased. She nodded.

"Good. Just so you know, your juicer is now fixed, the kitchen tap is no longer leaking, and your dinner's in the oven, waiting."

Did he have to be so nice to her?

"I noticed the faulty boiler, too. Your landlord will need to take care of it. I don't want you having cold showers."

Ha. Her landlord didn't address any problems. He'd say, "Oh, I'm starting to think I may have to sell the house, I can't afford to keep repairing it," which was, of course, an indirect threat—if she didn't deal with the problems herself, she'd be out of a home very soon. "I'll call him tomorrow," she said casually, though she knew the conversation would amount to nothing.

"No need. I called him while you were sleeping. He promised he'd take care of it."

She gaped at him. "You called him? How did you even know his number? And what do you mean 'he promised'?" Oh hell, what had he done?

Nick shrugged, his gaze on the TV. "I got his number the same way I got yours—I have contacts in the right places. Admittedly, he wasn't so cooperative to begin with. Cried poverty and talked about selling the house, but when I mentioned that his bank balance didn't quite back that up and just how important you are to me, he had a change of attitude."

"You know his bank balance?" She was beginning to think Nick could find out just about anything about anyone. He simply shrugged again, like it was nothing. "I suppose you threatened him too." He looked suitably offended.

"I didn't need to. He was spooked enough knowing I had access to his personal information—including the little detail of him having an affair with his sister-in-law."

She could only gape again. Then she shook her head, groaning. "You scare me sometimes."

He rubbed his hand up and down her thigh. "You never have to fear me. You're the one person who'll never be harmed by me, no matter what."

She believed that. A week ago, she wouldn't have believed a single word he said about anything at all. But now, she did. That told her he was getting under her skin. And that was dangerous. But how could he not? The fact was that, whether she liked it or not, it was hard not to like having him around. He made her life easier by doing the littlest things, and he tried his best to take care of her despite her grumbles and protests. No one had ever done that before. No one had ever been so completely focused on her. Not even her parents.

"Now that you're feeling better, I'll get out of your way." The last thing Nick wanted to do was leave, but he wasn't going to stay unless she asked him to. He didn't want her thinking that everything he'd done for her today had been in an effort to earn an invitation to stay. He'd done it because he wanted to. But as he wasn't as well behaved as she'd like, he didn't resist the temptation to plant a kiss on her tempting mouth. "If you need me for anything, you know where I am." He had only taken two steps when he heard her voice behind him.

"Nick . . . thanks . . . for helping," she awkwardly said. He flashed her a sexy smile that made her wolf shiver, and then he left . . . and Shaya found herself wanting to call him back. Yep, he was under her skin all right—under a lot deeper than she'd thought. Crap.

# CHAPTER EIGHT

After three weeks of Nick doing his best to immerse himself in her life, Shaya was about ready to cry . . . because it was working. To her dismay, he was utterly consistent in everything he said and did. Each morning, he would be waiting at his car with a coffee and an offer of a ride, which she had given up on refusing. Each day at work, a gift and a text message would arrive that brought a smile to her face and made her want to laugh. Every lunch hour, he came to take her to lunch wherever she wanted to go. At the end of each day, he was there to collect her from work with a meal he'd cooked for her. And every Sunday, he helped her with grocery shopping and offered to do any jobs around the house.

Although he touched her often and teased her with the things he'd like to do to her, he never pushed for more, never took advantage of the arousal that was coming close to ruling her body. That same arousal was responsible for the dreams she had every night. There was nothing vanilla about them. The one she'd had the previous night had been particularly hot. Not only was she naked on her back in bed with her hands bound above her head, but she had a butt plug up her ass and Nick was fucking in and out of her hard and deep. She blamed Kent and all his "I bet Nick's just as dominant in the bedroom" comments. That and Nick's constant teasing.

As such, when he walked into the salon at midday looking so freaking hot it wasn't fair, she wasn't sure whether she wanted to snap at him or jump on him. She went with the first. "I told you this morning that I wouldn't be able to make lunch today—Fridays are always busy here."

"I know," said Nick soothingly, smiling. Her snippiness never bothered him. "I brought you something—I wanted to make sure you didn't miss lunch altogether because you were busy." Not only did the female eat like a bird, picking at everything, but Nick knew she occasionally missed meals, and he'd be damned if he let her neglect herself like that. It particularly wasn't good for shifter metabolism.

Shaya might have rejected the bag he held out to her if the Subway sandwich didn't smell so unbelievably good. Begrudgingly she took it, silently cursing him for once again being nice and trying to take care of her. He did that a lot. Of course Kent thought it was unbelievably sweet, as did her regular clients, who had all met Nick at least once by this point and thought he was fabulous—in fact, the client in front of her was at that moment greeting him and talking with him about the freaking weather.

Finally, Nick turned back to Shaya and gestured at the sandwich. "Make sure you eat it." In a voice so quiet only shifter hearing would pick it up, he added, "If I find out you haven't, I'll spank your ass."

Perching a hand on her hip, she gaped at him. Just as quietly, she asked, "Who do you think you are, bossing me around and threatening to spank my ass?"

"I'm the person who owns that ass, baby. And I don't like it when you're not taking care of it." With that, he planted a brief kiss on her cheek and left.

Shaya, still gaping, looked at Kent, who was working at his station beside hers and would have easily heard Nick with his shifter hearing. "Can you believe that guy?" Kent simply shot her another look of disapproval. Why? Because she had accepted the offer of a date for tonight from a client she'd had that morning, who was new in town. Ordinarily, she wouldn't date a client, but she'd made an exception here. She could lie to herself all she wanted about why she was going—she could say it was because she didn't want Nick, or she could say it was because she had a huge thing for her date, but the truth was that she was testing Nick.

He was fast becoming important to her. She couldn't help being comforted by his presence and confidence. He made both her and her wolf feel safe, cosseted, and protected. For too long, she'd felt alone. Even before the whole Nick extravaganza, that loneliness had been there . . . like a cold draft in her chest. When he was around her, when his scent was filling her senses and he was touching her, that loneliness subsided.

He had made himself a part of her everyday life to the extent that if he left again, it would have a huge impact on her—an impact she wasn't sure she could bear. If that was going to happen, she would rather he did it sooner instead of later. If one thing could succeed in making him give up, it was her going on a date with another guy. If he still didn't give up . . . well, there would be no denying that he deserved a chance. It was a huge gamble, and it could blow up in her face, but she *needed* to know how committed he was to sticking around before she even properly considered giving him a chance.

After her client left, Shaya was cleaning her station when she again heard that frustrating noise. "Will you stop growling at me," she whispered abrasively to Kent.

"What you're doing is wrong, Shaya, and you know it."

"I need to know if he'll leave again."

"No, you want to punish him."

Okay, a part of her did want him to hurt as she had, but she was starting to think that he had been hurting as much as she had all this time. "If I can't trust him not to leave, we can't move forward. You know about my history with Mason—trusting is really hard for me. Considering Nick, *my own mate*, abandoned me once, I'd say it's not all that surprising for me to be so hesitant."

Kent's face softened. "I know. But Shaya, there's a strong possibility that Nick will kill your date. Do you want that on your conscience?"

"Why do you think I haven't told him anything about it and don't plan on doing so until after the date? I'll send him a text to say that I'm going to your place after work."

Kent gaped. "Why am I being dragged into this?"

She rolled her eyes. "Stop being a Nancy. He won't know that you knew anything about the date because I won't tell him."

He gave her a petulant look. "Is there no other way of testing Nick?"

"Testing Nick for what?" asked a new voice. Paisley.

Groaning inwardly, Shaya shot her a sweet smile. "Nothing."

"I have to say, I'm surprised he's interested in you. I mean, I look at him . . . and then I look at you . . . and it just doesn't make sense."

"Paisley," cautioned Kent.

"I'm not being insulting." For once, it seemed that Paisley wasn't being intentionally offensive. She appeared genuinely confused. "He's clearly a very dominant guy—I'd be surprised if he doesn't enjoy the D/s lifestyle. Someone like you, Shaya, well . . . I just can't see you being able to cope with Nick as he is. You're like the watered-down version of what he'd want—too testy and defiant, not to mention inexperienced. You . . . you'd be better with a guy who's practical, sensible, sensitive, and gentle and all that stuff. Maybe a librarian or someone like that."

"A librarian?"

"You know . . . someone safe and timid." Paisley shrugged. "Now Nick, well, he's far from that. I can't imagine that you have experience with guys like him. And you might be sort of pretty, and you may have gotten his attention, but seriously, you can't honestly think you'll be able to keep it."

Actually, Shaya didn't think she could. And that was also a huge problem in all this. She had discovered over the past three weeks that it wasn't just her distrustfulness that held her back. It was her insecurities. She couldn't help wondering if he would one day regret that she was his mate due to her submissive status. Most alphas preferred females whose strength matched their own. Shaya knew she had the inner strength to match his, but was that enough for him, or would he prefer someone like Amber?

Amber . . . Now *that* was a female she despised. The healer had been a big, fat pain in the padded ass since she arrived. The amount of times she had "coincidentally" turned up wherever Shaya and Nick were was truly unreal. Of course she always made a point of hugging him or touching him in some way, touching him with a familiarity that was way too intimate.

Then there were the times she turned up at Nick's motor home—oh yeah, Shaya had noticed and watched carefully from her window. He never let Amber inside, always kept her on the doorstep as they briefly chatted. Whenever Shaya had asked Nick about it later, he'd told her that Amber liked to keep him updated on what was happening with Roni, but she got the feeling there was more to it.

Amber wasn't mean to Shaya. No, she was something much worse—sickly sweet and friendly, and if Shaya hadn't seen the occasional flash of jealousy and contempt in Amber's eyes, she might have bought the act. Shaya would have preferred bitchiness, because then she could have said a few choice words to the female and insisted that she stay away from Nick. But while Amber was being friendly, Shaya would simply look unreasonable, mean, and even irrational if she began mouthing off at the healer . . . and maybe that was why Amber did it. This way, she got to be around Nick more.

When Paisley returned to the reception desk to answer the phone, Kent said, "Well, if you're set on going on this date, you can at least tell me about him."

"His name's Simon. He's a web designer."

"Sounds boring."

"All you've heard is his name and occupation."

"Exactly. Already he sounds boring. Now, if he was a tall, ash-blond alpha male with an inner wolf—"

"Kent," she groaned.

"Fine. So where are you going on this date?"

"We're going to the Moroccan restaurant near your place."

One of his brows lifted. "Oooh, maybe I'll pop in then."

"No. You'll grill him like he's being interrogated for a murder charge."

"Yes, for your own good. For all you know, he *could* be a murderer. An ax murderer, even. There could be bodies hidden under his patio."

She growled, "You're a pain in my ass."

He continued to be a pain in her ass all day—dedicated it to poking fun at a guy he hadn't even met, calling him dull and wimpy as well as possibly homicidal. But she still made him give her a ride to the restaurant after work. She had changed clothes in the salon, ready for her date. Of course Kent wished her luck, despite his disapproval, but as he drove away from the restaurant, there was a strange glint in his eyes that she hadn't liked—guilt, maybe?

Shrugging off the matter, she entered the restaurant to find that Simon was already there. He had politeness down to a tee—helping her remove her coat, pulling out her chair, letting her order first. Yes, this could work.

Nick was watching TV with Bruce when his cell phone rang. Derren. "Yup?"

"We have a situation. And you're not going to like it."

Instantly Nick was on his feet. There hadn't been any panic in Derren's tone, but there was anger there. "What is it?"

"I followed Shaya to make sure she got to Kent's place safely, like you asked." There was a short pause. "On the upside, none of the Nazi's guys or the extremists are on her tail."

"The downside?"

After another pause, Derren sighed. "She didn't go to Kent's place. She's at a restaurant. According to Kent here—who had apparently noticed me following him and came straight to my SUV in the parking lot to ask me to call you—she's on a date."

"A date?" Nick bit out. *Son of a bitch.*

Again Shaya had to resist the urge to fiddle with her new violet-black skirt. It had been one of those love-at-first-sight purchases. She loved how the outer edges, running from her hips to just over mid-thigh, looked to be laced up—as if just a tug would have the whole thing on the floor. She also loved the feel of the black silk underskirt against her skin. Shame it hadn't had some kind of warning label to alert her to the fact that whenever she sat down it was going to creep up her thighs.

She smiled at Simon as he poured more wine into her glass. The guy had been okay so far. The date, as a whole, had been okay so far too. Therein lay the problem: it was "okay." There was no sexual tension, though he had given her compliments that indicated he would happily take over for her vibrator. There was no teasing between them or banter. He seemed to be too nervous to joke.

She had to give him credit where it was due, however—he was doing a fantastic job at not staring at her breasts, despite that her top showed off her cleavage. Whenever his eyes did drift down to them, a blush would stain his cheeks and he would instantly look away. As she gazed at him now and took everything into account that she had learned about him, she realized something: He was exactly the librarian-type of guy Paisley had described as perfect for her.

But this was what Shaya wanted, wasn't it? Someone sensitive whom she could rely on not to hurt her the way she had already been hurt enough times before. Yes, he was missing the dominant streak that her submissive nature craved, but sometimes people had to compromise. So he would never take control and make her wet with just a look the way a certain alpha wolf could, but so what? Anyway, for all she knew, Simon could be a real Casanova in the bedroom. He could. Given the chance, there could be real passion between the two of them. They could be explosive.

Or she could be living in a fantasy world.

Maybe she was just one of those women destined to go through life traveling from one bad relationship to another. If that was the case, maybe sticking to flings would be better—no emotions, no strings, no rules, no pressure. It was just something based around the primitive need for sex. But a lifetime of that seemed sort of . . . cold. Shaya wanted warm. No, she wanted hot.

Looking at Simon again, she acknowledged that there wasn't going to be anything hot between them. But there could be warmth. If that was all she could have, maybe she should accept that, maybe—

The sounds of chairs being moved and the feeling of being crowded stole her from her thoughts. Then all of a sudden there were three other people seated at their table, and the one practically fused to her side had braced his arm over the back of her chair and fisted a hand in her hair in a shifter gesture of ownership. *Well shit.*

"Hello, Shay," rumbled Nick, though he didn't look at her. He only had eyes for the nervous male opposite him. Despite the dark emotions circulating through Nick, his voice was surprisingly even. He couldn't believe that she'd done this. He'd thought he was making progress, thought she was coming to accept his part in her life. And he'd hoped to God that meant she'd soon let him in—even if it was only slightly. He was fine with letting things move at her pace, despite how much it was killing him not to claim her. But he wasn't fine with her dating other guys. And if she'd thought differently, she didn't know him at all.

Shaya chanced a look at Nick's flawless face, and it verified what his stiff posture hinted at. He was boiling with anger. As he met her gaze, his eyes warned her not to challenge him. Her wolf shrank away—not out of fear, but because she had no intention of taking any blame here; her wolf hadn't liked being around the other male and had done nothing but growl at him. Both Derren and Kent were lazed in their seats with their arms folded over their chests, glaring at Simon like he had tried to assault her or something.

"Um . . . is, um, everything o-okay?" asked Simon nervously.

Feeling overwhelmed by Nick and the dark energy spilling from him, Shaya tried to shift away from him, but he growled and clamped his hand around the nape of her neck. When she stilled, he gently massaged her nape, almost as if he was rewarding her. Her wolf relaxed slightly at his touch.

"Why don't you introduce us, Shay," said Nick.

She cleared her throat. "Guys, this is Simon. Simon, this is Kent, Derren, and Nick." Picking up her wine glass, she took a long, comforting gulp.

"Nice to meet you all." Simon's eyes danced from her to Nick repeatedly, obviously noticing Nick's proprietary behavior.

"What do you do for a living, Simon?" asked Nick casually, needing to know every detail about this person, needing to create a profile in his head so he could figure out what the fuck it was that made Shaya want him over her mate. *Her mate.*

"I, well, I'm a web designer," replied Simon. Shaya thought he was most likely wondering why Nick's tone was that of a job interviewer.

"A web designer? Really? I bet that's exciting." He ran his hand through Shaya's hair, because although he was infuriated with her, she was literally the only thing that could ever keep him calm in a situation where his control was being so severely tested. If he didn't calm down, the human was dead. "Have you always been a web designer?"

"Well, I used to be a librarian when I—"

All conversation halted as Shaya almost choked on her drink. *Librarian?* No, the universe couldn't want to play *that* much of a joke on her, surely. Nick patted and rubbed her upper back.

"You ever been married?" asked Nick.

"Married? Oh no, never."

"Got any kids?"

"No."

Seeing that Simon's expression was begging for an explanation as to why he was being questioned, Shaya went to end this whole thing. "Nick, I—" She gasped as he bit her earlobe punishingly.

Nick continued, still smiling at Simon. "What word would you use to describe yourself?"

"What word would *you* use to describe *your*self?" she snapped at Nick.

He met her gaze. "Pissed."

The sound of Simon clearing his throat nervously had them returning their focus to him. His smile was anxious. "Um . . . you two seem . . . close." It was obvious to Shaya that he was dying to just ask Nick outright why he was behaving so possessively with her, probably worried he had unknowingly gone out on a date with another guy's girlfriend. But Nick really had that school principal "don't speak unless spoken to" vibe going on at the moment.

"Yes, we're close." Nick punctuated that with a nip to her neck.

The second Shaya's head whipped around to glare at him, his eyes cautioned her not to fight him. The stubborn part of her wanted to, but the glint of betrayal in his gaze halted her. As his eyes turned wolf for a split second, Shaya saw that his wolf was just as angry with her. And rightly so, she accepted with an inward sigh. Her own wolf was angry with her, in fact. This was one more date to add to those she'd been on back in California after he'd found and failed to claim her—more betrayal, from his point of view.

"How about you tell me how you two met."

Simon shifted uncomfortably in his seat. "Um, we met this morning in the salon when Shaya cut my . . ."

The rest of Simon's words were lost as a sharp pain lanced through Nick's head. Great. Another headache was coming on. Not that it was particularly a shock, given his current stressful state. He needed to get out of this place now. He sure as shit wasn't going to leave Shaya behind. "Well, it's been great talking to you, Simon. Baby, say bye to Simon."

Not sure if it was a good idea for them to be alone together right now, Shaya cautiously began, "Nick—" But he wasn't listening. He cupped her elbow, gently pulling her to her feet as he rose to his. His eyes were locked on her like a predator watching its prey that it suspected was about to flee . . . which wasn't far from the truth.

A part of her was thrilled about the effect this had had on him—it showed that he cared, that he considered her to be as important to him as she needed to feel that she was, that it wasn't just all a "mine" thing and there was more to his actions than a sense of ownership. But a part of her was nervous as hell. Not that she thought he would harm her. No, never that. Still, the guy could be unnerving at the best of the times. Now, it was bad.

With his hand caging her wrist, he guided her at a brisk pace out of the restaurant and into the Mercedes. Bracing herself for a typical dominant male explosion, Shaya clicked on her belt and waited. But that explosion didn't come. Nick calmly started the engine and calmly drove out of the parking lot. Then he calmly drove along the main road en route to her home. And she quickly discovered that the silence was much worse than a rage.

She kept expecting him to begin yelling any second, but he didn't. He remained silent the entire journey. Pulling up outside her house, he was out of the car before she could say a word, and then he was opening the passenger door for her. But he didn't look at her. Fine. If he wanted to brood, she'd leave him to brood. She stomped up the driveway and unlocked her front door, intent on letting him stew. But then she changed her mind. Twirling sharply, she growled. "Why did you drag me out of there if you're going to give me the silent treatment? If you've got something to say, say it. If you want to yell at me, do it."

"Go inside. We'll talk tomorrow. I'm not arguing with you in the middle of the street, and I'm definitely not doing it when we've got an audience." The Nazi's wolves were parked on the opposite side of the road, and the humans were about five car spaces away from the motor home.

"So come over here then." It was a dare, and she wasn't sure where the hell it had come from. No alpha would ignore a dare, and it seemed that her alpha—yes, *her* alpha—was no different.

Despite that Nick badly needed his pills, he ignored the pain and slowly began to cover the distance between him and Shaya. He half-expected her to run inside and shut the door, but she didn't react in any way—didn't cower, didn't lower her eyes, didn't fidget or back away. Instead, she remained where she stood in the doorway with her head held high, shoulders straight, and maintaining eye contact. *Good girl.*

"Now if you want to subject me to a lecture, do it."

"I have no idea what to say. I've been patient, Shay. I've let things move at your pace even though it hurts on every level to hold back. And what do you do? Go on a date with a goofy web designer who blushes even more than you do. The only reason he's still conscious is that Derren and Kent managed to calm me down to some extent before I got inside the restaurant. Why didn't you tell me about your date? Had you planned to keep it from me altogether?"

"I was going to tell you afterward."

"You know, Shaya, if you'd wanted to hurt me, you could have just stabbed me in the fucking chest and got it over with."

Guilt nibbled even harder at Shaya as she heard the despondency in his voice. She also found that she didn't like that he'd called her "Shaya." She'd been getting used to him shortening her name, and she even kind of liked it. *He abandoned you, remember,* a voice inside her snapped. Yes, he had. But he had also apologized to her, had also been gentle with her, and had never once lost his patience with her no matter what she said or did. Even when she'd physically hurt him that first night, he'd never hurt her, never tried to intimidate her, and never tried to suppress her with his dominant vibes. More importantly, he hadn't left her no matter what she'd done. "It wasn't that I wanted to hurt you."

"Oh, really?" His voice dripped with skepticism.

"Okay, maybe I wanted you to hurt a little. But I needed to know you weren't going to abandon me again."

"Ah, I see; well I'm so glad I passed your little test," he said bitterly. At this point, his head was starting to pound so hard that the sound of his own voice hurt. "What you're saying then is that, basically, everything I've done since I got here hasn't made an ounce of difference to you."

"That's not what I meant. If you want the truth—"

"Oh yeah, I want the truth."

"—it's working. But don't you get it? I never *wanted* it to work, but it has. I never *wanted* you to worm your way into my life, but you have. I never *wanted* to care if you left, but I do. I never *wanted* to dream about you, but I do, and then I wake up horny with no relief in sight."

"You want relief?" Quiet, gruff words.

She tensed. Before she could even think to answer, he'd pushed her inside the house, kicked the door shut, and slammed her against the wall. Then his mouth was on hers and he was devouring her. There was nothing gentle or coaxing about the kiss. His mouth ravished hers, his tongue forcefully thrust into her mouth, and he kissed her like it was the last thing he would do before he died. It was deep, commanding, devastating. The force with which he took her mouth should have scared her, but instead she was on fire, and all she could do was kiss him back. He wouldn't have settled for anything else.

Both his hands threaded into her hair, angling her head exactly how he wanted it. There was no denying that just then his lips and tongue completely owned her. It felt like a claiming, a promise, and a warning. Then he was sucking on her tongue while digging his hips into hers, crowding her with his body in a way that had her level of arousal spiking. As one hand splayed possessively over her stomach, the other suddenly yanked on her hair, forcing her head back and breaking the kiss. His face loomed over hers; his expression was fierce.

"I'm not going to fuck you." As he spoke, he slid the hand on her stomach down to the hem of her skirt and bunched it up around her waist. "I'm not going to be some casual encounter. I want you to want me, *your mate*—not sex. But if you need relief that badly, I'll give it to you." He cupped her hard. Gasping, she reflexively snapped her legs together, effectively trapping his hand. He shook his head, his gaze chastising. "Open your legs."

"What?" she squeaked at the very firm command, feeling off-balance by his sudden change of mood. He didn't repeat himself, just raised an expectant brow at her. Gulping, Shaya slowly did as he'd asked.

He pushed two fingers past her panties and drove them into her. So hot and wet. "Mine, Shaya. Understand? You're mine, and this pussy is mine. And if you ever again think about giving another guy what's mine, I'll kill him. I will. I'll fucking tear him apart, and then I'll spank your ass so goddamn hard, you won't be able to sit down for a week."

Shaya would have told him that she'd never intended to sleep with Simon, but then Nick was on his knees. He'd hiked one of her legs over his shoulder, and he was tearing off her panties.

Only an idiot would distract him from what he was doing. She was a bitch, but she wasn't an idiot.

When she felt the tip of his tongue swirl around her clit, her head fell back just as her eyelids drifted shut. She had been so damn aroused for so damn long that that one touch had her melting against the wall, moaning. As his tongue fluttered between her folds, she moved the hands she'd braced against the wall to his hair and pulled, needing more. He growled against her flesh, making her womb clench. She was glad he was gripping her thighs hard because she strongly doubted she'd be able to stand without help.

His tongue branded her with every stroke, reducing her to a sensual state that was so intense, she was almost afraid of it—almost afraid of her body's equally intense response. Everything other than the feel of his mouth faded away as he licked, sucked, nipped, and fucked her with his tongue. And she moaned, gasped, groaned, whimpered, and sobbed. But he didn't let up, didn't give her any reprieve, practically torturing her with pleasure. He might have been the one on his knees, but it wasn't Shaya who was in control. With his unrelenting grip, Nick controlled her every movement. With his talented mouth, he controlled her pleasure and her body's responses.

"Nick . . . I need to . . ."

He growled again, and the reverberations heightened the sensations. Her legs shook as he suddenly thrust two fingers inside her and began suckling on her clit, *demanding* that she come. He got what he wanted. She screamed as her climax forcefully slammed into her, shattering her. Nick bit down hard on her inner thigh, prolonging her orgasm.

Panting hard, she watched as he fixed her skirt and got to his feet. He gave her another possessive kiss, overwhelming her mouth and biting down punishingly on her lower lip, making it clear just how pissed he still was. Then he was gone. And she was realizing that Nick had been holding back his dominant side big-time.

As Nick tossed back a handful of pills and Derren sat at the dinette frowning in disapproval, Nick was thinking that this was becoming too familiar. Either the headaches were becoming more painful or the pills were becoming less effective, because he now had to take a higher dosage to dim the pain. The bitch of it was that the dosage and the pain thrown together acted as one hell of a sedative. Any minute now, he'd be in the land of the fairies. It wasn't until Nick slumped on the sofa, eyes closed, that Derren spoke.

"That's three headaches you've had today." His voice was quiet, which Nick appreciated.

"Yeah, well, it was a stressful day."

Derren cursed. "Nick, you need to go back to Amber for more healing sessions."

"No."

A heavy sigh. "Nick—"

"They're just headaches. Besides, you know as well as I do that if the sessions didn't work the first time, they aren't going to work a second time."

"It's always worth a shot. Or maybe you could go find another healer."

"I'm not leaving Shaya."

"I hate to say it, Nick—and I really, really hate to say it, because you deserve to be happy—but you're fighting a losing battle here." More sensitively, he added, "Shaya's not going to come around."

Nick was thinking he might be right about that. She had said that what he'd been doing was working, but she'd also said that she didn't want it to work. Still, he wasn't ready to admit it could be hopeless to himself, let alone to anyone else. "Leave it, Derren."

"You know I'm right. Christ, Nick, she went out with another guy."

"The reminder isn't necessary."

"If that doesn't tell you that you're making no headway here, I don't know what will."

"Derren, I can't have this conversation right now." He couldn't have *any* conversation right then. The sounds of their voices were blurring together, and it felt like someone was striking his head repeatedly with an iron rod.

"Let me call Amber and have her look at—"

"No."

"If I have to, I'll ask her to come when you're asleep—nothing in this world could wake you."

Nick was in front of him in a second. "You do that, and I'll kill you. You know as well as I do that if Amber touches me even once, I don't have a chance in hell with Shaya."

"It's possible that you don't have a chance anyway."

"I mean it, Derren. Do it, and that's it with you and me. Now I'm going to bed." Going to a room free of noise and light where he could fall asleep with the taste of his mate on his tongue and the smell of her on his hands.

He hadn't meant to unleash the full force of his arousal on her, but he had lost control the second his lips had touched hers. They had been so soft and pliant beneath his. Christ, she had been so responsive—moaning, writhing, and clinging to him. Moreover, he had tasted that natural submissiveness of hers, and it had only made him want her more.

Every cell of his body was urging him to go back to that house and take what was his. His wolf was clawing at him, annoyed with him for not claiming her there and then, despite how angry he was with her and how betrayed he felt. His wolf refused to consider what Nick was thinking, refused to accept that the whole situation was hopeless and that his own mate might never want him.

# CHAPTER NINE

The next morning, Shaya was ready to slip on her shoes and jacket when her cell phone rang. Digging it out of her purse, she saw that the caller was Kent. "If you're calling to check if I'll be late, the answer's actually no, so—"

A snort. "Well that would be a first. But that's not why I'm calling. I want you to take the day off."

Surprised, she paused in her movements. "What? Why?"

"I'm going to go out on a limb here and guess that you and Nick have some serious talking to do. He was severely pissed last night, Shaya, and I can't say I blame him."

She didn't blame him either. "You told him about the date, didn't you?"

"Yes. But Derren was following us anyway, and it wouldn't have taken much thinking on his part to work out what was going on. What happened when you got back home?"

Sighing, Shaya fell back onto the sofa and told him everything.

"Is he as good with that mouth as I've been betting he is?"

A half smile surfaced on her face. "Better."

He sighed. "Shaya, I understand why you've been protecting yourself so much, I understand why you've needed Nick to prove himself to you, and I understand that he hurt your pride in a big way when he didn't claim you and pretty much ignored you. But you're forgetting that that male has pride too. As an alpha, he'll have plenty of it. During the past three weeks, you've stomped on it in more ways than one. Also, you've hurt him. Badly. So if you don't want him to leave, you need to swallow your pride and give him that chance he's earned."

He was right. And Shaya knew it.

With Kent's advice still ringing in her ears, she headed to the kitchen to place her empty mug in the sink. As she passed the dining room, she noticed the two movie tickets sitting on the table—gifts from Nick. When he'd heard that there was a movie she wanted to see, he'd bought the tickets for her and Kent to go together, not even hinting for her to take him along instead. God, she'd really been a bitch. It was time for that to stop.

Opening her front door, she went rigid as she looked over at Nick's Mercedes. He wasn't there waiting for her with a coffee, as usual. Had his car not been there, she might have thought he was simply still at Starbucks. No, something was wrong. Anxiety slithered through her and over her, making her as nervous as her wolf. Taking a deep breath, she advanced down her driveway, expecting him to come out of the motor home any second. It was only when she neared the vehicle that the door opened. But it wasn't Nick who stepped out. It was Derren. She frowned when he closed the door behind him and stood in front of it like a protective barrier.

"I'll be driving you to work this morning," he said stiffly as he came forward, making her shuffle backward.

"I want to see Nick."

His expression hardened. "You'll have to wait until later."

"I want to see him now."

He arched a brow. "Why? So you can hurt him even more than you already have?"

She inhaled deeply. "I understand you're mad at me, I know how protective you are of Nick—"

"Then we don't need to have this conversation."

What was bugging her more than Derren's reprimanding tone was the fact that Nick hadn't come outside. He had to know that Derren was trying to keep her away; he had to hear what was going on, but he wasn't interfering. That meant one of two things: Nick genuinely didn't want to see or speak to her, or he had something to hide. A dark suspicion whispered into her mind. Was he with another female? Had he sought comfort from someone else? Amber? She actually wouldn't blame him, but she'd kill the bitch for sure.

It was only at this second that she appreciated just how hard last night had been for Nick. Just how deep her actions must have cut him. She really had some apologizing to do. And she needed to do it now.

"My SUV is behind Nick's car," said Derren, waving a hand toward it.

He thought he could keep her away from her own mate? *Pfft.* Acting as compliant as he obviously expected her to be, she nodded and walked toward the SUV. Sharply, she swerved, ramming her elbow into his throat, and then followed that up with a punch to his jaw. Then she was dashing toward the motor home.

Derren quickly made a grab for her as he came up behind her, but she'd expected that. She twisted slightly and kicked him hard in the chest, making him stumble. Then she opened the door and barged inside the motor home. She passed the sofa, dinette, small kitchen, bathroom, and continued to the rear of the vehicle where there were two doors. Taking a gamble that the one on the left was Nick's bedroom, she opened it wide. And stopped dead.

Nick was lying on the bed on his stomach, fully clothed, pale, and sleeping deeply. So deeply that his shifter senses hadn't been able to waken him, despite that they would have picked up the argument outside, the tension in the air, and also her scent. His wolf would sense all of that too, but clearly he was having no luck with waking Nick either. Even Bruce, who was sprawled beside the bed and licking the golden-tanned arm that was hanging over the mattress, wasn't managing to wake him.

Just then, Derren came up behind her and grabbed her shoulders gently but firmly, pulling her back and leading her away. Distracted by her concern, she didn't fight him. "Why is he lying there like that?" she asked quietly in a shaky voice. "What's wrong with him?"

She thought Derren wasn't going to answer, but then he sighed and said, "He gets headaches. Bad ones."

"That doesn't explain why he's not waking up."

"The worse the pain, the more pills he takes. Yesterday, he had three headaches, and the pain was agonizing each time. Put that pain together with a whole lot of pills, and you've got someone who's so deeply asleep, he's close to unconscious."

Suddenly unsteady, she took a seat on the sofa. She'd noticed the occasional tint of pain in his eyes, but she hadn't prodded him about it, determined to hide her concern for him . . . like an insensitive bitch—something out of character for her. She'd let the anger she harbored change her behavior in some ways. No more of that. That wasn't the person she wanted to be. "I didn't know about the headaches."

"Why would you? I'll bet you haven't taken the time to try to know him at all."

"Look, you can take as many potshots at me as you want. But not now, okay. I need to understand what's happening with Nick. And if you're not going to let me wake him up and talk to him"— not that she really would disturb him, but Derren didn't need to know that—"then you're going to have to be the one to tell me."

He snorted. "After what you did last night, I'm not in the mood to tell you shit. I'm guessing part of the reason you went on that date was because you wanted a reaction. Well, here's your reaction. I hope you're happy."

Panic fluttered through her. "You're saying that the bad headache he had last night was my fault? That I caused it?"

"If Nick's right, yes. He believes they're triggered by emotional stress. And he's sure had a lot of that lately, hasn't he?"

Shaya flinched and bowed her head. "I was hurt."

"Yes, you were. But you were so wrapped up in your own pain that you didn't notice his—or if you did, you didn't care. Did you know that being around you when he can't claim you physically hurts him?" That made her head snap up. "The mating urges make *you* uncomfortable. They put *him* in pain. It was bad enough when he wasn't around you. Being close to you makes the urges worse."

She ran a hand through her hair. "I didn't know."

"Would it have made any difference to you?" His tone communicated that he believed the answer was no.

Exasperated with both herself and Derren, she met his gaze unflinchingly—not caring that he'd find it odd for a submissive wolf to face the brunt of his anger. "I know you're pissed at me, but you can't judge me when you haven't found your own mate. You don't know what it's like to finally find the person who's so important to you that he's supposed to make every bad thing that happened before not hurt as much. You don't know what it's like to have that person who's made just for you completely reject you and cold-shoulder you. You can't know how being abandoned by your mate makes you feel dead inside."

Derren's expression and tone softened. "So can we agree that you've both suffered enough?"

She exhaled heavily. "Yes."

"If you're too hurt to accept him in your life, you need to tell him that, Shaya. Yes, I know you've been saying that to him since he got here, but you haven't totally meant it, and he sensed that. If you really want him gone, tell him, and this time *mean* it."

Hearing movement in the bedroom, Derren said, "Here's your chance. I'll take a walk, give you both some privacy."

Shaya got to her feet, waiting anxiously. Seconds later, Nick came out of the bedroom with Bruce by his side. Relieved that he wasn't staggering weakly, her wolf settled slightly. Spotting her, he double-blinked.

"Shay? What are you doing here?" Of course Nick had picked up her scent, but as he'd fallen asleep with the scent of her and of her arousal on his hand, it hadn't occurred to him that she was there.

A sigh of utter relief left her—he'd called her Shay, which meant his anger had lessened to some degree and he hadn't frozen her out. Also, although he sounded startled to see her, his tone wasn't unwelcoming. "Why didn't you tell me about the headaches?"

Confused, Nick began, "How did you—" Quickly understanding, he sighed. "Derren." Discomfort rolled through him as he wondered just how much Derren had told her. "I get headaches at times of stress." He shrugged as if it was nothing. That clearly annoyed her.

"Don't bother trying to play it down in that typical alpha male way. Derren told me how bad and frequent they are."

Wanting to leave this topic of conversation, he said, "We'll talk about it later. Come on, I need to get you to work before you're late."

"I'm not going to work." She cleared her throat. "I came here to speak to you." When he simply looked at her blankly, she added, "I wanted to apologize."

Nick felt his brows fly up. It wasn't just her words that had surprised him; it was the guilt and concern on her face. "Apologize for what?"

"Last night. And for trampling over your feelings and pride during the past three weeks. I can't say I'm sorry for telling you to leave and for being reluctant to believe the things you said. When you didn't claim me, it devastated me. Then I built you up to be this big, bad prick in my head . . . so when you started doing nice stuff and making a real effort, it didn't fit with the image I'd had of you—an image that had made it possible for me to try to hate you. I convinced myself you were fake and full of shit. I tried to keep you at a distance. But you made it impossible, you asshole."

He slowly went to her and tucked a curl behind her ear. "I'm not sorry that my efforts are paying off. But I am sorry that I hurt you."

"If it's been so simple for you to step down from Alpha, you would have done it back then. There has to be more to it." An emotion she didn't recognize flickered across his face. "There is more, isn't there?"

It was at times like this that he wished his mate wasn't so perceptive. "Sit down," he told her gently, gesturing to the sofa. Without invading her personal space, he sat beside her and twisted so that he was facing her; she mirrored the move. Moment of truth. After a long moment, he began. "I was five when my wolf surfaced for the first time."

Completely taken aback, Shaya gaped. "Five? But . . . why did your wolf surface that early?"

"There was a car accident. Only my parents and I were there. My dad died instantly. My mom was unconscious, but someone in a passing car stopped and managed to drag her out. That was when the car went up in flames. I was trapped in the rear passenger seat, and I couldn't get out. My wolf panicked, just as I did. But I'd hit my head really hard—everything was blurry, and my limbs felt heavy—so I wasn't putting up as much of a fight to get out as I otherwise would have done. So my wolf burst to the surface in an effort to protect me. Then he squeezed through the gap in the seats and got out through my mom's door, jumping through the flames. He's had a thing about fire ever since."

Too shocked to speak, Shaya just stared at him. As his eyes took on a faraway quality, Shaya knew he was back there, seeing those flames surrounding him all over again. Wanting to bring him to the present again, she said, "Nick?"

His gaze snapped to her. "You've heard of shifters whose animals have surfaced early before, right?"

She nodded. "I don't know any. But I've heard that it can happen."

"Do you know what happens to them in later life?"

At his hard tone, a blast of cold traveled down her spine. "What?"

"Healers aren't sure why it happens, though they speculate that it's because the body and the mind were forced to deal with changes they weren't ready for at a young age and that those changes put too much of a strain on them. It causes the cognitive functions to degenerate later on. When I found you, I was having healing sessions to try to fight it. The sessions worked. But I had that fear that the improvement was only temporary. I didn't want you to be my caregiver. It didn't feel fair to claim you and then have you burdened with someone you had to take care of—a patient instead of a mate."

There was almost a click in Shaya's head as everything he'd done or said since they first found each other fell into place for her. She finally understood. But . . . "Nick, you're a fucking idiot." There was no anger or harshness, just pure and utter exasperation. "Why the hell didn't you tell me this in the beginning?"

"You would have insisted on sticking by me."

"And you wouldn't have done the same if the situation was reversed? Don't dare tell me that that's different! It's not! You should have told me! You should have given me the choice to stand by you, to be there for you!"

"When I found you and realized I couldn't claim you without endangering you, it seemed . . . fitting. It made sense that I wouldn't be allowed to have my mate, considering the shit I've done and not regretted. And you're so damn sweet and perfect, whereas me . . . I have more coldness in me than I care to admit."

"You still should have told me! Why in God's name didn't you mention this to me three weeks ago?" To think how much of a bitch she had been to him when all he'd been trying to do by not claiming her was, in his own warped way, protect her.

"I didn't want a chance out of pity. I wanted it because I'd earned it."

Dominant males and their pride. "You still shouldn't have kept this from me."

"And you don't have your secrets? Don't think I don't know that you're keeping things from me, Shay. You have a huge issue with being alone. I haven't pressed you about it because I didn't feel I had a right to when I was keeping things from you. But I'd say it's only fair that you tell me."

"I don't like talking about it."

The ache in her voice made Nick's hackles rise. "I don't like talking about what happened that day in the woods . . . but I told you when you asked."

Okay, that was fair. It was a long moment before she spoke. "I was a twin. An identical twin. My sister, Mika . . . she died in the womb."

His eyes fell closed, and he cursed. He took one of her hands in his. "Baby, I'm sorry."

"Even then, before we were born, we'd bonded. That probably sounds dramatic and impossible. But it's no different from saying that babies can hear their parents' voices from the womb and can find them soothing. Mika and I had each other all those months. As I was growing up, that 'empty' feeling was always there. That feeling of being alone." She smiled as a memory came to her. "When I was little, I used to pretend that Taryn was my twin."

The image of a small version of Shaya feeling so lost and empty that she used her friend as a substitute sister almost broke his heart. "I'll bet Taryn was happy to be part of that game."

Shaya's smile widened. "Yeah, she was. She never had any siblings, so we both got a lot of fun out of that little fantasy." Her smile faded as she continued. "But maybe I would have coped a lot better if it hadn't been for what happened when I was four."

It was a struggle for Nick to keep his voice even when anger was riding him at the idea of anything hurting her. "What happened, Shay?"

"For the first four years of my life, my parents and I didn't live on pack territory. The Alpha—Taryn's dad, Lance—didn't approve of my mom mating a human, even though my dad was her true mate. So they lived in a house close by. But my parents . . . See, my dad was a Navy SEAL, so he went away a lot. My mom wasn't very good at handling it—not that I can blame her. It must have been hard. Every weekend, she'd go out with her friends to bars and clubs. She used to leave me alone in the house while she went, even when I was little."

Leave a child alone? "But surely there were members of your pack who would happily have taken care of you while she was gone."

"Of course there were. But she liked leaving me there alone because she knew I didn't like to be alone. She liked to hurt me. Maybe it was that when she looked at me, she always remembered that there should have been two of me. Or maybe it was because she felt my dad paid more attention to me than to her when he *was* home. Or maybe it's just because she is, naturally, a very self-centered person." And a hypochondriac, to boot. "Your guess is as good as mine."

Keeping his touch gentle was a struggle, but he managed it for her, massaging her hand with both of his. "Go on."

"I remember I used to sit on the stairs, crying, waiting for her to come home. Sometimes I'd fall asleep like that. Other times I'd stay awake until she was back. But one Friday night she went out . . . and she didn't come home that night. Or the next night. Or the next night. The longer she stayed away, the more I panicked—not just because I was alone, but because I was really worried that something bad had happened to her, that she'd been hurt or worse."

Her pain was so deep it felled him. His wolf growled, hating it. "Shay, what happened to her?" Her answer surprised him.

"Nothing. She was fine. She'd stayed away because she wanted to—she was laughing at how shook up I was. I swear, Nick, by the time she got back I felt like the walls were going to close in on me." When he pulled her onto his lap and held her tight to him, she didn't fight him. She melted against him and greedily took that comfort. "My dad hit the roof when I told him. I wasn't supposed to tell him, but I was so angry with her that I did. He insisted we all move to pack territory, because he wanted to be sure that I was safe whenever he was away. Lance didn't want us to move there, but Taryn's mom raged at him until he allowed it. Then I met Taryn, and I was never alone again after that."

Nick exhaled a long breath. "Shit." And now he understood just how badly he had hurt her by not claiming her, by abandoning her—even if he believed he'd done it for the right reasons. "I really did fuck up big-time, didn't I?"

"That's not the only thing I've kept from you." Pulling back to meet his gaze, she nibbled on her lip. "I'm a salient submissive."

Nick's brows almost hit his hairline. Salient shifters could be dominant or submissive and were very rare and unique in that they existed near the periphery of dominant and submissive. The fact that they were almost a perfect blend of both gave them an advantage over all shifters—their submission couldn't be forced. Even Nick, despite how powerful an Alpha he was, could be forced to submit if the dominant vibes being directed at him were powerful enough to do it. But neither salient submissives nor salient dominants could have their submission forced . . . which explained why Taryn had looked shifty when Nick mentioned that dominant females could defeat Shaya simply by throwing their dominant vibes at her. As it was, such an attack would have no effect on her.

It didn't change any of his worries about her safety as an Alpha female, but it at least meant that she couldn't be intimidated into submitting. "You must be proud to be a salient submissive."

"I often wonder if it means Mika would have been a salient dominant." Watching as his brow creased, she asked, "Another headache?"

He shook his head. "No. I hate hearing pain and tears in your voice. It cuts through me. You're not ever allowed to cry. Ever. I really can't take it when you cry."

"There's something I don't get. If you're so worried about whether you're truly healed, what made you come here? What changed?"

"I found out you'd gone. The idea that I'd never see you again, never get to touch you . . . It made me realize just how important you are to me. All of a sudden, all that other shit fell away, faded into the background. My pack, my issues . . . they didn't seem significant anymore. And that's because, compared to you, they're not." He cocked his head as he studied her intently. "Have you really been happy these six past months, Shay? Really?"

"If I said I was . . . ?" She wasn't, of course.

"I'd still want the chance to see if you can be happier with me." When wariness entered her expression, he kept one arm tightly locked around her while sliding his free hand through her hair and around to her nape. He squeezed lightly, as if it would help him get through to her. "You can trust me." He dabbed a light kiss on her neck. His wolf growled in approval as her scent washed over him. "You can trust me." He dabbed another kiss on her neck and then licked his way to the hollow beneath her ear. He scraped his teeth over the spot and then sucked at it. Releasing a soft moan, she dug her fingers into his shoulder, and he thought she'd shove him away. She didn't. "I'll never leave you again, Shay."

Lifting his head to examine her expression, he saw several emotions flash across her face—all of which had come and gone too quickly for him to identify them. "Not ever, I swear." He brushed his mouth against hers and nipped her lip. "I'm not asking you to let me claim you straightaway if you're not ready for that yet. But I'm asking you to let me in a little."

Looking into those dusky-green eyes, Shaya saw a possible future there. She saw everything she would ever have wanted. With all the things she'd said and done to him these last few weeks, she'd pushed him to the brink; she'd hurt him and his pride, but he was still here. And now that Nick had told her everything, now that she knew the complete truth and understood all of why he hadn't claimed her initially, the pain inside her eased. Oh, she still wanted to smack him over the head for not telling her all this before, but knowing Nick as she did, she could understand why he hadn't. More importantly, she understood that he'd never meant to or wanted to hurt her. Still . . . "Fuck up this one chance and I'll cut off your balls, put them in a blender, and make a margarita out of them."

He winced, smiling. "Understood." Sweeping the pad of his thumb across her velvety soft bottom lip, he asked in a whisper, "Does this mean you're willing to let me in a little?"

"Yes."

Satisfaction, exhilaration, and triumph rushed through him. "I need your mouth, Shay," he growled. "Open for me." His tongue shot inside to find hers, groaning at her taste. It wasn't a kiss. It was an explosion. An explosion of need, of heat, of desperation.

Needing to go deeper, Nick knotted a hand in her curls and angled her head how he wanted it. When she tried taking control of the kiss, he growled into her mouth and tightened his hold on her hair. She softened slightly, and he growled again—this time in approval. He slid his other hand down to her ass and cupped it possessively. It was the hottest ass, and it was his. He rocked her hips against his, making them both groan. At the sound of a heavy knock on the front door, they broke apart.

"Nick, you need to get out here," called Derren.

"What is it?" Nick gritted out.

"Trust me, you need to get out here."

Squeezing his eyes closed as he dug deep for self-restraint, Nick took a long breath. "I'll be right there." Opening his eyes again, he nearly groaned aloud at the heated expression on Shaya's face. "We need to postpone this for now, baby. But later, when I've finally got you in bed, nothing will stop me from getting inside you." It was as much a warning as it was a promise. Shaya's nod of acceptance settled something deep inside him. "But until then . . ." He bit her. Bit down hard in the crook of her neck, wanting and *needing* to mark her in some way, just as he'd been aching to since first laying eyes on her. She moaned and held his head close. He took the hint and sucked hard, ensuring it was a definitive mark that no one could miss.

Keeping Shaya behind him, Nick opened the door. Whatever he'd been expecting to find outside, it hadn't been the rebels.

"We thought you might want to know," began one of them, "someone vandalized the salon where your mate works last night."

# CHAPTER TEN

Before Nick's car had fully come to a stop, Shaya was attempting to jump out of the passenger seat. She might have been successful if Nick's arm hadn't clamped around her waist.

"Wait." He didn't release her until she nodded.

Shaya thought it was strange how he could sound so unyielding yet so gentle at the same time. Taking a proper look outside, her mouth fell open in horror as she saw the front windows of the salon almost completely shattered and the door hanging from its hinge. Pieces of broken glass littered the sidewalk like glistening diamonds, and the salon's sign had been splashed with black paint. "Oh my God." Her wolf whined, anxious and angry.

Once Nick had opened the passenger door, Shaya was out of the vehicle and dashing toward the salon only to, once again, be hampered by an arm around her.

"It's okay, baby, Kent's not inside. He's over there."

Kent caught sight of her at the same time as she spotted him, and then they were hugging each other hard. "Thank God you're okay," said Shaya. Her words came out in a rush. "When I heard what happened I started panicking that maybe you'd been hurt and then you weren't answering your cell and my mind was just running away with me and I was imagining you dead, covered in blood and—"

Kent poked her shoulder. "For God's sake, woman, breathe. I'm fine, really. The damage was done last night. I sent Paisley home a few minutes ago. She was white as a sheet."

Draping a supportive, comforting arm around Shaya, Nick gave Kent a half smile. "What about you?" At that moment, Derren appeared at their side.

"I don't think there are words to describe what I'm feeling right now."

"How much damage is there?" asked Nick.

"Damage is a mild word for this," said Shaya. "It looks like a tsunami hit it." Nick's hand slid around her throat, and his thumb massaged her nape soothingly. His presence and his touch anchored her when she wouldn't have believed anything could at such a time.

"Shaya's right, this is beyond damage or vandalism. This is . . ." Derren broke off, searching for an explanation that seemed to be just out of his reach. But it wasn't out of Nick's reach.

"Personal," finished Nick. "It seems personal."

"How bad is it?" Shaya asked Kent.

Kent puffed out a long breath. "Bad. Bottles of shampoo and conditioner have been poured everywhere. The mirrors have all been smashed. The leather chairs have been slashed with scissors. To add to that, broken mugs and plates are scattered all over the kitchenette, and the contents of the fridge have been thrown around. And then there's the office—it looks like a hurricane hit it. Papers and magazines and notebooks and files are all over the places. The computer hard drive, monitor, and keyboard have been completely wrecked. What's baffling the police is that the safe hasn't been touched and neither has the till. But I have a pretty good idea why that is." Noticing Nick's confusion, Kent added, "For the same reason that the vandals entered through the back door. That's right: The damage to the front door wasn't done out of a necessity to get inside—they basically did it for sport, along with the rest. The reason for that is the extremists are involved. I recognized a few of the scents."

"The extremists?" echoed Shaya.

Kent's voice was gravelly with emotion. "All I can think is they discovered I'm a half-shifter."

Before Kent had even revealed the extremists' involvement, Nick had known they were responsible, because he could clearly see Logan among the gathering humans. His expression was smug and daring. *Little bastard.* Vandalizing Nick's mate's—or girlfriend, as Logan believed—place of work *definitely* counted as personal and was definitely one very good way to rile him.

As both Shaya and Kent tracked Nick's hard gaze, they each snarled at Logan as the same realization dawned on them.

"He's got balls, showing up here after what he's done," hissed Kent, moving toward him. Derren's hand on Kent's arm stopped him.

"Not balls," said Derren. "He's hoping Nick will react." Derren briefly explained the situation. Nick had expected Kent to be pissed with him, to blame him to some degree for bringing this trouble to his salon. But Kent gave Nick a look of sympathy.

"I can't imagine what you must have gone through in that place. A lot of shifters don't last in juvie."

"You're not going to blame me for what happened to your business?"

Kent frowned. "Why would I do that? He did what he did because he's a bastard, not because of you. Besides, I was expecting it to happen sooner or later—though I thought it would be because they discovered I'm a half-shifter."

As Nick's eyes again locked on Logan, Shaya could almost feel his fury. Enraged though she was, she knew better than to confront Logan, particularly right now in front of all these people and a news reporter—oh yeah, any crime that might possibly be related to shifters counted as news. "Nick, don't give him what he wants." He didn't respond. "Look at me." Finally, he did. "Don't play into his hands."

"Right now, I need to make some calls," announced Kent. "I need to get some people out here to deal with this mess." He patted Shaya's hand. "You need to go home." When Shaya opened her mouth to object, he raised a hand. "There's nothing you can do here. All you'll be doing by sticking around is upsetting yourself. Now go. You'd say the same thing to me if it was the other way around."

Sighing in defeat, she nodded and gave Kent another hug. Then Nick was leading her back to his car, his eyes again on Logan. "Nick, don't play into his hands," she repeated.

Oh, Nick had no intention of doing that, despite how livid he was. Still, that didn't mean he wouldn't have a little chat with the human. "Baby, I need you to get inside the car."

"Nick, don't."

"I'm not going to touch him. I just need to have a little talk with him."

"Your version of 'talking' is often fighting." He stubbornly didn't budge. "Promise me you won't rise to anything he says."

"I promise. Now get in."

She sighed. "I'm trusting you to keep your word. Don't abuse that trust."

Once she was inside the car, Nick slowly made his way to Logan, who gave Nick a mockingly sympathetic look that made his wolf growl. "This place looks bad. I'll bet your girlfriend and her friend are pretty upset."

Drawing on every bit of control and experience he had at suppressing his emotions, Nick kept his face blank.

When Logan didn't get a reaction, he continued, "The police think it's something to do with the turf war that's going on between the shifters." He pursed his lips. "It makes sense. You know, you'll want to be careful that your redhead isn't targeted next time."

His wolf growled at the veiled threat, but he didn't urge Nick to lunge at the human because he knew as well as Nick just what game Logan was playing. "You haven't thought this through."

A frown marred the human's face. "Haven't thought what through?"

"You may have done this to piss me off, but it won't have been only me this has affected. As you said, the police are speculating that the local shifters are responsible. The local shifters won't like that. They'll know that if they want to find out who *is* responsible, all they'll have to do is take one footstep inside the salon—the scent of the perpetrators will be right there for them to sense."

Logan swallowed hard in a nervous movement.

"Then, naturally, they'll seek out said perpetrators for not only implicating them in a crime they didn't commit, but committing that crime on their turf. Congratulations, Logan, you not only just succeeded in uniting all the local shifters on something, you earned yourself more enemies than you'll know what to do with. Trailing the Nazi was one thing. But this?" Nick shook his head, *tsk*ing. "I wouldn't like to be you right now."

Logan's voice was shaky as he spoke. "If you or any of the others touch me, I'll—"

"Be dead before you even knew anyone was there. They might not do it straightaway, but it'll be done eventually—you're a walking dead man. You accuse shifters of being violent, aggressive, and disrespectful. But it hasn't occurred to you that the shifters you've been following could have killed you at any time; you wouldn't have even seen it coming. But they haven't. They've chosen to ignore you . . . whereas you and your little gang are not only harassing shifters but pulling shit like this. The word 'hypocrite' comes to mind, but so does the word 'motherfucker.'" With that, Nick turned his back on the pathetic excuse for a human and returned to his car.

"What did he say?" asked Shaya.

"He was boasting," growled Nick. "I'm sorry you won't have a job for a while, baby. I get this is my fault, so—" When she slapped his shoulder hard, he flinched. "Hey, what was that for?"

"You don't get to blame yourself for other people's actions." Her wolf fully agreed. "I won't allow it."

The fierceness in her tone surprised him so much, he found himself smiling. "Is that right?"

"Yes, Beavis."

"I am *not* stupid."

She patted his chest patronizingly. "No, of course not. You just have bad luck in the thinking department."

Scowling, he turned on the ignition and began heading back to her house. Unfortunately, he got there to find his mother, Roni, and Amber waiting outside the motor home. Surprised by their anxious expressions, he exchanged a confused look with Shaya. No sooner had they got out of the car than the three females were in front of them.

"My God, I saw what happened to the salon." Kathy studied Shaya, rubbing her arm. "Are you okay, honey?"

"You saw what happened?" Nick asked, scratching between Roni's ears.

"It's all over the news," Amber answered, standing a little too close to him for Shaya's liking. Making that clear, Shaya went to his side and laid a proprietary hand on his chest while smiling pleasantly at Amber. Maybe things were doomed for Shaya and Nick, but if anything was going to separate them, it wouldn't be some interfering bitch.

"The reporter said there's a pack war here. Why didn't you say anything to me about it?" Kathy chastised.

"Because it's a load of shit," replied Nick, curling an arm around Shaya. "There's no war going on."

Amber folded her arms over her chest. "Then what *is* going on?"

At that moment, Derren appeared at Nick's other side. "Where's your phone?"

Nick frowned and patted the pockets of his jeans. "I must have left it in the motor home."

"Don't be surprised to find that you have a ton of messages. I've just taken at least fifteen calls since we left the salon because you weren't answering your phone. A lot of people saw the live footage on TV—you and Shaya are in the background. Apparently, there's also footage that shows you and Logan talking in the background. As you can imagine, a lot of our friends remember that face. They all wanted to know what's happening and if you need them to come here."

"Who's Logan?" asked Kathy.

"I hope you told them it's not necessary," Nick said to Derren. He had enough people hanging around as it was.

"I explained there's no pack war and that you don't need any backup, but a number of them are concerned about what's going on with Logan. I'm guessing you'll be getting a lot more calls from our friends."

"Nicolas Axton, you need to explain a few things."

Seeing that his mother was doing that hands-on-the-hips thing, he sighed and gestured to the motor home. "We can talk inside." They all piled in, one by one. His mother and Amber seated themselves at the dinette while Derren plonked himself on the sofa beside Nick, who'd pulled Shaya onto his lap. Roni settled near Bruce in front of the TV.

"Well?" pressed Kathy.

"The problem around here isn't the shifters, it's the human extremists." Nick spoke about the Sequoia Pack and the false rumor surrounding its Alpha, though he omitted the detail of the game preserve. He wanted to keep it as quiet as possible for as long as possible. Plus, he didn't want Shaya, his mother, or Roni worrying. "The leader of this particular group, Logan . . . He worked as a guard when I was in juvie." Kathy shuddered.

"He's intent on provoking me into reacting, most likely intending to use me as evidence of just how violent shifters can be to support the extremists' argument. Vandalizing the salon where Shaya works was part of that."

"But you don't intend to retaliate." It wasn't so much a question as an instruction from his mother.

"Not right now, no."

"Nick, please don't risk yourself."

"I won't. But I have no idea how he'll react when the court hearing is over. If he gets the verdict he wants, he may be smug enough to leave me alone. If the ruling of the judge goes in our favor, I can't see him accepting that. If he comes at me, I won't stand there and take it." He'd never taken Logan's shit before, and he wouldn't start now.

"Maybe it's best if you leave here, taking Shaya with you of course."

"It won't make any difference," Derren told Kathy. "Logan has people following Nick constantly. He'll have them follow Nick wherever he goes. Besides, running away from extremists isn't the answer for any shifter. It'll only encourage their behavior."

Kathy sat in silence, considering that. When she eventually met Nick's gaze, it was to give him an accepting nod. Then her eyes danced from him to Shaya, and she half-smiled. "I take it this means you two are making a go of things."

"But you haven't claimed each other," said Amber tonelessly. Nick kissed Shaya's hair. "Yet."

Shaya smiled sweetly at the bitch. "I'm sure you wish us all the luck in the world."

When Derren's phone began ringing, he fished it out of his pocket and glanced at the screen. "Looks like another of our friends is interested to know what's going on. I'll take the call outside, give you guys some privacy." He looked at Kathy then. "Hint, hint."

Kathy's eyes widened, and then she nodded. "Well of course.

Roni, Amber, let's go." Roni gave Nick's hand a brief lick before following Derren and Kathy outside.

Amber slowly rose from her seat at the dinette and shot Nick and Shaya what was clearly a forced smile. "See you both later." It sounded more like a threat than a farewell comment, but Shaya once again gave her a sweet smile and waved.

When the bitch was finally gone, she breathed a sigh of relief. "I can't blame her for wanting you, but it doesn't change the fact that I'd like to sneakily pour bleach into her shampoo and watch what happens with glee."

Laughing, Nick twirled Shaya around to face him as she straddled him. "Vengeful. I like it. But, baby, don't let her bother you. She's not important."

"At least you're no longer denying that she wants you."

Nick might have continued believing otherwise if he hadn't seen jealousy briefly shimmer in Amber's eyes at one point. "You know, it could be *you* that she wants."

Shaya snorted. "I'm pretty sure it's you, Beavis. Are you sure you wouldn't prefer someone like her? Dominant with the physical strength to match yours?"

Though Nick's expression was reprimanding, he kept his voice low and sensual. "Don't make me bite you again." Her pupils dilated, and she took an unsteady breath. "Oh, you liked it, did you?" Her snort said, *Don't flatter yourself.* He placed his mouth to her ear. "I can smell your arousal, Shay." The tips of her ears were suddenly as scarlet as her cheeks. "What I really want is to taste it again. What I want more than that is to be inside you. You have no idea how badly I need it."

"Then what are you waiting for?"

He smiled against her lips. "For you to beg." Because he needed an element of surrender on her part—he knew he wouldn't get her total emotional surrender yet, so if he had to settle for this, it was enough for now.

Her mouth fell open. "That's *so* not going to happen."

"We'll see." He cocked his head, running his finger along her collarbone. "You didn't give away the movie tickets I gave you, did you?"

"No. Actually, I was going to suggest we go see a movie together."

"Then that's what we'll do tonight."

The deviousness in his tone made her narrow her eyes. "I don't like the way you said that."

He just smiled before kissing her hard. "I'll be at your door at six. Be ready."

"Huh?" She'd thought he would be eager to answer those mating urges that had been riding them both so long.

He cupped her chin and rubbed his thumb along her jawline. "Baby, I want you more than you know. But you've had a shock this morning, and it was a blow to your system. What you need to do is go inside, take a long bath, and relax for a little while." And then she'd be in an emotional state where she could deal with him, because Nick wasn't "nice" or "tame" in bed. "Then later, you can get ready for our date."

"Where are we going exactly?"

"We'll get something to eat—you can choose where we go. Then we'll go watch that movie you want to see, although I can't guarantee you'll be able to concentrate because I fully intend to make out with you the entire time."

"Sounds promising. And then?"

"There'll be foreplay. Lots and lots of foreplay."

"I don't like foreplay. I say we skip it and go straight to the main event."

He shook his head. "Don't worry, you'll like the foreplay. Then as soon as you beg, I'll give you what you want."

She should have guessed he'd be the type to love begging. He was a dominant male after all. Although she'd been with dominant males before, she knew without a doubt that it would still be nothing like sex with a very dominant alpha male—particularly when this male was her mate. She had to admit that she was beyond intrigued.

She knew that some people thought females who enjoyed sexual submission were weak, but Shaya didn't believe that. How could it make her weak when it took a lot of strength to give up that level of control, to entrust herself and her safety to someone else? Despite that Shaya enjoyed submitting in bed, it didn't mean that she could easily give up control. No, the male had to be someone she was comfortable with.

Her wolf was just as intrigued about tonight. Having a strong, powerful, dominant mate was what her wolf needed, what made her feel safe and secure. Being sexually dominated by her mate was an extremely attractive idea to her wolf. But Shaya had no intention of making it easy for Nick. Where would be the fun in that? "You really think I'll beg? Aw, bless your little heart." Complying was one thing, but begging was a whole other thing.

"Oh, you'll beg, baby. I can promise you that."


Shaya snarled at the woman sitting a few seats away who was ogling Nick . . . just like Shaya had snarled at the waitress in the restaurant, and at the girl who served them popcorn, and at the group of young women who had been behind her and Nick in the line. Annoyingly, the guy was ogled wherever they went. Although it was perfectly understandable, Shaya—much like her wolf—did not like it.

Most of the time, he didn't seem to notice the ogling, though that was probably because his focus was on Shaya. When he *did* notice, he never reacted other than to come closer to Shaya or to touch her, almost as if he sensed that it bugged her and that the reassurance eased her irritation. Maybe he did sense it. After all, she wasn't exactly discreet with her snarls.

The ogling had been a little easier to deal with when she'd rejected the idea of giving him a chance and had kept an emotional distance between them; it had dimmed the possessiveness slightly. But now that she had made the choice to include him in her life, this shit was getting annoying *real* quick. And so she was cranky.

Maybe her level of crankiness wouldn't have been so high if Nick wasn't doing his best to make her so freaking horny she couldn't stand the feel of her own clothes. At every given opportunity, he was touching her. He licked the bite mark on her neck, or nipped at her mouth, or sucked on her earlobe, or kissed her. Even when he simply brushed a hand through her hair or splayed a proprietary hand on her lower stomach, there was a sensuality and teasing quality to it that made her shudder. In essence, the foreplay had begun the very second she had stepped out of the house to find him waiting on the doorstep. Right now, she wasn't sure whether she wanted to slap him or straddle him. Her wolf liked the latter idea better.

True to his word, he'd spent the majority of the movie kissing and touching her, but each kiss and touch was featherlike—designed to frustrate her, designed to make her push for more. She had, clinging to him, sucking on his tongue, and unsheathing her claws to dig into his skin and keep him in place. But never did he give in, and she quickly came to understand why: He was communicating to her, her body, and her wolf that *he* was the one in control; that though he wouldn't expect her to hold back, and though he didn't want a puppet, he wouldn't be pushed into handing over dominance—that the control was his.

In short, he was ensuring there would be no misunderstandings when they got home.

When the movie finally ended, a sigh of relief left her. At this point, her face was flushed, her body felt restless, and she was so wet that she would bet even a human could smell her arousal. Nick's smile was smug as he noticed her discomfort. If it hadn't been for the fact that she could scent how much he wanted her, she might have thought he was totally unaffected. Marching down the aisle of seats, she gave him a sideways glance. "You're an asshole."

Nick slid an arm around her waist and pulled her back against him. "I told you there would be lots and lots of foreplay."

"I thought you meant when the date was over—silly me."

Smiling at her snappiness, Nick spoke into her ear as they walked down the rest of the aisle with his arm still locked around her. "There'll be foreplay when we get back too." He subtly ground himself against her, letting her feel just how hard he was.

"I vote for skipping it."

"Of course you do. You have no patience."

"So?" she snapped.

He chuckled and meshed his fingers with hers as he led her out of the movie theater. As he made his way to the car, he passed two of the Nazi's wolves waiting in a vehicle: his bodyguards. He gave them a wave, which made them roll their eyes—they didn't seem to like him much as he always insisted on losing them.

A few car spaces away from them were two of the human extremists in a white van. So Nick gave them a wave too, which made their faces turn interesting shades of purple. Derren, who was waiting in his SUV near Nick's Mercedes, had his window down and was talking with the rebels.

Shaya shook her head. "If they weren't so dangerous, it would actually be funny the way all three groups are watching you like this. Particularly since you have absolutely no interest in bothering any of them."

"Yeah, ironic." As Nick arrived at his car, the rebels turned studious gazes his way and nodded in greeting. Nick returned the nod before sighing at Derren. "Why are you still following me when I fired you again earlier?"

"I just wanted to park up and admire the evening sky."

Rolling his eyes, Nick urged Shaya into the car.

"The rebels want to introduce themselves," announced Derren. Turning his focus to the three males, Nick waited.

"I'm Jesse"—the well-built male with dark eyes and stubble for hair was clearly the leader of the three—"this is Bracken"—a tall male with playful eyes and an equally playful smile nodded at Nick—"and this is Zander." The blond, athletically built male gave a slight incline of his head.

"I'm not interested in trying to take over here, if that's what you're wondering."

"Yeah, we noticed you haven't joined Hadley," said Jesse. Quietly—most likely because the human extremists were close by—he added, "He believes the humans are running a game preserve where they hunt shifters."

Nick also kept his voice quiet. "I know, he told me."

"Do you believe him?"

"Yes. You should be careful that you aren't the next shifters to be taken."

Jesse exchanged a look with the others. "We aren't sure we can trust him."

"I can't vouch for his nature; I don't know him. But I do believe he's being honest about the game preserve. In any case, you guys need to watch your back, because if Hadley's not after you, the humans will be." Finally, the three males nodded and walked away. As Nick went to hop into the driver's seat, he asked Derren, "Do you think they'll stop hovering around us now?"

Smiling, Derren shook his head. "You really don't know why they linger?"

"If I knew, I wouldn't ask."

"They see you and all the power radiating off you, and they're drawn to you, just like their wolves are. You could provide them with the guidance and direction they need, and they sense that."

"I'm not here to form a pack. I'm here for Shaya."

"I know that, and I've explained it to them."

"Good." Nick slid into the car and was just about to close the door when Derren spoke again.

"Have fun."

Nick grinned. He'd be having all kinds of fun.

Neither he nor Shaya said a word during the journey to her home. Anticipation built inside him and licked over the surface of his entire body. Shaya's own anticipation was like a buzz in the air, seducing his wolf with its intensity. The scents of their arousal filled the car, which suddenly felt much smaller than it was. As such, it was a relief to finally get out of it.

Having helped Shaya out of the car, he let her take the lead as they advanced up the path. When she unlocked the front door and held it open for him, he paused. "Be sure that you want this, Shay. Be absolutely positive. I can hold off on claiming you until you're ready . . . but if I walk through that door, I *am* going to fuck you. Not soft and slow, but hard and deep. Over and over, until neither of us can move. Are you ready for that?"

He hoped to God that the extent of his dominance didn't unnerve her because he was who he was, and he truly didn't know how to tone it down. He half-expected her to fidget nervously, considering his words. What she did instead was shoot him a sexy grin and stroll inside, leaving the door wide open in invitation. That was all Nick needed.

Shaya was a calm, practical female who was *not* reduced to being tongue-tied and shaky at just a guy's presence. But as she and Nick stood in the hallway like two cowboys about to have a showdown, it was exactly what happened. His intensity and power wrapped around her like a cloak—not just his power as an alpha, but his masculine power. It seized and overwhelmed both her body and her mind, and she felt totally captivated by it and by him.

Shaya's need to have him and be taken by him was primal and potent, making it hard to keep her breathing even and her hands steady. Her mouth was suddenly bone-dry, and her heart was pounding. He hadn't even touched her, and yet she felt owned at the possessiveness now blazing from his eyes. Then he spoke, and his even, deep, authoritative tone made her and her wolf snap to total attention.

"Come here. Last night, I pounced on you. This time, I want you to come to me."

And she had every intention of doing just that, but she also wanted to test him, wanted to see exactly how much she could get away with. It was in her nature to push boundaries.

"Shay," he drawled warningly. "Come to me. Show me this is what you want. Show me you can handle this." Pride filled him when she straightened her spine before coming toward him. When she was finally before him, she boldly met his gaze. "Very good."

The drive to possess her in every way had him wanting to hungrily ravish her again. The only thing that kept it in check was that, having waited so long for this, he wanted to savor every minute. He wanted to familiarize himself with every inch of this body that had been made for him. He could sense that Shaya, on the other hand, was too highly strung to last through the savoring. She needed the edge taken off.

When his hands roughly slid into Shaya's hair and he licked along the seam of her mouth, she gladly opened for him. Immediately his tongue delved inside and he groaned. He didn't coax a response from her, he took it. Took it with the confidence of a guy who owned his sexuality and knew exactly what he wanted and just how to get it. Took it like no other guy had come close to doing before now.

Shaya sank into the kiss, locking her arms around his neck and scratching at his nape. A growl rumbled up his chest, teasing her pebbled nipples. As his hands palmed her ass and lifted her, she wrapped her legs around him. The breath left her lungs as he abruptly pinned her against the wall, snuggling his hard cock against her clit. She moaned and scratched at him as he rocked against her, irritable and restless as the tension that had been building within her all evening reached boiling point.

He whispered hotly in her ear as he agonizingly slowly lowered her zipper. "I'm going to fuck you, Shay. Very soon I'm going to bury every inch of my cock inside you. And I'm going to do it as many times as I want. Because I can. And you're going to love it, baby, I promise you. But right now, I need you to come for me right here." Then he slid his hand inside her panties and speared two fingers inside her. That was all it took: she'd been hanging on the edge so long that she shattered with a loud cry. He held her there until the reverberations stopped racking her body, dabbing soft kisses on her face, and then he carried her upstairs.

The second they were inside her bedroom, he slowly lowered her feet to the hardwood floor. Shaya swayed slightly, double-blinking—that had been one disorienting orgasm. She held still as Nick slowly removed her silver sequined top, black pants, and white lacy underwear, like he was unwrapping a delicate birthday gift. Then he was circling her with a predatory glint in his eyes, making her feel like prey, and it sent a shiver running through both her and her wolf.

Raking his gaze over every bare inch of her delectable body, Nick swallowed hard, and a surge of possessiveness swamped him. She was amazingly beautiful, all smoothly shaped muscle and curved in all the right places. Her breasts would fit just right in his hands, the same way her luscious ass did. Coming to stand in front of her, he bit her lip. "I have so many plans for this pretty mouth, but they can wait for another time. Now, I want you to lie on your back on the bed for me with your arms above your head." She backed up until she reached the bed and then slid demurely onto the white satin sheets, but the usual impish benevolence was in her eyes.

When he didn't do anything other than stare at her, she asked, "Are you going to join me, or shall I take care of myself?"

He arched a brow at her, his expression stern. "You don't get to touch yourself unless I say you can. Now be a good girl and spread your legs for me." Instead, she stared at him. He knew she was testing him, and he had every intention of starting as he meant to go on. "I don't like repeating myself, baby. Don't make me flip you over and spank your ass."

"That actually sounds promising, especially when the alternative is you just staring at me."

He loomed over her. "How's this for an alternative: I'm going to explore every single inch of you until I know your body better than you do. I want to know what makes you moan, what makes you squirm, how much pain you like." Every shifter liked the bite of pain, but he wanted to know just how much Shaya liked and could take. He stood upright. "Now, I believe I asked you to do something for me." After a few seconds, she finally spread her legs. He loved that she was completely bald and smooth.

With his intense gaze still trained on Shaya, he began removing his clothes. She knew her eyes were roving over him hungrily. The angles and slopes and indents of his amazing body all spoke of pure power. She had a particular urge to trail her fingers along the slim line of golden crispy hairs on his well-defined, solidly built chest that led to an impressive yet intimidating erection. Hmmm, maybe she should.

When she sat up and reached for his cock, Nick caught her hand and shook his head. "Lie back and put your arms above your head. I don't want you touching me until I'm done exploring."

She gave him a sympathetic look. "Aw, do you suffer from premature ejaculation? Will one touch set you off?"

His brow lifted. "Taunting me, baby?" He shook his head disapprovingly. "You really don't want to do that. Now, do as I asked."

The order rang with enough dominance to make her wolf shiver in delight. "Can't we just skip the exploring part?" Shaya complained, though she did as he said.

Nick got onto the bed and crawled on top of her, placing a hand on either side of her head. "I'll give you what you want soon. Just a little longer, and then you can have it." When he looked at her expectantly, she gripped the bars of the headboard. "Very good," he praised, nipping her lip.

Shaya shuddered as his body finally settled over hers, loving the skin-to-skin contact. His powerful build blanketed her own petite figure, making her feel crowded yet safe—both of which increased her arousal. He took her mouth in a scorching, lingering kiss while cupping and shaping her breast, feathering his thumb over her nipple. Then he tweaked and pinched and plucked at it, making her writhe and moan. God, he was good.

"I love that little noise you make. Let's see if we can make you do it again." Switching to her other breast, Nick lavished it with the same treatment, applying just the right amount of pressure to her nipple that he'd learned she liked. "And there's that sound I love again." He slowly glutted himself on her body, licking, kissing, nipping, stroking, and massaging—learning her, marking her, memorizing everything she liked and how she liked it.

Drawn by the scent of her, he settled himself between her legs, and growled at how wet and swollen she was. "I love the way you smell." Spreading her folds, he blew on her clit and then bit it gently; she practically jumped from the bed. Driving one finger deep inside her, he swirled it around and then withdrew it to circle the puckered hole lower down. "Has anyone ever been here before, Shay?"

He'd asked it so casually that Shaya could almost believe her answer was inconsequential. But she knew better. Male shifters liked to claim their mates in every way possible, including anally, and dominant males in particular liked for that to be virgin territory. They wanted their mates to have saved something for them to be theirs and theirs alone. "No."

Satisfaction welled up in him. "One day, I'm going to take you there. We'll work up to that. Now, I'm going to taste you. But I don't want you to come. Not yet."

Over and over, he licked and sipped, drowning in her flavor— he'd discovered last night that she *did* taste as sweet as she smelled, and it was intoxicating. Then he stabbed his tongue inside her and flicked at her walls teasingly. Each time she moaned his name, he growled softly and approvingly. Soon her leg muscles began to quiver, and she was whimpering. Sensing that she was about to come in spite of his order, he nipped her thigh and held those sparkling gray-blue eyes. "Fight it."

"Stop being a teasing prick!"

He *tsk*ed, smiling. "Now that wasn't very nice."

"So? Are you suddenly sensitive?"

Chuckling, Nick drove one finger inside her. She gasped and arched. "No, baby, but your body clearly is right now." Her low growl made him chuckle again. As her walls began to flutter around his finger, he withdrew it. "Fight it."

"You total ba—" She broke off as she was suddenly flipped onto her stomach and a hand twice came down sharply on her ass. She jerked and gasped as the burn turned to the most delicious pain, making heat explode in her stomach and bloom lower. Glancing over her shoulder, she scowled.

"I'll do it again if I have to," Nick warned her, blowing on the red mark left by his hand—a brand. "What you haven't quite accepted yet, baby, is that this body is mine. All mine. You'll only come when I'm finished playing with it. Of course, if you really want to come that badly, one little word will be enough to get you what you want." When he flipped her back over, he collared her throat and gently but firmly pressed her down onto the mattress. Keeping a tight grip on her throat, he used his free hand to thrust a finger inside her. "For someone who doesn't like waiting or being spanked, you're pretty damn wet."

Shaya growled at the combination of amusement, appreciation, and smugness in his voice. "I won't beg. And I don't like being spanked for having my own mind."

"Really? Look how wet you are." He brought his finger to her face, showing her how coated it was in her own juices.

*Two can play the sexual torment game.* Hoping to drive him to the edge, Shaya flicked out her tongue and licked his finger.

His grip on her throat flexed. "Sly little bitch."

She did it again, this time closing her mouth over his finger and sucking.

"Fuck." He forcefully thrust his tongue into her mouth in a mimic of what he intended to do to her body. He pinched her nipple hard the way she liked it, again wrenching that amazing fucking sound from her throat. Then he was sucking the taut bud into his mouth, loving the taste and texture of her. "If you want to come, all you have to do is say please."

"Keep dreaming, Beavis." She wanted to slap herself for how breathy she sounded. Oh, she was pathetic.

Nick shrugged carelessly. "If that's the way you want it." Then he drew her nipple into his mouth and suckled.

For what could have been hours—Shaya had absolutely no idea—he tortured her. Tortured her until her entire body was trembling and covered in a fine sheen of sweat. He'd worked her into a sensual frenzy until she was so sensitive that the slightest contact had her arching from the bed. She hadn't thought it was possible to feel so *empty*. She had never been more aware of that part of her body. But no matter how much she whined or cursed him, he wouldn't let her come.

"All you have to do is say please, baby," he reminded her before biting the curve of her breast and sucking to leave a mark. "One word . . . and you can have what you want."

Shaya tried to ignore his seductive voice. Tried to ignore his mouth on her breast and his teeth plucking at her nipples. Tried to ignore it when he thrust against her and pinched her clit. Tried, but wasn't successful. Maybe she should just say please this once. She wouldn't really be begging, she would just be repeating what he asked her to say, right? That wasn't the same thing at all.

Watching her squirm and writhe and hearing her seductive moans, Nick knew he wouldn't be able to hold out much longer. Looming over her, he fisted his other hand in her hair and wrenched back her head, forcing her to look at him. His eyes pinned hers. "Say it, Shay."

"Please."

He smiled at how begrudgingly it was said. "I don't think that was very sincere. You know what I want from you."

She did. It wasn't about the begging, it was about what the begging signified—he wanted her to submit, to accept that she was his.

Nick kissed and bit his way down her body and settled between her legs again. Her sweet scent lured him like nothing else could. "Don't make me leave you hanging and come all over you instead. Don't think I won't do that."

Oh, she believed him. The promise to do that was right there in his expression.

He flicked her clit with the tip of his tongue. "Say it. Now."

She quivered at the dominance coating that demand. After a long pause, she submissively went lax. "Please." Suddenly his mouth latched onto her clit at the same time as one finger plunged into her. Her entire body seemed to convulse as her long-awaited orgasm hit. She cried out and clenched her fists hard around the bars of the headboard as it tore through her. Once the aftershocks eased, she sagged into the bed, feeling drained.

"Look at me, Shay." The second she met his gaze, he slammed into her, groaning as her muscles tightened around him. "*Fuck.*" Jaw clenched, he fucked her hard and deep, pounding her into the mattress. After only three harsh strokes she came, but he didn't let up. He continued pumping his hips at a frantic pace that had Shaya crying out and clinging to him, just like he wanted. "Your pussy is squeezing me so tight. Like it never wants to let go."

*That's probably because it doesn't,* thought Shaya. The feeling of finally having him inside her was incredible. He was heat. He was strength. He was intensity. She shaped his back with her hands, liking how his sleek muscles bunched under her touch as he pumped in and out of her. The ravenous hunger that had been haunting and riding them for *so long* was now finally being quenched and slaked . . . and it felt a hundred times better than she could ever have imagined.

"Only I can make you feel this way, Shay. Only me, only your mate."

She heard what he didn't say; that it wouldn't matter if she refused to accept his claim and lived her life with someone else—never would anyone fit her or satisfy her the way he did. She knew that was true. It had never felt like this before. Not once. This was what it was to be truly taken. As much as she feared the power it gave him, he did own her on some level, and she would always belong to him whether he was in her life or not. "That works both ways, Beavis."

Nick bit her lip. "Yes, it does." He groaned as she clawed at the skin of his back. "That's it, Shay, mark me." He groaned again as she dragged her claws across his upper back, deep enough to leave permanent brands there. Satisfaction filled both him and his wolf—she might not intend to officially claim him yet, but she cared enough to leave her brands on him.

He wanted to leave his own on her, wanted the knowledge that even if she walked away at some point, her body would still be marked by Nick—she could never forget him, could never forget their time together, and anyone who touched her afterward would always remember that she belonged to Nick first and always.

"Nick," she rasped, clinging to him and arching against him, wanting more of him until she was stretched to the point of pain and filled beyond capacity.

Nick slipped an arm beneath her and curled it around her ass, tipping her. Then he was plowing into her that much deeper and she was almost sobbing. "Shall I make you come now?" She nodded, whimpering and digging her claws into his back. "You want me to come inside you? You want me to mark your throat again where everyone will see it?"

"Yes," she hissed. "Please, Nick, I need to come."

"Then come for me," he commanded.

As his order rang through her and his teeth sank into her throat, pleasure whipped through Shaya, locking her spine and wrenching a scream from her throat. She felt it as her inner muscles clamped down on him, triggering his own release.

Nick slammed into her one final time, pulsing deep inside her. "Fuck yeah," he growled. "Take all of it, Shay." He rocked against her, wanting every bit of his come inside her, wanting to mark her in as many ways as he could. He might not be able to claim her, but she could bet her hot little ass that he'd be marking her often and thoroughly. To his surprise, he felt a set of teeth suddenly clamp down possessively on his shoulder before a tongue licked over the small brand there. He arched a brow at his mate, amused by her self-satisfied expression.

Shaya shrugged. "Tit for tat."

Cupping her face and staring into her glazed eyes, he kissed her deeply—it was a kiss of triumph, satisfaction, possessiveness, relief, and total adoration. This female had the power to break him like nothing else ever had or ever could. He just hoped she didn't.

# CHAPTER ELEVEN

Shaya woke to the feel of a hot mouth kissing her nape and a large hand sliding up and down her bare thigh. Images of last night flashed in front of her eyes, feeding the need that was building in her system. A moan slipped out of her when Nick's hand dipped between her legs and his finger slid between her folds. But when she shifted to try to take that finger inside her, he withdrew his hand—a message that *he* was leading here. Cheeky shit had done stuff like that all night.

When an impish idea whispered into her mind, she smiled. "God, that feels so good, Kade," she rasped. Instantly she was flipped onto her back and there was an extremely pissed male draped over her.

As she laughed uncontrollably beneath him, realization dawned on Nick. He narrowed his eyes. "That was sneaky. And who the fuck is Kade?"

"No idea. I was just paying you back for teasing me—again."

He spoke against her lips. "You like it when I tease you." There was a twinge in his chest as he thought of how much time they'd missed together, how he could have had her with him, laughing and bantering with him like she was now, if he'd only claimed her when he first saw her.

Seeing the light in his eyes dim, Shaya was about to comment when his cell phone rang.

Having retrieved his cell from the pocket of his jacket, Nick saw it was Derren. "What?"

"You have visitors." Derren sounded slightly amused.

"Well then tell them to go away." He had a mate to explore, taste, bite, and fuck all over again.

"I think you might want to speak to them."

"Is it a matter of life and death?" Nick gritted out.

"Possibly." The smile in Derren's voice had him and his wolf intrigued.

"I'll be down in a minute."

As Nick ended the call and began pulling on his clothes, Shaya decided to do the same. She'd heard his phone call, and she wasn't reassured by Derren's apparent amusement—she'd come to learn that he had an offbeat sense of humor. If it was Logan, she wanted to be with Nick to ensure he didn't let the human provoke him.

Dressed, Nick landed a kiss on her lips. "Stay here for me, baby."

"Oh no. If someone's here, I want to know who it is." Seeing that he was about to object, she added, "This is *my* home. If shit comes to my doorstep, it's my right to be part of dealing with it."

*Fair point*, thought Nick with a sigh. Neither he nor his wolf was worried about her coming along because both he and his wolf knew that if there was any true danger, Derren would have warned Nick about it. "Fine. But if, for any reason, I need you to go inside, don't ignore that." Only when she nodded did he take her hand in his and lead her out of the room and down the stairs.

Keeping Shaya slightly behind him, Nick opened the front door . . . and almost gaped. Derren and the rebels were standing on the doorstep. But the rebels weren't the visitors. No, the rebels appeared to be joining Derren *against* the visitors. Visitors who had his wolf on alert, growling and ready to pounce.

At the sight of Taryn, Trey, Tao, and Dominic all scowling at Nick, Shaya gawked. "What are you guys doing here?" Oh shit.

"No, what's *he* doing here?" demanded Taryn, though she didn't look surprised to see Nick, simply pissed—Shaya could only assume Taryn had also seen the news footage that featured Nick and Shaya together in the background. Great. The members of the Phoenix Pack all briefly moved their gaze to Shaya, shot her a teeny smile, and went back to scowling at her mate. Shaya's wolf didn't like that. Oh God, oh God, this could get really, really bad.

"If you're here to take her," began Nick, his voice a deadly growl, "you've had a wasted journey." His wolf growled, backing Nick up on that. No one was taking Shaya anywhere.

"I already explained that." Derren sounded a mixture of bored and amused.

Taryn snarled at Nick, clenching her fists. "I told you to stay away from her."

"You knew I wouldn't," said Nick, his voice deceptively patient. "She's my mate. Nothing's going to keep me away from her."

Tao snorted. "Really? Strange. Because you stayed away from her for months of your own accord."

"Leaving *us* to care for her and comfort her," added Dominic, which made Nick growl—he really would like to kill that wolf. "Call us odd, but we don't want you around her when there's every chance you'll upset her again."

"And you *will* upset her again," maintained Taryn, glaring hard at Nick. "Because you're a cruel, insensitive shithead—something you've proven by even thinking of coming here! You lost the right to see her when you ignored her instead of claiming her! Don't you think it's a little late to come knocking now?"

Nick raised a brow. "Don't you think that's up to Shaya to decide, who I'm sure isn't liking that everyone's speaking on her behalf?"

Her mate knew her well. As his arm lifted in invitation, Shaya let him tug her to his side. He wasn't forcing her to remain behind him—he was treating her like an equal. She hadn't expected that. Sensing that Taryn's anger was increasing, which in turn was increasing the anger of the Phoenix wolves—of course, all of that was feeding Nick's anger and putting his wolf on edge—Shaya decided it was past time to defuse the situation.

Petting Nick's chest to calm him, Shaya smiled at her best friend. "Taryn, I really appreciate your concern for me—it was the same concern I showed for you when you first mated with Trey." Ignoring Trey's affronted look, Shaya continued, "But I'm asking you to give me the same support I gave you." When both Dominic's and Tao's mouths opened, Shaya gave them a dark look that made their mouths snap shut. "You've made your opinions clear. I don't need to hear them again." She swept her gaze over all of them as she said, "This isn't a negotiation. If you're not willing to give Nick the same chance I'm giving him, you need to leave."

When Trey's eyes moved to her neck and narrowed, Shaya knew he'd seen one of Nick's many marks. "You haven't officially claimed her," noted Trey, studying Nick curiously.

"Yet," Nick quickly said. "When Shaya's ready, I will."

Lips pursed, Trey considered that for a moment, and then nodded in satisfaction. Tao did the same while Dominic shrugged.

Taryn gawked at her mate. "You're okay with this?" she practically screeched.

"Baby, you knew this would happen." Trey ran a hand through the various shades of blonde that made up his mate's hair, clearly trying to calm her down. "Nothing in this world could keep me away from you, and nothing was going to keep him away from Shaya."

"He should have claimed her when he had the chance!"

"Yes, but he didn't." Trey gestured to Shaya's neck. "And look, he still hasn't. He's waiting for her to be ready. That's more than a lot of shifters would do, and we all know it."

After a thoughtful pause, Taryn turned to Nick again. "I want to talk to Shaya alone." Her eyes dared him to say no.

"Then you need to ask Shaya," said Nick. "I'm her mate, not her boss."

Taryn's brows rose in surprise, and Shaya saw a hint of approval in her eyes.

"Why don't you all wait inside while Taryn and I talk out here?" When Nick tensed almost imperceptibly beside her, Shaya knew he didn't like the idea of her being completely out of his sight with Taryn when it was clear that the Alpha female wanted her away from Nick. She laid a reassuring hand on his chest and rubbed her jaw against his side. That easily, the tension left him. Looking up at him, she said, "I'll just be a few minutes."

Common sense told Nick that Taryn wouldn't attempt to sneak away with Shaya because that would mean leaving without her mate and pack members. Common sense also told him that Taryn was too brazen to do "sneaky"; she'd do it right in front of him and expect him to deal with it. But he couldn't help being anxious. It was one thing for the two females to talk where he could *see* them. It was another for him to wait inside. But as he looked down into gray-blue eyes that were begging for the same trust she was trying to give him, there was no way he could object.

Dropping his arm, Nick nodded. Shaya's beaming smile was reward enough for him. "Don't leave the yard unless you want our little followers to hear your conversation." As Shaya nodded and then went to the Alpha female, he caught the blonde's eye and held her gaze. "Try to take my mate from me, and I'll take yours from you."

The blonde just blinked at him, before asking Shaya, "Is he always delusional?" Nick tracked their movements as they went to stand at the bottom of the yard, satisfied when they didn't walk any farther.

"Who are the people watching the house?"

At Trey's question, Nick sighed. "I guess you'd better come in."


As Nick, Derren, and the Phoenix wolves went inside the house, the rebels insisted on waiting outside. The trio stood monitoring Taryn and Shaya, and she had the feeling that they intended to ensure on Nick's behalf that Taryn didn't attempt to kidnap her. It was kind of touching. "So, to what do I owe the pleasure of your visit?"

"We saw you and Nick on the news," said Taryn, arms folded across her chest. "We left Dante and Jaime to hold the fort while we came here. The reporter said there's some kind of shifter war going on, but that made no sense to me—every shifter in the world is on their best behavior right now, not wanting to give the human extremists anything to work with."

Shaya sighed. "You can thank those extremists for what happened. They did it to get a reaction from Nick. It turns out that the guy running the local extremist group was one of the prison guards when Nick was in juvie." When Taryn showed no surprise about Nick having been in juvie, Shaya frowned in confusion. "You knew about his past?"

"Only what Dante told me: that he killed a human and injured two others while defending himself and his sister."

Shaya inwardly sighed in relief. She was sure Nick wouldn't like all his past to be common knowledge.

"You can't seriously be thinking about mating with him, Shaya."

"There was a lot I didn't know about him." Aware that Nick's pride would balk at others knowing about his health issues, that

Nick wouldn't want to be viewed as having weaknesses to anyone, she didn't elaborate. "And nobody can say he hasn't earned
a chance, Taryn. I put him through an alpha's version of hell—
rejected him, stomped on his pride, and even went on a date with
another guy."

"No way!" Taryn seemed pleased about it.

"But he's still here. He's apologized, he's done sweet stuff for
me, he's bought me gifts, he's fixed the little messes in my life,
and he's just generally been here for me. It's like, wherever I look
he's there, just like—"

"A mate," finished Taryn with a sigh. "Okay, I get it; he's been
a good Boy Scout. But how do you know that will last?"

"I don't. I can only give him the chance he's earned."

"And if he messes it up?"

"I make a margarita with his balls."

Taryn laughed. "I have to say I was impressed when I heard
he'd given up his position for you. I'd expected him to return to
his pack at some point. But he never did. He kept searching for
you. What are you going to do about your living situation? You
only took on the lone-wolf lifestyle to hide from Nick. Does this
mean you'll come home now?"

Shaya ran a hand through her curls. "I don't know. Nick
offered to join the Phoenix Pack."

Taryn's jaw almost hit the floor. "You're shitting me. He
hasn't asked you to go back to his old pack?"

Shaya shook her head. "He knows his wolf would find it hard
to obey someone less dominant than him, and he doesn't want
the position of Alpha, so he has no intention of returning. I'm
just going to take things one step at a time. If things turn out
badly, I'll probably come home. But if they don't . . . well, that's a
decision Nick and I would have to make together. But I couldn't
ask him to join the Phoenix Pack, Taryn. I couldn't ask someone
as powerful as him to serve and obey someone else."

Taryn nodded in understanding. "It wouldn't be right. Well,

there's no denying that he's trying hard to win you over. I still don't like him for how miserable he made you."

"But you'll give him a chance just like I am. You'll wish me luck, like I did for you and Trey," prodded Shaya.

Rolling her eyes, Taryn said, "Fine."

Smiling, Shaya threw her arms around her best friend, who returned the hug. "I've missed you." She pulled back. "And I've missed Kye. How is he?" Although the fact that she chatted with her pack over Skype at least once a week meant that Shaya had watched Kye grow, it wasn't the same as being *with* him.

"You can find that out for yourself," said Taryn, urging Shaya to follow her to the pack's Toyota Highlander that was parked behind Nick's Mercedes. "Now that I know there's no chance of a fight breaking out and no blood will be shed, I can get him out of the SUV." When Shaya's face lit up, Taryn snorted. "I wouldn't get so excited if I were you. Old Mother Hubbard, who has spent the past five hours driving me insane in the SUV, is waiting with him—she insisted on coming." Taryn was referring to Trey's grandmother, who was very possessive of Trey, Dante, Tao, and the enforcers and didn't like females around them. "She hovers around him unhealthily like she does with Trey and her other 'boys.' It's disturbing."

As Taryn slid the side door open, Greta huffed at the Alpha female. "I heard that, hussy. No respect." The arguing that went on between them happened daily.

Taryn gave Trey's grandmother a sweet, mocking smile. "Oh, I'm sorry, was I supposed to break the habit of a lifetime and bring joy to your day?"

Cuddling a sleeping Kye to her chest, Greta huffed once more at Taryn before turning to Shaya and smiling fondly. "Shaya, sweetheart, how are you?"

"Oh, you're nice to her because she's not going to mate with one of your boys." Taryn growled. "Give me my son before your old-lady breath bleaches his hair." As Taryn took the adorable eight-month-old baby into her arms, his lids fluttered open to reveal a set of arctic-blue eyes exactly like his father's. As Nick had once said, Kye was literally Trey with Taryn's hair—which made him one absolutely gorgeous baby who would undoubtedly break many female hearts when he was older.

"Hey there," whispered Shaya, playing with his hair. "Recognize me?"

"Of course he does," said Taryn. "It's so cute how he points to the laptop and waves—I know it means he wants to wave to you on Skype. Can you do it for Auntie Shaya again now?" Taryn waved her hand slightly, and Kye mirrored the move, flashing Shaya a huge smile. "Now that I can visit you without worrying that Nick will have people following me who will then know where you are, we can come see you whenever I want, and you can visit us whenever *you* want."

A smile spread across Shaya's face. She liked that idea. After only a minute of gentle coaxing, Kye went willingly into Shaya's arms. "He's such a sociable kid."

"It's only natural given that he's part of a pack that spoils him rotten and treats him like he's at the center of the entire universe," said Taryn. "He's used to being handled by different people."

With Kye in her arms, Shaya led Taryn and Greta into the house. She found the guys all gathered in the dining area. Her eyes instantly went to Nick, who was sitting at the table. His smile had a hint of relief to it, and she realized just how worried he'd been that she might leave. As she entered the room, Dominic straightened from where he'd been leaning against the wall and came toward her wearing a devilish grin—yep, he had every intention of flirting with her to annoy Nick, just like he did to all the mated females to provoke their mates. Well, it wasn't so much flirting as delivering cheesy lines, but it had the desired effect on the mated males.

She halted him with a look. "Dominic, if you value your life, you won't aggravate him right now." Not while Nick was being forced to cope with her being in the presence of a number of males, particularly when two of them were unmated. Possessiveness would be haunting him, just as it did her when Amber was around.

Dominic, to her surprise, raised his hands in surrender and dropped his smile. "Okay, fine, but I was just going to give you a little kiss. If you don't like it, you can always return it."

"*Dominic.*"

"Watch it, blondie," warned Nick, his voice like a whip.

"You sure like to live dangerously, don't you?" said Tao, shaking his head at his packmate.

Dominic just grinned. "There's no better way to live." Noticing Nick's evil smile, he asked, "What?"

"I'm just thinking how much fun your pack is going to have when you meet *your* mate. I could be wrong, but I'm guessing the males will be getting some payback."

Nodding, Trey said, "Damn right." At that moment, his son held out his arms to him, and Trey took him gladly.

"Hey, I'm a breath of fresh air," maintained Dominic. "Besides, why would I want a mate yet when there is such a wide variety of females out there to sample?"

Shaya wasn't buying that act for one minute. Oh sure, Dominic loved women, and women loved Dominic—it was impossible not to love that wicked grin, his caramel skin, and those impressive abs—but he wasn't quite the slut he pretended to be. She had yet to figure out what his act was all about, however. Just as she had yet to figure out why he bothered with lines, given how easily he reeled in females.

As Greta came to stand beside Shaya, the old woman scowled at Nick. "*You* I'm not in the least bit happy with," she told him in her usual witchy voice. Nick's brows rose in surprise. "It doesn't matter that you had your reasons—you hurt our Shaya, and I don't like it. You should be thankful that you have a mate as wonderful as Shaya and not a hussy like *her!*" She tipped her head at Taryn, who just smiled.

"You love me really, Greta." Taryn elbowed her gently. "Admit it, I hold a place in your heart of solid concrete."

Trey rolled his eyes and then turned to Shaya. "Nick and Derren have told us what's been happening around here with the humans. It's not safe."

"Which is why I recommended that you take your pack and leave," Nick told him.

Sensing his understandable tension, Shaya went to Nick. Without moving his gaze from Trey, Nick looped an arm around her waist and pulled her onto his lap.

"Shaya told me a little of what's going on too." Taryn went to stand beside Trey and their son. "If she's in danger, we're not leaving without her."

Nick went to argue, but then he considered that for a moment. The idea of Shaya around Logan didn't sit well with Nick any more than it did for Taryn. Looking at Shaya, he said, "Maybe you should leave." Her eyes flashed with fury.

"No."

"Shay—"

"All you have to do is keep a low profile until the court hearing. Then you can do whatever the hell you want."

"But keeping a low profile will be hard to do if the guy is doing his best to provoke Nick," Tao gently pointed out, shrugging.

"We could always head off in the motor home and lead the humans away," Derren suggested to Nick.

"No," insisted Shaya shakily, earning Nick's instant and undivided attention. "You said you wouldn't leave me again."

"And I meant it." He nipped her lip and ran a hand up and down her arm, knowing the source of her fear and hating it.

"I'm not talking about leaving for good," Derren assured her. "I'm talking about leading the humans on a merry chase."

"Nick's not leaving, and neither am I," Shaya firmly stated with utmost authority, which seemed to amuse everyone in the room. Okay, she could admit she'd sounded every inch the Alpha female, but whatever.

"Then neither are we," declared Taryn. "We're sticking around until the court hearing—we need to be sure that Logan doesn't manage to rile Nick or harm you. There's strength in numbers."

Familiar feminine voices outside were quickly followed by the entrance of Nick's mother, Roni, and Amber. He had to assume that Jesse, Bracken, and Zander had let them pass. Although there was really no *letting* Kathy Axton do anything.

"We saw the Highlander outside and thought there might be trouble," said Kathy, eying up the strange newcomers.

Shaya quickly introduced them. "Kathy, this is Taryn and Trey—my old Alpha pair. And these others here are members from their pack. Guys, this is Nick's mom, Kathy; his sister, Roni; and their pack healer, Amber." The latter word almost came out a growl.

Everyone froze as Taryn and Amber suddenly walked toward each other, looking like two cowgirls about to have a showdown. Great—a standoff between two healers. It was kind of like "Mirror, mirror on the wall, who's the most powerful of them all?" Both females considered themselves to be quite powerful healers and had reputations that backed that up. But there was an ongoing debate about which of the two females was the most gifted among wolf shifters.

"Taryn Warner, I presume," drawled Amber.

The Alpha female studied the other healer from head to toe. "I'm guessing you're Amber Lyons."

"It's a pleasure to meet you." Amber's smile couldn't have been more false.

Taryn's smile was even more unpleasant. "No, the honor's all mine."

Shaya exchanged an amused look with Nick.

"Shaya didn't introduce us all properly, did she?" Greta said to Kathy, coming forward to shake her hand. She was the picture of courtesy. "I'm Trey's grandmother, Greta." She said it like it made her the president or something. Kathy shook her hand gladly, totally falling for the gracious act. "And these are two of my other boys here, Tao and Dominic."

"Oh, so they're all your grandsons?" asked Kathy, giving both males a sweet smile.

"In my heart they are." Greta placed a hand over her chest, wearing a proud smile. "I've always looked out for them, always been there for them. They think the world of me." She sighed wistfully. "Of course, I wish Trey and Dante, our Beta, had chosen better mates, but you've got to let them make their own mistakes, haven't you?" Kathy's smile said, "I know what you mean."

Taryn rolled her eyes. "If you're done with the dramatics, Mother Goose, we'll—"

"Nick," called Jesse from outside, "there's someone here to see you."

"Who is it this time?" Nick growled.

"The Nazi and some of his wolves."

Nick groaned. "Great." All he wanted was to be alone with Shaya. Instead of people leaving, more and more kept appearing.

Dominic cocked his head. "Who?"

"The Alpha of the local pack," replied Nick.

Dominic's forehead creased. "Why is his nickname the Nazi?"

"Because he's a Nazi." Was it really that confusing?

Standing, Shaya took Nick's hand in hers. "Come on, let's go deal with this." She waited for him to tell her to remain inside, to let him speak to the Alpha alone and be extremely overprotective due to her submissive status . . . but he didn't. Instead, he walked with her to the door, willing to present a united front despite that his overprotective streak would be screaming at him to do otherwise. That delighted both Shaya and her wolf.

Conscious that everyone other than Kathy and Greta had followed him and Shaya to the front door, Nick shook his head. Nosy bastards. "If you don't want what you say to be heard by the humans in the van across the road, you might want to talk quietly," he told Hadley.

The Alpha ran his eyes along Nick, Shaya, and the crowd behind them. "My wolves informed me that you've been gathering some of your alliances together. I had nothing to do with the destruction of the salon, if it's me you're intending to war with."

"I have no issues with you. I'm aware that the human extremists are responsible for what happened to the salon, but I can't do shit about that right now."

"But you *will* do something at some point," Hadley surmised. "There are many more to their group than what you've seen. Although a certain number of them actively support their argument, there are still many more. If it came to a confrontation, their number will well exceed the number you have here."

"I suspected as much."

"Have your contacts uncovered any information about the game preserve?"

"Game preserve?" repeated Shaya.

Nick cursed silently. Now his mate was going to be extremely pissed at him for not telling her about it. Worse, he'd have to worry her with this shit. He really wanted to hit someone right now . . . preferably Dominic. "Not yet. You?"

"I think we're close to locating it," said Hadley, "but I can't be sure. If we don't find it before the court hearing, we could be in deep shit. Even if the extremists' argument is ignored, this won't end well. The extremists—particularly the ones around here— would most likely confront us."

Nick could agree with that. "If it comes to a confrontation with the humans, I'll be at your side."

"As will I," announced Derren. The rebels nodded.

"Me too." Shaya held Nick's gaze, letting him see just how

seriously his life depended on him not arguing with her on that. She might be submissive and therefore not as physically strong as the dominant shifters around her, but she could still defend herself—particularly against humans.

Deciding he'd argue with her in private later, Nick simply kissed her temple to relax her. Hearing Roni growl beside him, he had the feeling that his sister was offering to stand with Nick in a fight. Great.

"And me," said Trey. Tao and Dominic nodded their support.

"If Nick's going to be there," began Amber, "I'll be there." Shaya had to grit her teeth at that response, which was much like something a loyal and very close friend would say.

"And me," said Taryn. "And, of course, Greta." When Trey looked at her oddly, she shrugged. "What? How else am I supposed to get rid of the old crone?"

"I heard that, hussy."

Taryn turned and called out, "Damn, Greta, did someone leave your cage open again?"

Shaking his head and wondering why the universe would insert these crazy people into his life, Nick turned his attention back to Hadley. "I'll have Jesse call you if my contacts uncover anything."

The Alpha advanced down the path, nodding. "Good. Likewise, if I find out anything, I'll let you know."

When the Sequoia wolves had driven away, Shaya turned to Nick. "Now you can explain what he meant by 'game preserve.'"

So Nick led everyone back inside the house and begrudgingly did just that, which led to a lot of cursing and shouting—they all found the idea as repugnant as Derren and Nick did. Then, naturally, he received a lecture from Shaya for not telling her sooner. But after some apologizing, neck kissing, and soothing touches, she eventually forgave him . . . though she did inform him that he should think twice before keeping something from her ever again because she knew where he slept and she had a nifty bat. "I need to go for a run," Nick then told her, winding a curl around his finger. "Come with me."

Shaya led him to the rear of the house and outside. Reaching the small cluster of trees at the end of the backyard, she started to remove her clothes as Nick began to remove his. "See the little gap in the fence? I made that so I could go run in the little wooded area here in my wolf form."

"You know that I'm going to chase you, don't you?" said Nick, smirking. "I'm going to chase you, catch your ass, and mount you."

"Not a chance," she chuckled, now totally naked. Then she let her wolf free, enjoying the familiar pleasure/pain that came with the shift.

Nick smiled down at the graceful red wolf and went to pet her, but she bounded off into the woods—it was a challenge. He shifted seconds later and loped after her.

For hours the wolves played: chasing, ambushing, mock fighting, and jaw wrestling, making up for the time they had lost due to the behavior of their human halves. When the sky started to darken, the large gray male wolf ushered the red she-wolf through the fence where they entered.

Once they were back in their human forms and fully dressed, Nick kissed her hard and deep, leaving no doubt in her mind that he believed she was his. Patting her ass, he said, "Come on, let's go inside. I need food. And I have to make sure Derren doesn't cook dinner again. The guy could burn water."

"A little like me then," admitted Shaya as she began pulling on her clothes.

"Then it's a good thing I can cook." As they were walking up the path toward the house, the door opened and a familiar figure came strolling out. Nick wasn't surprised when Shaya tensed beside him.

"Oh, hi," said Amber with a bright smile, "I was just about to come and hunt you both down. We've all decided to go out for dinner." She cocked her head as she regarded Nick. "You look a little more relaxed now."

"You can thank Shay for that."

Catching movement in her peripheral vision, Shaya spotted Roni sprawled on the grass by the small shed.

"Sometimes she likes to go off and be alone," explained Amber before turning and heading back into the house.

Shaya looked up at Nick. "I'd like to talk to Roni alone for a minute."

"She's not being bitchy by not shifting to talk to you, Shay—"

"Hey, I know that," she assured him. "I'd just like a minute alone with her. I know her wolf won't understand the words, but she will."

Shrugging, Nick said, "Sure, if that's what you want. I'll be inside."

Cautiously, Shaya made her way over to where Roni lay. Sitting beside her, she smiled. "Hi there." The wolf didn't react other than to briefly glance her way. "Guilt's a funny thing, isn't it? It lingers, even when it doesn't make sense to feel it. I was a twin, you know. She died in the womb. I know it's not my fault, and I know I couldn't have helped her and that for me to survive when she didn't isn't an awful thing. But I hated myself for a long time. Even now, I *know* I shouldn't feel guilty. Mostly, it's gone . . . but a tiny bit still stays. Whenever the guilt and the sadness got too bad, I'd stay in my wolf form for days on end. Because though the guilt's still there, it's dimmed when you're in that form, isn't it? Staying as a wolf . . . it was my escape. And it's yours too." She had Roni's full attention now.

"I know that really I have no reason at all to feel guilty. None of it was my fault . . . just like what happened that day in the woods wasn't your fault. Nick doesn't realize you shift to escape the guilt. He thinks you stay in this form a lot because you're escaping the memories of what happened, that he traumatized you. Maybe if you guys talked . . . maybe you could help each other out with the unnecessary guilt you both feel." Giving Roni one last stroke, Shaya got to her feet. "See you soon."

Entering the house, Shaya found that Amber was doing her best to lounge over Nick, and Taryn was therefore throwing peanuts at her. Of course Amber's attention quickly switched to Taryn, ridding Shaya of the need to march over there and make it clear that Nick was hers. Shaya observed with a frown as Nick dodged Kathy's touch in the same way that he dodged Amber's; his mother didn't appear surprised or offended by how uncomfortable he seemed with her attempts at affection. It occurred to Shaya then that Nick wasn't just like that with Amber, or even just with Kathy. He didn't seem to like being touched in general, which was pretty odd—as odd as him disliking company, in fact.

"He's always been like that, according to Kathy."

Derren's voice snatched her from her contemplations. "What?"

"He's never been particularly affected by social touching. Kathy said that even when he was a baby, he didn't like to be cuddled much or rocked to sleep or anything—he always liked his space, liked to sprawl on the bed like a starfish. Even now, he hugs Roni and Kathy, but that's pretty much it. It's only you I've ever seen him be truly affectionate with."

"In other words, I don't need to worry about Amber. Does everyone buy her sweet friendly-friendly act? I see a lot of deviousness there."

"Yup, a lot of people buy it." He sighed. "She's very cunning. A word of warning: She'll try her hardest to become a close friend, but you can't let her get friendly with you—not even to humor her. If you do, you'll make it possible for the communication between you and Nick to become triangular with her as the go-between. I'm sure you know as well as I do that if that happened, she'd be passing on messages to both of you that would be twisted or false."

"Ah, and then it would make Nick and I upset with each

other, and we'd both turn to her for advice, enabling her to interfere in a big way." Sneaky. So sneaky it was almost worthy of respect. "That won't happen. You're on my side, right?" She had the feeling that Derren was a good person to have on her side.

"Are you planning to hurt Nick again?"

"No."

"Then yes, I'm on your side." As Roni butted his leg, Derren reached down and petted her. "And you'll have Roni on your side, too. She can see right through Amber's act. Unfortunately, Kathy can't, but she wants Nick to have his mate—and that's you."

"I guess all I can do is ignore her. If that fails, I have rat poison and a shovel." As Nick then came over and locked his arms around her, Shaya smiled and sank into his arms. Over his shoulder, she noticed that Amber was watching her from the far side of the room. The female shot her a friendly smile, but Shaya hadn't missed the anger that had momentarily sparkled in her eyes. Still, Shaya returned the smile while at the same time tightening her hold on Nick, conveying a clear message that he was hers. That wasn't enough for her wolf; she wanted Shaya to bite him. So Shaya did, right on his pectoral.

Nick winced, peering down at his mate, who was grinning in self-satisfaction. "Did you just bite me, baby?"

"Yep."

The possessive glint in her eyes made him smile. Leaning down, he bit Shaya's bottom lip hard and then licked across it to soothe the sting. "You're never going to get away from me, you know. You're mine. I'm keeping you. For good." He'd expected her to snort at him or maybe look wary, but she surprised him by relaxing slightly in his arms. His wolf growled in contentment, convinced that his mate was coming around to the idea of being claimed. But Nick often found himself wondering if it was something she would ever be ready for.

# CHAPTER TWELVE

---◈---

S haya had always been good at defusing situations and calming tempers, which was ironic considering her own temper
was pretty bad. However, defusing any arguments that occurred
between Taryn and Amber took a great deal of effort—something
Shaya had quickly come to learn over the last four weeks. As such,
she was tapping her foot impatiently while she stood between the
two females in the living area who ranted at each other, pointing
fingers and scowling. Meeting her mate's gaze, who was sitting on
the sofa looking both amused and exasperated, Shaya struggled
not to laugh at the insults being exchanged.

Amber had done exactly as Derren had said she would—
she'd tried extremely hard to become close friends with Shaya.
But when that hadn't worked, she had instead taken to trying to
provoke Shaya with sugar-coated insults and backhanded compliments that had been so cleverly delivered they sounded totally
innocent to most people. Taryn, however, knew exactly what
Amber was doing. Whereas Shaya's response to Amber had been
to act sickly sweet rather than snap—which would have made
her seem unnecessarily bitchy and hostile toward Amber—Taryn
was much too direct to cope with her shit. And now the bitch had

done what she knew would piss Taryn the hell off: She'd touched her mate.

Amber threw her hands up in the air. "All I did was touch him with my fingertip—I was trying to heal the cut on his hand!"

Taryn sniggered. "Well thanks, E.T., but I can heal him myself! Touch him again, and—"

"Girls, girls," intervened Shaya, sighing. She kept her tone even and calm as she spoke. "You've both made your point. The solution here is clear: Amber, it would be extremely smart if you didn't touch Trey again."

"It was just his hand!"

Taryn pointed hard at her. "That's not the point, and you know it. Don't think I don't see you for the cunning little bitch that you are."

"I just wanted to heal him." Oh, Amber's innocent act was good. "Nick, surely you're not going to let Taryn speak to me this way!"

Nick simply shrugged. "I'm not your Alpha anymore, Amber. Your problems are yours to deal with."

*Right answer*, thought Shaya.

"But I just wanted to heal him! It's part of who I am."

Playing along to end the whole thing by being impartial, Shaya nodded. "And kind though it was, it truly wasn't necessary—Trey's paper cut was certainly not fatal, and Taryn was right beside him in any case, so she could have healed him if necessary. Plus, touching a mated male when you're not mated yourself isn't totally wise."

Amber planted a hand on her hip. "Dominic touches you all the time. What's the difference?"

"Maybe you haven't noticed that the pervert is covered in nettle stings after I threw him in the bush for kissing Shaya," said Nick, not even bothering to stifle his smile. Annoyingly, Dominic found the whole thing funny too. To Nick's surprise, he'd actually come to like the pervert over the last month. The guy was pretty smart, very observational, and extremely loyal to his pack . . . but he just couldn't resist provoking Nick from time to time.

"Now I think it would be wise if both of you stayed out of each other's way until you're both calm," said Shaya. They looked about to protest, but then they gave each other one last scowl and waltzed away in opposite directions. Blowing out a heavy breath, Shaya went to stand between Nick's legs. His hands immediately landed on her hips, his thumbs tracing her hipbones. "I think it's safe to say that those two will never get along."

Tugging her down so that she was straddling him, Nick kissed her lightly. "You're really good at that." At her questioning look, he explained, "Easing tension and stopping arguments." So good that not only had she managed to calm two dominant females, but they had listened to her—not bristling at a submissive wolf interfering. Also, she had managed to remain impartial despite that she'd known how badly Amber was in the wrong *and* despite that she truly disliked her.

"I guess so," she agreed a little breathlessly as his tongue licked at a mark he'd recently left on her throat. "Still, I can't guarantee Taryn won't one day launch herself at Amber and scratch her eyes out." The thought was pretty appealing. The bitch was always lingering, uninvited. Not that Amber was the only one, to be fair. As Derren went wherever Nick went, the only time Derren wasn't around was when he was sleeping in the motor home—it was empty other than for Bruce, as Nick now stayed with Shaya.

Although the Phoenix wolves all stayed in the shifter motel like Nick's family, some of them visited at least once a day. Roni hung around a lot too, though she mostly remained outside. Not only that, Jesse, Bracken, and Zander patrolled the perimeter of the house "on guard"—and totally of their own accord. They returned home to bathe and change when they needed to, but that was pretty much it; they had apparently decided to attach themselves to Nick, though it was hardly surprising to her. As Derren had said, Nick drew people to him and inspired them—he just didn't see it. Expectedly, having all these people around annoyed the shit out of Nick.

"You know," began Nick, "I'm actually surprised that Amber was ballsy enough to touch Trey. The Alpha female isn't someone anyone should go out of their way to aggravate. In fact, I'm equally surprised Taryn didn't draw blood."

"Personally, I think Amber was hoping that Taryn would try to attack her so you would fly to Amber's rescue—after all, it'd be pretty instinctive for you, considering she was once under your protection." That would then have resulted in Shaya going ballistic at Nick for siding with Amber, as Shaya's loyalty lay with Taryn.

Recalling how Amber had turned to him for support, Nick thought Shaya might just be right. "Well, if she honestly thinks I'll jump to her defense, she's very mistaken."

"The woman's getting on my last nerve, trailing after you all the time. And her playing the 'close friend' card is annoying too." Shaya cringed at how every word had dripped with jealousy.

"I don't have friends, you know that."

"Yes, you do. You just don't realize it." When utter confusion flashed across his face, she rolled her eyes. "Derren doesn't stick with you just because he wants to guard you. He does it because you're his friend. And what about all those friends who helped you track me down?"

"Contacts. They are *contacts*."

"I suppose these people who repeatedly call you and Derren, asking if you need backup against the humans, aren't your friends either," she said dryly.

Nick shrugged. "I don't bond."

Shaya shook her head, sighing. "You're a hopeless case, Nick Axton."

"And *you're* being jealous for no good reason," he assured her gently as he collared her throat and then tipped her head backward. "I only want you." He ran his tongue along her collarbone, loving the taste and smell of her. "When you're finally ready to trust me totally, I'll prove that by claiming you. Until then, I'm going to spend my time kissing you and biting you and fucking you 'til you accept that you're mine."

She didn't say what she was thinking, that she had already accepted that she was his, and that the problem was she couldn't fully accept and trust that he would always be hers. It was becoming less and less about the fact that he had once left her, and more and more about her own insecurities. How could she not worry that he would one day look at her and find her lacking because she didn't match him in strength on every level? If he had been merely a dominant male, it wouldn't be so much of an issue. But he was a born alpha. How could she not worry that he might one day resent her for being the reason he had left his pack and couldn't hold an Alpha position anywhere? It would torture and stifle Nick's wolf to obey someone else when he was a natural-born leader.

It was fair to say that he hadn't given her any reason to believe that these insecurities were rational. In fact, over the past month he had made her feel nothing but cherished. Not with soppy words or actions, but by the way he gave her his total and utter attention—an unwavering focus that both ate her up and comforted her. When he thought she needed or wanted something, she suddenly had it. When he believed there was a problem, he took care of it.

She'd been right to think he wasn't a guy who could ever be "managed"—his iron will wouldn't allow it—but he didn't try to manage her either. He didn't try to walk all over her as other dominant males had done, and he was quick to snap if he thought anyone else tried to do it. He made her happy. But could *she* make *him* happy? Could she really hold someone like Nick? Could a mating bond ever truly be enough if it might mean he and his wolf were forced to live packless and with no territory to call their own? When it would mean that any children they had would also be forced to live that life?

"You're thinking too hard." Nick lifted her head and bit her lip. "Stop."

"Like it's that simple."

"If it's a distraction you need," he began with a devilish smile, grinding her against him, "I can happily help you out with it." Taking her upstairs, he did just that.

A few hours later, Shaya was sitting on her sofa drinking coffee and watching with a smile as Roni lay protectively where Kye was playing with his toys on the carpet with Dominic and Taryn. Although Kye wouldn't be able to use his gift of healing psychological scars until he was much older, he still oozed a feeling of safety that attracted anyone with such scars. It was safe to say that Roni had some.

As was often the case, the living area was pretty crowded. Shaya, Derren, and Trey were on the sofa. Greta and Kathy had each taken an armchair. And Tao and Amber had each dragged in one of the dining chairs. Amber had also brought in a spare chair, and Shaya was pretty sure it was supposed to be for Nick—who was currently in the kitchen speaking with Eli on his cell phone. Shaya had to give it to her, the bitch was certainly persistent.

She supposed that in Amber's eyes, it was Shaya who was the one interfering. Amber had most likely viewed Nick as hers for a very long time and may have even convinced herself they had a chance of imprinting one day. Having felt the sting of rejection, Shaya would have sympathized with Amber—okay, she *might* have sympathized with her—if Nick hadn't made it clear to his entire pack that he didn't intend to mate with anyone but his true mate. If Amber had convinced herself otherwise, it was her problem.

"This is bad, isn't it?" asked Kathy, referring to the news report that was practically dedicated to making shifters seem like a species that needed to be completely eradicated. "The extremists might just win this fight and have the laws put in place."

"They won't win the bigger fight," stated Derren. "No shifter is going to allow themselves to be chipped or confined somewhere. All this is about control. It's in our nature to want freedom—we need it."

"You think a war will break out between us and the humans?" asked Dominic.

Derren raised a brow at him. "Would you be prepared to let them take away your freedom like that?"

"Hell no."

"Then there's your answer."

"But the humans *have* to know how bad things could get," said Tao. "They can't be so stupid as to pass laws that will lead to a war."

"Why not?" Derren snorted. "They battle among themselves often enough—much more so than shifters do. And they're arrogant enough to believe they'll win because they know there's a higher population of them than us. What they *don't* know is that not all shifter packs have come out of the closet. There's a lot more of us than humans can even imagine, and many different species of shifter."

Trey exhaled a heavy breath. "The problem is, though, that although we're stronger than them, it won't mean shit in a full-scale war. They have all kinds of fancy weapons. *We* fight with tooth and claw. There's likely to be more damage done to us than them."

"You're right there," said Greta with a sigh. "But spending our time grumbling about it isn't doing us any good. I say we find something to take our minds off it instead of watching this garbage."

"Like what?" asked Tao.

"I don't know . . . something constructive and fun."

Taryn smiled cheerily. "Great, I'll help you pack."

Greta narrowed her eyes at Taryn, who simply shot her another cheery smile.

At that moment, Nick entered the room, and Shaya's wolf lolled onto her side, happy. As always, his presence *demanded* attention. It certainly got Amber's attention, who flashed him a huge smile and patted the chair beside her. But it was Shaya he went to. He carefully lifted her and then took her seat before placing her on his lap. Content, she lounged against him, enabling him to nuzzle her neck.

"How's Eli doing?" Derren asked Nick.

"Wishing he could be up here, part of the action," replied Nick. It was typical of his brother—the guy feared nothing and loved any kind of action. "Other than that, he's fine." Nick couldn't resist licking over the fresh bite he'd delivered to the soft flesh of Shaya's neck earlier. She shuddered, satisfying both him and his wolf.

"When are you going back to work, Shaya?" asked Amber pleasantly, most likely looking forward to Shaya and Nick being separated during the daytime so she could get him alone. Tramp.

"Not until the place is fixed up," replied Shaya just as pleasantly. The insurance company was dragging its heels, which was infuriating Kent.

Unlike with Amber, Kathy's friendly tone was authentic. "Have you thought of applying for another job?"

"That's already covered."

At her mate's shocking words, Shaya slowly turned her head to look at him. "Already covered?"

"Yes. You've already applied for another job."

"What does that mean? And did it occur to you that I might want to keep the job I have?" She couldn't help feeling slightly affronted.

Nick merely shrugged. "If you don't want the other job, you don't have to take it. It's simply an option for you to consider."

"What job?" asked Taryn, curious.

"I'm not prepared to say anything until I'm absolutely positive that the interview process isn't already over."

Shaya frowned. "So it's an interview? Not a guaranteed position?"

Nick cupped her chin. "I know you, and I know that if you want this job, you'll want to have it because you were the best person for the job—not because of contacts I have. Besides, you don't need my interference. I have every confidence in you."

That made things a little different, and hearing he had such faith in her warmed her. "Thank you." Right then, all she wanted was to straddle him again and kiss him hard in gratitude . . . but as usual, they didn't have much privacy, and Shaya wasn't an exhibitionist. "I have an idea."

"If it involves getting naked, I'm game."

She rolled her eyes, despite that her thoughts hadn't been far away from his. The guy could so easily have her pining for him, even if it had only been a matter of hours since he had last been inside her. "Let's go out somewhere—*just* you and me." Of course she understood that Derren would still tag along, but he'd be polite enough to keep a fair distance away and pretend he couldn't hear their conversations.

Nick grinned. "I like that idea."

She whispered low enough for only him to hear. "I can take the butt plug out before we leave, though, right?"

He laughed. "How can I say no when you were such a good girl for me earlier?" They had gone from using fingers to butt plugs and slowly increasing them in size. Some would say it wasn't necessary since, as his mate, she was made to take him everywhere and he'd automatically fit snugly there. Still, he didn't want her in even the slightest bit of pain when he finally took her.

Not so long later, they were sitting in an ice-cream parlor, sharing a caramel sundae. Mostly, though, he just watched—totally enraptured—as Shaya licked and swirled her tongue around the ice cream, wearing a teasing smile, knowing exactly what she was doing to him and exactly how jealous he was of that sundae right then.

After that, they went shopping and—no surprise—Shaya bought a pair of stilettos. No more than twenty minutes later, she'd bought another two pairs. Not that Nick was complaining, since she looked sexy as hell in them. And she'd known just how much she was tantalizing him by modeling them for him in the store. In fact, she'd drawn several male gazes, and naturally, Nick had snarled at every one of those males.

Hours later, they were at a Mexican restaurant, and Shaya was driving him insane by picking at her food like a bird rather than eating it properly. When she'd ignored his insistence that she eat more, he'd given her a look that swore repercussions. Then, figuring she deserved it, he'd teasingly nibbled and licked at her fingers and hand, whispering the things he fully intended to do to her when they were finally home. Flushed and horny, she'd turned a little cranky until she saw just how hard he was. Realizing she wasn't alone in her desperate state and realizing just how well her teasing had worked, she'd gone from cranky to smug.

The time alone had been just what they needed, in Nick's opinion—and not just because he disliked company unless it was Shaya. It was kind of hard to spend time trying to win her complete trust and faith when people were hanging around, depriving them of privacy. He understood why the Phoenix wolves did it; they wanted to be nearby in case they were needed. And, naturally, they'd all missed Shaya since she left their pack, just as Kathy and Roni had missed him. Taryn in particular spent a lot of time with them, and he knew it was because she was deliberately trying to make things hard as hell for him. He could understand it, but it still made him pissed, because not having her best friend's total support was hurting Shaya.

Whether Taryn realized it or not, Nick had never worked as hard for anything as he had for Shaya . . . because nothing had meant as much to him as she did. Sure his mom, Roni, and Eli were important to him, but he *needed* Shaya. Even with his family around him, he'd always felt alone somehow. Always felt slightly apart from them. Maybe he'd created that distance himself because he felt to blame for how damaged Roni was and for how they had all felt the need to leave their original pack after what had happened. On the other hand, the emotional distance could just be a result of his inability to truly bond—he didn't know.

With Shaya, it was different because he didn't want any distance. How could he? She understood and accepted him in a way that no one had done before, not even Derren with his ability to relate to Nick due to their past in juvie. She saw his faults, knew his mistakes, was aware of what he was capable of, yet she didn't judge or fear him. She stood up to him, she kept him on his toes, and she was a living, breathing challenge—Nick had always loved a challenge. She gave him hope that it might be different this time, that for once in his life, he might truly be able to bond with another person. But that all depended on her, on whether she was willing to accept his claim on her, because a bond required both of them.

Having finished their meal, they both left the restaurant hand in hand. They had only taken a few steps into the parking lot when it happened—a *knowing* hit him, a feeling of foreboding, an itch at the back of his neck. Slowing his steps, he stretched out his senses and discovered that there were people lurking . . . but not just in front of him; they were also lurking behind and on either side of him. "Shit." He dug his cell out of his pocket and pressed the speed dial for Derren's phone. Quietly, he said, "We have some visitors. Be careful."

"What's going on?" asked Shaya in a low voice.

He kissed her temple. "Humans. Don't worry, we'll—" That was when four humans began to gather a short distance ahead of them. Another two were then on either side of Nick and Shaya while three more came up behind them. The humans were keeping a fair distance away, but they were also trapping Nick and

Shaya. He recognized a few of them as extremists, and though Logan wasn't present, Nick would bet he was behind the whole thing. He and Shaya were standing back-to-back and being circled by eleven humans.

Any other time, Nick would've felt nothing but bored. He'd handled humans before, and he could handle them again. He didn't relish the idea of harming anybody, but he'd defend himself and his mate in an attack. But this wasn't just an attack. It was a trap—an attempt at provoking Nick into violence. What male, human or shifter, wouldn't turn aggressive at the thought of his female being attacked? But humans wary of shifters wouldn't look at it that way, because it wouldn't suit them to do so.

He knew how Logan's mind worked: The bastard would no doubt produce photographs of his fellow extremists—clawed and bitten and wounded badly—to reporters or the court and spin a nice story to accompany those photographs. As such, when Nick fought these extremists off, something he fully intended to do in order to protect Shaya, he would be playing right into Logan's hands. But there was no other choice, because the very idea of Shaya being hurt wasn't at all acceptable to him or his wolf. The animal was currently growling and flexing his claws, honing his senses on the humans.

Nick was aware that Derren wasn't far away, and he would imagine that the humans would be aware of that too, as they knew Derren accompanied Nick everywhere. He would bet they wouldn't be fazed by that at all—the more shifters involved in the attack, the better for them.

"You should have listened to Logan in the beginning. You should have left town long ago," the human directly in front of Nick said. Hatred swirled in his blue eyes, twisting his thin face into a scowl. "And you *really* shouldn't have pissed off Logan the way you did. So you could say that you brought this on yourself . . . that it'll be your fault your girlfriend's about to be very badly hurt. Don't worry—she might just enjoy what we have in mind for her."

Barely restraining himself from bloodying the prick, Nick realized just how good a trap Logan had set. Logan knew Nick's past, knew what had gotten him sent to juvie. He'd be hoping that if they threatened to do to Shaya exactly what was done to his sister that day, Nick would for sure react. A cunning plan. And it had every chance of working.

Sensing Nick's control quickly splintering, Shaya brushed her hand against the back of his thigh. She kept her gaze trained on the humans in her vision, registering every move they made, fully prepared to defend herself if any one of them took a single step toward her. So far, they had done nothing but glare at her, clenching their fists in an attempt to intimidate her, but that could quickly change.

"I still can't work out whether she's a shifter or not," continued the human. "But if she's going to fuck one, the slut might as well be."

A growl poured out of Nick. Reflexively, he moved to rip the asshole's limbs off, but then there was the sound of the only thing that could have gotten through to him—Shaya's voice.

"Don't, Nick," she said, low enough for only him to hear. She spoke in the same calming tone she used with Taryn and Amber. "He wants you to charge at him so that I'm standing here alone. He's trying to separate us."

She was right, Nick realized as the red haze blurring his thoughts began to disperse. "He called you a slut," he gritted out quietly.

"What's the big deal? I'm *your* slut." Her voice held a tint of amusement.

"You know, coming forward and announcing your existence had to be the dumbest thing your species ever could have done," said the human. "What made you think you would ever be accepted? You're exactly what those religious fanatics say you are—abominations. And you need to be destroyed."

Like Nick hadn't heard this spiel before.

Clearly bugged that Nick wasn't reacting, the human snickered. "Not so brave and cocky now that you're surrounded like this, are you?"

"Don't mistake my silence for fear," Nick told him, vibrating with anger. "I can spot a trap when I see one. I know exactly what you hope to do. Don't worry—you'll get the response from me that you're aiming for. But if you think you'll all get out of this alive, you're very much mistaken."

There was a slight unease in the air that made Shaya smile inwardly. There was no doubting that Nick meant every word. The scent of fear surrounded them, pleasing her wolf, who—though not a fan of confrontation—had every intention of standing by her mate.

"If you know anything about shifters," continued Nick, "you'll know how vigorously we protect females and children. You're threatening my female, you intend to cause her physical harm, and I can't allow that. So if you have it in your head that all that will happen is some of you will go home wounded, you're very wrong. I've killed a human before to defend someone, and I won't hesitate to do it again. If I turn my attention to you, know it means you're about to die. Those who value your life over Logan's plans . . . you might want to step back."

Fear wafted from the human, and it was clear that his snigger was forced. "You're no threat against all of us."

"There may be strength in numbers, but not against a shifter protecting his female. That has a way of amplifying a man's strength. I'd tear apart anyone who tried to hurt her. And she's not exactly an easy target—you should be aware of that before you think of cowardly targeting her rather than me."

In spite of the situation, Shaya found herself smiling. He had never once disregarded her strength and her capability of taking care of herself, had never once treated her as anything but his equal. Even now, while she was in clear danger, he wasn't treating her like a damsel in distress.

"Well, well, well, look what we have here."

At the sound of Derren's voice, Shaya's head whipped to the right, and her brows rose in surprise. There he was, slightly outside the circle, smiling in amusement . . . and recording the whole thing with his smartphone.

"Eleven humans boxing in and intimidating a shifter and his girlfriend—two people who had been minding their own business. Not just humans, but human extremists." Derren shook his head in reprimand. "What will the world think when they see this on YouTube, I wonder."

Three things suddenly happened at once: One of the humans lunged at Derren, making a grab for the cell phone. Nick snatched Shaya's hand and pulled her to the ground, yelling "Down!" as two bullets whizzed past. And the humans all scrambled away into the dark night. All but one, Shaya quickly realized, as she saw that Derren was not only still in possession of his phone, but he also had an extremist by the scruff of his neck.

Derren tipped his head at the human. "I'm thinking he can answer some questions for us."

Shaya didn't enjoy seeing anyone in pain, she really, really didn't. But as she watched with Taryn and Trey as Nick and Derren circled the human tied to a chair in her spare bedroom, she didn't feel in the least bit disturbed to know he would soon be in bad shape.

For one thing, the guy—Lee-Roy was his name, according to his driver's license—was pure evil. He'd spent the past half hour boasting about how many shifters he'd beaten up in his time and about how easy it was breaking into the salon and how much fun he'd had smashing it up. Then there was the little detail that he kept calling her a slut and condemning to hell any "spawn of the devil" she was impregnated with. And why would he be so bold? He was convinced that Nick wouldn't hurt him for fear of repercussions. Also, he was too crazy to be smart enough to be scared.

"It's a shame Dante's not here," said Taryn. The Beta's skills as an interrogator were well known. "He could have this guy singing like a canary in no time."

"We don't need Dante," Trey told her. "A male whose mate has been threatened is a force like no other. That son of a bitch over there would have happily hurt Shaya. Nick will easily have him talking. And he won't let him live long, either."

As Derren studied the gun he held in his hand that he'd found in Lee-Roy's pocket, the human smiled evilly. "If you're thinking that watching you play with it will make me nervous, you're wrong. You won't kill me."

Nick cocked his head at him. "Why would we use your gun when we have these?" The human jerked in surprise as Nick's claws shot out. He barely refrained from slitting the man's throat right then and there. The need for information was the only thing that had kept the human alive to that point.

Still, Lee-Roy shook his head, repeating, "You won't kill me."

Nick crouched in front of him. "I noticed the ring on your finger. Do you love your wife, Lee-Roy?"

The human's eyes bulged. "If you hurt her—"

"That thing you're feeling right there, that clump of emotion . . . Nothing comes close to it, does it? Fear, fury, and desperation all tangled together. That's exactly what I felt when you and your friends threatened to hurt Shaya." Nick's face hardened, and his voice turned guttural. "So don't think for one minute that your life means anything to me. I'll cut your throat without a care in the fucking world, believe me."

Lee-Roy gulped audibly. "The others will know I'm missing, and they'll know you have me. They'll come for me."

Derren smiled, amused. "You really think so? I wouldn't be too sure of that. At this moment in time, you and your friends are all very famous. Yes, that's right. The little video of what happened earlier is on YouTube as we speak. No shifter is going to like that. Every one of your friends now has a big, fat target on their back. They'll do the smart thing and go into hiding from shifters and the police. If your friends can't contact you, they'll assume it's because you're hiding just as they are."

Lee-Roy was silent for a moment, but then he snickered. "My wife won't accept that I'm gone."

Derren *tsk*ed. "Not if she receives some text messages from your cell phone to say that you'll be hiding for a while. She's part of your group, isn't she? She's hardly going to go to the police and announce that you're missing in case they link you with the incident on YouTube. In other words, Lee-Roy, it would be quite simple for you to disappear."

"And considering my mate was shot at," rumbled Nick, "I'd like nothing more than for you to disappear." In fact, Nick was looking forward to it. He knew he wouldn't regret it either.

Looking slightly nervous, Lee-Roy said, "It wasn't me who shot at her."

Nick snorted and got to his feet, beginning to once more circle the human. "Had you been the male who shot at Shaya, you'd be nothing more than a bad smell right now. Trust me on that. I'm curious: Were you planning to attack us *before* you shot us, or had the plan been to just take us out with a bullet all along?"

"Logan told us to take the guns in case you went too wild or we were disturbed."

"And he wanted you to shoot Shaya too, right?"

"Our order was to shoot her if you didn't react." He jumped at Nick's growl.

"Tell us about the game preserve," ordered Nick.

Eyes wide, Lee-Roy gawked. After a moment, he finally spoke. "I don't know what you're—"

"Don't play with me, Lee-Roy," growled Nick. "I really don't know how much longer I can stay calm. Answer me."

"I don't know where it is—we're blindfolded the whole way there." He sounded smug that he didn't have the answer.

"So you've been there?" Derren's question dripped with anger.

Lee-Roy smiled at Derren. "You really shouldn't knock something until you've tried it. It's surprisingly addictive. The shifters are drugged at first—something that stops them from shifting for a little while. Then they're dumped in the middle of nowhere. When they wake up and are finally on the move, a group of us begin to hunt. Slowly at first, not letting them know we're there. Then we amp it up. Guns, knives, whips, sledgehammers—you name it, we use it. They always beg in the end."

*Oh, the sick bastard.* As if he'd sensed Shaya's impulse to slap the asshole, Nick shook his head slightly at her. She knew why: He didn't want Lee-Roy's flow to be interrupted.

"And then they scream," continued Lee-Roy. "God, how they scream. Especially the females. It's one of the perks of working for Logan."

"Youmotherfuckingtwistedpieceofmonkeyshit!" snapped Taryn. Only Trey's hold on her arm held her back.

Shaking with rage, Nick gritted out, "So Logan is the one behind it?" The crazy bastard laughed. "Something funny?"

"Here you are judging me, calling me twisted, when the person who created the preserve is one of your own."

There was a boom of shocked silence.

Finally, Nick spoke. "Repeat that."

"Oh, I was shocked too." Lee-Roy shook his head, incredulous. "I was just as shocked that Logan would associate with any shifter. But this guy doesn't consider himself a shifter—hates the race as much as we do, and he's promised to stand with us against you all."

"Bullshit," bit out Shaya.

Lee-Roy laughed again. "Want to know what's even funnier?" he asked Nick. "You know him." His smile was cruel and taunting.

"Nick, if you don't kill him," rumbled Trey, "I will."

"That won't be necessary. This one's mine." Then Nick sliced open the human's throat with his claw. The bastard deserved much worse than a quick, merciful death, but Nick had already traumatized his sister by unleashing his temper in vengeance. He wouldn't do that to Shaya too. She had a huge heart, and he wanted only to protect it. Worried that even this swift execution had been too much for her, Nick looked at her. There was no revulsion on her face, only concern. For him, he realized. She was concerned that he wasn't calming.

Knowing and hating that Nick expected her to judge him, Shaya went to her mate and curled her arms around his waist. "He deserved worse."

Accepting the paper towel Derren handed him, Nick wiped the blood from his claw and then retracted it. Wrapping an arm around Shaya, Nick breathed her in, using her to center him. "I think the bastard was insane."

"But not a liar," said Trey. "When he said the preserve was being run by a shifter, he was telling the truth. And he wasn't kidding when he said you knew him."

Nick nodded, aware that Trey was right. "That doesn't exactly narrow it down. I know a lot of people."

Shaya looked up at Nick. "But if the shifter's closely allied with Logan, it makes sense that he's local. At the very least, I'd say we can narrow it down to male shifters in Arizona."

"Then we need to get a list of the male shifters residing in Arizona," said Derren.

Nick turned to Derren. "Call Donovan, he'll be able to get that info for us."

"Let me guess," drawled Shaya. "One of your contacts—not your friends." Derren chuckled while Nick frowned down at her.

"The question bugging me is," began Taryn, "why would a shifter hate his own kind?"

Puffing out a breath, Derren shook his head. "I'm pretty sure said shifter wouldn't be dumb enough to let other shifters know about it."

"If we're going with the theory that he's someone local," said Taryn, "you do realize that places Jesse, Bracken, and Zander under suspicion, don't you? I mean, think about it: They've been supposedly standing guard, but they could just be here to keep watch over us. It also means Hadley's a suspect. After all, most of the shifters going missing are from his pack, and he's got a reputation for being a ruthless bastard. Plus, he's got people supposedly guarding you too, people who are just as capable of reporting back to him."

Nick nodded, rubbing a hand up and down Shaya's arm. "When I get the list of names, we can go through them. Until then, we'll be extra careful about what we allow the rebels and Hadley's guards to see."

# CHAPTER THIRTEEN

Watching from his spot on the patio step as the wolf with the salt-and-pepper fur—Dominic—earned himself a swipe from a dark wolf with creamy markings—Ryan—Nick could only laugh. Despite Dominic's wolf's efforts to tempt the other wolf to play, he wasn't successful. Ryan's wolf was much too serious for that, just like his large gray Alpha who was currently watching two jet-black wolves—Derren and Tao—wrestle playfully. Similarly, the red she-wolf and the dark-gray she-wolf—Shaya and Roni—were leaping at one another playfully.

Many of the wolves had decided to go on a short pack run on the land behind Shaya's home, sticking close to the house, but Nick was much too wary to shift while it was quite possible that one, if not all, of the rebels were in fact a threat. Over the past three weeks, he had watched them closely without giving any indication that he suspected them of anything. He'd come to learn that Jesse was surly and militant yet admirably composed. Bracken was flirty and a regular joker, but—unlike a certain blond pervert—he understood boundaries. Not only was Zander one of the shrewdest sons of bitches Nick had ever met, he was incredibly strong and fast. Not one of them had given him any reason to believe that they might be allied with Logan, but Nick wouldn't risk Shaya's safety.

Also, despite that the extremists no longer hovered outside Shaya's home—wisely keeping a low profile—that didn't mean they weren't out there somewhere. When the video of the extremists' attempt to attack Nick and Shaya went on YouTube three weeks ago, it hadn't been long before the footage was featured on the news. Seeing the extremists demonstrate the type of violence, complete with flying bullets, that they repeatedly accused shifters of perpetrating had lost them a lot of support and credibility. Nick knew that Logan would hate that, would blame Nick for it, and he fully expected the asshole to retaliate by going for his only weak spot: Shaya. As such, Nick intended to stay on high alert.

Despite receiving a list of all the male shifters residing in Arizona, Nick was no closer to working out who was behind the creation of the game preserve. The only ones he knew personally were Jesse, Bracken, Zander, Hadley, and a guy called Flint who was born in the same pack as Nick. But Flint was a decent guy, mated and with two pups—it made no sense for him to endanger his own family.

Taryn had said she wouldn't be surprised to find that her father was responsible, that she believed he was capable of just about anything. However, that didn't ring true for Nick. Sure Lance was a bastard—so much of a bastard that he had been responsible for Shaya and her parents spending the first four years of her life packless—but he was known for his disdain for humans. He believed shifters to be the superior race.

Pulled out of his thoughts by a familiar yapping sound, Nick looked to see that his mate was snapping her teeth in warning at a russet she-wolf. *Amber.* It was a clear "fuck off." Shaya might be reasonably patient with Amber, but her wolf sure wasn't. Normally, a submissive wolf wouldn't even entertain the idea of displaying such antisocial behavior at a dominant, but that wouldn't mean shit to her wolf while she viewed the other female as a rival—her possessiveness and jealousy would drive her to make her point. The russet she-wolf stood tall, growling low at the red she-wolf in an attempt to intimidate her. And what did his mate do? Lifted her head haughtily and turned her back on the dominant female, swishing her tail in her rival's face for good measure—dismissing her with utmost contempt. He could only chuckle. But then the russet she-wolf growled again and moved toward his mate. Before he had the chance to react, his sister was there, blocking her path. She curled back her upper lip, displaying teeth and gums, at the threat to his mate. Roni was much more dominant than Amber, and they both knew it. Wisely, the russet she-wolf loped away.

"It seems the bitch has a sense of self-preservation," commented Taryn as she sat beside Nick. "I find myself disappointed."

"You're not going on a run with Trey?" Nick asked her.

"There's no point. Kye should wake up from his nap soon. Why, trying to get rid of me?"

He snorted, turning his gaze back to his mate. "There's no such luck. But I have to admit I don't much like talking to you."

"Why? I'm a very nice person."

"Because it's like being arrested—everything I do and say can and will be used against me."

She laughed. "How are things going with you and Shaya?"

He snorted again. "Like you don't watch us like a hawk and quiz Shaya ten times a day."

"She won't tell me why her submissive status is suddenly no longer an issue for you. It makes no sense. According to Jaime and Dante, when they spoke to you about it, you insisted you couldn't claim Shaya."

Nick shrugged. "I changed my mind."

"Huh. What did you do with the diaper?"

He threw her an exasperated look. "Don't you have anything better to do than irritate me?"

"But it's fun."

He rolled his eyes. "On a serious note, must you really try to make things difficult for me where Shaya's concerned?"

"Yup. You weren't the one who held her while she cried, Nick. What you did devastated her." She cocked her head, eyebrow raised. "What, nothing to say to that?"

"I don't have to explain myself to you, Taryn," he reminded her. "Shaya, yes. But no one else."

"She's my best friend."

"Then be her best friend and support her instead of making things hard for us." When Taryn went to contradict him, he asked, "Remember that time you came to my old territory to see your uncle? Remember how he behaved toward Trey? Don's your uncle, and you love him, but when he was an ass to Trey instead of being supportive in your choice of mate, what did you do? You chose Trey over him. You put Trey first, because that's what mates do. Don't put Shaya in a position where she feels she has to choose." He wasn't just saying that because he worried she'd choose Taryn. He hated to see his mate hurting in any way. "Support her."

"I am supporting her." But he could tell that Taryn was now realizing that her behavior had, in fact, been anything but supportive. "I told her I'd give you a chance."

"But you haven't. You're determined to hate me. To be quite frank, I couldn't give a shit what anyone other than Shaya thinks of me. But it's hurting *her*. And I know that's something you'd never want to do."

Taryn was silent for a moment, which was new. Then she turned perceptive eyes his way. "Do you care about her? I don't just mean as your mate, the person who's made for you—it's instinctive to be fond of your mate. I mean do you care about Shaya the person?"

He looked again at the red she-wolf, watched as she bounded around with Roni. "Yes. It's kind of hard not to."

Taryn tilted her head, conceding that. "True. Do you know why she's holding back?" Her tone communicated that she did. He knew Shaya confided in her a lot.

Nick sighed heavily. "She thinks I'll suddenly decide I want a dominant female and then leave her."

Taryn's expression morphed into one of surprise. "She told you?"

"No. I've come to learn how her little mind works, realized how many insecurities she has—it isn't surprising, given how her own mother constantly puts her down. I've told Shaya over and over that she's all I want, but another thing I've come to realize about her is that words mean shit to her. The only way she'll believe me is if I *show* her that she's all I want." Although Nick wasn't sure what more he needed to do to convince her he was sticking around.

After a short pause, Taryn sighed. "I guess it's fair to say that you've been pretty perseverant up to this point. But if you get what you want and she gives in, will you suddenly feel bored? That's *my* question."

Nick gestured at the snippy red she-wolf, who was now approaching him—even her walk was sassy. "How could I get bored with all that sassiness?" The wolf came to stand between his bent knees, nuzzling his hands. Taking the hint, he began to pet her. Apparently the wolf didn't like that another female was sitting so close to her mate, because she snapped her teeth at Taryn.

The Alpha female gaped. "Hey! Not cool."

Smiling in amusement, Nick continued to happily stroke his mate and rub his face against hers. She licked at his chin and then snuggled up against him.

"I didn't expect her to be that possessive." Taryn looked at them curiously for a minute before releasing a sigh of resignation. "Fine. I'll stop being a pain. Not that I'll stop coming around here—I want to be here for her. But I won't poke my nose in or be a bitch. However . . . know that if you hurt her I'll shove a beer bottle up your ass, use your sphincter to twist the top off, and laugh along with everyone as you scream in absolute agony."

"People would find that amusing?"

She shrugged one shoulder. "Well, I'd be laughing."

When the she-wolf gave his chin another lick and then trotted inside the house, followed quickly by Roni, Nick guessed his mate was going inside to shift and get dressed.

"She'll make a good Alpha female."

It took a few seconds for Taryn's words to sink in. He looked at her oddly. "What?"

"Are you going to let Kent join your pack too? I heard him talking to Shaya on the phone, saying that he'd happily—"

Nick held up a hand. "Whoa, whoa, whoa. What're you talking about? I haven't started a pack."

Her smile was sympathetic. "You kinda have, sweetie." She paused to nod at Derren as he came—now back in his human form—to sit at Nick's other side. "You know, I wouldn't be surprised if my uncle asks if he can switch from the Ryland Pack to yours. It's safe to say your brother will definitely join."

"There's nothing to join."

"Are you sure?" Taryn raised a brow. "Because if you count you, Shaya, Derren, Kathy, Roni, Amber"—said with a growl—"Jesse, Bracken, and Zander . . . Hmm, looks like the beginnings of a pack to me. By the time Roni and the unmated shifters have all found their true mates, your numbers will be—"

"Enough." Beyond exasperated, Nick sighed. He didn't have the patience for this. "Derren, you deal with her."

Derren shrugged. "Taryn's right. This is virtually a pack."

"I know you think you can't make Shaya your Alpha female without endangering her," began Taryn, "but it truly wouldn't make any difference if she was a dominant female."

"What do you mean?"

"I mean that, yes, it will put her in physical danger, but it's no different for me. In fact, I'd say it's worse for me. The fact that I'm powerful makes a lot of dominant females consider challenging me—defeating me would quickly and significantly bump up people's opinion of them. Shaya would be in similar danger if she was dominant."

Huh. He hadn't thought of it that way before. Nick wasn't sure how he himself felt about being an Alpha again, but he knew that his wolf would leap at the challenge. He was born to lead; it was what he did best, and it was what he enjoyed doing. But his wolf wanted Shaya more than he wanted any position, just as Nick did. "In any case, I don't think she'd want to be an Alpha female."

"You won't know unless you talk to her about it. One thing I know for sure is that she'd make a better Alpha female than many I've known."

Nick could agree with that. Still . . . "My aim right now is to win Shaya's total trust. If we decide to form a pack, it can be something that comes much later." With that, he stood up and headed for the kitchen, intending to make some coffee.


With Nick out of earshot, Taryn turned to Derren. "Am I right in thinking that part of his problem is that he doesn't want to share Shaya?"

"Yup. Plus, Nick prefers being alone." Derren sighed. "If he had his way, the two of them would be holed up somewhere together and no one would ever bother them. But that's never going to happen. Nick's strength draws people to him, always has and always will. If you had seen the way he organized all the groups in juvie . . . Even the older ones followed him. There was only one guy, Merrick, who wouldn't—Nick had to challenge him, and though he never meant it to go that far, he killed him. Nick never elected himself as leader, never tried to be one, but everyone made him one. And I'm going to do the same now. If he won't take on the position, I'll make him do it in my own subtle way."

"He's not going to like it," said Taryn, but she was smiling. "How can I help?"

As her mom did her woe-is-me routine complete with degrading comments, Shaya was wishing she hadn't answered the phone. Feeling guilty for the fact that she had completely ignored her mother's calls for the past two weeks, she'd answered it . . . and now she was close to smashing her own phone. While Gabrielle Critchley was still ranting, Shaya placed her cell phone on the bed and pulled on her blue denim cutoff shorts and strappy black top. Unfortunately, her shifter-heightened hearing meant that she could hear every word clearly. Once Shaya had slipped on her black stilettos, she retrieved her phone. Time to end this quickly and cleanly.

"Mom, I know but"—she faked a static noise—"I have to"—another noise—"Something must be wrong with my"—more static—"I can't hear"—more static—"I'll call you tomorrow and—" Then Shaya ended the call with a sigh of relief.

She was just heading for the stairs when the bathroom door swung open and a strange female wrapped in a white towel walked out. Both of them froze, gasping. Shaya was just about to demand to know who the hell this woman was when she realized that the dusky green eyes were very familiar—eyes that were just like Nick's. "Roni?"

She gave Shaya a wobbly smile. "Yeah. Hi." Tucking the long, wet, ash-blonde ropes behind her ear, she cleared her throat. "Um, I sort of need clothes. I can ask Amber—"

"No, no, it's fine." Recovering from her brief moment of shock, Shaya pointed behind her. "Just follow me to my bedroom." Once inside, Shaya closed the door behind them and gestured to the bed. "Take a seat."

Gingerly, Roni perched herself on the end of the bed and gave Shaya a slight smile.

"It's nice to meet you properly."

"Yeah," chuckled Roni—it was a rusty sound, suggesting she hadn't made it for a while. "If I'm honest, I hadn't thought about shifting back to my human form until you talked with me a couple of weeks ago. The things you said stuck with me, played on my mind over and over."

Shaya couldn't figure out whether Roni found that a good thing or a bad thing. If she was anything like Nick, the girl was the type to hold her cards close to her chest. "You and Nick really do need to talk. He thinks you stay in your wolf form a lot because you're haunted by the memories of what happened—it breaks his heart and makes him feel awful. But it's not that, is it? You're haunted by a senseless guilt that you're responsible for the downward spiral his life then went on."

"Perceptive," said Roni, catching the hairbrush that Shaya threw to her. "I didn't realize he felt guilty. That's stupid." Dragging it through the tangles, she continued, "How could he think I was anything other than grateful for what he did for me?"

"Nick's not exactly great with understanding 'feelings.'"

Roni nodded her agreement. "He never has been. I'd be bad with emotion too if my wolf had surfaced so early. His mind wasn't anywhere near ready for it, was introduced to a stage of life that his development simply wasn't equipped to deal with. Can you imagine that? As young as he was, he found it hard to cope, and his wolf was so angry and cold. Having to deal with that at any age would be hard. I know because my wolf became so angry after what happened that day in the woods, but she healed."

But Roni hadn't, Shaya knew. "Nick's wolf didn't heal?"

"With my wolf, the anger was tangled up with trauma. With Nick's wolf, it's not trauma. He was born in anger, and it shaped his personality. You can't 'heal' someone's personality. You can change it to some degree, but not heal it."

Shaya retrieved a long-sleeved T-shirt and a pair of jeans from her wardrobe and laid them gently on the bed. "They should fit you fine."

Roni fingered the soft material of the white top as she quietly confessed, "I'm nervous about going downstairs and facing all those people."

"How long has it been since you were last in this form?"

"About six months."

Wow. "And that's by choice? Your wolf doesn't hound you to stay in wolf form?"

"Oh no, she's quite happy to stay in that form for months at a time, but she doesn't fight the change. She understands there has to be a balance."

Right now, it wasn't a very good balance in Shaya's opinion. There wouldn't be one until Roni healed. "The lingering guilt . . . it'll get better . . . but only if you want it to. Sometimes we cling to the guilt because we think we deserve to suffer. That's not the same as being truly guilty of something, is it?"

Roni frowned thoughtfully, but she didn't answer.

"It's not that you need to forgive yourself. It's that you need to realize there's nothing to forgive."

"Have you forgiven Nick for not claiming you in the beginning? It wasn't that he was abandoning you. If you had seen the state he was in when his cognitive functions started degenerating . . . It was horrible. We all panicked, scared we'd lose him. I remember the day he first met you. He came home that night, and he was in the foulest mood. He told me about you, about how it had killed him to leave you behind. I've honestly never seen him look so upset—not even when he was sentenced to time in juvie. Not even the times we went to visit him there. When he met you, he was in the middle of his healing sessions and his future was so unsure; he didn't want to be your patient. I think he also worried that if he claimed you and then slowly became someone you didn't even know—worse, someone who didn't know *you*—you would then hate him."

"Idiot."

"Yeah, but Nick's a good person. The best. He'll drive you insane sometimes because he's stubborn and likes having his own way, but he'll do everything he can to make you happy."

Shaya couldn't deny that—he'd been doing it since he first turned up, wanting to claim her. He guarded Shaya with a ferocity that was more than protectiveness and possessiveness. It was in his tone, his posture, his gaze, and the way he liked to tuck her into the cradle of his shoulder, sheltering her while communicating "mine." The intensity of it all made her feel totally safe and secure while still not stifling her on any level. And although Nick wasn't, by any means, soft-shelled and could be quite cool and remote in general, he could be indulgent, thoughtful, patient, warm, and unselfish with her. He was safe and solid—exactly what a submissive wolf needed, exactly what Shaya wanted. "I have forgiven him. How could I not?"

"But you still haven't allowed him to claim you."

"Like I told Taryn, I worry he'll decide he wants a female who matches both his physical and inner strength."

Roni considered that for a moment before speaking. "I know you probably won't want to hear about Nick's past, but you should know that he never sought out only dominant females; his past flings include submissive wolves too. Status was never something that was an issue for him. He never treated any of those females the way he treats you—never looked at them like they were all that mattered. You could fix him, Shaya. But you could also break him totally. And don't forget, if he wanted a dominant female that badly, he could have claimed Amber." She said the female's name through clenched teeth.

"You guys aren't really friends, then?"

A snort. "No, she hangs around me to get to Nick."

"You know what I don't get? Nick is a really astute, observant person, yet he's never—until now—picked up that Amber wants him."

"Ah, but she's been clever," Roni said. "See, he was very clear to all the females that he'd never imprint with anyone. Many of them tried to seduce him into changing his mind, but Amber's approach has been to become close to him in another way. To wriggle her way in by first becoming his 'friend'—although if you were to ask Nick, he'd say he doesn't have friends, because he doesn't realize that people naturally like and look up to him. Anyway, she obviously hoped they could be friends and it would grow into something more. It hasn't worked, because Nick doesn't bond with people easily. He's grateful that she's good to me, but he doesn't realize that she's good to me just to impress him and earn his loyalty and a spot in his life."

Shaya folded her arms across her chest and cocked her head. "Does she care about Nick?"

"Yes, I think she does. And it can't be nice to watch someone you care about with someone else. I'd imagine it's agonizing. But if you mate with Nick, she won't try to steal him from you. She's not delusional; she'll know that the claiming has solidified the mating. And if she cares deeply for him, she'll back off and wish you both luck. If not . . . well, just be careful. Whether we like it or not, she's physically stronger than you, and she'd love to hurt you."

Shaya smiled. "That's okay. I'm good with a bat. And if all else fails, I can always show her my knife trick."

Roni grinned. "You and I are going to get along *so* well."

Wondering why Shaya was taking so long, Nick intended to go upstairs in search of her—followed closely by Amber, who was jabbering on about something or other. When he reached the hallway and heard footsteps on the stairs, he was expecting to see Shaya. His mouth dropped open at the sight he found. "Roni?" Reaching the bottom of the stairs, she smiled a little awkwardly, as if unsure what reception she'd receive. He pulled her into a huge hug. "Hey." When her arms went around him, he swallowed hard. Seeing Shaya smiling at him, he mouthed, "Thank you." He didn't have to ask to know that she had something to do with it.

Shaya was enjoying watching Nick and Roni chattering away and doing that sibling teasing thing . . . until Amber came to her side, making her automatically tense slightly. Her wolf bared her teeth.

"It's so amazing," said Amber, gesturing to Roni. "We don't see her in her human form often. Even when she changes, she often keeps to herself. It's great to have her being sociable like this. Thank you." She laid a hand on Shaya's arm, the image of sweetness.

Shaya patted Amber's hand a little patronizingly. "You're so welcome." Amber didn't like that. Ha.

At that moment, Taryn, Trey, Dominic, and Tao entered the hallway and stopped dead, growling. Shaya quickly realized they weren't too happy to see Nick hugging another female. "Guys, this is Roni." Like that, the growling stopped. One by one, they each came over and greeted her.

Then Roni did the oddest thing. She cocked her head at Dominic and slowly made her way to him. Stopping in front of him, she scratched a nail over his collar almost tantalizingly. A mixture of surprised and curious, he smiled. In the same tone Dominic reserved for his cheesy lines, she said, "Are you religious? Because you're the answer to all my prayers." After giving Nick a conspiratorial wink, she then waltzed away, presumably to find Kathy. Well, it seemed that Roni was getting some payback for her brother.

Wide-eyed and gaping, Dominic pointed at her retreating back. Turning to Shaya, he spluttered. "She just—" He shook his head. "Did you hear—?" He exhaled heavily. "Dear God, I hope she marries me." As he ran after her, they all laughed.

Nick held Shaya against him. "She'd eat him alive. What you'll soon learn about my sister is that she can handle just about any guy. I've yet to see her tongue-tied or blushing—she's resistant to charm."

"Oh, you don't need to worry about Dominic." Tao shook his head. "He'll tease your sister and flirt with her, but he'll never touch her."

"What makes you so sure?"

"Because it's clear that she's someone he could like as a friend, and Dominic doesn't sleep with girls he likes."

Shaya realized that Tao was right, and she was about to comment when Nick flinched beside her. Seeing his face scrunched up in pain, she asked, "Another headache?" He'd been having at least two a day lately. No doubt it was due to the strain of being unable to locate the preserve or find out the identity of the shifter who was running it.

He pinched the bridge of his nose, squeezing his eyes shut against the blinding pain. "It's okay. I've got some pi—"

"Here, let me help." Amber stopped in front of him and went to touch his head, but a pointed look from Nick made her freeze.

"No."

She sighed. "Don't be stupid, Nick. You're in pain."

"It's no big thing, leave it."

"Why would you want to suffer?"

"I have some pills upstairs. I'll be fine."

She turned to Shaya, huffing impatiently. "Tell him, Shaya. Tell him to stop being silly. You don't want him in pain, do you?"

Oh, now that was smart. And cunning. And made Shaya want to kill the bitch. Of course she didn't want her mate in pain. To tell Amber to stay away from him when she could heal him would be cruel and petty. Shaya was backed into a corner, and there was no other answer she could give. "It's fine, Nick."

"No, it's not," he immediately countered. He knew *exactly* what Amber was doing.

Taryn stepped forward. "I can heal him, if you want."

"*Nobody* is healing me. Leave it." Pulling away from Shaya and simultaneously avoiding Amber's attempt to touch him, he made his way up the stairs.

"He'd sooner suffer than let me touch him?" Amber's expression turned sulky.

Taryn pursed her lips. "Well . . . I'm liking Nick a little more now."

Rolling her eyes at that, Shaya followed him up the stairs. Hearing someone coming up behind her, Shaya turned when she reached the landing. "Everything okay?" she asked Taryn, who looked shifty and unsure—totally unusual for the Alpha female.

"I'm sorry."

Shaya frowned. "For what?"

"Being a bitch to Nick all the time, and trying to get in the way." Taryn came a little closer. "At first, I was doing it because I wanted him to put in all the effort you deserve. But then I carried on doing it because I was trying to punish him a little for hurting you. Best friend or not, I had no right to do that to your mate. And I sure as hell would have hated it if you'd behaved like that with Trey."

Smiling a little, Shaya rubbed her upper arm. The whole thing had been bugging Shaya to the extent that she had almost snapped at her friend a couple of times. The only thing that had stopped her was the knowledge that Taryn's heart was in the right place. "It's okay. I know why you did it. I know you meant well."

"That doesn't make it fair, though. I just hate how badly he hurt you."

"Yeah," sighed Shaya. "But I hurt him badly too. Just like Trey once hurt you badly and Dante once hurt Jaime badly. It happens when you're in a relationship. They can get complicated and difficult because people can be complicated and difficult. But imagine how different your life would have turned out if you had rejected Trey because he hurt you. You guys wouldn't be so happily mated, and you wouldn't have the adorable little boy sleeping downstairs."

Taryn nodded. "I just wanted to say I'm sorry, and that it's going to stop."

"Thank you." Shaya hugged her best friend tightly, feeling a weight fall from her shoulders.

"You should know something. I talked to him earlier. . . . He knows you worry he'll leave you for a dominant female."

It annoyed Shaya that her mate was so astute. "It's only natural for me to worry," she said defensively.

"I don't think it is. You're an amazing person, Shaya. Why would you think that you're not good enough for him exactly as you are? Look, I know your mom's done a number on you, and I know that what Mason did made it all ten times worse, but don't let it mess this up for you. Don't let *her* and Mason make you hold back from Nick. I wouldn't root for him if he hadn't just told me he cares about you. You deserve to have that."

Shaya scrubbed at her forehead. "I want to trust him. I just . . . I don't know how. I honestly don't know how to totally trust another person. I trust you about as much as I'm capable of trusting someone. But Nick . . . he's my mate, and he'll want more than that, it's only natural. I just can't yet."

Taryn was silent for a moment. "Okay. Just think about what I've said. Oh, and you should probably know something else too. Derren has every intention of making Nick into an Alpha and forming a pack."

Shaya smiled a little. "I can't say I'm surprised."

"It would make you an Alpha female, if you mated with him. Would you want that? Don't say you couldn't manage that position. You could, and you know it."

"I don't really know how I feel about that yet."

"Then I guess that's something else for you to think about. And now I hear my son crying."

"Go. We'll talk again later." As Taryn skipped down the stairs to tend to Kye, Shaya trailed after Nick, knowing he had gone into the bathroom to retrieve some of his pills from the cabinet. To her surprise, she found him lounging in the bathtub, eyes closed. His lids lifted when she shut the door behind her.

"Hey, baby." Nick tried to play it down as he always did, but his pain was even in his voice, which was undoubtedly what made Shaya wince.

"You should have let Amber heal you," she admonished quietly, knowing his hearing was always sensitive when he had one of his headaches. Having kicked off her stilettos, she crouched beside the tub and dipped her hands in the hot water. "I admit I don't like her touching you. But I prefer *that* to you being in pain."

Yeah, well, he preferred the pain to her being upset at seeing another female touch him, especially Amber. "The headache's already fading." When she began massaging his temples, he groaned and closed his eyes again. "Now I understand why my dad used to lock himself in his room when he had one of his headaches." Every little noise was like a hammer to his head.

"I don't like how many pills you take a day. It can't be good for you." The feeling of helplessness plagued her and her wolf. "What can I do?"

"Come here. You're better than any pill." Slipping a hand behind her head to tangle in her curls, he gently brought her face to his and slowly took her mouth, sipped from it, licked at it, and sucked on her bottom lip. Tightening his hold on her hair, he tugged hard and, without breaking the kiss, slid deeper into the water, effectively urging her inside the tub. She compliantly followed as he'd known she would, coming to straddle and drape over him. Needing her skin against his, he slid her top up and over her head and removed her bra. Then he flattened her upper body to his, feeling her pebbled nipples stab his chest. Releasing her mouth, he ran a hand through her curls. "So beautiful." She blushed cutely.

Massaging his scalp with both hands, Shaya lightly kissed him. Hoping to distract him from the pain, she said, "May I just note for the record that it would be great if you could stop leaving bite marks all over my breasts? Most of them are in spots that are easily visible to others."

A self-satisfied smile spread across Nick's face. "I was marking them as mine. And I like looking at your breasts and seeing my brands right there, just as I like knowing that if anyone else *dares* to look at them, they'll know you're taken."

The latter word sounded so final and absolute—a balm to her lingering insecurities and her worry that he would leave her alone again. "It would also be great if you could give the dozens of marks on my inner thighs time to fade before leaving any more. I can hardly wear a bikini when I look like I've been assaulted."

"You won't be wearing a bikini unless we're alone. No, baby, I've seen how skimpy your bikinis are. As much as I approve, I'm not going to deal well with other guys drooling over you worse than they already do."

"There has been no drooling. That's just you being paranoid and possessive."

She really didn't see how beautiful she was, and Nick didn't understand it. "Believe me, they look, and they drool. Not that I can blame them." He skimmed his hands up and down her back, clutching her close.

"I'm too thin and pale," she contradicted, echoing Paisley's claims. They weren't insults she hadn't heard before—her mother informed her of this on a regular basis.

Nick gave her a stern look. "No, you're perfect. The most perfect thing I've ever dared to touch. Every single inch of you is delectable, especially this." He slid his hands inside her cutoff shorts to cup her ass. "It's every guy's fantasy." So many females these days didn't seem to have an ass; there was nothing to hold and clutch and squeeze. But the one in his hands . . . Perfect.

"The one who gets drooled over is *you*," she insisted. "And it's freaking annoying."

"I wouldn't know about that. My attention's always on you."

That would have sounded like a pathetic, kiss-ass comment if it wasn't for the fact that Shaya knew it was true. His focus *was* always on her. When he did notice another female was ogling him, he would touch Shaya or pull her close, as if to reassure her that *she* was the one who mattered to him. She hated that she needed that reassurance so much, but a part of her would always be locked away until she felt she could totally trust him.

As she started to shift away, Nick could feel her emotionally withdrawing a little. "Why do you hold so much of yourself back, Shay?" he asked softly, tightening his arms around her to keep her close. It was another thing he had come to learn about her. "You don't just do it with me. You can bond so easily with people, but you never give them all of you. Why?"

It was disconcerting just how well he could read her. "When I was sixteen, I met this guy, Mason. He was ten years older than me."

His wolf growled, not liking another male's name on her lips. Nick didn't like it much either, but this was important. "Go on."

"He had all the right words, said exactly what a sixteen-year-old girl with an empty space inside her would want to hear. If I hadn't felt so starved of a connection, maybe I wouldn't have fallen for it, maybe I wouldn't have let him convince me we were mates. I wasn't the first girl he'd done it to. The weird asshole had a thing for virgins. When I realized I'd given my virginity to a complete asshole, I hated myself and I swore I'd never be that naive again. I became pretty distrustful and wary, not intending to give so much of myself again unless it was my true mate— someone I was confident wouldn't betray me."

As guilt and shame slithered over him, Nick's eyes fell closed. "I don't know who I'm angrier with—me or Mason." He kissed her neck. "As much as you avoid deep connections, it's what you really want, isn't it?"

Yes, it was. She had been her own worst enemy, really—craving a soul-deep connection but at the same time avoiding forming one because she didn't want to risk feeling the pain of losing it. "I want to feel indispensable to someone."

His hands framed her face, seizing her gaze. "You're indispensable to me—essential to me on every level. I wouldn't be here, suffering the company of your old pack and listening to some pervert constantly hit on you with cheesy pickup lines if you weren't."

She would have chuckled if his mouth hadn't mashed with hers. "You know, I once shook hands with Jaime on a plan to get a gun and assassinate you." Without moving his mouth from hers, he laughed. "And I planned on getting 'Nick Axton Is a Fuck-Ass' tattooed across my forehead. It was just that . . . when I found you, it was terrifying and electrifying, pain and pleasure, and then . . ." And then utter agony when he'd walked away. When he looked about to apologize, she put a finger to his lips. "It's okay. Roni told me how hard it was for you to walk away that night."

Hearing her be so understanding actually made it worse. "Fate should have given you someone better than me."

She gave him a look full of censure and disapproval. "You're a deserving person."

He cupped her chin. "If you really believed that, you'd want me to claim you—I'm not bringing it up to push you, I'm just pointing out an important fact. You're beautiful and perfect, and you deserve better. Any shifter would be proud to have you. But none of them can have you—you're mine, even if you don't want to be."

Before she could say a word, his lips were on hers and his tongue was shooting into her mouth, sweeping away any intention of speaking, any intention of telling him he was wrong and she *did* want to be his, of easing the hurt in his voice. His hands cupped her ass again, pulling her tight to him. Even through the denim, the feel of his hard cock against her clit made her gasp. Sliding her hand between their bodies, she fisted him and began to pump, making him groan.

Pulling back, Nick stared at her red, kiss-swollen mouth . . . and had only one thought going on in his mind. "Tell me . . . whose mouth is this?"

Shaya swallowed hard. "Yours."

"That's right. It's mine." Swiping his thumb across her lips, he met her eyes. "I want this pretty mouth wrapped around my cock, Shay."

It wasn't a request, she knew. And it vibrated with enough dominance to make both her and her wolf quiver.

"I want you to step onto the mat, take off your shorts, and dry yourself off. Can you do that for me?"

Nodding, she did exactly as he asked—all the while, he held her gaze, refusing to let it go. Then he stepped out of the tub and she patted him dry, their eyes still locked. Abruptly his fingers tunneled into her hair as his tongue drove into her mouth, stroking her own. As always, his kiss took her over, demanded everything from her but at the same time gave her everything back—a give and take that she wouldn't have expected from this alpha male who could at times be so remote and distant with others.

"I want your mouth now, Shay." With the hand knotted in her hair, he pushed down gently but firmly on her head.

Shaya slowly went to her knees, finding herself level with one hell of a hard-on. Knowing that she could induce this response from such a darkly sensual male sent a sizzling thrill through her body.

"Clasp your hands behind your back." Without moving her eyes from his cock, she did as he'd asked; the action elevated her breasts the way he liked. Tightening his hand in her hair, he said,

"Lick it." Without hesitation, she ran her tongue along the length of his cock from base to tip and then lathed the head. Christ. "Open your mouth." The second she did, he eagerly surged inside, and the feel of her hot mouth surrounding him was too good.

She was his living, breathing sexual fantasy. She was always game for whatever he wanted to do, always eager to please him, and always trusted herself to him. It was the one time that she didn't hide or hold back from him. Her cheeks hollowed as she repeatedly took him into her mouth, dancing her tongue along his shaft as she did. "Fuck, that's it. Look me in the eye, baby." Her gaze flicked to his, searing him. "I'm going to fuck you, Shay. I'm going to fuck you so hard. Do you want that?"

Shaya paused in her sucking to nod. His eyes flashed with approval.

"Very good." He traced the outline of her mouth. "You're going to scream for me when my cock is in you, Shay."

Yeah, she most certainly would, she thought. She always did. As she began sucking harder while cupping his balls, his face scrunched up in a kind of pleasurable agony.

"Fuuuuuuck." Close to the edge, Nick roughly speared his free hand into her hair so that both his hands then held her captive. He angled her head slightly and held her still as he pumped his hips. She didn't fight him; she stayed still other than to scratch her nails along his thighs. Then she moaned around his cock, and he couldn't take any more. With a guttural groan, he exploded into her mouth. "Swallow it all, baby. All of it." It was another way to mark her, another way for her to accept that she was his to mark.

When Shaya felt him begin to go flaccid in her mouth, she pulled back and sat on her heels, peeking up at him.

He rubbed a hand down his face. "Christ. That was too good, baby." Again, he traced her mouth. "Now get up and sit on the edge of the tub while I take the rest of what's mine." It wasn't until he'd licked her to orgasm twice that he sat back and lifted her, impaling her on him fully. When he exploded inside her, he came much too close to claiming her right then, consequences be damned. Not because of how possessive he felt or how determined he was that she accept that she was irrevocably his. But because he realized just how much he'd come to care about her, knew he was nothing and no one without her. He really couldn't let her go, and he hoped to God she didn't ask him to. He'd give her anything she wanted, but not that one thing.

# CHAPTER FOURTEEN

W aking up at dumb o'clock to find Shaya draped over him on a diagonal angle, Nick might have smiled if it wasn't for the pounding on the bedroom door. Carefully rolling a sleeping Shaya onto her side, he pulled on his jeans and made his way to the door. Opening it, he found an edgy-looking Derren. Stepping outside the room, Nick quietly closed the door. "What is it?"

"I just got a call from Donovan. He hasn't found the location of the game preserve yet, but he's managed to track down the place where the extremists hold their meetings. I'm guessing they're mostly just 'we hate shifters' chats, but it might be worth attending one."

Later that evening, they did just that. From his spot in the wooded area surrounding the isolated warehouse, Nick closely watched the people gathered in the open building, waiting for the meeting to begin. Derren, Trey, Tao, and Dominic were squatting near him, studying the place just as intently. The great thing about their shifter senses was that they didn't need to get close to hear and see what was going on.

Dominic shook his head in disapproval. "It's wrong to bring kids to something like this."

Tao looked at him incredulously. "It's wrong to *do* something like this."

"You know what I mean—if someone's going to become a prejudiced shithead and go to meetings like this, they don't need to pass on that ignorance to their kids and drag them along."

Derren nudged Nick. "Hey, the blonde on the front row . . . Isn't that the girl who works in Kent's salon?"

Seeing that he was right, Nick nodded. "I guess it's a good thing that Kent and Shaya kept the fact that they were hybrids from Paisley."

Shaya hadn't been at all happy when he'd asked her to remain behind, but she'd been placated by his promise not to act on anything he heard or saw at the meeting. But he guessed that if Taryn hadn't agreed to remain behind, it wouldn't have been so simple to make Shaya do the same. Jesse, Bracken, and Zander had wanted to come along, but Nick had needed to know that she was closely guarded. Although Taryn was still slightly wary of them, Nick's gut and his wolf told him they weren't involved. It had only been later that Nick realized he'd given the rebels an order and they had obeyed him like he was their Alpha. Groan.

"Logan is walking to the podium," announced Trey. The humans clapped at the sight. "He doesn't seem too happy, oddly enough."

Nick shrugged. "He probably doesn't like that what he did was plastered all over the Internet and TV."

When Dominic shifted to lie on his side with his head propped up on one hand, casual as anything, Nick frowned at him. "What are you doing?"

The pervert's expression was all innocence. "There's nothing wrong with getting comfortable."

"Is he always like this?" Nick asked Trey and Tao. They both nodded, sighing.

Logan raised his hands, gesturing for silence. "Friends, thank you for coming. Your dedication to our cause and your unfailing attendance hasn't been unnoticed. You'll see here the leaders of three local groups. Tomorrow night, there'll be another. Yes, that's right, the groups that are most local to the Sequoia Pack are banding together. And every single one of us will be ready—ready to finally act, ready to finally take on the responsibility of ridding the world of the abominations among us when they attack."

Trey growled. "The prick's basically formed an army."

"If I know Logan like I think I do," Nick said, listening to his gut again, "he won't stop at destroying the Sequoia Pack."

"And that could trigger a domino effect, make other human groups do the same," Derren pointed out.

"We all know that they will never consent to being chipped," continued Logan. "Nor will they accept a life of being confined to their territories. They had the chance to do that without our knowledge, but no, it wasn't enough for them. They announced their existence and tried to infiltrate our communities, mating with our race and breeding hybrids. How many men and women have lost their partners because they believe they're a destined match for animals? How many of our people have been lost to these 'packs' that are more like cults? How many more need to be attacked or raped and forced to produce offspring for these animals before the government acts?" There were a lot of supportive murmurs.

"So he doesn't know that shifters can only reproduce with their mates," mused Derren.

Trey snickered. "There's a lot the humans don't know. Many of them don't bother to find out—too eager to fear and reject us."

Logan held his hands up in a helpless gesture. "Let us be realistic—a war is inevitable. When the hearing is held in two days' time and the verdict comes back in our favor, the shifters will be enraged and begin to attack our communities. We must be prepared to defend our town, prepared to protect our people." The crowd was getting riled now. "We have gathered enough weapons to make that possible. Unified with several other groups, we have the numbers we need."

"But what if the hearing doesn't give the verdict we want?" another extremist asked, nervous and awkward.

Logan's smile was truly unpleasant. "Then *we* attack. If the government refuses to act, we will do it alone. We will wipe out the Sequoia Pack and, most importantly, the small assembly of wolves living here in a local house. The group is run by an extremely dangerous shifter, one of the most dangerous I've ever encountered. He once murdered one of our own, and yet he walks the streets. As if that's not bad enough, he is trying to mate with a female of our race and has drawn her into his cult. The shifters in her house have been gathering in number—it is clear that they plan to attack if the verdict goes in our favor. When that happens, we'll be ready. And if it doesn't happen, we'll make it happen."

Back in Shaya's dining room, Nick held her in front of him—her back to his chest—with his arms curled around her as he relayed Logan's speech to everyone. As he sensed her anxiety increase, he was sure to run his hands through her hair or trail his fingers up and down her arms or lick over his mark—anything to soothe her and her wolf.

When Nick was finished talking, there was a momentary silence. Then everyone seemed to be talking at once, and his mom and Greta were suggesting finding where Logan lived and burning him alive.

"You have to come back to California," Taryn said to Shaya. The Phoenix wolves all nodded their agreement. "You have to get away from those psychos."

"I'm not letting anyone run me out of my own home." Shaya set her jaw and lifted her chin. Yeah, pride could be a dumb thing but, dammit, she was sick of feeling the need to run from other people. Maybe it was time she dealt with it differently. "They're the ones with the problem. Why should *I* be the one to leave?"

Taryn appealed to Nick with a look. "*You* talk to her."

Shaya had fully expected Nick to back her up on this one . . . but he didn't, the asshole.

"I say we leave."

She snorted at her mate. "So you can keep me safe from Logan?" His overprotectiveness was freaking annoying at times.

Sensing that he'd nicked at her pride, he lightly toyed with her curls. "It's not just that. Yes, it will mean I get to know that you, Roni, and my mom are safe"—his sister and mother didn't appear to like the protective move either—"but it will also mean dividing the huge group of humans."

Mollified slightly on realizing there was more to his decision, Shaya asked, "What do you mean?"

"From the things Logan said, he isn't going to be happy until Nick's dead," Derren replied for him. "If Nick leaves town, he'll follow. Sure, many of the humans will follow Logan. But many of the humans have grief with the Sequoia Pack, and they won't be so concerned with a group of shifters who aren't even in their town anymore—they'll see us as the problem of whichever extremists live in the town we then head to."

"Divide and conquer," drawled Tao, nodding in approval.

"I can warn the Sequoia Pack about the planned attack." Nick tucked his head into the crook of Shaya's neck. "That will give them time to gather any contacts—I'm guessing the Nazi has plenty of them and they're all plenty dangerous. They can deal with the humans who remain when Logan leaves, and I'll deal with Logan."

"*We'll* deal with Logan," corrected Derren. "You're not alone in this. Don't forget, Nick, you're not the only one set on seeing that man dead."

Nick nodded. "Fine. Now we have to decide where we lure them to. I was thinking—"

Taryn snorted. "We lure them to our territory."

"You can't be serious." Nick shook his head. "This problem isn't yours. You would risk your home, the safety of your pack?"

Another snort. "Of course I wouldn't. But Shaya *is* pack to me. More importantly, *she's family*. I won't risk her safety. That makes this just as much our problem as it is yours. As far as I'm concerned, there's no safer place than our territory."

Anticipating that Trey would insist his pack stay out of this mess, Nick turned to the Alpha. To his surprise, the male nodded his agreement. Nick's wolf was impressed and pleased.

"She's right." Trey cuddled his sleeping son closer against his chest. "We've stepped up the security measures. The place is now tougher to get inside than Fort Knox."

"So we're going to lure the humans there . . . but hide?" Roni frowned, looking confused and disappointed.

When an evil smile surfaced on Trey's face, Nick understood where his thoughts had taken him. "You intend to let them think they've breached your territory. You want to let them inside, seal up the opening so they can't get back out, and deal with them on your own turf." Trey's smile turned even more evil. The guy was just as ruthless as everyone said. Nick's wolf approved.

Amber didn't appear convinced it would work. "They have guns."

"And we have Ryan," said Trey. "The guy might only be one man, but he's like a fucking ghost. Add in Jaime—who can sneak up on anyone without being sensed—and you have a way of moving in on the humans before most of them even know they've been discovered."

"And let's not forget that Shaya is an excellent marksman." Taryn smirked.

Nick turned his mate's face to his. "A marksman, huh?"

"My dad was a Navy SEAL, remember. He taught me stuff."

Roni cocked her head at Trey. "How large is your pack? I heard it was a relatively small one."

"It is. And I can't seek support from my alliances as there may be extremists planning to attack them too—they need to be with their packs in case that happens. So there'll only be us."

"From what we heard at the meeting, it's just Logan who intends to attack without provocation," Tao reminded Trey. "The other extremist groups are simply on guard in case shifters attack first."

Trey nodded. "I know, but do you think Nick would ask Jon to stand beside him in this war and risk his old pack—which still includes his brother and Taryn's relatives—being adequately protected?"

Nobody responded, because the question didn't need addressing: Nick definitely wouldn't risk his old pack.

"Then there isn't any other choice but to take care of this shit ourselves." Trey shrugged.

Dominic sighed. "Yep. We can't afford to just hide and ignore what the humans have planned."

That was true, Nick could concede. He didn't relish the thought of having more blood on his hands, but they couldn't allow the humans to live and do the damage they intended to do, particularly as it would inspire other extremists to act in the same way. This was about more than just them. What decision they made would affect the lives of many shifters.

"Their large number doesn't worry me," said Taryn. "They'll be on our territory where our rules apply, and whereas we know that land well, they won't have a goddamn clue how to get to us. Even if that asshole Logan forms a huge army of extremists and turns up at the gates of our territory, he's as good as dead."

"He's as good as dead anyway," growled Derren.

"Then we agree that if he follows, it isn't a problem." Taryn and Derren exchanged nods.

Trey spoke then. "Their deaths will send a message too. Logan, boastful as he is, will have told his plans to the other extremist groups. When his gang of armed humans enters shifter territory never to be seen again, it won't be forgotten."

"Um," began Jesse, "what about me, Bracken, and Zander? Do you want us to keep guarding the house while you're gone?" he asked Nick and Shaya.

"I assumed you were coming with us," said Derren, grinning.

Nick was ready to object, but the rebels were grinning as wide as Derren, and Nick didn't have it in him to disappoint them. They clearly wanted to be part of this, and he guessed they would rather stand with the shifters here than with the Nazi. Still . . . "If you guys want to come, that's your choice. But everyone needs to be clear that I'm not forming a pack."

Derren waved a dismissive hand, all reassurance. "We're all aware of that."

If Shaya hadn't known about Derren's plan to make Nick into his Alpha, she would have bought that act. She wasn't yet sure whether she wanted the plan to be successful or not. On the one hand, being an Alpha was natural to Nick and would make his wolf content. On the other hand, Nick had been loaded with responsibilities for a very long time. If he wanted a breather, he deserved one.

While the others continued discussing the extremists, Nick turned her in his arms and brushed her hair from her face. "You're thinking very hard about something."

"Just wondering what to do about the house. I mean, are we going back to California for good?"

Pursing his lips, Nick shrugged. "That's up to you." He had never felt bonded to any particular place—not even to the land where he'd once been Alpha. As such, neither he nor his wolf was being tugged in a direction other than Shaya.

"No, it's up to *both* of us." If the idiot wasn't making decisions for her, he was handing them completely over to her—unreal. It struck her then that being a partnership was uncharted territory for Nick. As Alpha, he'd been used to making decisions alone and putting what everybody else needed before himself. She didn't want him always putting her needs first. A relationship was about finding middle ground. "It has to be something that works for us both."

"I know that, baby, but I don't see the point in being fussy about something that means more to you than it does to me. I don't feel drawn to any particular place. Maybe you do."

"Actually, no. I've always wanted to travel. My dad used to tell me stories of all the places he'd been, and I'd always wanted to see them when I was old enough to go traveling."

"Then maybe you'll be happy to finally learn what the job you've applied for is."

"Go on."

"Dean Middleton is soon retiring from his position as one of the wolf shifter mediators. If you want the job, it'll mean you'll need to travel a lot." In Nick's opinion, no position would suit her better.

Shaya could only gawk. Then she was smiling widely and wrapping her arms around him. "Thank you!" It was, in fact, a job she would love.

"Dean's contract doesn't run out for another four weeks," he told her when she released him, "so you have time to still go through the interview process. I'm confident they'll adore you and decide you're best for the job."

Clearly Shaya's delight had caught Taryn's and Derren's attention, because they both appeared. "What's going on?" asked Taryn.

Excited, Shaya told them. "I would love it." And it would give her a sense of purpose—another thing she would enjoy having. Grateful, she snuggled against Nick.

Taryn nodded approvingly at Nick. "Good call, Axton. I actually wouldn't have thought of that, and I've known her for forever."

"What kind of mate would I be if I didn't know her inside out?" Nick dropped a kiss on Shaya's head.

"An Alpha female as a mediator," drawled Taryn. "Even better."

Nick shook his head in exasperation. "How many times do I have to say it? I'm not starting a pack. You're almost as bad as . . ." Nick stopped, frowning. His mouth repeatedly opened and closed, but the name of the guy he was talking about, the guy in front of him who he had known for a long time, wouldn't come out. It wouldn't come out, because he couldn't remember it. He reached for it again and again, feeling like it was on the tip of his tongue . . . but it didn't come. His wolf growled and instantly began pacing, knowing this wasn't good.

Shaya frowned in confusion, unsure what was wrong. "Hey, you okay?" Nick looked at her, but he didn't answer. He seemed to be struggling with something. Totally baffled, she turned to Derren and raised a questioning brow. The guy was pale. What the hell was going on? "Nick, what is it?"

Nick shook himself out of it, determined to hide his panic from Shaya. How could he not panic? The memory lapse was a too-familiar feeling—a sign that his cognitive functions were again degenerating. That could only mean one thing . . . a thing he had dreaded and feared and hoped would never happen. And there was really only one thing he could do if he wanted his mate—the only thing that mattered to him—to live a full, happy life: leave that life.

His wolf didn't agree with Nick's decision, as the animal was too elemental in his way of thinking. Shaya was his mate, she was his, and so Nick must claim her—things were really that simple to his wolf. As such, he was raging with Nick for his decision to leave, pacing, growling, tearing into Nick with his claws. But Nick ignored his protests. This wasn't something he would budge on, no matter how much it enraged his wolf, or how much it would hurt them both to do it.

Forcing a smile for Shaya, Nick kissed her gently on the mouth, wishing he could deepen it, take his time, and enjoy this one last taste of her. But his Shaya wasn't stupid; she would know something was wrong, would sense the desperation in that kiss. Worse, she would insist that he stay, would demand that they face this together because that was who she was. So fucking brave and with such a big heart and a stubborn will.

He didn't want her to one day find herself looking into the eyes of a person she had mated with and seeing nothing of that person there. He didn't want her to spend her life without someone being there for her, loving her, and caring for her. She had already lost her twin, had been through enough. She needed and deserved to have somebody who could take care of her, not for it to be the other way around.

"I just remembered I haven't let Bruce out of the motor home for some air today." Most likely because he was uncomfortable being in a house full of strange shifters, Bruce preferred to stay in the motor home most of the time. "I'll be back in a minute," he added, running his finger from her temple to her jawline, needing to touch her, needing that contact . . . and bracing himself to give it up.

Suspicious and, for a reason she wasn't sure of, suddenly anxious, Shaya nonetheless nodded. "Okay."

"I'll be back in a minute." He took one last moment to drink in the sight of her, drink in every single detail of her face, despite that each one was already committed to memory—a memory that would disintegrate until it eventually didn't include her. The idea of that was enough to put a lump in his throat.

Ignoring his wolf's raging, Nick forced another smile for her and then strolled out of the house. It hurt to do it. Hurt to do the one thing he'd sworn to her that he'd never do. Hurt to know he'd never again see her, never again hear her laugh, and never again experience the calm that only she gave him. But he'd do it for her. And it *was* for her, though he doubted she'd see it that way.

He hadn't been inside the motor home for more than five seconds when Derren abruptly barged in. "What are you doing?"

Nick threw Derren an impatient look. At least he could remember his name again. "Is that a serious question?"

"I thought you didn't want to leave her."

"I don't. But I won't fuck up her life."

"Don't you think Shaya gets some say in this? Or don't you think you owe it to her to at least consult another healer?"

"If a healer as strong as Amber can't help, no one can. And you know it."

Derren bowed his head, inhaling deeply. When he looked up again, there was pain in his expression. "If you run, you'll lose her forever, Nick. She'll never forgive you."

"I'd rather she hated me than for her to watch me slowly become someone I'm not, become her patient. That's not a mate." And at least this way, she would remember him as he was. "The upside of leaving is that I'll lead Logan away from her. No doubt some of his followers are still watching from a distance. They'll see me leaving."

"I'm coming with you."

Nick shook his head. "No."

A snort. "Surely you've learned by now that arguing with me over this gets you nowhere."

"I want you to stay with her," he said through his teeth. "I want to be sure that she's safe." He trusted Derren with her.

Arching a daring brow, Derren folded his arms across his chest. "If you want to be sure she's safe, stay."

*Son of a bitch.* "Why are you doing this?"

"I'm your friend, and I don't want you to make a mistake you'll regret for the rest of your life."

Nick snickered. "How could I regret anything when I probably won't even remember her after six years or so? It would hurt her to see that happen."

"So you're going to cut and run?"

Hearing the new voice—a female voice filled with hurt, betrayal, and fury—Nick squeezed his eyes shut. He'd been so wrapped up in his own panic that he hadn't sensed her come in.

Shaya advanced toward them, arms folded. It hadn't taken a genius to work out that something was seriously wrong, particularly when Derren had dashed out after Nick. So she'd followed and remained outside the motor home, eavesdropping on the conversation between the two males. A part of her was hurting for Nick, sympathized with him, and even understood why he had made this decision and why he believed this was his only choice. But the other part of her was too torn up and felt too betrayed to give a flying fuck—he was her *mate*, he'd sworn that he wouldn't abandon her again, and now he was going back on his word. Her wolf wasn't angry; she was too busy freaking the fuck out, panicky and anxious.

Without moving her eyes from Nick, she gritted out, "Derren, leave."

The authority in her voice made Nick's wolf stop in his pacing, surprised. Even more surprising, Derren's wolf didn't appear to have bristled at a command coming from a submissive wolf. Nor did Derren; he coaxed Bruce to follow him out of the motor home and closed the door behind them . . . leaving Nick alone with a totally pissed-off female wolf who looked ready to bloody him—again.

Shaya smiled bitterly. "Here you are again making decisions for both of us, deciding what's 'best' for me and leaving me, all in the name of that."

"Are you telling me you wouldn't do the same if the situation was reversed?"

Okay, yeah, she probably would, but while she was hurting this badly, she wasn't concerned with being fair. "If I want to be here for you and stick by you through all this, then that is *my* choice."

His face hardened. "I'm supposed to protect you, Shay. I'm supposed to protect you, care for you, and be a pillar of strength for you. It shouldn't be the other fucking way around."

A snicker. "Sounds like pride talking to me."

Yes, his pride was taking a huge blow, but that hadn't been what he'd meant and she knew it. "I can't give you what you need," he said quietly, his voice gravelly with emotion.

"You promised me," she hissed.

"Shay—"

"*You promised me.* You swore you wouldn't leave me again! I trusted you!"

"That was before I knew I wasn't healed. And you've *never* really trusted me, Shay."

The sadness in those latter words made her want to cry. He looked and sounded so lonely, and it broke her and her wolf inside. "You don't get to do this. You don't get to make this decision for me. I *choose* to stand by you through this."

"Why? So you can watch me slowly deteriorate and become someone you don't know? Well fuck that. I *choose* to not make you go through that." And then she was punching the shit out of his chest. He locked his arms around her, grunting through clenched teeth as she dealt his ribs blow after blow. After a minute or so, she finally stopped. She didn't move away, kept her forehead leaning against his chest as she tried to calm down, panting and clenching her fists. He gently kissed her hair, loving the softness of it and knowing he'd miss it.

She didn't look up at him when she spoke. "I'll hate you forever if you go now."

Cupping her face, Nick lifted her gaze to his. "I would rather you despised me than for you to be without a mate. I wouldn't be a mate, Shay. I wouldn't even be someone you knew." He ran the pad of his thumb across her bottom lip. "You deserve better than me anyway. You always knew that. It's why you don't want me to claim you."

No, it wasn't; she *did* want him to claim her. And maybe she hadn't known exactly how much she wanted that until right then, but it was true. She had come to trust him as much as she trusted Taryn—which was saying a *lot*—had come to depend on him, and had come to finally accept his place in her life. And now he wanted to leave. Not a chance. If the situation had been reversed, nothing would have made Nick leave her. He would never have made her go through such a thing alone; he'd have supported her every step of the way. She'd be damned if she'd behave any differently. He was hers. Ill, healthy—it didn't matter. And if he didn't like her decision, he could kiss her wolf's furry ass.

Dropping his hands from her face, Nick stepped back. "I need you to go inside now, Shay."

Her eyes flared with defiance and anger. "No."

Nick sighed. "Baby, please—"

"No."

He arched a brow at her. "Don't make me put you unconscious again, Shay. If that's what it takes, I'll do it. You know I never make a threat I don't intend to follow through on."

That was true. And fighting him off wouldn't be easy; he was bigger and far stronger, and Shaya knew from past experience just how capable he was of taking her on. But she'd made her decision, and she'd stick to it. All she had to do was get close to him. Of course that was a little difficult right now while he was on guard, braced for her to fight him. Still, there was more than one way to skin a cat—or a wolf, in this case.

Just as she had that first night he came when he'd cuffed her wrists, she played the miserable victim accepting of her fate. "Can I at least get a hug before you leave me again?"

Guilt pierced his chest. "Come here."

*Worked like a charm.* Fixing a desolate look on her face, she stepped into his open arms, which curled tight around her. She buried her face into his neck, being sure to sniffle.

Another arrow of guilt shot through Nick. "It's for the best, baby. Really. I know you don't think that right now, but it—" He flinched as her teeth sank down hard into the juncture of his neck and shoulder. "*Fuck*." As she sucked hard on the mark she was leaving, Nick quickly realized she wasn't marking him one last time. Shaya was trying to claim him.

# CHAPTER FİFTEEN

"Shay . . . Shay, you have to stop." She really, really did, because the sensations crawling through him and over him were threatening Nick's self-control. His wolf, his body, his soul—they all rejoiced in what she was doing, and they wanted one thing, and one thing only: to claim her right back. So did Nick, but he knew better, knew he couldn't keep—

He groaned as she sank her teeth deeper. "Shay . . ." Then the tricky bitch was tearing open his fly and fishing out his cock. He sucked in a breath at the feel of her soft hand wrapped around him. He was hard and hot and aching, and she was fisting him with a possessive grip that was making him forget why he wanted to fight this.

Tangling a hand in her hair, he tugged hard in an attempt to dislodge her. She was having none of that. She simply bit down harder until she drew blood, growling. And God, that fucking possessive growl made the whole thing worse. His wolf approved of her strength, of her defiance. Nick yanked harder on her hair this time, but it was like she'd locked her jaw because he couldn't make her release him. Then she was pumping him faster, stealing more and more of his control with each stroke, and sucking on the bite in time with her strokes. If he didn't stop her, if he didn't make her release him, there wasn't a hope in hell that she'd leave this vehicle unclaimed. "Shay, *stop*," he ordered.

The depth of authority in his tone almost made Shaya falter. Almost. This was her mate. He was *hers*. And he wasn't going anywhere. When he tugged again on her hair, she responded by increasing the pace of her strokes, and smiled inwardly at the sound of his sharp intake of breath. She could sense his resolve weakening, could sense his temptation to claim her slithering all over him, and could sense just how little self-control he had left. It thrilled her wolf to know she could do this to him, to have this power over him. *Submissive, my ass.*

When the hand she'd knotted in his T-shirt released him, Nick peered down and watched as she opened the snap of her jeans and slid her hand inside her panties. Christ. Then she made that moaning sound that drove him fucking crazy. "Shay . . ." It wasn't a sound of complaint or censure anymore. It was a plea for mercy. He was drowning in the sensations she was causing and the primal urge to *take*, to own, to claim. "Baby, you have to—" His sentence was cut off as the hand she'd jammed down her pants rose and inserted one wet finger into his mouth. Her taste exploded on his tongue. *Fuck.*

In seconds, Nick had shredded her jeans with his claws, lifted her in his arms, slammed her against the wall, and thrust deep inside her. She released his neck with a shocked gasp, raising determined eyes to his. He held himself still, searching for the control to withdraw, because if he fucked her right now, he'd claim her. No question.

Anger . . . he needed anger—it was a fuel that had always worked for him in the past. He didn't have to dig for it, not while both he and his wolf were already raging at fate. His hard gaze drilled into hers. If he had to make her detest him so that she'd leave, then that was what he'd do. "Why would you want this, baby? Because you feel sorry for me? Because your conscience is

telling you that it's what you should do? I don't want your fucking pity. I don't want you."

Did he really think she wouldn't know what he was doing?
*Pfft.* Shaya was well aware that he wanted to piss her off, to drive
her away, to make her hate him enough to run out of this motor
home and never look back. What an idiot. "I want this because I
care about you, dumbass."

"Care about me?" He didn't have to force the snort—that
was something he truly didn't believe. "Nothing I've done since
I got here has meant anything to you. Nothing. The only reason
you gave me a chance was because you felt bad about going on
a date—a date you never would have gone on if you cared—so
don't give me that shit."

She ran her fingers through his hair. "It won't work, Nick.
You won't push me away."

It pissed him off that she'd seen right through him. That
didn't mean he'd give in. "I already have pushed you away. I did
it the second I found you by ignoring you instead of claiming
you. It put up a barrier between us, and that barrier will always
be there, no matter what."

She shook her head. "Not true." That barrier had come down
weeks ago, she now realized. She'd just been too bowled over by
her insecurities to take this final step. Faced with the idea of him
leaving, she realized that being without him would actually hurt
more than if she took a chance and it didn't pay off.

"It is, and you know it." When she writhed and her pussy
tightened around his cock, Nick grasped her hips hard to still
her. "We never had a chance of making this work—you knew
that from the beginning, I just didn't want to accept it. But you
were right; I get that now, and I'll leave you to live your life just
like you wanted."

She gave him a gentle but self-satisfied smile. "It's too late,
Nick. I've claimed you. It's done." She didn't think she'd heard
of a submissive wolf being the first one out of a pair of mates to

lay claim. The idea of that made her smile widen. Oh yeah, not only had she claimed a dominant *alpha* male before he'd claimed her, but she was now going to totally seduce that alpha male. This was a story to pass down to the grandkids—when they were old enough to hear it, obviously. Taryn was going to love it.

"It means nothing if I don't accept that claim. *And I don't.* Do you hear me?" Nick went nose to nose with her. "I don't want you." His wolf took a swipe at him for that. Nick didn't blame him.

"Yes, you do," she softly insisted, sliding her hands over his tense shoulders. "The truth is that the one misguided here is you. I claimed you for the right reasons. You're trying to push me away for all the wrong ones." She clenched her inner muscles around him, satisfied by his thick groan. "You want this, Nick. Stop fighting it."

"Shay."

It was a tortured plea that made her chest ache. "We'll find a way to stop what's happening to you. There are other healers out there. But you have to be prepared to battle it instead of rolling over onto your back and accepting it. Some dominant male you are."

He growled. "Taunting me?" Even his wolf didn't like that.

"Just pointing out a fact. No dominant male—especially a born alpha—would give up like this. But you are; you're doing it. If you're a dominant male, act like it."

"I'm not going to fall for that." Not when it concerned her well-being.

"And I'm not going to fall for your attempts at making me hate you."

He shrugged. "Stalemate." She squirmed slightly and, Christ, it was like his brain shut down for a second. Then a rush of her cream bathed his cock, wrenching a guttural groan from him. When she went to squirm again, he tightened his grip on her hips and warned her with a look. "Don't fucking move." He was too close to losing it.

"I can't help it." She truly couldn't. Figuring some dirty talk would help, she said, "I need you, Nick. I need you to claim me."

So did he; he felt like he'd go out of his goddamn mind if he didn't.

"Please, Nick." Oh, he appeared to like the begging. Ha. "Please, I need to come."

His eyes flared at her. "You should have thought about that before."

She raised a daring brow. "Then punish me."

"Dammit, Shay."

Seeing how well her efforts were working, she smiled inwardly. "Shall I lick you clean when you're done?" His cock jerked inside her, and his hand abruptly collared her throat.

"Don't think I won't make you. They're brave words, baby, but I don't think you could back them up."

"Is that one of the plans you said you had for my mouth?"

Nick squeezed his eyes shut, cursing. The sly little bitch was good at this, pushing all the right buttons.

"We'll fight it, Nick."

The sensitivity in her voice made him open his eyes; ones full of determination and arousal were staring back at him. "You're stronger than anyone I know."

Seeing that the fight had almost gone out of him, she pressed in a whimper, "Come on, Nick. Fuck me. Do it like you own me."

"I do own you," he said through clenched teeth, feeling his control slipping away, feeling her pulling him into a place where there was only Shaya and the need to claim. His wolf was urging him to give her what she wanted, to make it clear to her once and for all that she belonged to him and ensure that she could never dispute it again. Never had Nick been balanced so precariously on the edge of his control. When she drew his tongue into her mouth and sucked on it eagerly, it naturally had him remembering her sensual lips around his cock. Shit.

"Prove it."

"You know what will happen if I do." He'd claim her and she'd be tied to someone who—

He groaned as she again squirmed. More of his control slipped away.

"I don't care, I want this. I want you to claim me. Now, Nick, I need to come. Please."

With his mate's gaze holding his, offering everything she had and everything she was, the will to fight this any longer left him. His worries and his reservations left him. All that mattered was Shaya and finally claiming what was his.

Growling, Nick slammed his mouth down on hers, eating at it, plundering it with his tongue. She went pliant under the assault, making him growl approvingly into her mouth. Pulling back, he bit her bottom lip hard enough to draw blood. "How bad do you want to come?"

Relief and triumph surged through Shaya, invigorating her. The uncertainty and anxiety had disappeared from his eyes; there was now only pure male need blazing at her. It thrilled her wolf just as much as it did Shaya. "Bad." She gasped as he cocked his hips, giving her a shallow thrust.

Extending his claws, Nick easily stripped her of her top and bra. "I'm going to fuck you hard, Shay." He rotated his hips, putting pressure on her clit until she whimpered. With one hand still gripping her hip, he let his free hand roam over her body. "But you're not going to come." He clutched her ass and shifted her angle, flexing his cock inside her and making her gasp. "You're going to fight it until I say you can come."

Oh that so wouldn't be possible, not while she was hanging on the edge. Not while the need to be claimed was like a fever in her blood. "Nick—"

"You taunted me, baby," he reminded her, pinching her nipple just right until she released that amazing moan. "You can't taunt me and expect to get away with it. And you tried to take the dominant role here too, didn't you? Tut, tut, tut. You knew I wouldn't like that, you know I like to have the control. To make matters worse, you lied to me."

"I didn't—"

He cut her off with a hard, punishing thrust. "Oh, you did. You told me you wanted a hug. But you wanted to get close enough to claim me, didn't you? You tricked me." He shook his head in reprimand, thumbing her clit once. "I can't have that."

Seeing his eyes blazing with resolve and heat, Shaya knew that this mating was going to be every bit as rough and hard and explosive as the claiming between true mates was reported to be. It would be no-holds-barred. The idea excited and unnerved her in equal measures.

Leaning forward, Nick licked the crook of her neck. "I'm going to mark you right here." He sucked at the spot. "Here, where everyone can see it, so that everyone knows you're mine, that you belong to me. So everyone knows this pussy belongs to me, and only I can have it. Do you understand that? Only I can have you. Say it."

Shaya swallowed hard at the authority pouring from him, heating her entire body. Her wolf was melting from it. "Only you can have me."

"That's right. Very good." He rewardingly cupped her breast with the right amount of pressure, knowing what she liked. "No one else will ever be inside you. And if anyone even tries to touch what's mine, I'll strangle them with their own spleen." And then he was powering into her at a frantic pace, staring into her glazed eyes, not letting her look away. She clawed at his back as if trying to anchor herself, tearing into his T-shirt and branding him at the same time. Her legs squeezed him so tight that her heels dug into his ass, which only spurred him on. When he felt her inner muscles begin to flutter around him, he snapped, "Fight it."

Shaya whined. "I can't."

"But you will."

Before Shaya knew it, he'd jerked her away from the wall, withdrawn from her, lowered her to her feet, and then spun her around. Suddenly she found herself facing the small table of the dinette. Nick sucked on her earlobe. "Bend over."

If anyone else had spoken to her with that amount of authority, with such expectation of her total and utter submission, she would have scoffed at their order and slapped them. But not with Nick. Never with Nick. He'd earned her submission on every level. She knew she could never have given up this depth of control to anyone but him, could never have been this comfortable with anyone else, or felt this safe with anyone else.

"Don't make me repeat myself, Shay."

Shivering at the dominant growl, she obediently bent over and gripped the table. The cool of the wood against her breasts made her gasp. When a hand abruptly came down hard on her ass, she jumped.

"That was for ignoring me when I told you to fight your orgasm, trying to escape your punishment." Again he spanked her ass. "That was for almost taking my head off with a baseball bat—oh no, baby, I haven't forgotten about that." He made the third spank extra hard. "And that was for going on a date with the web designer and almost tearing my heart out of my fucking chest." He lightly massaged the prints he'd left on her ass, blowing on them. Then he drove one finger inside her and swirled it around, loving the look of her bent over, submitting to him and finally fully accepting that she was his. "Christ, you're so wet."

Withdrawing his finger, he ran it to her puckered hole and circled it teasingly. "This is another place I'll be claiming soon, baby." They had been slowly getting her ready for it. "Very, very soon. But right now, I have other plans." He knotted a hand in her hair, snatched her head back, and buried himself inside her in one long, smooth stroke. They both groaned. Her pussy clamped down on him, tight as a fist and so fucking hot and wet. Folding over her, he spoke into her ear. "Remember: Don't come yet."

As he suddenly began pounding into her, bliss tinged with relief rocketed through Shaya. *Finally* he was taking her. It was wilder than the other times he'd been inside her—more intense, more uninhibited, more everything. His pace was literally feverish as he fucked in and out of her. With him blanketing her body and pinning her in place, all she could do was take it. The feel of the denim of his jeans rubbing against the sensitive skin of her ass heightened the other sensations. The tension inside her kept building and building, making it more and more difficult to hold back her orgasm.

"Are you ready for me to claim you?" She nodded, releasing a broken moan of assent. Nick's voice was almost harsh as he continued. "You know what it'll mean, Shay, don't you? I won't let you go. Not ever. Not for anything or anyone. There'll be no more holding back from me—I won't stand for that. I want everything that you are, everything you can give. Can you handle that?"

Shaya gave him a sideways glance. "Only if I get the same."

Nick grinned. There was that sassiness he loved. "That's my girl."

As he licked the crook of her neck, Shaya's entire body tingled in anticipation. Her claws shot out, making deep grooves in the cherry wood table.

"Shall I let you come now?" When she began to sob, Nick frantically slammed in and out of her, wrenching loud cries from her. "That's it, baby, let me hear you. You know how much I love hearing those noises you make." He slid his free hand around her body, finding her clit and circling it with his finger. "Come. Now." She did; her pussy clutched and rippled around him as she screamed his name, making him explode inside her. It was right then that he bit down hard and deep at the crook of her neck, sucking hard and licking so that there was no mistaking what that mark was to her or to anyone else: the ultimate irrevocable brand, a claiming.

A zing bowed Shaya's back as a sharp pain lanced through her head, but it was quickly gone and replaced with warmth, and calm, and a sense of "home." She'd never felt so safe, so sheltered, so utterly complete—and maybe that meant so much more to her because she had felt so broken her entire life. Not now. The cold loneliness was gone—she could feel him inside her and surrounding her. There was only her bond with Nick, and it was much stronger than she would have expected. Not totally complete, but it was by no means weak. Maybe it was because they had both wanted this for so long, or maybe it was because the claiming had been a total surrender on both parts. She didn't know, and she was too content and at peace to ponder much over it. She wondered if this was what it felt like to be high.

Drawn to the mark on her neck like it was all that existed, Nick licked it again and again, filled with self-satisfaction and elatedness and a sense of completeness. He could *feel* what Shaya was feeling—it was the same things that he himself was feeling. His wolf felt at peace for the first time. Oh, he'd always be moody and remote in many ways, but he no longer found the world so bleak. How could he when Shaya's warmth was filling the empty spaces inside him?

A dark voice whispered in Nick's mind, reminding him of why he'd been fighting this, but Nick wouldn't let fear creep in and fuck with this. He'd do what Shaya said, he'd battle this with everything he had. And now he had the biggest incentive possible—his mate's happiness depended on him winning that battle.

"I'll be right there with you the entire time," said Shaya.

Yeah . . . this sensing his feelings thing would take a little getting used to. "I know." He kissed her mark, licking over it one last time before standing upright. Surprised to find that he was steady on his feet considering that it felt like his whole world had tipped on its axis, he slowly withdrew from her and stepped back. When she, too, was standing, she turned to face him and smiled up at him—a free, easy smile he'd never seen before. "I hope you meant it when you said you could handle this, Shay, because I'll never let you leave."

"Same here, Beavis."

"For the millionth time, I'm *not* stupid." Before she could tease him further, he loosely collared her neck with both hands and shook her playfully. She laughed—a sound as free as her smile. And he knew right then that he'd do whatever it took to keep hearing that sound and seeing that smile.

Half an hour later, Nick and Shaya returned to the house, where she quickly dressed in fresh clothes . . . clothes that were then removed so he could be inside her again. They then made their way downstairs to find that everyone had gathered in the backyard. Nick could only gape at the sight. Many of the shifters were swimming in the pool while music was playing and lots of food was being passed around. Nick turned to Shaya. "They think this is a summer camp or something, don't they?"

Shaya could only smile at the consternation on Nick's face. He'd apparently had enough of their constant company and was on the verge of snapping. "Guys? Guys?" Finally they all turned to look at them both, smiling. Then eyes zoomed in on the claiming marks, and everyone was talking at once.

"*Finally*," drawled Derren, grinning, from his sun lounger.

Simultaneously, Roni, Kathy, and Amber hopped out of the pool and all hurried over to hug Shaya and Nick. Not liking even the thought of another female with her hands on Nick—particularly when said female coveted him and was only dressed in a skimpy bikini—both Shaya and her wolf wanted to slash Amber's face. But Shaya pasted on a smile, settling slightly when Nick stepped away from Amber and curled an arm tightly around Shaya before kissing her temple.

Trey, Tao, Bracken, Jesse, and Zander came over to pass on their congratulations, shaking Nick's hand and merely nodding at Shaya—they weren't dumb enough to hug her right now. From her spot on a lounger, Greta raised her teacup and smiled. Shaya tensed the second Dominic came over, knowing he had no sense of self-preservation. But he wasn't wearing his usual flirty smile.

When Nick growled warningly at the blond pervert, Dominic raised his hands in a gesture of peace. "I only want to pass on my congratulations like everyone else. I won't lie—I had my reservations about you, Nick, but Shaya's a good friend of mine, and I want her to be happy. If you make her happy . . . well, that's good enough for me." He offered his hand to Nick, who slowly shook it. Dominic then gave Shaya a nod, just as the others had.

"So just like that, you're fine with this?" asked Nick, skeptical.

Dominic shrugged. "I learned a lot about you today. Not really personal stuff. But your mom talked about you a lot, told me how you pulled through for your old pack at a time when they needed you, even though you'd only just got out of juvie. I can respect that." He tilted his head. "Your mom told me you had some Portuguese in you. I never would have guessed. I have some Irish in me, like Shaya."

Frowning, Shaya shook her head. "I don't have Irish in me."

"You don't? Really?" That flirty smile crept onto his face. "Would you like some in you?" Anticipating that Nick would make a grab for him, Dominic quickly jerked out of the way. But Nick was too fast; he grabbed him and launched him into the pool. When Dominic burst to the surface of the water, he shouted in exhilaration and went into a fit of laughter.

Trey growled at his enforcer. "Could you try being normal for just a little while? I'd rather not have to take you home in a fucking casket."

Shaya moved her attention to the person whose support she needed most. Taryn was sitting at the patio table beside Trey, her expression slightly sulky. "You're uncharacteristically quiet."

"If you're going to tell her she rushed into this or some shit like that," began Nick, "you should—"

Taryn snorted. "Easy there, Axton. I'm actually happy for you guys. I'm not saying I think you're good enough for Shaya— *no one* will be good enough for her, in my eyes." A huge sigh. "But it just occurred to me that this means Shaya will never be part of my pack again. Face it, Nick, you can't obey Trey—or any other wolf, for that matter—and we all know it. But that means I can't have Shaya back, and I hate that. Yeah, that's selfish, but I never claimed I was unselfish."

Nick stifled a smile at her petulant expression. "It's not like you're losing her. She'll still be visiting you and stuff."

"Will you be coming, too?" Taryn smirked—she knew the answer.

"I'll be waiting for her in the car. You people annoy the shit out of me."

Taryn leaned forward in her seat, her face imploring. "Please say you guys will have your mating ceremony on Phoenix territory? That's your real home, Shaya. Nick's family and Caleb can come too, obviously."

Shaya looked up at him. "I'd like that. Is that okay for you?"

Nick shrugged. "If you want us to have the ceremony there, I'm good with that." Trey chuckled, drawing Nick's attention. "What's funny?"

"I just find myself reminded of that time when you visited my territory and the subject of a mating ceremony for Taryn and me was brought up. I said if she wanted to have one, we'd have one, but that if she didn't, we wouldn't. What was it you said? Oh, that's it. You said I shouldn't let my mate have her own way all the time. Hmm. Right back atcha."

Nick scowled at him. "Whatever, asshole—you mated a psycho." Trey nodded in agreement, looking proud. *Twisted.*

Chuckling, Shaya shook her head against Nick's chest. When she nipped it, he peered down at her. "I'll be back in a minute." His arm contracted around her. "Where are you going?"

"To make some coffee. Want some?"

"Sure." For the hell of it, he bit her lip hard before she pulled away.

Giving him a mock frown, Shaya turned and waltzed back into the house. She had only just switched on the coffee machine when she picked up Amber's scent. Her wolf growled.

"I just wanted to say congratulations once again," said Amber as she appeared beside her. Her eyes bulged as she added excitedly, "We have to get started on the plans for the mating ceremony!" Not only was she effectively inviting herself to the ceremony, but she was doing the BFF thing. Shaya had had enough of it.

As everyone was still outside and the music was blaring enough to keep the conversation private, Shaya figured that now would be as good a time as any to get things straight with her and Amber. "Listen, I appreciate the offer, but we both know that it wasn't made out of the kindness of your heart." Amber looked appropriately offended. "You don't want to befriend me. My guess is that, on the contrary, you hate me . . . because you want Nick and I have him."

Amber's expression darkened, and her eyes became diamond hard, no longer hiding the hatred she had. At least she wasn't going to play the "Oh, you've got it all wrong" game.

"I can't be pissed at you for wanting Nick—it would make me a huge hypocrite. But if you care about him, you won't try to mess things up for him. I say 'try' because it's not something you'll succeed in doing if you do make an attempt at it. But hopefully, you won't want to."

In a sickly sweet voice full of contempt, Amber said, "Of course I wouldn't mess things up for Nick. I want him to be happy."

Shaya gave her a beaming smile. "Great. I'm glad that's settled."

Amber turned on her heel and marched away, but then she suddenly halted and pivoted to face Shaya once more. Deviousness twinkled in her eyes. "I really do hope you two will be happy. I know a few mated dominant/submissive pairs. They're all happy. Even the ones whose bond hasn't completely snapped into place. Not *totally* happy, but happy enough, given the circumstances. Oh, did you not know that *fully* mating can be a problem for dominant/submissive pairs?"

No, Shaya hadn't, and her expression must have given that away because there was a glint of smugness in Amber's gaze.

"No one knows exactly what the issue is," she said as she did a cocky strut around the room, "but it seems to be that taking the very last step is hard because it requires both shifters to accept what that means. Dominants often have to give up any ambitions of being Alpha or holding positions of authority within their pack. Submissives have to accept that they hold their mate back and that their strength will never match that of their mate. Some dominants are okay with that, but the submissive of the pair isn't always so okay with it because knowing they hold their mate back is hard. Especially if it's the guy who's submissive, or if the dominant of the pair is a born alpha. But hey, don't worry, it doesn't mean that will happen to you and Nick."

But Amber would try her best to ensure it did happen, Shaya understood. It wasn't an uncommon thing for jealous ex-partners or shunned pursuers to try to stop the shifter they wanted from fully bonding with their mate. It was the ultimate form of revenge and, in a lot of cases, it could work. In this case, it had a high chance of happening without Amber's help because the difficulties Nick and Shaya faced were exactly those she had described.

"Can you imagine how hard that must be to have your mate so close but for him to never totally want and accept you? That would be a hell like no other, wouldn't it?"

Yes, it would. If a bond seemed to be taking too long to click into place, resentment and anger and depression would build—not a good combination. That combination would then make it more difficult for the bond to fully form. Shaya had seen it happen. But she wouldn't let it happen to her and Nick. "I guess I should make it clear to anyone who thinks of trying to interfere with the development of the bond that I won't stand for it."

Amber gave a short laugh, regarding Shaya like she was ridiculous. "What is it you will do to these people? Other than cower and submit, I mean."

Shaya smiled. "I'd warn them that they *really* don't want to find out the answer to that."

"But for them to defeat you . . . all they would have to do is this." Amber's dominant vibes crashed into Shaya, attempting to force her to submit. When that didn't happen, Amber's eyes widened in both surprise and anger.

"Hopefully that would be enough to make those people think twice about coming at me. What do you think?"

Clearly too infuriated to remember to keep up her sweet, friendly-friendly act, Amber curled her upper lip at Shaya . . . and it was apparent *exactly* what Amber intended to do. Before the dominant female had the chance to charge at her, Shaya quickly grabbed the knife block beside her and whipped out a knife, hurling it in Amber's direction. Just as quickly, she threw another, and another, and another, and another . . . and smiled at the end result.

As Nick walked into the kitchen in search of Shaya, he came to an abrupt halt at the sight he found. There was Amber, plastered against the wall with five knives stabbing into the wall and framing her body. And Shaya . . . well, she was smiling cheerily and somewhat sweetly. "What's going on?" he asked dubiously. His mate shrugged, still the image of innocence.

"I was just showing Amber my knife trick," Shaya told him, pulling the knives from the wall. "Cool, huh?"

Pretty certain there was a *lot* more to this, Nick narrowed his eyes at Amber. But then Shaya was in front of him, kissing and holding him . . . and he decided that if she didn't care, fuck it. Having shot Amber a cautioning look—which received a gulp and made her quickly depart—he locked his arms tight around Shaya. "Are you sure everything's okay?" Her smile wobbled slightly. "What's wrong?"

"Nothing. Or, at least, nothing I want to talk about right now."

Pleased that she wasn't trying to blow him off, Nick planted a firm kiss on her mouth. "Then we'll talk about it later."

As Taryn then entered the room with Roni close behind, she smiled awkwardly at Shaya. "We might have a problem. A problem other than that Greta's still alive and kicking, that is."

Shaya rolled her eyes. "What?"

"When I spoke to Caleb on the phone yesterday, I told him about how Nick tracked you down—he was harassing me and making me feel guilty, saying we were leaving him out of everything."

"I don't mind you telling Caleb." When Taryn's awkward expression remained, Shaya narrowed her eyes. "That's not the 'problem' you mentioned, is it?

"No. He called me just now and, well . . . Remember I said he complained we were leaving him out of everything? Well, he thought it was only *him* who we hadn't bothered to tell about Nick finding you. So he sort of might have mentioned it to your parents, thinking they already knew."

"*What?*"

"And they sort of might have demanded to know if he's claimed you yet and when the mating ceremony is."

"Taryn!"

"It's not *my* fault. Blame Caleb."

Running a hand over Shaya's curls, Nick asked, "You didn't want your parents to know you're mated?"

"Not until after the ceremony, because then my mother couldn't insist on going." She grimaced.

Roni cocked her head. "Why wouldn't you want her to go?"

"My mom isn't like yours."

Confused, Roni frowned. "In what way?"

"She's evil," supplied Taryn. "Her dad's okay, though . . . albeit a little unbalanced." Shaya couldn't deny that.

Nick tightened his hold on his mate, rubbing her back. "She's not coming to the mating ceremony."

"I doubt she wants to," said Shaya, "but she'll go for the sake of appearances. In any case, my dad will want to be there, and he'll force her to do her motherly duty and attend."

"I don't care what *they* want." Nick leaned his forehead against hers. "If you don't want them there, they don't go—that's it."

"It's not that I don't want my dad there. It's just that I know he won't leave my mom behind."

"Then they both stay behind."

"I agree." Taryn nodded. "Now I'm going to save my son from Yoda—he's due to have a nap soon. If you guys are going to go upstairs again, try not to make too much noise, okay?"

"We're not that loud," maintained Shaya, blushing.

Taryn's expression said, "Sure you're not." Aloud she said, "By the way, Nick, I have to say you're good at the dirty talk—you could give Trey a run for his money. You know who else is good at it? Cam."

Shaya gasped, shocked. Cam was a reasonably quiet mated Phoenix wolf with the cutest baby face. "Really?"

"Really." Taryn shook her head in disbelief. "To look at him, I wouldn't have thought he had it in him. I think Derren would be good at it too. What do you think?"

Before Shaya could answer that, Nick slapped a hand over her mouth. "Just in case you say something that could get Derren killed," he explained to Shaya. He threw a warning look at a departing, laughing Taryn, who had clearly been baiting him.

287

He looked into his mate's amused eyes. "You have a very strange friend. I shouldn't like her, but I find that I do." When amusement fled from Shaya's eyes and they became more like lasers, he dropped his hand and kissed her hard on the mouth. "Not the way I like *you*, baby. I told you, you never have to feel insecure about us."

"Maybe you should reassure me a little. In the bedroom. Naked."

A grin spread across Nick's face. "I'll reassure you anytime you want."

When a soaking-wet Dominic appeared at Shaya's side, fidgeting with a weird grimace on his face, she looked at him questioningly.

He wiped a hand over his brow. "Is it hot in here, or is it just you?" Naturally, Nick's fist went flying at his jaw. Laughing, Dominic barely dodged it. He *had* to be suicidal.

# CHAPTER SİXTEEN

While the males loaded the vehicles early the next morning, Shaya pulled Taryn aside in the front yard and told her all about Nick's cognitive functions degenerating. She'd wanted to do this since last night but hadn't been able to get her alone while the house was so crowded.

"Jesus." Wide-eyed, Taryn blew out a long breath. "Well, that sure explains a hell of a lot. And now I certainly no longer feel like strapping him to a bed and smashing his ankles with a sledgehammer like Kathy Bates in *Misery*." She sighed, her expression sympathetic. "You want to know if I can heal him."

"Yes. Amber's powerful, but so are you." Seeing reluctance on Taryn's face, Shaya quickly added, "All I'm asking is that you try."

Taryn dragged a hand through her hair. "It's not that I don't want to heal him—it's that I'll hate myself if it doesn't work and I've let you down this badly."

Shaya hugged her reassuringly. "I would never see it as you letting me down." She pulled back and held her best friend's gaze. "Not ever, I promise. Will you please try?"

Exhaling heavily, Taryn nodded. "Let's get back home first. Then I'll try, okay?"

"Thank you." Seeing that Nick was approaching wearing an exasperated expression, Shaya smiled. Her wolf practically melted—she was so pathetic. Once he was up close, he pulled her against him. "You look totally pissed off."

"Of course I'm pissed off." He gestured to the vehicle behind him. "My motor home is full of a number of wolves, and I'll have to deal with them for the next five hours." Dominic, Greta, Kathy, Amber, Kent, Jesse, Bracken, and Zander had all decided they would prefer to travel in the luxury of the motor home rather than any of the other vehicles. "Thank God I'll have you to keep me calm. You have to sit up front with me or I'll lose it."

"How did you cope with being an Alpha for so long when you don't like having lots of people around you?" asked Taryn, genuinely flabbergasted.

"Like I told Shaya, I'd killed the pack's old Alpha, and no one wanted the position. I did what was fair to them." He looked at Shaya then. "And now that I've finally got free of that life, I have Derren doing his best to make me form a pack. Oh, don't think I hadn't noticed what he's been doing by deferring to me and involving Jesse, Bracken, and Zander more."

Shaya gently ran her nails down his chest, trying unsuccessfully to stifle a smile. "In Derren's defense, those guys follow you like you're a guiding light anyway."

At Taryn's chuckle, he growled. "I'm glad you find this so amusing."

A passing Greta, who had clearly picked up on Nick's frustration with Taryn, patted his arm consolingly. "Don't pay any attention to Tiny Tim." She tossed Taryn a scowl and then carried on walking.

Taryn snorted, trailing after the woman. "At least I'm not so old that my birth certificate has expired."

A laugh burst out of Shaya, making Nick's own burst free. When her laugh abruptly died and her smile faded, Nick followed her gaze to find Amber staring at her from across the yard. The female flashed him a smile, but not before he'd seen the contempt for Shaya in her eyes. It made his wolf snarl.

Dismissing Amber with a look, Nick cupped Shaya's chin. "Whatever she said to upset you, ignore it." He'd offer to deal with Amber for her, but he had come to learn that—dominant or submissive, human or shifter—females liked to deal with shit that involved other females.

"Did you know that dominant/submissive pairs have difficulties with fully bonding?"

Nick released a heavy breath. "Yes. But we won't have that difficulty."

To her surprise, he looked and sounded absolutely positive. "What makes you so sure?"

He dropped his forehead to hers and swept the pad of his thumb over his claiming mark, liking her answering shudder. "If we can get past our other issues, we can get past this too."

She supposed he had a good point, but she wasn't sure if that made him right. "And we'll get past this other business too. We will get you healed."

"You're not healed?" asked Roni, having overheard.

Turning to face his sister and seeing the panic in her expression, Nick inwardly groaned. Respecting her too much to blow her off, he told her about the headaches and the memory lapse. "Like Shaya said, this is something we'll get past."

Roni put a hand to her forehead, her eyes sad and anxious. "God, this is horrible."

With cautious steps, Kathy suddenly approached, obviously worried about Roni's panicky state. "What's wrong, honey?" She ran a hand over Roni's hair. "You look pale. Is everything all right?"

"You have to tell her," Roni told Nick. "She deserves to know."

"Know what?" asked Amber.

*Great*, thought Nick. Taking a preparatory breath, he once again explained the situation.

"You're not healed?" echoed Amber, stunned and panicked. "That can't be possible. I healed you. I healed you; I did."

"It hasn't worked," Shaya told her gently. It was hard not to be gentle when Amber looked genuinely distraught. "His cognitive functions are degenerating again."

Amber shook her head in denial. "No, I healed him."

"You *tried*, but it hasn't worked."

Tears now swirling in her eyes, Amber turned back to him. "Nick, I'm so sorry. I know I warned you the improvements could be temporary, but I was pretty sure you were totally healed. I'm so sorry."

"It's not your fault," he assured her, not being good with crying females. "It is what it is."

"Let me try again. It'll work this time, I'll make sure it does."

He held a hand up. "Amber, if it didn't work the first time—"

"Just let me try."

"Taryn's going to try," announced Shaya, which made hope enter both Roni's and Kathy's expression.

"She's not more powerful than me," maintained Amber.

"You better hope she is, or Nick's in shit street."

Shaking her head in denial again, Amber quickly scampered. A concerned Kathy went after her.

"If Taryn can't heal you," began Roni, "we'll find someone else. You can't give up, Nick."

"I won't," he vowed. Satisfied yet still understandably anxious, Roni nodded and walked away.

Shaya jabbed him in the chest with her finger. "They better not be empty words. You've made that promise to both me and Roni, and we intend to make you keep it." Her wolf was in full agreement.

Nick cupped her face. "I have never given you empty words. Ever."

"Just sayin'." As he cuddled her close, his cell began to ring.

After a brief conversation, he returned the phone to his pocket with a sigh. "Everything okay?"

"That was Jesse. There are humans watching us closely from a house farther down the street; he recognizes them as extremists. They'll either follow us or report back to Logan that we've left."

"Do you really think the plan to divide the group and get to Logan will work?"

"Yes, I do. Let's find out for sure."

After a very long journey to Phoenix Pack territory in a vehicle full of talking people, Nick had wanted nothing more than to take Shaya somewhere inside the caves where they could be alone. But that hadn't been possible. First the pack had wanted to make a huge fuss of Shaya while at the same time scowling at him for originally failing to claim her. Defensive on his behalf, Shaya had told them all about how his wolf had surfaced early and what was happening to his cognitive functions as a result. At that point, the scowling stopped, and now Jaime was following him everywhere, claiming she was able to empathize with him as she knew how hard it was to have a scarred wolf. That was nice and all, but Nick wasn't the type to need empathy. He liked privacy, peace, quiet—and he soon learned that none of these things could be found in this territory.

The meal that had awaited them went a long way to improving his mood. Their packmate, Grace, was a good cook. As they ate, Trey and Taryn had explained the entire situation surrounding the human extremists. Rhett, who was the ultimate geek and also Grace's mate, planned to try to uncover what he could about the game preserve with his hacking skills, but Nick wasn't optimistic that Rhett would uncover much—if Donovan couldn't, no one could. As Nick had expected, two of the extremists had followed them to Phoenix Pack territory and would undoubtedly tell Logan their location. So far, everything was going to plan.

That would have pleased him if it wasn't for the fact that now that the wolves all knew a little about his time in juvie, Nick was receiving nods of respect and pats on his back—particularly from the enforcers and also a mated pair, Cam and Lydia, whose old friend hadn't made it out of juvie alive. Also, Jaime's brother, Gabe, and his mate, Hope, were apparently as empathetic as Jaime. Great. Further annoying him, Jaime's ugly, chunky cat kept charging at Bruce. Even more annoying, the damn dog wasn't standing his ground.

Probably more irritating than all of that, however, was that Marcus kept trying to flirt with Roni. Where Dominic was sleazy-flirty, Marcus was smooth-flirty. The only thing stopping Nick from growling at the asshole was that Roni was simply looking at the guy blankly, totally bamboozling him. Given how uncomfortable she was around all these strangers, Nick wouldn't be surprised if she returned to her wolf form sometime soon. He had hoped that she would go home to the Ryland Pack with his mom and Amber. Unfortunately, she had refused. Even more unfortunate, so had his mom and Amber. And now—to top it all off—his beautiful mate beside him was totally pissed off because Amber was sitting on his other side. Not even the fact that Kent was throwing fries at Amber was cheering Shaya up.

Wanting to soothe her and reassure her that *she* was the only one who mattered, Nick lifted Shaya and sat her in his lap. After a moment, she melted against him, and he locked both arms around her. "Please tell me your bedroom is on a completely different floor than everyone else."

Hearing the frustration in his voice, Shaya couldn't help but smile. Her mate was in hell with all this attention and offers of friendship. "Sorry to disappoint, but it's only a few doors away from Jaime, your new best friend." His growl made her chuckle. "They're just all feeling bad for their behavior toward you when it's clear you had your reasons for not claiming me in the beginning. They'll stop smiling at you within the hour."

He bit her ear for teasing him. "I can't believe we've only been here an hour and already all the females have our mating ceremony totally covered and have scheduled it for tonight." It was tradition that the other females of the pack organized the ceremony, but he'd never heard of one being so swiftly planned. "Maybe they just want it over with quickly because they don't trust me not to abandon you again."

"You didn't truly abandon me. And the reason they want us to have it quickly is so that the humans don't interrupt it with an attack. Dante and Jaime's ceremony was spoiled by Glory and her relatives infiltrating the territory and attacking everyone. You do want to have a ceremony, right?"

"Of course I do, dumbass."

She spoke against his mouth. "Good. Because if you don't turn up at that ceremony out of some misguided attempt to protect me from what's happening to you, I'll hunt you down and beat the shit out of you with my bat."

He smiled. "Feisty."

"Besides, I asked Taryn if she would try healing you. She said she would."

"It might not work, Shay," he told her gently.

"I know, but you promised you wouldn't give up."

"And I won't; I'm willing to let Taryn try. Although, I have the feeling that Taryn would sooner cut my throat than heal me."

"I think she's warming to you."

He snorted at that and was about to comment when Derren, who had popped out of the room to take a call, suddenly barged inside the kitchen.

"Nick, I just got off the phone with Donovan. He said to turn on the TV."

"Why?"

"He found the location of the preserve. And he called it in."

Everybody quickly piled into the living area, but no one spoke as the news of the preserve was aired live. Nick had encountered much evil in his life, known cruelty and violence, but he had never seen anything like this. It was worse than even Lee-Roy had described. Dead bodies of shifters ranging from the age of seven—fucking *seven*—had been dumped on the land, all maimed, brutalized, and decaying. Some of the bodies were even frozen mid-shift while others were missing their eyes or limbs. Even the human reporter, the same reporter who had days ago portrayed shifters as animals, was horrified and close to tears at the sight of the bodies—particularly those of the children.

Nick understood why Donovan hadn't notified him before contacting the police; he'd known that when Nick saw how bad it was, he wouldn't have been happy to let the police deal with it and that he'd have wanted to go after Logan and those other bastards himself. As such, Donovan was right not to have told Nick first. This was about more than just them. This was about shifters worldwide.

Although many had been arrested in connection with it, Logan's name hadn't been mentioned, and there had been no mention of a shifter being involved either. Nick knew, however, that Lee-Roy had been telling the truth when he said the person running the preserve was a shifter. That meant the bastard was still out there, free as a bird.

*Feeling* Shaya's desolation and realizing she was crying, Nick moved her from her spot beside him on the giant sofa to his lap. He cradled her against him, rocking her. Most of the other females were crying too. The sickening sight of the preserve almost brought tears to his own eyes. The more the reporter revealed, the more nauseous he felt. Until they worked out who the shifter responsible was, they couldn't be sure another preserve wouldn't be set up somewhere else . . . and they couldn't make sure the prick paid for what he'd done.

"Nick," croaked Shaya. "After seeing this . . . I don't know if I can—"

She cut herself off, but Nick knew what she was thinking: She didn't know if she could go through with a mating ceremony and throw a celebration when this was on her mind. He was feeling the same way. The images were stuck in his head, and he couldn't get them out and didn't think he would anytime soon. It didn't seem right to throw a party on the heels of something like this. "Me neither, baby. We'll do it after this is all over, okay?" Nodding, she snuggled even more into him.

Kent brought his hand to his mouth. "I honestly think I might be sick."

Derren looked at him, his expression grim. "You know what this means."

Nick nodded. "It means the extremists' case will be dismissed on Thursday morning. And it means they'll be here Thursday night for sure—they'll take this into their own hands, just as Logan planned in the meeting."

"That's okay," growled Trey, "because we'll be waiting. I can't wait to get my hands on those motherfuckers. They deserve whatever happens to them."

"I have a feeling the shifter behind all this will come with them," said Ryan. Nick was surprised to hear him speak.

"Me too," said Trick. "He hates shifters anyway, and now that he's no longer making money from charging humans to kill our kind, I'd say he'll be pissed enough to join Logan in the attack."

"Let's hope so," growled Taryn. She rose from her armchair and approached Nick. "It's time. We need you at top strength. I can't guarantee I'll be able to heal you, but I can certainly do my best." She then turned to her pack. "Grace, you know what I need. Ryan, the window." While the short brunette nodded and left the room, the grumpy-looking enforcer opened the window wide.

Determined to only think positive thoughts, Shaya rose from his lap. "Lie down on the floor, flat on your back."

"That's usually my order," rumbled Nick, smiling at her blush. Hoping against hope that the Alpha female would be successful where Amber wasn't, Nick did as Shaya asked.

"Everyone other than Shaya step back," ordered Taryn, all business. The depth of authority and seriousness in her voice had everyone immediately backing up, giving her plenty of space. As she knelt on his left side, Shaya knelt on his right and took his hand in hers. She exchanged a reassuring look with him, knowing he felt a little awkward.

Shaya watched as Taryn placed her hand on his forehead; just like that, patches of luminous lights were gleaming through Nick's scalp, indicating where the damage was. Taryn then leaned over and placed her mouth to his like she would give him the kiss of life. Although the sight of another female's mouth touching his made a part of Shaya balk, her concern for his well-being was far stronger than that.

Taryn inhaled deeply, then lifted her head, turned it toward the window, and blew out a heavy breath; a whoosh of black particles escaped from her mouth and zoomed out of the window. She repeated the move again and again, not stopping until the luminous patches of Nick's scalp had completely faded.

"Done." Puffing out a breath, she toppled backward, and would have landed on the carpet if Trey hadn't been in position, waiting to catch her. He pulled her so that she was sitting between his legs, her back to his chest. She was pale and a little tired, but otherwise fine.

"As usual," said Trey, "you now look like shit."

Her voice hoarse, Taryn snapped, "Ass." As a cough seemed to burst out of her, Grace gave Taryn a bottle of water and an energy bar. "Thank you."

"How do you feel?" Shaya anxiously asked Nick as he slowly sat upright.

Rubbing his head, he considered lying to Shaya, but their bond would allow her to pick up on it. "Honestly . . . I don't feel any different."

"That's because you weren't in pain or feeling dizzy or weak," Derren pointed out.

*Good point,* thought Nick. He looked at Taryn. "So you've healed my cognitive functions?"

Taryn pursed her lips. "That's not quite how it works with me. All that foul crap I took out of you . . . that was, like, the *badness.* It's hard to explain. If you take away the negativity that pollutes a positive situation, the situation is then no longer polluted—it's pure again. The same thing applies here. Your cognitive functions are no longer 'polluted.' Hopefully, it stays that way. If this was the first time you had been healed, I wouldn't even question whether or not the effect would be permanent. But as you've had a number of healing sessions before now and the problem still came back, I can't guarantee it won't come back again."

Shaya leaned her head against his shoulder, and his arm instantly came around her. "It always amazes me when you do that," she told Taryn. "Thanks."

"Yeah, thanks," said Nick.

"Unnatural, that is," muttered Greta.

Clearly offended on Taryn's behalf, Jaime frowned at the old woman. "So is your life span, not to mention your moustache."

Keeping Taryn in his arms, Trey got to his feet. "Come on, you need to have a small nap." After that, she would be her normal hyper self again.

"But Kye—"

"Is half the reason you're so tired," finished Trey. "He kept you awake for most of the night. He'll probably still be asleep when you wake up. If he does wake early, he'll be absolutely fine with all these people to fuss over him."

"I know, but he looks for me, so I feel bad when I'm not there for him," whined Taryn. The kid, though extremely sociable, was very tightly bonded to Taryn, just as Taryn was to him—which was most likely why she continued to complain as Trey strolled out of the living area with her in his arms, en route to their bedroom.

Shaya turned to Nick, who was clearly attempting to smile at a talking Jaime, but it looked more like a grimace. Taking pity on him, she said, "Come on, let's go take our stuff up to my room." Nick's relief was visible in his expression, which made Jaime smile.

Entering Shaya's bedroom, Nick studied his surroundings and noticed that the room was a lot like the bedroom in the house she'd been renting in Arizona—pine furniture, gold and cream color theme, satin sheets, and a bed adorned with decorative pillows. He still had yet to figure out why anyone would bother with decorative pillows, but the last time he'd complained about it, she'd smacked him over the head. So he would stay quiet about it this time. Instead, he tugged her to him and ravaged her mouth like he'd been dying to do since they arrived. "We need to christen that bed."

In the aftermath of a session of wickedly slow, leisurely sex that made Shaya come so hard she saw stars, she simply lay—totally sated and somewhat resembling a limp noodle—in Nick's arms, content. "I don't think I can move for a while."

"Good. Let's just stay here until it's time for the evening meal."

She chuckled. "So you don't have to interact with the others?"

"That and I like having time with just you." He nipped her bottom lip. "I don't like sharing you."

"It's a good thing I have no intention of asking you if we could live here permanently—it would kill you."

The total lack of privacy would in fact drive him insane. "If you really want to, I could try." This was the only family Shaya had ever really had, and he wouldn't take her away from it if it would devastate her. "Any other ideas of where you'd like to live?"

"I don't know. I guess that depends on whether or not you've decided yet if you want to be an Alpha again?"

Rolling onto his back, he groaned. "Not you too. You're supposed to be on my side."

"I *am* on your side." She rested her chin on his chest. "That's why I'm bringing it up. You need to talk about it." When he didn't speak, she said gently, "Hey, if you don't want us to form a pack, we won't."

"But . . . ?" he prodded, sensing there was one.

"*But* I think that you do. You're a natural alpha. I think, deep down, a part of you must want it, must want to be part of something and want to give your wolf the sense of purpose that any alpha likes to have."

"My wolf does want it," he admitted, "but he wants you more, so it doesn't matter." She smacked his shoulder. He winced. "Hey!"

"Of course it matters. I don't want your wolf feeling in any way unfulfilled." She didn't want their bond to always remain incomplete.

"He doesn't feel unfulfilled. Besides, you don't want to be an Alpha female since you'll need to travel a lot for the job I'm confident you'll get. I'll be traveling with you." He was no longer worried that her being an Alpha female would place her in danger, not after witnessing her strength over and over, and not when he knew that the people who were sneakily trying to make him their Alpha would never challenge her anyway. They saw her strength, and they respected her. Plus, they knew she was talented with weapons, and they didn't want to die.

"That doesn't mean you can't be an Alpha. There are some dispersed packs out there. I know usually shifters don't like their packs to be that way, but if people are trying to influence you into forming a pack while knowing that's the only way it could be, it's obviously not going to be something they'll care about. I can't promise I'll be any good at the Alpha female thing."

He dropped a kiss on her mouth. "You could do anything." He was certain that she'd make a good Alpha female, just as

Taryn had said. Shaya wouldn't be loud and forward like dominant Alphas; she would lead in a diplomatic, calming, supportive way. He could give the pack the feeling of physical safety, and she would give them the feeling of emotional safety. Providing the people in his pack could totally accept that, it could work. "I thought you wouldn't want that position."

"Miss a chance to boss people around?"

Toying with her curls, he told her, "It's not something I need, Shay. Wanting something and needing it are two different things. You're what I need."

"Ah, but if you can have what you want *and* what you need, why shouldn't you?"

Unsure what he wanted, he said, "Let's talk about something else."

"Like what?"

"Like the fact that I don't want you fighting against the humans with us on Thursday night."

She narrowed her eyes. "I knew you were going to say that." She wasn't exactly surprised. He was her mate; he wouldn't want her in any form of danger. "I know you like to have your own way, and I know that sometimes I compromise, and I know that sometimes you sneakily talk me into consenting to what you want"—he smiled, not in the least bit apologetic—"but I won't budge on this: I *will* be part of what happens Thursday night."

"Shay—"

"I'm just as angry as you are about that preserve. Those bastards did things they deserve to die slow, agonizing deaths for. On top of that, one of them tried over and over to rape you in juvie. Then there's the little fact that he wrecked the salon and had someone shoot at us. I'm not letting that slide." To her surprise, he wasn't scowling, he was smiling. "What?"

"You should hear how righteous and very Alpha-female-like you sound."

She blushed. "Females feeling vengeful on their mate's behalf can sound a lot like that."

"It's not just me who has a problem with this. Your wolf doesn't like it either, does she? She's nervous at just the idea of it."

Her wolf was, indeed, pacing anxiously. "Granted, she's not keen on the idea of being in a situation that violent. But she's also reassured"—okay, *slightly* reassured—"by the fact that I have no intention of shifting and expecting her to deal with it."

He frowned, confused. "You don't intend to shift?"

"It'll be kind of hard to use my rifle with paws and claws."

"Rifle?" he echoed disbelievingly.

"Thanks to my dad and our hunting trips, I'm a really good shot. I deserve to be a part of this just as much as the others do. The other males haven't asked *their* mates to stay behind—it's unfair to expect me to stay behind just because I'm submissive and—"

He silenced her with a look. "This has nothing to do with your submissive status, so don't even go there." He was becoming increasingly offended by her repeated accusations of him thinking less of her due to her submissive status. "Trey and Dante aren't asking their mates to stay behind because the situation isn't personal for them. My wolf has wanted to get a grip on Logan for a *long* time for a *long* list of reasons, and he's none too happy with the shifter who created the preserve either. During the attack, his sole focus will be on getting to them. You're the only thing that could distract him, the only thing that would matter more to him than ripping those fuckers apart."

"You're saying I'll place you in danger."

He cupped her chin. "You're my only weak spot, Shay. Logan will know that. On that battlefield, it'll be you who he's looking for. If you're there, my wolf will be distracted and anxious and won't be able to focus on getting to Logan or the shifter—and that will make it easier for them to get to one of us."

Well, when he put it like that . . . "What if I promise not to enter the battlefield? What if I promise to stay on a spot out of sight? It's not like I need to get close to use my rifle."

That placated him and his wolf slightly, but the idea of her being anywhere near Logan still turned his stomach.

"You can even help me choose which spot."

He scrubbed a hand down his face. "I don't like it, Shay."

"Of course you don't. Just the same, I don't like the idea of you playing a part in the battle, but I haven't asked you to stay out of it, have I?"

Twisting the situation to get what she wanted? "Baby, that's sneaky." Because she made a very good point.

"This is my fight too, Nick." He was silent for a long time, and she thought he was going to object again, but he instead released a sigh of resignation.

"I can't deny that your skills will be needed."

Knowing that was Nick's version of an "oh, all right," she kissed him hard. "I appreciate you not being an overprotective caveman. Dante used to do it to Jaime a lot in the beginning— God, they argued like cats and dogs about it." Although Nick was even more overprotective than Dante, he didn't play the "I'm a male, I have a dick, and therefore I will make all the decisions" role like the Beta male had.

"This doesn't mean I'm happy about it. My wolf's pretty pissed with you too."

She petted his chest patronizingly. "Don't worry; when we go down for dinner later you can tell your best friend, Jaime, all about it and she'll—"

"You keep that woman away from me. She's chatty and does that sympathy thing."

"And that's bad?" chuckled Shaya. Although Jaime genuinely did sympathize with Nick and liked being around someone who could sort of relate to her predicament with her wolf, Jaime also found it hilarious just how uncomfortable it made him.

Nick moved Shaya so that she lay on top of him, fitting her body to his. "I don't want sympathy, and I don't like to chat unless it's with you."

"Why? What's so different about me that my company is okay?"

He smoothed his hand up and down her back. "You're perfect to me. They're not. You're important. They're not. You're mine. They're not."

"Your family is important to you," she reminded him.

"But not in the same way you are. I care about them, but you're something I need." That was the only way he could explain it.

It scared Shaya that he needed her, felt so strongly for her. She knew that he'd kill for her, die for her, and do anything he had to do to keep her, no matter what it cost him. She had never been that important to anyone before. No one had ever *needed* her like that—it was scary, but it was also fulfilling. "Then prove it." Entering her a second time that day, he did exactly that.

# CHAPTER SEVENTEEN

A knock at the door the next morning was quickly followed by Trick's voice. "Shaya, you've got visitors. If Taryn's right, you might not be too happy about it."

As those words penetrated her sleep-dazed brain, Shaya groaned. She didn't have to ask who the visitors were. Her mother had been trying to contact her nonstop over the past two days, but Shaya had ignored her calls. Caleb would have told her that Shaya had returned to Phoenix Pack territory. It had only been a matter of time before the woman showed up. Sleepily, she called out, "I'll be down in a minute."

"They're waiting for you in the kitchen." The sound of Trick's footsteps faded down the tunnels.

Any other time, she would have been stumbling around the room on just waking. But knowing her parents were here was enough to galvanize her into action. Hopping out of the bed, she told Nick, "It's got to be my parents. You might want to sit this one out."

Frowning at the anxiety rushing through her, Nick instantly jumped out of the bed. "Your parents are here?"

"It's okay, just stay here, I won't be long."

Following her into the en suite bathroom, Nick said, "No way. I don't care how upset they are with me for not claiming you in the beginning, I'm not letting you deal with them alone." Like her, he quickly washed up and brushed his teeth.

"It's not just about that," she told him as she returned to the bedroom and retrieved some clothes from her wardrobe. "My mother . . . she's difficult, Nick. She likes to belittle me and insult me. I don't want you to lose it with her—all you would be doing is giving her the drama she loves so she can act the victim of the world."

Shooting her an incredulous look, he began pulling on his jeans. "I can't just sit there and say nothing while someone insults you."

"Exactly—so you're better off staying here."

Not a chance would he remain behind at a time when she'd need him at her side. "I promise I won't lose it, okay? I can't promise I'll stay quiet if she's upsetting you, but I won't lose it. I'm not letting you face her alone."

Appreciating his support, she smiled. "Thanks."

When they were fully dressed, they walked hand in hand through the tunnels. The thought of seeing her mother again made her stomach sink, but the thought of Nick meeting her father made her heart pound. She could easily recall the times Stone Critchley had met her boyfriends, and just how those meetings had gone—just how *badly* those meetings had gone. "Um, when you meet my dad . . . if he scowls at you, don't worry, you're fine. If he smiles, well, be on your guard. And no sudden movements. And try to make eye contact with him as little as possible. Oh, and don't—"

"Shay, relax." He squeezed her hand reassuringly.

Relax? Ha. Not going to happen. Finally, they reached the large kitchen. Roni and Marcus were standing in the doorway, regarding her parents with studious eyes. Clearly Roni had wanted Nick to have an ally nearby. As for Marcus . . . well, she wasn't sure why he was there. Although it was fair to say that he'd been a good friend to Shaya when she was going through all that crap with Nick in the beginning.

Instantly, the two people seated at the long dining table were on their feet. Her mother was, of course, looking the victim as usual. Her father's expression was as indulgent as always.

Coming around the table, Stone took Shaya into his arms. "Hi, baby girl."

She returned his tight hug. "Hey, Dad." Pulling back, she said, "This is my mate, Nick."

Stone's expression immediately turned assessing. "Is it now?"

"Nick, this is my dad, Stone."

"Pleased to meet you," said Nick, shaking the human's hand. He had the same eyes as Shaya, but there was none of her impishness there—instead, there was ruthlessness and danger. He and his wolf recognized a predator when he saw one, and the male before him was certainly one. He also knew that Stone would recognize Nick as a fellow predator, and that was important because he had no intention of letting anyone try to intimidate him.

"Likewise," drawled Stone, sounding not at all honest.

Nick then turned his attention to Shaya's mother, and he wished he hadn't. The woman was practically sneering at her daughter, a statue of disapproval. His wolf growled, wanting Nick to warn her against hurting his mate. Nick was about to do just that when Shaya slipped her hand into his again and gave it a double-squeeze—a clear "please leave it."

"Mom, Nick. Nick, this is Gabrielle."

He merely exchanged a curt nod with the female. "Shall we sit?" Without waiting for a response, Nick took the chair opposite the one her father had claimed. The others quickly returned to their seats. Before anyone could speak, the door opened and Taryn entered. Going to stand beside Roni, she nodded at Stone in greeting, who returned the nod.

"Hello, Taryn," said Gabrielle, flicking her braid of red curls over her shoulder.

Taryn gave her a withering look. "Mmm-hmm."

Stone leaned back in his seat, arms folded across his chest. "So . . . you've finally decided to claim Shaya. I'm interested to know what took you so long." It wasn't a query, it was a reproach delivered with a snarl.

"Then you should ask Shaya in private," advised Nick.

"I'm asking *you*."

"Yeah, but I don't explain myself to other people—only to Shaya."

Stone narrowed his eyes, his gaze studious, but he said nothing. Nick had the feeling that his answer had won a little of Stone's respect . . . or maybe the guy just liked that although Nick was a bastard, he wouldn't be one to Shaya.

"How've you both been?" Shaya asked her parents, smiling, breaking the awkward silence. The tension in the air was practically crackling. Having Nick's arm draped over the back of her chair and his fingers playing with her hair was a comfort she *so* needed right then.

Gabrielle answered instantly. "If you must know, I don't feel good at all—not that you truly care. I haven't slept in weeks. No doubt it's stress, seeing as my own daughter has left me and barely answers my calls."

Shaya held her smile in place. "Forgive me if I don't enjoy being insulted and sent on a guilt trip for having my own life."

"You've always been selfish and difficult," Gabrielle claimed. "Never sensitive to my predicaments."

Sensing Nick's irritation building, Shaya squeezed his thigh under the table. "Have you consulted a healer?" It was second nature to feign interest.

"Yes. He said there's nothing wrong with me." She huffed. "Can you believe that?"

Well, yeah, Shaya could.

"What is it you believe is wrong with you?" rumbled Nick, wanting the woman's focus away from Shaya. He had no tolerance for people who faked ill-health when there were so many people out there who were truly ill.

"I have a thyroid problem, I know I have. I don't care what the healer said, I know my own body. *And* I checked my symptoms on the Internet. Maybe Taryn can take a look at me while I'm here."

The Alpha female merely made a noncommittal sound.

"So you no longer believe you have heart failure, deep vein thrombosis, and a fractured ankle?" asked Shaya dryly. She hated herself for being frustrated and angry with her mother, but she'd really had enough of the emotional manipulation. The number of times Shaya had heard the words "I think I'm dying" was unreal, but there had never been a single thing wrong.

In the past, Shaya had over and over rushed Gabrielle to a healer; by the time they arrived there, her mother had gone from weak and pitiful to excited and chipper—she loved the attention. It had gotten to the point where Shaya's life had revolved around Gabrielle and her "conditions." It was part of the reason why Shaya had switched to the Phoenix Pack, though she had still gone to visit her mother at least every other day, feeling guilty if she didn't.

Of course when Shaya moved to Arizona, there was no one to fuss around Gabrielle—Stone certainly didn't "entertain her dramatics," as he referred to it. As she'd expected, Gabrielle hated that. She believed she was entitled to Shaya's time, attention, and aid. Gabrielle looked about to reprimand Shaya, but then Stone was speaking again. Not to Shaya, but to Nick.

"Tell me about yourself."

Nick recognized that deceptively friendly tone all too well. He'd used it himself with the web designer. "I'm not applying for the position of being your daughter's mate. I *am* her mate. We've claimed each other. If you want to ask me questions for no other reason than that you'd like to get to know me, I'd be happy to answer them."

Stone smiled, making Shaya tense. "I tried to do a background check on you." His tone was even, calm—that meant bad things, she knew. "No one would tell me anything. Why is that?" Nick didn't answer. He just smiled.

"If you have more contacts and allies than I do—and I have a *lot*—you must have won the loyalty of many people. All I'm really interested in knowing is if you've won the loyalty of my daughter and if you plan to give her the same in return."

"Shaya's always had my loyalty."

"And he has mine," Shaya told her father, leaning against Nick for a few seconds.

"You believe he deserves it?" It was a genuine question from Stone.

She nodded. "He hurt me, but he had his reasons for not claiming me—good ones. It's complicated."

Stone sighed, grumbling, "It always is with male shifters."

Nick noticed his mate's smile of amusement and gave her a mock scowl.

"What about you, Taryn?" asked Stone. "If anyone's as protective of Shaya as I am—other than Nick here of course"—said with so much patronization that Marcus almost choked on a laugh—"it's you. Is he worthy of her?"

Taryn snorted. "No one's worthy of Shaya. But she's right—he had his reasons for not claiming her initially. He's proven over and over that she comes first. Also, he's *totally* whipped, if that makes you feel any better."

Nick scowled at the blonde. "I'm not whipped."

"Of course you're not," placated Shaya, patting his arm, "you're just well trained." She laughed at his low growl. Turning to her father, she said, "I wanted to tell you, I have an interview for a mediator position. If I get it—"

"You'll get it," insisted Nick with utter confidence.

"—it'll mean I get to go traveling. Maybe I'll even see some of the places you used to tell me all about when I was little."

Stone's smile was genuine this time as he took Shaya's free hand in his. He gave Nick a small nod, which could be translated to "I'll accept you *for now.*" It might not be a gushing reception, but it was enough to lift her spirits. Then Gabrielle went and spoiled the moment.

"Traveling? Have you not learned anything from watching my relationship with your father? Mates shouldn't be separated for long periods at a time." She looked at Nick then. "You'll soon have an idea how I've felt all my life."

"I'll be going with Shaya," Nick told her, barely refraining from snapping at the woman. "Where she goes, I go."

"Nice idea," said Stone.

Gabrielle turned to her mate, spluttering. "You never took me with you."

"I couldn't have taken you into war zones, despite that it was an appealing idea at times. Then you'd have known what suffering *really* is. And maybe you would have stopped being so self-centered and paid attention to our daughter."

Gabrielle gasped in outrage, but it was Shaya she snarled at. "It's difficult to give attention to an ungrateful, inconsiderate—"

"Enough," said Nick quietly, his voice still filled with authority. Gabrielle's eyes widened. "*No one* speaks to my mate like that. Not even her mother. In my opinion, though, I shouldn't have to order her mother not to do so."

"You don't know what it's been like for me," claimed Gabrielle. "You don't know how hard it is to lose one child and then find that the other is selfish and—"

"One more insult," rumbled Nick, "and you leave."

Shaya rubbed her jaw against his upper arm, hoping to calm him. "I've never asked you for anything, Mom. But I'm asking you now . . . if you can't be happy for me, if you can't be part of my life without trying to hurt me, leave me alone."

"Trying to hurt you?" echoed Gabrielle, her tone incredulous, but Nick was aware the female knew what Shaya meant.

"You displaced your guilt onto Shaya."

Gabrielle gawked at Nick. "Excuse me?"

"You were heartbroken when your other daughter died in the womb—of course you were. You felt responsible, felt guilty. But you couldn't handle the weight of that guilt, so you transferred it onto Shaya. And she's carried it all her life, and you let her. The times you left her alone in the house . . . you did that because that was what your mate did to you, left you alone. You wanted someone else to suffer. All your life you've escaped your own pain by dumping it on Shaya. No more. As she said, if you can't be in her life without hurting her, you need to leave it."

Gabrielle spluttered again and looked at her mate, expecting him to defend her. He didn't. Nick knew it wasn't because the guy feared him; it was most likely that he knew Nick was right and that Shaya deserved better than what Gabrielle had to give.

"Well, what will it be?" Shaya asked, her voice strong.

Gabrielle averted her gaze, concentrating on a spot on the wall. She was quiet for a minute. "When is your mating ceremony?"

"In a couple of days."

Without looking at Shaya, she said, "We'll be there."

Shaya knew that was the equivalent of Gabrielle saying she was backing down and wished to stay in her life, but it wasn't the "sorry and I love you" that she would have preferred—not that she had expected, or would ever expect, to hear that, but a girl could dream.

Abruptly, Gabrielle rose to her feet and headed for the doorway, where she waited as Stone said his good-byes to Shaya and Nick.

Just as she was about to leave, Nick called out, "If you hurt her again, Gabrielle, the choice of whether or not you remain in Shaya's life will be taken out of your hands."

Again Gabrielle looked to Stone for support. Again, she got none. Still, she claimed haughtily, "Her father would never allow that."

"I wouldn't be too sure of that. Like me, he has Shaya's best interests at heart. But you wouldn't know anything about that, would you?" Swallowing hard, the woman left with her mate following behind her, who was shaking his head at the woman—looking exasperated.

Nick turned back to Shaya, pulling her into the cradle of his shoulder. "Okay, baby?" When she nodded, he nipped her earlobe. She gave a cute little yelp. "Don't lie."

She sighed, shrugging. "What do you want me to say? Sure, I wish things could be easier between my mother and me, but they're not. At least she's willing to try. That was more than I would have expected. It's a relief my father seems to like you."

"I'm not so sure he likes me, but he's reconsidering the idea of shooting me with the Glock he's carrying, which is good enough."

Shaya smiled. "I wondered if you'd notice. He carries it everywhere." She waved a hand. "No more about them. We have more important things to worry about."

"Yes, unfortunately, we do."

As it was important that Nick knew every inch of pack territory in preparation for the attack, Shaya took him on a thorough tour of the land while they were in their wolf forms after breakfast. She showed him every lake, every clearing, every hidden entrance to the caves. She even showed him the "hut"—the small building where trespassers were taken to be interrogated by Dante.

When they stopped at a particular lake, she shifted back to her human form. "This is my favorite spot on Phoenix land. Come on, I want to swim."

Back in his human form, Nick glanced around, taking in his surroundings. Instantly, he understood. "You used to come here to be alone, didn't you?" he asked, smiling. It was almost funny, considering she was so sociable.

"Yes," she admitted, slowly going deeper and deeper into the lake. "Sometimes a girl likes a little alone time."

He gasped in mock outrage. "All this time you've been poking fun at me for preferring solitude, and you actually have your own secret spot. I feel so betrayed."

She laughed. "The main reason I used to come here a lot is that it reminds me of a spot in the land my dad and I used to go hunting on."

Nick joined her in the water and pulled her against him, wanting her skin against his. "Tell me about these hunting trips."

"Well, you know all shifters take their kids hunting; they shift into their animal forms and teach their kids how to hunt rabbits and other animals. Of course Stone couldn't do that because he's human. So he took me hunting with him in my human form. We used different weapons, eventually working up to shotguns and rifles. I like rifles best."

"Your Alphas let you do that? Most shifters hate the use of weapons."

"No, we weren't allowed to hunt on pack territory. Occasionally, my dad would take me to a place called Oakdon Creek and rent the private hunting lodge there for a week. Well, 'lodge' isn't really the right word. It was more like a huge rustic mansion. I used to love it—it was literally my favorite place in the world. It was peaceful and relaxing, yet wild and untamed. And it was my refuge too—or, at least, that was how it felt because they were the times when I wasn't required to run around after my mother."

"She had you doing that even as a kid?" Nick barely held back a growl.

Shaya shrugged, sliding her arms around his neck. "I was just a supply of attention to her."

He rubbed a soothing hand up and down her upper back. "Do you and your dad still go on these trips?"

"No. When I was seventeen, the place was bought by a human company that hated shifters. They knew my dad belonged to a wolf pack and that I had to therefore be a half-shifter, so they saw him as a traitor and refused to let us rent the lodge anymore."

Assholes. "How often did you used to come out here for some alone time?"

"I didn't always come alone. Sometimes I'd bring Taryn. I also came here a lot with Marcus." At Nick's low growl, she quickly added, rolling her eyes, "We didn't go swimming together. We just came and sat on that fallen tree over there whenever I needed to talk."

"About what?" He found he didn't like the idea of her confiding in another male.

"You. See, I never told anybody in the beginning. It was for two reasons, really. One, I was embarrassed and ashamed that my own mate didn't appear to want me. Two, I knew that Taryn would break your nose and then the pack would force the claiming—I wanted you to come for me because you *wanted* me, no other reason. So I kept it to myself. But Marcus . . . He'd guessed I was upset about something, and he *hounded* me until I told him. Not out of nosiness; Marcus just has a very protective streak. He's so easy to talk to that I found myself telling him about you being my true mate and stuff. Despite being an enforcer and very close to Trey, he kept the secret for me from even them."

The idea of her feeling so embarrassed, of her carrying that painful secret around and feeling so unbelievably alone, almost put a lump in his throat. It also made him want to punch himself. "I'm glad you had someone here for you when I wasn't."

"Stop feeling guilty. You had your reasons; let it go."

Like that would ever happen. Whether he'd meant to hurt her or not, he'd still caused his mate pain, and that was something he couldn't forgive himself for. "Anyway, you don't need Marcus anymore, you have me."

"I can have friends too," she chuckled.

He slid his hands down to cup that ass he loved. "Of course you can, and I'm sure you'll still confide in them about things, but I'd like to think I'll be your first port of call if you need to talk."

That was when Shaya realized something—something she couldn't believe she hadn't noticed before. "You feel threatened by my close friendship with Taryn."

"Not threatened exactly. But I see how much more open you are with her than with anyone else." And it hurt that she wasn't that open with him. He'd told her when he claimed her that he wouldn't allow her to hold back from him anymore, that he wanted all of her. And he *did* have all of her . . . but he didn't have her total trust, and that was one of the most important things to him.

*Feeling* that it wounded him, she softly said, "I trust you as much as I trust her."

"But?" He could tell there was one.

"But . . . it's different with Taryn. I don't mean she's more important to me than you. It's hard to explain." After a short pause, she spoke. "She was there for me when I needed someone—since I was four, she's been that one constant thing that I knew I could rely on. But really, I never relied on her; I wouldn't let myself rely on anyone. She gave me the comfort of knowing that if I *did* want to rely on someone, she was there. But she would never demand it from me, so there was no pressure.

"With you . . . it's something I have to give you at some point, but I don't know how to emotionally rely on another person, how to trust them. I *know* I can rely on you, and I do in some ways. But holding back a little . . . it's like my safety cushion. It means that if things mess up, I've kept a part of me safe, so it won't utterly destroy me. I don't know how to trust that I don't need a safety cushion; that you're all the safety I need. But I am trying. I really am."

To some extent, Nick could understand that. He'd never relied on others either. As a child, it had been an act of defiance, a determination to be independent in every sense—most alphas were like that as kids. But then he'd gone to juvie and there had been no one to rely on; all he'd had was himself. When he'd been released from juvie, it was to be thrust into the position of Alpha and have others relying on him.

It could be said that Nick had ignored his own needs for a very long time, which had been helped along by his inability to fully connect with people. But with Shaya, he *wanted* that connection; he didn't resent that she would be someone who would need to be able to rely on him. He liked the idea of being her source of security, just the way he liked how she balanced him out. Where he was unsociable and withdrawn, she was outgoing and had an ease with people. Where he was hard and remote, she was life and sensuality. Where he was often too serious and intense, she was light and laughter. She made him *live*, forced him to crack the shell he had around himself and try to accept others in his life.

No one else had ever gotten so close to him, because he hadn't wanted them to. But he didn't hold back with Shaya, never had. That was why it pained him so much that she didn't feel totally safe with him. The fact that she considered him in some way a danger to her caused an ache in his chest.

Sensing how bad he was hurting, Shaya wished she wasn't so messed up. "I'm sorry."

He held her even tighter to him, giving her a pointed look. "Hey, don't you dare apologize for what you can't give me. It's my own fault anyway."

"No, it's not. Even if you had claimed me that very first night we met, this trust issue would still have been there. As if that isn't bad enough, there's the fact that dominant/submissive pairs find completing the mating link hard."

"Only those who believe that a difference in status is a problem and feel that they can't complement each other. I know you worry I'll grow to resent that you're not dominant, but that's just dumb. I want you exactly as you are. I've never seen you as weak.

You don't hold me back in any sense; you make me stronger because you balance me out. And *I* balance *you* out."

"You do?" she said with a smile, amused by the utter confidence in the latter words.

He nodded, nipping her lip. "You've always made me think of a butterfly. Vibrant, graceful, colorful. But there's another reason why you make me think of a butterfly—you're damn hard to pin down." She chuckled. "It's true. I used to watch you, see the way you flitted from place to place and person to person, never still . . . because you're trying to live your life for both you *and* your sister." He could tell she hadn't thought of it that way before. He stroked the curls away from her face, cupping her cheek as he softly continued. "You can't do that, baby. You can use her as motivation, but you can't live for two people."

Stunned, Shaya struggled to find words. "I didn't realize that was what I was trying to do. But you're right; I was."

"And if I hadn't pointed it out, you would probably always have done it. This is what I mean when I say I balance you out. I keep you settled in one place—with me. I anchor you, ground you, make sure you don't neglect your own needs, stop you from feeling alone, and give you and your wolf the security you need . . . but I don't smother you in any way or try to take away your independence in doing that."

And all of that was exactly what she needed, Shaya knew. "I still can't believe I hadn't seen this with Mika before now. It's not like it's a little thing."

"She wouldn't want you to be doing this, because it would mean you weren't living a full life."

It would also mean she and Nick weren't living a full life *together*, and that wasn't acceptable. "I guess, in some ways, I did it because I always felt guilty for being alive when she wasn't."

"Your mother made you feel that way, Shay." He'd happily cut that toxic woman from Shaya's life if he didn't think it would hurt her not to give her mother a second chance. "It was wrong of her to do that. But you can't carry on trying to live for both of you." Jokingly, he added, "After all, I can't deal with two mates. One's enough."

Narrowing her eyes, Shaya slapped his shoulder and reflexively snapped, "I don't share." Realizing how dumb she'd sounded, she groaned inwardly.

"I'm glad to hear it, because neither do I. You're all I want. And you're not something I'm prepared to lose. Ever. I already know how it feels to try to live a life without you in it. I don't want to feel that ever again."

"You tried to leave me the day you had the memory lapse," she pointed out.

"Not leave you." He kissed her lightly. "Protect you, put you first. I'll always do that."

"But not by trying to leave me again." It was half question, half statement.

He shook his head. "No, baby, not that. It might have worked before we'd claimed each other, but it wouldn't work now. We're linked, for better or worse."

"You're healed," she insisted, knowing what he meant by "worse."

He hoped so, because the alternative was that Shaya would spend her life with a mate who didn't even know who she was. "Come here." Sliding a hand into her hair, he angled her head and brought his mouth down on hers. The kiss was slow, leisurely, and soft enough to be teasing and make her push for more. It wasn't long before her claws pricked into his back—a demand for more. As if she quickly understood the demand would only make him prolong the featherlight kiss, she retracted her claws and released a sigh of frustration into his mouth.

"Shh," soothed Nick. "It's okay. I have no intention of making you wait." Not when an attack was looming—it brought with it an acute awareness of the fleeting nature of time. Tucking Shaya's leg over his hip, he thrust deep inside her. His eyes didn't leave hers even once as he slowly claimed her all over again with each and every stroke. She clung to him with an almost desperate hold, and he sensed just how worried she was that by holding back from him, she'd drive him away.

He rested his forehead against hers. "Let me ask you something. When you turned psycho on me that first night and bloodied me, did it drive me away? No. When you rejected me over and over, did I leave? No. When you went on a date with that goofy human, did that drive me away? No. I've told you from the very beginning that you'll never make me give you up. Start believing that."

He kissed her again, hardening his thrusts as if it might just help him get through to her. When she finally came, triggering his own climax, she sank her teeth into his neck in a move that was as possessive as it was a reaffirmation to herself that he was hers. But the possessive bite wasn't what had his wolf growling in satisfaction a few minutes later. Frowning, Nick fought the sated fog and smiled in both smugness and contentedness as he understood. "Our scents have mixed." The head leaning on his shoulder suddenly shot up; her expression was pure wonder.

Shaya had been so deep in her dreamy post-orgasmic state that she hadn't even sensed it. Well that certainly explained why her wolf was so relaxed and tranquil.

Nick tucked a curl behind her ear. "It means the bond is advancing, Shay."

Maybe it was because they had talked some things through, or maybe it was because she had made the decision to stop clinging to Mika, to let her go, and, as such, it had given Nick the space to burrow deeper inside Shaya than he already was. She wasn't sure, but she knew one thing. "I find I'm possessive enough to be smug that now everyone will know by just your scent that you're taken and mine."

He laughed, burying his face into the crook of her neck. "You smell even better now than you did before. Like the ocean, and cinnamon, and me." He sucked her bottom lip into his mouth. "Mine."

She nodded. "Yours."

Entering the living area a little while later, they found Jaime, Dante, Roni, Marcus, Dominic, Grace, Lydia, and Amber. The smell of Nick and Shaya's combined scents seemed to hit everyone at once, because they were all smiling—even Amber, despite that it was fake.

"Well, well, well," said Jaime, delighted, as Nick and Shaya perched themselves on the gigantic sofa where everyone other than Roni and Dominic, who had each claimed an armchair, was sitting. "It would appear things are moving along nicely." Jaime swapped places with Dante so that she was then sitting by Nick, winking at Shaya when he stiffened at her proximity. "How's my BFF doing?" When Nick gawked at her, Jaime said indulgently, "Not you, sweetie, I was talking to your mate." Shaya would have been pissed by people continually poking at him if she didn't know this meant they accepted him.

"Fine, thanks." Shaya patted Nick's thigh soothingly.

"I'm glad things are working out for you guys," said Roni.

"Me too," said Grace. The others all nodded.

"Thanks. Where's Mom?" Nick asked Roni. His mother spent a lot of time with Greta, and he couldn't find it in himself to see that as a good thing.

"She went on a pack run with some of the others. I wanted to go too, but it seemed that Marcus, Dante, and Jaime suddenly found lots of things for me to do." She threw them a scowl, folding her arms over her chest. She wasn't stupid; she knew people were trying to keep her from shifting in case she disappeared in her wolf form again. They wouldn't be able to stop her doing it during the attack tomorrow, though. Nick only hoped his sister came back afterward.

"Imagine if it turned out that Gok Wan's actually straight as a ruler." Yeah, that was Dominic—totally random. His eyes still on the TV, he gestured at the show. "The guy would be my hero if that was the case."

Grace snorted at Dominic. "You don't need to trick women into getting naked. They're all too happy to oblige, from what I've heard."

Lydia nodded. "It's the same with Marcus, only the females are after his heart too because they fall for all that charm." Marcus winked and flashed her a grateful smile that made her blush.

Dominic frowned, affronted. "I have charm."

"But it's a twisted kind of charm, honey," said Lydia. "If you'd let Marcus teach you a few things, you'd be lethal."

"I'm not sure if I want to be lethal if it means females will want more than sex." Dominic shuddered.

"In other words, you're a slut?" asked Roni.

"I guess you could say I've been a bad boy, Roni. If you want to send me to your room and—"

"Shut up, jerk," said Marcus, rolling his eyes.

Hearing Taryn and Trey's voices coming along the tunnels, Shaya smiled, eager for her best friend to hear that the mating link was developing. Thinking she might have just picked up another voice, Shaya cocked her head to listen harder. Then, to her surprise and delight, Taryn and Trey walked into the room with Caleb behind them.

Shaya practically jumped from the sofa and darted to the person whom she thought of as a brother. "Caleb!" Wearing a smile as wide as hers, Caleb wrapped his arms tight around her and squeezed. Then he froze at the sound of two low growls. Roni and Nick apparently didn't like that another male was embracing her. Pulling back, she urged Caleb to follow her to Nick and took her mate's hand in hers. At her tug, he stood. "Nick, you remember Caleb from Taryn and Trey's mating ceremony, right?"

Nick's voice came out dry. "I remember." He awkwardly shook hands with the tall, brown-eyed wolf with stubble for hair. There was no desire in the guy's scent or eyes, which meant he didn't appear to have any interest in Shaya in a sexual sense; therefore, Nick could allow him to live. Still, Nick didn't like other males hugging his mate, so it was pretty impossible to drop his scowl . . . even though Shaya was jamming her elbow into his ribs.

As Taryn came close with Kye in her arms, Caleb leaned in to her and said quietly, "I didn't think I'd ever meet anyone who can look scarier than Trey."

"Hey, your scents have mixed," said Taryn, pleased—a total relief for Shaya. "It just proves that dominant/submissive pairs have every chance of fully bonding," she threw over her shoulder, meeting Amber's hard gaze.

"They're not fully bonded yet," Amber pointed out, "but I'm sure it will happen soon. They suit so well."

She smiled sweetly, but apparently Caleb wasn't fooled because he gave Shaya a look that said, "Seriously, what's up with that?"

Shaya merely smiled and mouthed, "We'll talk later." Out loud she said, "Caleb, this is Roni—Nick's sister—and Amber, the healer of his old pack."

As Caleb exchanged greetings with the two females, Nick sank back into his seat and looped an arm around Shaya's waist, pulling her onto his lap. Pettily jealous that her attention was on Caleb, Nick bit her ear. Clearly sensing he missed her focus being mostly on him, she gave him an amused sideways glance. But she didn't return her full attention to him, and that just showed how well she knew him—it wasn't at all good to let him have his own way all the time.

"When did you change your hair?" Shaya asked Caleb.

His smile fell, and irritation practically steamed from him. "When my little cousin decided to chop bits of it off while I was sleeping."

Taryn cocked her head, studying him. "It suits you."

He snorted. Then, his expression now serious, his eyes danced from Shaya to Nick and Taryn as he spoke. "When I heard what was happening, I had to come. I can help guard the entrances to the caves tomorrow night and make sure Kye's protected. I need to play a part in this. I couldn't sit home on my ass when I know something bad is going to go down here."

Respecting the male for his loyalty to his friends and his offer to help when many submissive wolves would have opted out of the dangerous situation, Nick gave him a nod of thanks. "It's appreciated." His estimation of the male had now gone up.

Taryn gave Caleb a smile of appreciation. "Thanks for caring so much for Kye."

"We're grateful for the support," said Shaya.

At the sound of the main door closing and two males laughing loudly, Taryn said, "Oh, Nick, that'll be your brother."

Nick arched a brow. "My brother?"

She shrugged. "Derren told me he was going to collect him and bring him here. Apparently the guy refused to miss out on whatever happens with the extremists."

"That's typical of Eli and his lust for action," Nick grumbled to Shaya.

"I don't like the idea of your brother in danger, just like I don't like the idea of anyone here in danger," said Shaya. "But if Eli's willing to help, it would be dumb to turn him away." A moment later, Derren entered the room with a powerfully built male who had the most enormous brown eyes. He wasn't as tall or as broad as Nick, but he had the same indomitable look about him. Everyone exchanged nods with him—they had all seen him before at one point or another, as he often went with Nick to pack meetings or social gatherings and had actually been one of the wolves who fought alongside the Phoenix Pack against Trey's uncle.

Grinning, Eli walked toward Nick, all self-assurance. "Hey. I tried calling to ask you to pick me up, but you didn't answer your cell." They exchanged one of those weird male body hugs, though

Shaya could see Nick found the contact a little awkward. Clearly his brother was too used to that to care, because he didn't comment or appear to be the slightest bit offended.

"I was a little preoccupied," said Nick.

Knowing just what he meant, Shaya almost blushed.

Nick curled an arm around her. "You guys haven't officially met. Eli, this is my mate. Shaya, this is the adrenaline junkie of the family."

Eli laughed and then turned his attention to her. "It's good to finally meet you, Shaya." He cocked his head, studying her for a minute with an analytical gaze. Then he nodded, apparently satisfied about something. "Derren's right. You'll make a good Alpha female."

Shaya frowned. "You don't even know me."

"Ah, but I know things about you. You evaded Nick for a long time, so you're clearly smart. A number of the wolves here went all the way to Arizona to check on you and refused to leave until they could be sure you're safe, which means you're good at earning loyalty, and that says a lot about a person. Also, Derren tells me you insist on being at Nick's side through all this, which proves that you're brave and believe in protecting those who matter to you. If you're Nick's mate, you must be as strong as he is. Not physically, no, but being physically strong doesn't make someone Alpha material. It's a good trait to have, but that's not the be-all and end-all."

Shaya looked up at her mate. "I like your brother." Eli gave her a winning smile.

Nick snorted. "Don't let that smile fool you, baby. He's a ruthless fucker."

Shaya could believe that. Eli was almost as dominant as Nick, but he wore that dominance in a very subtle way—much like Dominic. Eli's wolf, however, wasn't so subtle. Shaya's wolf could easily sense his wolf, sense his curiosity and edginess.

Eli's expression suddenly turned serious. "Derren updated me on what's been happening. In my opinion, it won't matter what the verdict is tomorrow morning. The extremists will attack in any case."

"But we'll be ready for that," announced Taryn. The others nodded.

"Ready and waiting," rumbled Trey.


The next morning, the court hearing was held to hear the case put forward by the human extremists. And every shifter worldwide celebrated as the case was dismissed.

# CHAPTER EIGHTEEN

It was eleven thirty in the evening when the humans finally came. Shaya and the others were all in position, planted in various spots—waiting, silent and still. While many were in their wolf form in the woods, Shaya was positioned on her stomach on a thick branch of a tall tree, allowing her to oversee whatever would come next. Despite the anxiety running through her body and mind, her hands were steady as she held the rifle. It felt right in her grip, made her remember the times her dad had taken her hunting when she was younger. For long periods of time, they would lie still as she was doing now, their senses on high alert. As such, this wasn't unfamiliar, but still her wolf wasn't so steady; she was too frightened for her mate's safety.

Most of the females, Kent, and, of course, Kye had remained in the caves, guarded by Caleb, Gabe, Rhett, and Cam. As such, there was a total of eighteen wolves—including Shaya—taking cover in what would soon be a battlefield: Nick, Derren, Eli, Taryn, Trey, Dante, Jaime, Roni, Tao, Trick, Marcus, Ryan, Dominic, Bracken, Jesse, Zander, and Amber.

It wasn't long before, one by one, the humans began to enter through the gap that Tao had deliberately made in the perimeter fence. Forty-six humans in total. The fact that they were all dressed in black made Shaya roll her eyes. Dark clothes worked well as camouflage, but black would make a person easier to see, as true black looked unnatural, outlining a person's silhouette. Even from her distance one hundred yards away, she could clearly see with her shifter-heightened vision that the humans were well armed with guns and knives. It wasn't unexpected, but it was still alarming.

Knowing his stature and posture well, she could easily spot Logan co-leading the group with another figure as they slowly and cautiously began to move. Could that be the shifter responsible for the creation of the game preserve? Quite possibly. Just the idea had her wolf growling.

Shaya's advanced hearing barely picked up much noise from them, but she guessed they were all quite experienced at going unseen and unheard if they had been enjoying themselves in the game preserve. Instantly, the images she had seen on the news flashed in her mind, making her sick to her stomach. Having a perfect view of Logan and his co-leader, it was so tempting to just shoot them both there and then. But that wasn't the plan.

The entire day in the caves had been spent going over the plan. It was simple. They had to lure the humans far inside the expansive territory, which served two purposes. One, it meant Tao could seal up the opening in the fence, thus trapping the humans inside. Two, everyone felt the humans deserved to be tracked and played with, just as they had done to the shifters in the game preserve. Only once the humans were deep in pack territory would the shifters all begin to attack. When images of the mutilated child shifters once again flashed before her, Shaya felt a surge of anger. Yeah, the bastards had this coming.

As the humans followed the trail Trey had left, Shaya thought they would undoubtedly believe they were getting closer and closer to the entrance of the caves. In reality, they were being led farther and farther into the woods. Shaya watched as, without the humans' knowledge, their hunters began to move into place until the large group was loosely circled as they walked, giving them no avenues of escape when the attack finally began.

It wasn't until the humans reached one of the many shallow lakes that the shifters made any moves. The three humans at the rear of the group were targeted first. There was no loud attack. Ryan, Dante, and Jaime—all in their human form—each stepped out from behind a tree and swiftly snatched a human and yanked them aside. Shaya knew exactly what they had done in the shadows: snapped the humans' necks instantly, taking them out of the equation.

Totally oblivious, the rest of the group continued onward. A few seconds later, Dante, Jaime, and Ryan repeated the move. They did it again and again, picking off the humans. They might have done it again, but then one of the group stepped onto a bear trap; his pain-filled cry echoed throughout the forest as the two jaws clamped around his foot and he dropped to the ground. Several humans gathered around him.

Panicked, one human crouched beside him. "Shit, what happened?"

"A bear trap." Logan.

"I can't get it off!"

Logan again: "Of course you can't. You're not supposed to be able to. Be careful, there'll be more around."

"Do you think they have the place rigged?" one asked him.

"I wouldn't be surprised if the closer we get, the more traps there are. And not just bear traps."

"We better get moving," said the co-leader. His voice didn't sound at all familiar. "The wolves will have heard him screaming. They'll come out here to look around."

Logan nodded his agreement. "Two of you help him up and support him as he walks. Filcher, any movement back there? Filcher? Filcher?"

"He's not there," another human said. "Shit, neither is Gavin or—"

"We're being picked off," drawled the co-leader.

"We're being hunted," corrected Logan. His voice held a telling tremor. "That means they know exactly where we are. Stay close together." Two of the group helped support the injured human as they all slowly continued ahead through the trees, constantly turning as they walked to cover every angle.

Twenty seconds or so later, another human triggered a thin trip wire that sent a spiked boulder swinging at his head. Grunting, he fell to the ground, crying out and cursing and bleeding like crazy. *Shit, that had to have hurt.* When the spiked boulder continued swinging and looked about to hit another human, the male dove out of the way . . . and stepped into another bear trap. While a few of the large group went to tend to the injured, everyone else seemed to freeze, wary of moving.

Whereas the group had before seemed nervous but confident, they were now cautious and fearful—just like the wolves wanted. It wasn't until right then, when the group was confused and disoriented, that the ambush began. There was gunfire, there was growling, there was screaming, there was yelling as the wolves came at the group from all directions. It was also the go-ahead for Shaya to act. Aiming for those who she judged the biggest threats and of whom she had a clear view, Shaya fired one bullet after another, gratified down to her gut as she disabled the bastards.

One of those bullets hit her target's arm rather than his heart, and he dropped his gun as he flinched with the pain. When Nick's wolf turned his attention to him, the human turned and ran in what could only be described as a blind panic. He suddenly screeched in pain and fell to the ground, having stepped on one of the barbed-spike plates that were planted around. Nick dived on him, closing his jaw around the asshole's throat.

The wolves were all merciless in their assault. Trey's wolf had gone feral by this point and was tearing into whatever human was near him. Although he'd taken a bullet to the leg, it wasn't stopping him—not in that state. Most likely disturbed about his injury, Taryn's wolf was staying near her mate as she pounced on the humans with equal vigor.

Now in their wolf form, Jaime and Ryan were fighting alongside Dante's injured yet relentless wolf, who kept bumping Jaime out of harm's way—all instinct at that moment. Jesse, Bracken, and Zander weren't far away, attacking with a rage that spoke of the pain of losing loved ones to these corrupted humans.

When Tao and Trick's wolves lunged at two now weaponless humans, they instantly turned and sprinted away . . . and fell right into a deep pit in the ground onto a cushion of spikes. *Ouch.* Similarly, Eli's and Amber's wolves chased another duo of humans into a second deep pit that was also cushioned by spikes.

One human was running backward and simultaneously firing in every direction. Had he been looking ahead of him, he might have seen the heavy rock that was supported by several branches, tilted on an angle. The second the human's foot hit the branch that served as a trigger, the rock collided into him, crushing him. Dominic's wolf then delivered a killing bite to his throat.

Meanwhile, Shaya continued trying to pick off or, at the very least, severely injure the remaining humans. Unfortunately, two of those remaining were Logan and the co-leader, who were being protected by the others. Clearly determined to reach the two sick bastards, Nick's wolf was targeting their protectors. Roni's, Derren's, and Marcus's wolves were helping him, but the circle of protection was still strong.

Shaya didn't have a good angle on the remaining humans and it was pissing her the hell off. She thought about climbing down from the tree and moving to a spot that would provide her with a better shot, but she had promised Nick that she wouldn't step any closer into the war zone, and she'd keep that promise. If she didn't, it would distract him, and that would risk him being seriously hurt.

Watching as he suddenly stopped still, she frowned. His head turned her way, and she felt his confusion and anxiety. Then there was some kind of explosion. She could only guess that one of the humans had some kind of grenade—at that moment, the *who, what, why, when,* and *how* wasn't important; what was important was that the force had sent Nick, Roni, and Derren zooming through the air. Roni crashed into a tree, Derren flew out of her view, and Nick hit the ground hard—so hard that she *felt* as blackness overcame him. Fuck, he'd passed out.

Everything inside Shaya screamed at the sight of him lying there like that, unconscious and vulnerable. Her wolf froze in panic, howling. Drowning in emotions she couldn't even understand right then, Shaya ignored reason and rationality as instinct took over; she climbed down and raced through the maze of trees. With only Nick's safety on her mind, she hadn't registered the presence of three unfamiliar scents until an arm looped around her waist, a hand was clamped over her mouth, and the gun was yanked from her hand. *Shit!*

She struggled like crazy, hitting and head-butting and scratching, but her attacker—a shifter, she sensed—didn't release her. From the corner of her eye, she saw movement: Amber's wolf was finishing off a fleeing human. She caught sight of Shaya and froze in what was most likely surprise. Shaya appealed to her with her eyes, hoping that for just once, Amber would do what was right instead of what suited her.

She didn't.

The bitch loped away, leaving Shaya at the mercy of God-knew-who. Then the butt of her gun smacked into her head, and everything went dark.

*"For God's sake, shift! Now, Nick! I can't heal you until you shift!"*

It was not the voice of the Alpha female that woke the gray wolf. It was the feel of his mate's fear, her anger, her determination to be free of the danger she was in. Danger. He had *known* the danger was coming for her, had felt it just before the blackness came.

There was the sound of the Alpha female's voice again. But the gray wolf had no interest in her. His only concern was his mate. She needed him, and he would not, could not, ignore that. He tried jumping to his feet. His leg crumpled beneath him. He yelped with pain, unable to rise. He could feel Nick's panic, knew that Nick wanted dominance right then. Accepting for his mate's sake that Nick was the strongest at that moment, the wolf backed down.

The shift was agonizing; Nick clenched his teeth against the pain, worried he'd pass out again. His leg had not only taken a bullet, but it was broken in two places. He was bleeding badly in several places, had taken a hard blow to his head, and had knife wounds in his sides.

"Roll onto your back now!" ordered Taryn.

"Shaya," he panted. "She's—"

"*Now*, Nick! If you die, Shaya will kill me!"

Carefully positioning himself on his back, he again tried to speak, but Taryn's mouth was locked on his and she was healing him. It was the oddest feeling; each time she breathed out some of what she called the "badness," he felt lighter yet stronger, relaxed yet galvanized. The pain got worse before it got better as his leg snapped back into place. But then there was only calm and peace and power. Done, she sat up. Trey was instantly at her side, holding her.

Nick shot upright and turned to Derren. "Shaya's been taken."

"Taken?" growled Derren. "Taken by who?"

"I don't know." But whoever it was, they would soon be dead. "Where's Logan?"

"We can't find his body, but he was badly injured—there's no way he could have kidnapped Shaya when he could barely walk. She'd have easily overpowered an injured human."

Nick could agree with that. "What about the shifter? I haven't scented an unfamiliar shifter."

"Neither have I."

That meant the shifter was most likely the kidnapper. His panic increased at the thought of it, at the thought of anyone hurting this female he'd come to love more than he believed he was capable of loving anyone. He didn't fear the realization, didn't fear the all-consuming feeling or view it as a weakness. All he feared was anything happening to her. "I need to shift again. I need to find her." This would be the perfect time to have another one of his *knowings*, but oh no, fate had apparently decided that this was a situation he and his wolf would have to fight their way through alone.

"We can't come with you, Nick," Taryn told him, tears in her eyes. "I need to stay here. A lot of these people are injured." Nick nodded in understanding. "You make sure you bring her back," ordered Taryn. The tears were in her voice now too.

Oh, he'd bring her back. He'd never before let anyone keep him from Shaya, and he wouldn't start now. "Count on it." With that, he swiftly returned to his wolf form.

The gray wolf darted to the spot where his mate should have been waiting. He needed to follow her scent in order to find her. Near the tree, he picked up four scents: one belonged to his mate, two belonged to humans, and the last scent was that of a shifter. It was a scent that the wolf knew . . . a scent that belonged to a wolf who should be dead.

Shaya knew Nick would come for her. Knew it. But she truly didn't want him to. Not when it was obvious that she was bait—a bait that was sitting on the floor with her wrists tied behind her back, held captive in the "hut" on the other side of pack territory by a trio of mentally unhinged males. Worse, one of said unhinged males was pointing her own rifle at her.

Pissing Shaya off even more, Amber was sitting opposite her in the exact same position. The only good thing about that was that the bitch had a broken leg. No, it wasn't because she had tried to help Shaya after all. The trio had taken Amber so that she couldn't alert anyone. They had even injected Amber with a drug that stopped her from shifting—the same drug they'd used in the game preserve. Had they known Shaya was a half-shifter, they would most likely have done the same to her.

Was Amber now on Shaya's side? No, she was trying to bargain with the trio for her life, claiming she would heal their wounds if they agreed to free her. The bargaining didn't appear to be working. Shaya wouldn't have cared if it worked; the only thing she could think about was getting to Nick. But there were three of these shit-heads and one of her. She had to wait for the right moment, or they would most likely put her unconscious again. She couldn't escape if she was unconscious. And she *would* escape. It went in her favor that none of them knew she was a half-shifter. They didn't know she was much stronger and faster than she looked, nor that the knot tying her wrists might not be as effective as they'd hoped.

Her dad had taught her the trick of freeing herself from knots a long time ago, but it was a little different trying to do it when it was a life-or-death situation. Just thinking about Nick uncon-scious had the adrenaline pumping more rapidly around Shaya's body and her heart pounding even louder.

*Stay calm*, her father would have told her. *Be observant*. Okay. Well, two of the three males were human, they had all been visited by the Ugly Fairy—one was so ugly it was almost fascinating—and the one in the center was clearly the shifter behind the creation of the game preserve.

The trio hadn't come into pack territory at the same entrance as the other humans, so Shaya could only guess that they had taken advantage of the pack being preoccupied during the attack to force their way through the gap Tao hadn't yet had the chance to fully secure. Humans wouldn't have stood a chance against it, but another shifter could.

"So, I was just wondering," she began in a flat tone, "what's the plan?"

Eyes the color of a dark storm landed on her, twinkling with malice. "Logan wants Nick to find you. He wants him to watch you die. After what Nick did to me, I like that plan."

"What did Nick do to you?" He didn't answer. She cocked her head at him, noticing he had a very chimp-like face. "Why do you hate shifters so much?"

"You wouldn't understand. You wouldn't understand what it's like for me."

God, he sounded like her mother. "Then tell me." *And keep your mind away from Nick.*

His upper lip curled. "Imagine how it feels to have to share your own soul. Share it with an *animal*, no less—an animal that selfishly pushes its wants and instincts on you. You have to live in a pack with an Alpha for a dad—someone everyone looks up to, while they look down on you for not being as good as he is. Imagine how it feels to find that fate has dumped you with a true mate who is nothing but a slut. Yeah, that's right, she imprinted on someone else, even had pups with him.

"The only good thing about this life is the *power* and *strength*. I told my father to step down and give me his position, but would he? No. He said I didn't have what it took to be an Alpha. So I did what had to be done—I killed him in his sleep. Did the pack accept me as their Alpha? No. They threw me out. As I had no place to go and no money, it was no wonder that I soon found myself in juvie. That was a hell like no other."

"And that's where you met Nick," she surmised. She couldn't recall Nick speaking of anyone he'd severely pissed off in juvie, though. Or anyone who resembled a chimp, for that matter.

"Speaking of Nick, he should be here soon. He'll definitely come for you. I know that much." He turned to the humans. "Where the hell is Logan?" They merely shrugged. "I'm going to take a look outside, see what's going on." To Shaya's frustration, he disappeared out of the hut, closing the door behind him.

"What's his problem with Nick?" she asked the two humans.

"That's his business," said the chubby compulsive spitter who would look right at home on a porch swing with a banjo.

Shaya released a sigh of frustration and turned to the gangly guy beside Chubby. "What did Nick do to him?"

Without moving his eyes from her breasts, Gangly absentmindedly replied, "Merrick just wants to make Nick suffer—it's like a tit-for-tat thing."

*Merrick?* That name certainly rang a bell. "But . . . Merrick's dead. Nick challenged him in juvie; he killed him." And he'd spent most of his life feeling bad about it.

"Obviously, he didn't. I'm pretty sure Merrick would have left Nick alone if the game preserve hadn't been found and Logan hadn't been goading him." Gangly shrugged carelessly. "In any case, he intends to make your mate suffer."

"If you want Nick to suffer," began Amber, "all you have to do is kill *her*. Let me go, and I'll heal you."

"You hadn't really healed Nick at all, had you?" Shaya somehow *knew*. Amber's shocked expression told her it was true. "I have to admit, it didn't occur to me at first. You looked so genuinely devastated when he told his mom and Roni about the memory lapse. You even asked for the chance to heal him again. But you wouldn't have truly healed him. No. Keeping him sick meant that you could keep him coming back to you, didn't it?"

Amber's expression turned somber. "It was the only time he'd really let me touch him. The only way to make him—the guy I love—need me."

"That's not exactly an excuse, sweetie. You kept my mate *ill* to the point that he thought he couldn't claim me. But that was the whole idea, wasn't it?" Before Amber could answer, Logan came bursting into the cabin, hobbling and bleeding, with Merrick close behind him.

"Nick's unconscious," Logan told them all. "I managed to get away while the shifters were concentrating on helping and healing each other. But it won't be long before he wakes up. We need to be ready."

Merrick retrieved a can of kerosene—*kerosene?*—from the floor.

"Remember," said Logan, "don't splash the hut. We don't want the place to blow up or burn too quickly. Just dribble it around the perimeter of the hut. It'll spread to the hut quick enough, but not so fast that Nick doesn't get to hear, feel, and smell her burning to death." With that, Logan followed Merrick outside, closing the door behind him.

*Motherfuckers.* Logan would know a lot about Nick's past through his juvie records; he would know about the accident that killed his father and forced Nick's wolf to surface prematurely. Yeah, if there was anything that would make Nick suffer, it was this. *Fuck. That.* It really was time to go. One half-shifter against two humans was much better odds than if Merrick and Logan had been standing there too.

"I'll give you only one warning," she told the two humans in her gravest voice. "Release me, or I will kill you." Instead of heeding her warning, they both laughed. In fact, so did Amber. How dumb. Seeing that Gangly was still ogling her breasts, Shaya sneered at him. "Must you be a perv?"

He gave her another of his creepy smiles. "I'm just wondering what color your nipples are."

She raised a brow tauntingly. "Why don't you come over here and find out for yourself?"

"You know what, I think I will."

If she had been calling his bluff, Shaya would have been panicking right about then. But she hadn't been calling his bluff. She in fact wanted him to come to her, because what he didn't know was that her wrists were no longer bound.

Fueled by her rage at what had happened to her mate, Shaya

waited until he was close before supporting her weight on one hand as she sharply whipped up one of her legs and kicked the rifle out of his hands. Before he could react, she whipped up her leg again and booted him in the balls; he made a strange choking sound and fell to his knees. Abruptly, she snatched the knife her father had long ago given her that was tucked into her boot and speared it into his chest.

When a stunned-looking Chubby came charging at her, she rolled to the side and sliced both his Achilles tendons as he stumbled past. Like a sack of spuds, he fell to the ground, crying out. Rolling once again, she seized the rifle and twisted to see that Chubby was trying to crawl away. He froze when she cocked it and gave her a pitiful look. She shrugged. "I told you I'd kill you." The bullet hit him dead-center in his forehead.

It was then that Merrick swung the door open. But she had already cocked the gun again, ready to shoot, and was aiming it as his head. "You should have run, Monkey Boy." But the awkward bastard dove to the side, making the bullet skim his ear. "Fuck." Then a wall of flames suddenly formed around the hut, and Merrick slammed the door closed. "Double fuck." Before she could even think of acting, a hand shackled her ankle.

"You can't leave me here," growled Amber.

Shaya found she didn't have an ounce of mercy for this person who had deliberately kept Nick ill, who had made her almost lose her mate. "Of course I can."

"You bitch!"

"Personally, I think I'm more evil than that, but whatever. Give me one good reason why I should help you."

Instead of answering, she yanked hard on Shaya's ankle, making her lose her balance and crash to the floor. She lost her grip on the rifle, which went skidding away from her. "If I'm gonna die, so are you," snarled Amber.

Oddly enough, it wasn't her own life that Shaya was so frantic about saving. It was Nick's. Knowing he was unconscious and hurt was making both her and her wolf panic like crazy. Shaya knew that if the bond had been fully developed, she could have used her own strength to bolster his, to help him wake up. Trey had done the same thing for Taryn during the battle with his uncle: He had surrendered to the bond while she was unconscious, and when the bond clicked into place, Taryn had quickly come around.

Since waking up in the hut, Shaya had been trying to do the same as Trey had, trying to surrender to the bond, but she had no idea how. Over and over she'd tried with no success. She knew what stood in the way—her trust issues, her need to feel indispensable to him, her worry that he would come to resent her submissive status. But, she suddenly wondered, were those things really that important to her? Or had she just been finding excuses all along to keep a distance between them?

Over the past few months, he had given her all the assurances she could have needed, hadn't he? *You're stronger than anyone I know*, he'd told her right before he claimed her, echoing every act that communicated he considered her as his equal. Repeatedly he had assured her, *I don't want anyone but you.* and, thus, soothing her worry that her submissive status made her less desirable to him. She'd never forget when he said, *My life's worth shit without you in it.* And then there was the, *You're indispensable to me— essential to me on every level.*

He'd kept every promise, he'd gone at her pace, and he'd been as patient with her as she had needed him to be. Yes, he'd earned her trust with everything he said, with everything he did, with every promise he kept. She *did* trust him. And yet . . . the bond wouldn't snap into place.

Well of course it wouldn't, she thought with a snicker. It had never really been her difficulty to trust at all, had it? Sure that had played a factor, but that hadn't been the barrier between them. What had held her back all along had been fear—the fear of him leaving her, the fear of being alone, the fear of just what it would do to her to have to live her life without him being a part of it. And, most importantly, the fear of the power it gave him to admit to herself that she loved him. But clinging to that fear in order to protect herself wasn't fair to either of them, nor was keeping those words from him.

Ironically, it had been fear that had held Nick back from claiming her at the very beginning, but he had let go of his fear, determined to not let her suffer for that fear. Now, she needed to let go of hers. And she found that she could.

It was not the scent of fire, smoke, and wood burning that made the gray wolf skid to a halt. It was the sudden bang in his chest and impact to his head. He did not fear either. There was no pain. Only the feel of his mate *inside* him: the feel of her heartbeat, the rate of her pulse. Neither was as strong as it should be. He took no time to enjoy the satisfaction of knowing their bond was now unbreakable. He needed to get to his mate.

With a number of wolves following, the gray wolf allowed the bond to lead him to her. Seeing the small building alight, his mind immediately flashed back to a distant, painful memory—one that brought with it fear, panic, desperation, and the feeling of being trapped. Those same feelings taunted the wolf now, making him hesitate, making him howl. But then he heard his mate's voice, felt her sadness. She sensed his fear and wanted him to stay back. The wolf could not do that. She was his. She belonged to him. She needed to be safe. The sight of her in danger caused a different kind of fear—not the kind that made him hesitate, the kind that acted as fuel and made him act.

Feeling the bond click into place, Shaya's wolf and soul screamed with joy. But Shaya didn't have the time to rejoice about it, because she needed to be free of the evil bitch clinging to her ankle. And she needed to do it before the fire now attacking the wooden walls collapsed the building and killed them both. It was hot, it was dark, it was frightening. She couldn't hear a thing over the hissing, sizzling, crackling, and popping around her.

Coughing and panicking as her ability to breathe became more and more difficult, Shaya kicked at Amber's face and hand, wishing she was wearing her stilettos. Amber only tightened her hold and bit into Shaya's leg. "You weird bitch!" she croaked. Shaya reached down, fisted her hand in her hair, and pulled hard until Amber's teeth released her. She would have shifted forms, but her wolf was too spooked by the fire.

Using her hold on her ankle, Amber dragged Shaya toward her and went to claw at Shaya's face. But the move was clumsy and awkward—most likely as Amber was already weak from her injury. Shaya's hand shot out and snapped around Amber's wrist. Digging deep for every ounce of strength inside her, Shaya propelled Amber onto her back, pinning her arm to the ground. As a submissive wolf, her strength shouldn't have exceeded Amber's, but knowing what this bitch had done to her mate, Shaya and her wolf were close to feral—it gave her the added strength she needed.

With the hand still fisted in Amber's hair, she slammed the bitch's head down over and over until Amber gave a dizzy, hoarse moan. Had she been able to see anything, Shaya might have been able to find her knife or rifle and kill the bitch, but the black smoke made it impossible for even shifter vision to see much. She wasn't sure where the door was, or she might have tried to crawl toward it, but there was the possibility that she might simply crawl farther into the hut.

Sensing that her mate was now outside, Shaya would have smiled with relief if she hadn't also sensed the fear and memories tormenting his wolf. It broke her heart to *feel* just how deeply the accident so long ago had scarred him. She tried to communicate to him that he didn't have to put himself through this again, that she didn't want his scars to deepen, but she didn't have a freaking clue if it was working.

Caught off guard, Shaya found herself lying on her side as Amber tried to reverse their positions. She could tell that Amber was again attempting to shift, but apparently the drug Merrick had used on her still hadn't worn off. That or her wolf was just as spooked by the fire as her own was. Both coughing and close to passing out, they still continued wrestling with one another, weakly battling for dominance.

Then she heard the door suddenly burst open, and the scent of her mate entered the hut. Seconds later, strong hands slipped under her armpits and were attempting to lift her, but Amber locked her arms around Shaya's waist, using all her body weight to keep her in place. Amber clearly had no intention of trying to get out of the hut, fully aware that she was dead if she did anyway. She seemed to prefer to die of smoke inhalation than by being pounced on by a pack of pissed-the-fuck-off wolves. And she wanted Shaya to die with her.

Shaya, however, wasn't okay with that. She shoved hard at Amber's head, but the bitch released her claws and dug them into Shaya's waist to strengthen her hold. Not willing to give up, Shaya dug both of her thumbs into Amber's eyes, pressing hard. Meanwhile, Nick continued pulling, only slightly hampered by Amber.

"Get off me, you neurotic bitch!" It came out more of an abrasive whisper. With the last bit of energy she had left, Shaya pulled back her fist and crashed it into Amber's jaw. Her hold on Shaya then loosened, and the rescuing hands scooped Shaya up, breaking Amber's grip. Keeping her tucked against him, Nick hurried through the doorway. She had expected to have to go through a wall of flames, but the way was now clear, and the fire was quickly subsiding.

Finally outside, she dimly noted that fire extinguishers were blasting the flames—things that were kept inside the caves in case of forest fires. But as he sat her inside the SUV, her concentration was solely on Nick; she ran her gaze over every naked inch of him, searching for any injuries.

"Taryn healed me," Nick assured her. He blew out a breath, forcing one of the bottles of water Cam had brought into her hands. Shaya practically inhaled it. "Christ, baby, you scared the shit out of me."

"I didn't get kidnapped on purpose," she rasped. His tight hug would have hurt her if she hadn't needed that contact as much as he did. "How is everybody?" From her position in the vehicle, she could only see Jaime, Dante, Ryan, Cam, and Rhett. Shit, shit, shit.

*Feeling* the panic zooming through her, he pulled back and cupped her chin. "They're alive, don't worry. Unfortunately, they're not in great shape." He paused as a cough interrupted him. "But Taryn was in the process of healing them when I left. My guess is she's probably just half-healed them so she doesn't exhaust herself. Gabe and Caleb drove one of the SUVs out here and picked them up while Cam and Rhett came out here with the extinguishers and drinks."

"Speaking of half-healing . . . Amber didn't fully heal you, Nick. She purposely didn't, because she wanted you to keep going back to her. You know what it means, don't you? It means the only reason you got ill again was because of her. Taryn's healing should be permanent."

The betrayal didn't cut deep, as he'd never felt anything for Amber, but it still wasn't pleasant to know that someone who had once been a member of his pack could betray him that way. "In that case, I'm glad no one went back in to save her. What she did goes against the principles of every healer."

Realizing that a few people appeared to be circling something at the side of the hut, she frowned. "What's going on?"

Nick sighed. "Jesse, Bracken, Zander, and Derren went after Logan and Merrick, and brought them back." He cupped her face. "I need you to stay here for me."

Shaya bit her lower lip. "You're going to kill them, aren't you?"

"Yes." He waited for her to yell at him or at least try to talk him out of it, but she instead nodded.

"Make it painful."

Startled by her words, he almost smiled. "I'll be back in a few minutes."

Still vibrating with fury and fear for his mate, Nick strolled over to the group near the hut. They instantly parted, letting him through. He went to stand before Merrick and Logan. Their expressions were blank, but undiluted fear was wafting from both of them, pleasing his enraged wolf. They knew they weren't getting out of this alive.

Logan's voice was shaky. "If you kill me, the rest of my—"

Nick held up a hand to silence him. "I've heard it all before from your friend Lee-Roy. It never worked for him, and it certainly won't work for you." He looked at Merrick. "You're supposed to be dead." Under any other circumstances, Nick would have been glad to find out that Merrick was still alive, that he could let go of the guilt he had been carrying for a very long time. But not now; no, the son of a bitch really did deserve to die. "Know what's ironic? I always felt bad, since I never meant to kill you. But now I'm actually wishing I had."

Merrick laughed, but it was a nervous sound. "I don't doubt it."

"What I can't understand is how you're alive."

A slight shrug. "The day you almost killed me, I made a deal with Logan that if he brought in a healer to fix me up, I'd tell him everything I knew about you and the other prisoners in there— the codes you all used, what positions you'd all given yourselves, what everyone's weaknesses were. We're like-minded, he and I." The wolves all growled, disgusted by him.

Derren came to stand slightly behind Nick, glaring hard at Merrick. "You betrayed your own kind."

"They're not my kind. *My* kind wouldn't have ostracized me from my own pack."

"Trey's pack ostracized him," said Nick, "but he didn't decide to make his entire race pay. There are no excuses for the things you've done."

Apparently Merrick didn't care, because he ignored that. "I *should* have been Alpha of my pack! And I *should* have been Alpha in juvie!"

"No, you shouldn't have." Nick's voice was even and quiet. "You're everything that an Alpha isn't: cocky, cunning, self-centered, fickle, and bullying. Everyone saw it, and everyone hated it."

"They respected and followed me until you came along and challenged me."

"No, they existed in small, tight groups. And those groups feared you, sure, but an Alpha who tries to rule through fear and intimidation isn't an Alpha. It's that simple. And so is your fate."

"Nick," said Jesse. "We know this guy did you wrong, and we know he kidnapped your mate, but he's also responsible for the kidnapping and deaths of our family members—my sister, Bracken's cousin, and Zander's nephew."

And the three males needed vengeance, needed closure. Nick could understand that. He could. Had the situation been reversed, he'd have demanded the same. Besides, he'd be getting closure for every juvie member by killing Logan, who had also played a part in kidnapping and attempting to kill his mate. He could give this other piece of shit to Jesse, Bracken, and Zander if that was what they truly wanted; he'd beaten Merrick once before anyway. Nick's decision must have been obvious in his eyes, because Merrick's expression turned to a mixture of confusion and anxiety.

"You're not going to challenge me, one to one?"

"If I did that, it would be over quickly, wouldn't it? This way, you get to suffer for a little while. I find that I like that idea. You don't deserve mercy, Merrick. Neither of you do." He extended his claws, dancing his gaze from Merrick to Logan and back again. "You both tried to take from me the only thing I've ever loved. As you can imagine, I have a serious fucking issue with that." He stepped a little closer to the man who had raped and killed so many young shifters. "This might hurt a little."

# CHAPTER NINETEEN

THREE MONTHS LATER

A s Jaime yapped beside him at the dining table about some-thing or other, Nick forced a smile for her. Oh, she was a nice enough girl and stuff, but he just didn't do the friend thing, and apparently a person didn't have a choice in the matter when it was Jaime. He noticed that his mate, who was sitting on his other side, was stifling a smile of amusement at his discomfort—as usual.

*Just a little longer,* he reminded himself. Just a little longer, and then he and Shaya would be finished with their evening meal and leaving Phoenix Pack territory, and they would only be returning as visitors.

Since the night of the battle, he and Shaya had been living on pack territory temporarily. Although they had slept in the motor home outside the caves, they were still constantly harassed and, as such, had had very little time alone. Nick and Shaya weren't the only ones who had remained on pack territory. Derren, Roni, Eli, Kathy, Jesse, Bracken, Zander, and Kent—who had sold the salon—had remained too. Why? It wasn't that they expected Nick to start a pack. No, it was because they believed they already *were* a pack.

Hell, even Caleb thought he was part of this supposed "pack." To his surprise, Nick found that he actually liked Caleb despite the male's close friendship with Shaya. Although Caleb was protective of her, it wasn't to the extent that he imposed on Nick's role. Also, Nick was grateful to him for being there for Shaya growing up when her mother wasn't.

If Nick was honest with himself, he would admit that being an Alpha again would be a challenge he would enjoy, because this time he'd have his mate with him, and he would be an Alpha of a dispersed pack—something his "pack" had subtly hinted they would all be fine with. That meant he would have plenty of time alone with his mate. The "pack" all deferred to Shaya a lot, treating her with respect and acknowledging the inner strength that many people would have overlooked.

In essence, they had made her their Alpha female, and she was perfectly fine with it since it didn't interfere with her position as a mediator. She had gotten the job, just like he had known she would. Naturally, she was ecstatic. The only time he had seen her happier was the evening of their mating ceremony.

As planned, they had the ceremony a few days after the attack, when everyone was fully healed. Trey performed the ceremony for them, just as Nick had done for Trey and Taryn. Shaya had looked absolutely beautiful; he could vividly remember every detail—her halter-neck dress had been azure in color, all satin with a layer of silk beneath the skirt that had trailed slightly below the satin. As tradition, he had worn a simple suit, which had been a dark gray—the same color as his wolf's fur. And for the first time since he'd first surfaced, his wolf had been truly and utterly content. He still was.

The after-party had been pretty funny as Rhett had gotten so drunk he'd actually passed out near the music speaker. Seriously, how was that even possible for someone with shifter hearing? But then, Nick supposed it wasn't every day a male discovered his mate was pregnant. To Rhett's dismay, Grace was refusing to "take it easy," in spite of the fact that she had fussed over Taryn when the Alpha female was pregnant with Kye. Nick knew that the day Shaya became pregnant—something he would know just by a slight change in her scent—would be one of the best days of his life, but it would still shock the shit out of him, just as it had Rhett.

His mother, who was currently laughing hysterically about something with Shaya, Roni, and Eli, had been leaving not-so-subtle hints about him giving her grandchildren sometime soon. She absolutely adored Shaya, which was why she had spent a good portion of the mating ceremony snarling at Gabrielle—who had been extremely well behaved that night, not insulting Shaya even once. Stone had been pleasant enough to Nick, but he'd patted his Glock a few times and given Nick a look that said, "I'm watching you." Whatever.

Eli, too, had easily taken to Shaya. Of course he had. She had a natural ease with people that Nick was sure would make her fantastic at her job. She, Kathy, and Eli had been conspiring together about ways to keep Roni from returning to her wolf form for another long period of time. If anyone could accomplish that, it was Shaya.

A big relief was that, so far, he hadn't had a single headache since Taryn healed him. Not one. Nor had he had any other problems that might signify his cognitive functions were beginning to degenerate again. At Shaya's request, Taryn occasionally laid a hand on his forehead to see if any luminous patches showed up under his scalp. But there were none. If what everyone speculated was true, the only reason he had gotten ill again after his first healing was that Amber had deliberately failed to fully heal him. As such, Shaya was confident that he was healed for good now. His gut told him that she was right.

Nick was pulled from his thoughts when a chunky ginger cat sprang onto the table and then onto Jaime's lap, hissing loudly at Dante, who was opposite her. Nick looked down at the animal that always managed to scare the hell out of his dog. In Bruce's defense . . . "That is one motherfucking ugly cat."

Jaime gasped in horror while Dante nodded his agreement. Cuddling her cat close, Jaime turned on her mate, cursing him for being antisocial toward her pet. Gabe consoled her until she ended her rant with a huff, though he and Hope were chuckling to themselves.

"These disputes between them about her freaky pet are commonplace," Gabe told Nick, petting Bruce, who had taken a liking to the male. "Dante gets jealous of the attention Hunk receives from his mate." Dante didn't deny it.

Although Nick had initially disliked Dante for warning him away from Shaya—in fairness, he had been merely trying to protect Shaya—Nick had come to like the Beta male. Over the past few months, Dante and Tao had taken it upon themselves to subject Jesse, Bracken, and Zander to the training given to enforcers. Nick knew why; they were preparing them to be enforcers for Nick. Yep, the Phoenix Pack was also taking part in the plan to make him an Alpha again.

As Shaya stood and leaned across the table to retrieve the bottle of ketchup from Kent, Nick couldn't help but enjoy the view. "You truly do have the most perfect ass." His mate merely smiled brightly.

"I strongly agree," said Dominic, endangering his life once again. When Nick growled, he raised his hands. "Just kidding."

Kent sighed at Dominic before turning to Nick. "I'd hit him for you . . . but look how pretty he is."

Roni fingered the shirt Dominic was wearing. "Nice shirt. Can I talk you out of it?"

As everyone laughed at her teasing, Dominic pointed at her. "Stop doing that. If you're not going to marry me and let us be filthy-minded together—"

"You stop doing it to mess with my brother, and I'll stop doing it to you." As usual, Roni and Dominic then began to quibble. Nick noticed that Marcus didn't appear to like the byplay that often went on between Roni and the pervert. Marcus watched and flirted with Roni a lot, who just responded with blank looks. Unlike the other females here, she was resistant to his "charm," which was a good thing because it meant Nick didn't have to kill him. Sitting there now, Marcus looked confused more than anything else . . . like someone who felt as though he had lost his magical powers. And Trick appeared to find it hilarious.

When Grace took Nick's empty plate and topped up his coffee mug, he gave her a nod of thanks. He had to admit, he'd miss her cooking. Like Lydia, she was also good with injuries; they had both been a great help to Taryn when many had been wounded after the battle. Hell, Tao and Dominic had come very close to dying. Eli, Trey, Marcus, and Trick had also been badly hurt. Taryn had been totally and utterly pissed with Trey about it, as if he'd *wanted* to get shot or something.

At the moment, though, the Alpha pair was perfectly happy, sitting together at the table, playing with their son and laughing as Kye frowned at Cam's attempt to play peek-a-boo with him— as if the kid was offended that Cam thought such a game would be enough to entertain him. Nick felt a distinct pang of longing. He wanted that with Shaya one day. As if she sensed that, she smiled at him and placed a hand on his thigh. Her hand was nowhere near his cock, but it didn't matter—like that, he was rock hard. "Can we leave now?"

She laughed. Yeah, she probably shouldn't have found it amusing that her mate was in hell surrounded by people, or that she could make him hard that easily, but she *so* did. "Let me finish my cake and coffee."

In truth, Shaya was eager to leave, because Nick was finally taking her to see the house he'd bought for them. He'd refused to tell her anything about it—not even where it was—and she wasn't a patient person. Still, she wanted to enjoy this meal with the

Phoenix Pack because she knew that after that day, things would be very different. She'd be an Alpha female.

Though Nick was reluctant about being an Alpha again, she knew it was a given. Unlike with many other dominant males, he didn't have to showcase his alpha qualities, he didn't have to actively work to gain people's attention—he just *was*. And that was enough for people to notice and be inspired by him. He didn't have to demand to be obeyed, or respected, or followed—those things happened for him automatically. It was kind of annoying when people often sought him out for help or advice and seemed to gather around him. But it was also kind of funny considering he had such an aversion to company.

"Wrap up the cake with a napkin and bring it with you."

Grinning at the impatience in his voice, Shaya said, "No, I want to eat it now."

"But . . . people keep smiling at me."

"So smile back."

"I don't want to."

"Just so you know: They'll still be friendly to you, no matter how much you try to keep them at a distance. They're determined to break down your defenses and make you one of their own." Like Jaime, however, the guys also did it to irritate Nick. Yeah, the males of the Phoenix Pack—particularly Trick—lived to tease one another and everyone else around them. As Tao was so easy to provoke, he got it the worst. Ryan simply grunted in what looked like impatience whenever Trick tried it with him.

"Stop hogging my grandson," complained Greta at Taryn as she held out her arms to Kye, clearly expecting him to reach for her—he didn't.

"I think you mean *hugging*," said Taryn sweetly, holding Kye closer. He giggled, playing with her hair.

Greta placed her hands on her hips, scowling at Taryn. The old woman had spent the past half hour insulting the Alpha female and didn't appear to be done. "You know what I mean, hussy."

Taryn sighed tiredly. "Greta, I think you've delighted us long enough. Why not go select some favorite hymns and poems—it won't be long before the funeral. Have you put any more thought into whether or not you want an open casket?"

"*Humph.* I still have no idea why my Trey mated with you. Tiny, sarcastic, disrespectful—"

"Greta, seriously, careful your vile tongue doesn't get your false teeth knocked out."

Of course that made Greta ten times worse.

Nick turned to Shaya. "I really don't think I can take much more." These people were crazy. "You done yet?"

Chuckling, Shaya held up her index finger. Drinking down the last of her coffee, she nodded. "*Now* we can leave."

Both relieved and excited, Nick took her hand in his and helped her rise from the table. All at once, Derren, Roni, Eli, Kathy, Kent, Jesse, Bracken, and Zander rose from their seats. "Oh no. Shaya and I want some privacy for a change."

"We just want to know where we'll be living," said Derren innocently. The others nodded. Most likely in response to Nick's growl, he said, "You're not going to get rid of me, you know that. Nor are you going to get rid of these people. And you're not going to get out of being Alpha either."

As an idea came to mind, Nick crossed his arms over his chest. "Okay. You want me to be Alpha? You got it . . . as long as you're Beta—no more bodyguard shit."

Derren gawked. "Hell no. I don't want responsibilities. They scare me."

"Then I'm afraid I don't have a place for you. Derren, with regret, you're officially out of the pack. I'm permanently firing you."

"Hey, you can't do that. *I'm* the one who organized the pack," he more or less whined.

"Doesn't matter. If I'm Alpha, it's my decision. So, are you going to accept the position of Beta or not?"

Derren had the look of a sulky teenager. "Fine."

Smirking, Nick led Shaya around the table. "I'll show you the house tomorrow," he told his "pack." Being an Alpha again was going to take some getting used to. "Shaya and I want to spend our first night there *alone*." They all nodded respectfully.

After he and Shaya had said their good-byes and she had been molested by Dominic—which almost led to the pervert losing a limb—Nick and Shaya went out of the tunnels and down to the indoor parking lot. He held up something he'd taken from his back pocket.

Shaya tensed. "You want to blindfold me?"

"I told you, I want this to be a surprise."

"But . . . you want to blindfold me?"

"What part of 'surprise' don't you understand?"

A little irritated that she wouldn't even be able to look out the window and guess where they were going, she nonetheless nodded. He gently put on the blindfold, plunging her into complete darkness, and kissed her lightly on the mouth before guiding her into his Mercedes.

When Nick finally drove them out of pack territory, he released a sigh of relief. Those people had the potential to drive him insane. The only person he wanted to be in the company of was Shaya, and now he had her all to himself *finally*. He soon realized that he probably should have brought a gag as well as a blindfold, because she did nothing but quiz him throughout the entire journey—no doubt to annoy him. It worked.

When the car finally came to a stop, Shaya practically bounced in the seat in anticipation. She probably looked like a toddler in a playground, but she didn't care. Three long months of "it's a surprise" had her feeling beyond excited—as well as exasperated. "Can I take the blindfold off now?"

"No, that's my job. Wait there."

Sighing, Shaya waited as Nick exited the car and then came around and opened the passenger door. Taking her hand, he helped her get out of the vehicle. The familiar scents of pine, sun-warmed earth, and moss hit her nose. The place itself had a familiar scent . . . she had been here before. "Blindfold. Off."

Nick *tsk*ed. "No patience." He led her a short distance and then, standing behind her, untied the piece of black cloth. "*Now* you can look."

Blinking a few times to adjust to the light, Shaya fully opened her eyes and gasped. "Oh my God." Yeah, she'd been here before, been here many times as a child. It had been her favorite place back then. "You bought the hunting lodge I told you about?" It was just as she remembered it. The first level was made with large stone while the second and third levels had timber frames. The large glass dove windows took clear advantage of the natural light, practically illuminating it. To add to that, fairy lights now decorated the trees that surrounded the lodge. "I can't believe you did this." With emotion clogging her throat, the words came out in a whisper.

Surprising the hell out of Nick, she sharply pivoted and dived on him, wrapping around him like a clinging vine. He caught her easily and curled his arms around her. "Does this mean you like it?" Her "I love it!" made him inwardly sag in relief. Nick had believed he knew her well enough to know this was something she would love, somewhere she could think of as home, but a tiny part of him had been worried that he'd been wrong. His wolf was thrilled by her reaction.

When she finally untangled herself from him, he explained, "It's not just the only lodge here now. The owners built and rented out several other lodges on the land, which would be perfect for the 'pack' to live in. It means you and I will have our own space."

Touched to the point that she was tearful, she said, "I really, really can't believe you've done this. I never would have guessed. I suppose I should have—you always try to spoil me."

"It's my right, and it'll happen a lot, so you need to get better at accepting gifts."

She waved away that comment. "You know what else I can't believe? That the prejudiced humans sold the place to a shifter." When he opened his mouth to speak, she raised a hand. "Don't tell me . . . Your contacts got involved, right?"

"Right," he confirmed. "Want to go inside?"

"Do Dalmatians have black spots?"

"One thing first: I made a few . . . changes."

"What do you mean? And don't look so panicky about it. Just because you've made changes doesn't mean I won't still love it."

Smiling, he explained, "The place hadn't been properly looked after. It needed some work, so a contact of mine—"

"A *friend* of yours," she stressed.

"A friend of mine," he allowed, "who runs a business specializing in restoring and also modernizing buildings worked on the place. I told him what I thought you'd like, and he and his team have been working on it. He'll also work on the other lodges when they've each been claimed and the 'pack' tells him what they want. Ready?"

Nodding enthusiastically, she slipped her hand in his and let him lead her inside. The second she entered, she gasped again. It was very different from before; the living room, kitchen, and dining area was one huge, open space—the main feature being the living area with luxurious sofas and armchairs and a state-of-the-art entertainment system. Between the TV and sofas was an oval white fluffy rug that just made her want to go curl up on it. There was also a big stone fireplace that added to the rustic tone of the place. It had such a homey, spacious, warm feeling that hadn't been there before.

Nick led her up the golden curved staircase and gave her a tour of upstairs—showing her the large bathroom, the many guest rooms, and the game room with a cocktail bar. The master bedroom could only be described as sensual with its red, gold, and white color theme and the grand four-poster bed—the room made a person think of sex, pleasure, and desires fulfilled.

As if it wasn't great enough that there was a Jacuzzi in the stylish en suite bathroom, there was also one on the deck outside the bedroom balcony, overlooking the river and the sun that was setting beyond it. The whole place was like a peaceful oasis for her and her wolf. Turning, she found her mate in the doorway of the bedroom with his gaze locked on her. "I absolutely love it. But . . . no decorative pillows?" she teased, pouting.

He shook his head and began advancing toward her, intent on taking her on that bed as he'd imagined doing since he'd chosen it. "*No* decorative pillows." Finally reaching her, he trailed his fingertips up her arms. "As for the basement . . . it's now an indoor pool, but you can see that later. Now that I finally have you in this room, I'm keeping you in it for a little while." He took a single step backward. "Take off your clothes."

Shivering at that authoritative tone that brooked no argument, Shaya removed her tank top, stilettos, jeans, lacy bra, and matching panties. Eyes flashing with need raked over her, making her entire body tingle in awareness and anticipation. But he didn't touch her. Instead, he began to very slowly circle her predatorily in that way he sometimes did. Behind her, he licked along the curve of her shoulder and delivered a sharp nip to her earlobe. Then his deep, seductive voice was murmuring in her ear.

"Perfect . . . every single inch of you."

Coming to stand before her again, he still didn't reach for her. But his hungry gaze felt enough like a touch that a tremor rippled down her spine. As he slowly undressed, her breathing deepened as electricity arched between them and the silence seemed to stretch on and on. Every part of her seemed to ache for him; her breasts felt heavy, her nipples were hard, and her clit was pulsing. "Nick," she appealed.

His piercing gaze ensnared hers. "What do you want? Tell me, Shay. Tell me, and I'll give it to you."

Somehow, his dominant tone created a trancelike effect that made both her and her wolf total slaves. "You," she rasped. "All of you." It was an echo of something he had once said to her. And it got Shaya what she wanted: a growl rumbled up his chest as he fit her body to his, crushing her breasts against him and cupping her ass. His mouth, tongue, and hands were demanding, dominating, and possessive. She more or less liquefied under the assault to her senses, threading her fingers through his hair and tugging.

He closed his mouth around her nipple, sucking hard and raking his teeth over it. Moving on to the other nipple, he lashed it with his tongue and then drew it into his mouth. At the same time, his hand skimmed over her flat stomach and down to cup her hard. Then two fingers sank deep inside her and swirled around.

"I love how you get so wet for me." Kissing her again, Nick slowly thrust his fingers in and out of her, loving the moans she fed him, watching every expression that flashed across her face. Withdrawing his fingers, he moved one to circle the puckered hole where a butt plug was snugly positioned inside her. "I'm going to finally take you here tonight, baby. Do you want that?"

Shaya nodded, wanting her mate to have claimed her in every possible way—this was the only step they hadn't yet taken, because Nick had wanted her to be totally ready. Also, he'd explained that he didn't want her to surrender this way just to please him or out of curiosity, that he wanted her to want it as much as he did. She did, and she wasn't embarrassed to admit it.

"On the bed, baby." Once she clambered onto the bed and lay on her back, he crawled over her and took her mouth, branding it. He ended the kiss with a bite to her lip. "Spread your legs," he rumbled. "I want to taste this pussy that was made for me."

Once she'd followed his order, Nick kissed, licked, and bit his way down her body to dip his tongue into her navel before going lower still. He flicked her clit with the tip of his tongue, eliciting a sharp intake of breath from her. He might have made her beg a little, but the scent of her pussy was much too tempting. Sliding his hands under her thighs, he tilted her hips and hooked her legs over his shoulders. Then he licked, sipped, and drank from her, savoring her taste and her moans. Each one of his senses was filled with, and overwhelmed by, her.

One thing he loved about Shaya was that her responses were without deception or exaggeration; she simply allowed her desire to flood her veins, rule her, and take her where she needed to be. The way she writhed and arched, the way she pulled on his hair, the way she groaned and whimpered and dug her heels between his shoulder blades—all of it was real, and all of it sent an agonizing need rocketing through him. "I need to be inside you. Right fucking now. Turn over."

Those words caused quivers deep in her stomach. Needing to come *so* badly, Shaya obediently positioned herself on her hands and knees. He smoothed his hands over her ass as he came to kneel behind her, letting his cock rub against her slit. It felt good and all, but she really couldn't wait much longer. "Nick, I need to come."

He positioned his cock at the entrance of her pussy. Keeping one hand on her hip, he held her shoulder with the other. "When I'm ready for you to come, I'll tell you." He slammed home, groaning as her walls clamped down on him. Buried inside his mate, the aching need in his body eased. But then it exploded.

Shaya cried out as Nick began to ruthlessly hammer into her, thrusting hard, driving deep. His pace was feverish, frenzied, and was sending her into that same frenzied state; she was moaning, whimpering, and instinctively pushing back against him. Well, actually, she was *trying* to push back, but his iron hold prevented her from moving. Still, her attempts earned her a growl and the prick of claws against her skin—Nick's way of telling her to keep still, that *he* was in control and she'd take what he gave her.

"I love the feel of your pussy around me. Know what else I love?" Nick slid his hand into her hair and pulled, urging her upright so her back was to his chest, and bringing her face to his. "You. Every goddamn inch of you—inside and out. Can you feel it?"

She could. She could feel it flowing over her, centering her, sheltering her, and wrapping around her. Even if she hadn't known it with every cell and every bone of her body, she would have known it from the look in his eyes right then. He *loved* her. Loved her with an intensity that he would never have thought himself capable of—it was deep, and boundless, and true. It was also returned. She looped her arms around his neck. "And I love you."

The words made Nick pause in his movements. He truly hadn't expected her to give him those words, hadn't believed she felt that way—not yet. He could have used their bond anytime to find out for sure, but he hadn't wanted to delve that deeply in case what he found wasn't what he'd hoped to find. But now what she felt was radiating from the bond. So knowing that it was true, *feeling* it was true, Nick was filled with elation and a sense of completeness that only Shaya could have given him. It made something settle deep inside his wolf, gave the animal a peace he'd never otherwise have known.

"Come here, baby." Her mouth met his, and Nick devoured it, dominated it, but also cherished it. Then he placed a hand on her lower back and gently pressed forward until she was leaning on her elbows. "Now I'm going to make you come." With that, he began fucking her with hard, feral digs that made her cry out, made her gasp his name and tear at the bed sheets with her claws. "*Now.*"

The combination of his order, the feel of his teeth buried in her shoulder, and the light pinch on her clit had her body imploding. She threw her head back, screaming. That was when, in one smooth movement, he pulled out the butt plug and thrust into her ass. She screamed again as the sensation intensified her climax.

Nick didn't move one single inch as she came down from her orgasm. When she began to writhe, he cinched her hips and held her still. "You okay, baby?" He couldn't sense any pain from her, but he needed to hear her say it.

"Move, Nick; I need you to move. It hurts a little, but it's a good hurt."

Satisfied, Nick slowly withdrew until only the head of his cock was inside her, and then he thrust forward just as slowly. "Fuck, baby, that feels so good." He did it over and over, not picking up the pace until she became restless against him and begged for more. When she tried slamming back into him, he hardened his thrusts slightly, staying fully connected to her through their bond so he could make sure she wasn't in pain.

"Let go, Nick. I know you're holding back."

It seemed he wasn't the only one who was tapping into the bond. "I don't want to hurt you."

"You'd never hurt me. You've lost control lots of times, but you've never once hurt me, and you won't do it now. Let go."

Groaning, he began frantically pumping his hips, taking what he wanted and giving her what she needed. Every thrust was a brand, a reminder that she was his. Her noises drove him crazy and spurred him on until his pace was frenzied and relentless, offering her no mercy, ensuring she never forgot this, never forgot how good it felt.

"Nick, I need to come."

"Then come." As her body tightened and rippled around him, pure rapture tore through Nick—a pleasure/pain that went on and on—and he exploded inside her.

Shaya screamed his name as a blistering, white-hot fire tore through her mind, body, and soul—bowing her back and sending tremor after tremor ripping through her, obliterating every thought she had in her mind except for one: She loved the bastard.

"I'm not a bastard," Nick practically slurred as they sank onto the mattress, still joined.

She hadn't actually meant to say that out loud. "Sure you're not, Beavis," she panted.

He growled and nipped her shoulder, rolling them onto their sides. "I'm *not* stupid."

"No, you're just slow. And it's such a shame too."

"If I'm Beavis, you're Butt-Head."

She snorted. "You wouldn't call me that."

Smiling, he licked one of the marks he'd left on her nape. "Sure I would, Butt-Head."

Indignant, Shaya shuffled over so that his cock slipped out of her. "The fact you think you can get away with that just proves that you're dumb." Then she dashed for the shower. Of course he followed her, and of course he made her come with his mouth again. Having stripped off the shredded bed sheets, they eventually collapsed on the bed, still naked.

"I can't believe you've already ruined the brand-new sheets. You need to learn better self-control," he teased.

"I refer back to my earlier comment—you're a bastard."

Chuckling, Nick moved onto his side and pulled her to him. "Yeah, well, you still love me."

She could sense his utter surprise. "You should have known I love you. You've heard what they say: 'Love sucks; true love swallows.' As I recall, I've always taken every last drop."

He groaned. "Now I'm getting hard again."

"Sorry, stud, but we can't do anything about it until we've decided something important."

"What's that?" he asked, licking at his claiming mark. He couldn't think of anything more important than making her come all over again—it was his favorite thing to do.

"What are we going to name the pack? It needs a name."

"Huh. I hadn't thought of that. Any ideas?"

"Well . . . when Taryn, Caleb, Joey—that's the kid that Taryn thought was her true mate and died when he was nine—and I were little, we used to pretend we were a special ops team."

"Special ops team?" He chuckled.

"Taryn and I weren't girly as kids. Anyway, we used to call our team 'Mercury Ops.' I think that would be good for a pack name."

"The Mercury Ops Pack?" he echoed with distaste.

She slapped his arm. "No. The Mercury Pack. It would mean a lot to me. And to Taryn. And to Caleb. And to Joey, whose soul may haunt you forever if you say no." She fixed a pitiful look on her face. "Please?"

"Oh, I do love to hear you beg, Shay."

"I've already run it by Derren and the others; they all like it."

He narrowed his eyes as he realized something. "And here I thought they were working *on* you, but you've been working *with* them, haven't you?"

She shrugged unapologetically. "Your wolf will always feel like something's missing if he doesn't do what he was born to do. That's not good with me. So . . . the Mercury Pack—yes or no?"

"If I say no?"

"I'll harass you until you say yes." When a strange glint entered that dusky-green gaze, Shaya automatically became wary.

"I'll tell you what: I'll say yes if you agree to something."

That didn't sound good. "What is it you want?"

"I want you to drop this fantasy you have of me dressing like a sailor."

"Oh, but—"

He rolled onto his back, holding up a hand to cut her off. "No, no, I am *not* dressing like a fucking sailor."

She pouted. "Oh, come on! After the first few times, it won't even feel kinky anymore."

"No."

"But you'd look so—"

"No."

"Can't you at least think—?"

"No."

She growled and gave him the sulkiest pout ever. "Trey does it for Taryn."

Nick felt his face scrunch up. "Jeez, Shay, I so did *not* need to know that." The image came unbidden to his mind, and Nick feared it might just pop into his head whenever he was around the Alpha male in the future.

Her voice turned sultry. "If you do it, I may reconsider the pole dancing scenario you had in mind."

A short pause. "I'll think about it."

"That's all I'm asking."

# Acknowledgments

I have to firstly say thank you to my husband and children for being my inspiration and for their patience with me when I'm in "cave mode." I'd also like to thank my sisters for pulling me out of the cave occasionally to make sure I give myself the breaks I need.

A massive thanks to everyone at Montlake Romance for their help, support, and time—especially to my editor, JoVon Sotak, and also to Jessica Poore for answering my many questions.

And of course a humungous thank-you to everyone who has taken time out of their lives to read my book. If for any reason you would like to contact me, please feel free to e-mail me at suzanne_e_wright@live.co.uk.

Website: www.suzannewright.co.uk

Blog: www.suzannewrightsblog.blogspot.co.uk

Twitter: twitter.com/suz_wright

Facebook: www.facebook.com/pages/Suzanne-Wright/1392617144284756

# About the Author

Author Suzanne Wright, a native of England, can't remember a time when she wasn't creating characters and telling their tales. Even as a child, she loved writing poems, plays, and stories; as an adult, Wright has published five novels: *From Rags, Here Be Sexist Vampires*, and *The Bite That Binds* from the Deep In Your Veins series, and two books in the Phoenix Pack series, *Feral Sins* and *Wicked Cravings*. Wright, who lives in Liverpool with her husband and two children, freely admits that she hates housecleaning and can't cook but that she always shares chocolate.